IN THE TEMPLE OF MEHYT

MORE IN THIS SERIES

In the Court of Kemet
Ancient Egyptian Romances Book #1

The Draughtsman's Daughter
Ancient Egyptian Romances Book #3

AVAILABLE FALL 2016

Lady of the Caravan
Ancient Egyptian Romances Book #4

ALSO BY DANIELLE S. LeBLANC

Living with Oral Allergy Syndrome: A Gluten and Meat-Free Cookbook for Wheat, Soy, Nut, Fresh Fruit and Vegetable Allergies

Recipes for Unusual Gluten Free Pasta: Pierogis, Dumplings, Desserts and More!

Cooking and Baking with Gluten Free Beer

IN THE TEMPLE OF MEHYT

Ancient Egyptian Romances Book #2

By

Danielle S. LeBlanc

La Venta West, Inc.

For Alex

LA VENTA WEST, INC., 2015

www.laventawestpublishers.blogspot.ca
Vanouver, Canada

Print ISBN 978-0-9949751-0-2
eBook ISBN 978-0-9949751-1-9

Table of Contents

Quick Reference
for
Ancient Egyptian Words

Asastru – testicles
Hem-netjer – priest
Hemet-netjer – priestess
Hmww – carpenter / furniture maker
Hnrt – prison complex
Hwt – temple
Hul gil (Sumerian) – "Plant of Joy" a.k.a. opium
Ka – life force / spirit
Miu – cat
Nebet-i – my lady
Sekhet-Aaru – the fields of the afterlife
Senebti – be well, a way of saying goodbye
Sephat – regional divisions in Ancient Egypt, roughly equivalent to modern day provinces, or semi-independent city-states, comprised of several cities and/or towns. Ancient Egypt consisted of 42 sephats, later known by the Greek term, *nome*.
Tayi neb – my lord

Chapter 1 – A Reluctant Partnership

Kemet, 2974 B.C.E.

Satsobek eyed her sister warily across the low wooden table, not pleased with the turn the conversation had taken. She shifted on her cushion, uncrossing and re-crossing her legs, and avoided Amenia's question by reaching across the plates and bowls of food to grab a honey bun, tearing off a chunk, and popping it in her mouth. In the process, she flicked glances at her father and his concubine, each seated on opposite ends of the table between herself and her sister. Her father appeared engrossed in tearing the leg off a pheasant while his concubine, Kiya, intently picked through a bowl of nuts, plucking out the sweet tiger nut tubers she preferred.

The large tent they dined in sat atop the roof of their home near the queen's palace. Late morning sunlight filtered through the white linen walls, tinting everything – and everyone – with the cheerful orange-yellow colour of an egg yolk, lending her family a false appearance of affability. Despite the sun's rays, the rooftop was still cooler than inside the mud-brick manor, where the heat was oppressive enough to be trance-inducing. The temperature outside was, as yet, only sufficient to inspire a general apathy; the air hot, dry, and still. But the weather would only get hotter in the days to come and Satsobek had no doubt that in a couple of weeks – when the harvest season was over – she would look back on a day like today and wistfully recall its cool breezes and mild temperatures.

Amenia thrust a hand out and waggled her fingers under Satsobek's nose. She repeated her question in a simpering voice, "How could I *not* be happy with the husband our father chose for me? I have some of the most beautiful jewellery in all of Kemet." Amenia's gold rings glinted in the sunlight, blinding Satsobek and forcing her to blink and squint.

Digging her fingernails into her palms, Satsobek willed herself to keep silent. *If happiness means flirting with any and every man you encounter as soon as your fat old husband is out of sight, then yes, dear sister. You must be overcome with happiness. Truly ecstatic. Rapturous, even.* Indeed, Amenia seemed happy enough to let her husband spend four nights a week with his concubines, leaving her free to entertain her male servants in her own bedchamber.

Not that Satsobek would ever say that to her sister. Evincing how angry her family's sly criticisms made her accomplished nothing except to expose weaknesses for others to manipulate. She couldn't wait until their meal was over and she could steal away to the quiet, shaded gardens behind the mansion. She wanted to listen to the rustling leaves of the date palm trees, hear the birds call, watch some insects crawling. Anything to get away from her family.

So she flattened her lips into a stretched smile that she knew couldn't possibly reach her eyes and said, "Yes, Amenia. You do have beautiful jewellery. You must be *quite* proud."

Amenia patted a tentative hand over the braided wig perched high on her scalp, a smug smile curving her lips. "And look. I have the finest wigs in all of the queen's court. Everyone says so."

Amenia narrowed her eyes at Satsobek and took three quick sips of wine. *Her third mug of wine already and it is not yet midday.*

"It is true, Satsi." Satsobek cringed at the sound of Kiya's nasal voice. She hated the nickname her father's concubine had given her, along with the overly familiar way in which she used it.

Kiya's white linen wrap was pleated around her midsection, exposing both breasts. The style was not uncommon and Satsobek herself wore her own wraps that way from time to time, particularly on hot days. But in

Kiya's case there was something almost lewd about the way it laid her ample, wobbly bosom bare for all to see.

Kiya's bosom quivered now as her shoulders waggled slightly and she said, "Your father made an excellent choice for your sister. You really ought to let him choose for you. You cannot be expected to make these decisions for yourself. That would be silly."

Kiya threw a smile at Satsobek's father, the puffy, bald man seated on a cushion at the head of the table. He didn't notice, however, as he was busy ripping a greasy piece of flesh off a cooked pheasant's plump leg with his teeth. There was a slurping sound, then a wet chewing noise that turned Satsobek's stomach.

Satsobek raised an eyebrow. "I am hardly a child, Kiya. I am nineteen years old, and you are barely five years older than me."

Kiya dug her fleshy fingers into the bowl of nuts, heedlessly spilling a few on to the table. "I may not be much older than you, Satsi, but I *do* know what men like. You could certainly do a little more with your hair. It is very plain, and will not catch a nobleman's eye. If you would shave your head we could have you a nice new wig made."

In an automatic response, Satsobek smoothed a hand over her chin-length hair, which hung loose and unadorned, tucked behind her ears. Satsobek already knew she was plain. She'd been told so her whole life. A change in hairstyle would not compensate for the eyes that were just a little too large and black – "like an evil spirit's," according to Amenia – lips too full to be tempting, "too much like a fish's" – cheekbones too sharp, "no man wants a woman who is all angles and lips and eyes" – and her breasts were, apparently, too small to be of any use.

Even if she'd had such physical charms, she'd discovered – thanks to Inkaef – that men did not like women with tongues as sharp as their cheekbones. And she was no good at pretending to be otherwise. The one time she *had* caught a nobleman's eye things had ended badly for her. She had no reason to expect future endeavours would be any different.

So she said, "I am perfectly happy without the trouble of a husband. I would rather not have one." She knew she'd made a mistake as soon as the words were out of her mouth, but it was too late.

Her father's head jerked up, his beady black eyes narrowing at her, and she felt a qualm under his hard gaze. He swallowed and wiped the back of his hand over his mouth. His voice was a calm, deadly drawl. "You *will* marry and you will marry soon, whether you like it or not. I will not keep you under this roof forever. You are already almost too old for it. I intend to find you a husband before the end of the next season. If you insist on being difficult, I will marry you to a man who will not have the chance to see you beforehand, or hear your tart tongue." He tore another chunk off the half-gnawed pheasant leg clutched in his hand.

Satsobek's gut tightened and she placed a hand on her abdomen. The end of the next season was only four months away and she had no prospects. With her stomach in sudden rebellion, she feared she might disgorge her barely digested meal.

Kiya rushed in, speaking through a mouthful of half-chewed nuts. "Of *course* she will marry. She is just being quarrelsome, as she often is. But really, Satsi, perhaps if you were to be *a little* more agreeable it would be easier to find you a man." Her smile was dubious, but cheerful.

Amenia smirked. "Yeah, *Satsi*," she put emphasis on the nickname she knew Satsobek hated, "you *could* be more agreeable."

Pushing herself up from the table, Satsobek said, "Thank you all for the advice, but I believe I am quite full and have had more than enough."

Satsobek's father thumped a greasy fist on the table, stopping her in mid-action. "We are not done talking about this, girl."

Any further retorts were cut off by a servant clearing his throat behind her. Satsobek looked over her shoulder at Paser, the thin, bent man with short, curly grey hair standing in the doorway. The man smoothed his hands over his coarse white linen shenti, his eyes flitting between Satsobek and her father.

"Yes, Paser?" Satsobek prompted him.

The man cleared his throat again and looked up at her. "*Nebet-i,*" *my lady,* "an escort has come for you. Your immediate presence is requested by Her Majesty, the queen."

"Really?" Concern and misgivings replaced her queasiness. Satsobek had not been to see the queen of late. Given how busy the queen was, Satsobek didn't think she'd be missed. Six months ago, with the death of Pharaoh Wadj, Queen Merneith announced she was with child and, against any precedent, she intended to rule as regent for the unborn heir until the child – hopefully a boy – was old enough to rule.

Satsobek ignored her father's derisive snort at the servant's pronouncement. There were many who doubted a woman's ability to rule, her father amongst them.

"Yes, *nebet-i,*" Paser continued, lowering his voice so that only Satsobek could hear him. He knew of her father's disdain for the queen. "It seems there has been an *accident* in the *hwt* of Mehyt involving the high priest and priestess and the queen needs to see you. That is all the escort told me."

Satsobek drew in a sharp breath. Another two people she had not seen for some time. Her heartbeat sped. "Well then, tell the escort I will be there momentarily." Satsobek was moving to follow Paser out of the dining room when her father called her.

"Girl, you *will* be here tonight for dinner. We are not finished with this conversation."

Satsobek tightened her lips and inhaled before turning back to face him. "Then Father, would you care to send the attendants back to the queen's palace with an explanation as to why I cannot obey her command?"

He grunted, glaring at her as he put his oily palm up to his maw, sucking a piece of meat off of it. Satsobek nodded, knowing she had ended it. *For now.* She turned to her sister and Kiya and inclined her head. "My apologies, ladies, but I must attend the queen."

A small measure of guilty satisfaction curled in her chest at the envy written on their faces as she turned to walk out the door. Bad hair or not, the queen needed to see *her*, not her sister or Kiya. All the wigs in the world didn't change that.

But her smugness quickly dimmed when another thought hit her. *Dear gods, what if he is there?* "He" being Ebrium, the foreign pirate-turned-soldier of the royal guard who had saved her life eight months ago when two tigers broke loose during a banquet at the palace.

When she closed her eyes, Satsobek could see the forest of exotic animal tattoos that traced up and over his muscled back, shoulder, and chest rippling and shifting as he hovered over her. She shivered, as she always did, when she recalled how he'd thrown her to the ground and laid his body over hers when one of the beasts stalked near them, and how he'd fought the animal off even as it swiped at him, leaving him with a broken arm. A mingled thrill of fear and desire coursed through her each time she pictured Ebrium's large, sculpted body tangled with the powerful, furry mass of the tiger rearing up next to her. Ebrium, with his thick black wavy hair, chiseled jaw, and brilliant sea-blue eyes.

Ebrium. The man who had not even thought her worthy of acknowledging after she'd sent a messenger behind her father's back to thank him for saving her life. She'd even offered her services as a scribe, should he ever need anything written down. Eight months and all she knew of him had been gleaned in bits and pieces from servant's gossip. She berated herself for her curiosity about a man who clearly had no interest in her. *Why be curious?* She did not want anything from him. Especially not after the way he'd responded to her. *Still*, she thought, it couldn't hurt to make sure her hair didn't look like battered crow's feathers, and to ensure that the dark grey kohl that lined her eyes wasn't smudged. *Just in case.*

Ebrium was in a foul mood.

His skull felt like it was being crushed and the scorching heat of the mid-morning sun caused beads of perspiration to form on his brow and between his pectorals. On his way to the queen's palace, he wound his way along a narrow, dusty path near the bank of the great river – the Iteru. He'd only just returned home from the House of Iput when a messenger arrived with a mysterious summons from the queen. All he'd wanted to do was spend the late morning dozing in the shade on his rooftop, sleeping off his unsavoury memories of the night before. But whatever it was Merneith required must be significant otherwise she wouldn't have sent for him on his first day to himself in some time.

Nearing the palace, he greeted some of his fellow guardsmen with a nod. Normally he'd stop to chat and joke. Being second-in-command under Bey, Captain of the Royal Guard, and recently elevated to the position of the queen's unofficial investigator, hadn't changed the way Ebrium interacted with other soldiers. His height and size, along with the unusual tattoo that circled his shoulder, bicep, and chest, were enough to garner a foreigner like him a healthy amount of respect amongst the Kemeti troops, regardless of his demeanour. But today he was in no mood for idle talk.

Passing through the entranceway and the white-washed walls of the main hallway, he climbed the stairs inside the courtyard of the queen's palace. He strode across the granite slab that covered one section of the rooftop and came to a stop in front of a large white tent. Sweat prickled the skin between his shoulder blades. There was not one merciful cloud in the sky to stop the scorching sun from pounding into his head. He squinted against the brightness, wishing he'd rimmed his eyes with kohl before leaving the House of Iput to help shield them from the glare. At the very least he wished he'd had time to grab a scarf to wrap around his head.

Raking a big, calloused hand through his thick black hair and adjusting the white linen wrap skirt known as a *shenti*, he tried to put some semblance of order to his appearance. Before a servant could move to announce him the tent flap parted and a man stepped out, the linen fabric falling closed behind him. Pausing, the man looked Ebrium over, a cold glare hardening his brown-black eyes. His head was shaved except for a long, black side-lock which was braided and looped on the right side of his head. In his mid-thirties, muscled, broad-shouldered and narrow-waisted with a chin just a touch too soft to be called strong, he had the air of a man used to having his orders followed.

The man clenched his jaw and lifted his chin as if to indicate he expected Ebrium to move out of his way. Ebrium raised one eyebrow and a cynical smile twisted his lips as he inclined his head and stepped aside. The nobleman swept past Ebrium without another look, leaving Ebrium to stuff down the urge to wrap a hand around the Kemeti's throat and show him that, high-born or not, Ebrium was still the more powerful of the two. He was getting tired of being treated like a serving boy by Kemeti noblemen.

Ebrium waited a moment for the servant to announce him, then he pushed aside one of the tent flaps and stepped into the cool, dappled shade of the queen's tent. Bluish light filtered in past the potted plants outside and through the thin linen walls of the tent and it took a moment for his eyes to adjust. When they did, he saw Queen Merneith propped up on a large, cushioned bench that curved upwards behind her back. Her long curly black hair was piled atop her head with beads of turquoise braided into it. Bey, a large, dark-skinned man with green eyes and tattoos that mirrored Ebrium's own, sat on a low chair next to the queen. Arranged around the tent were several chairs, potted trees, a few small tables, oversized cushions, and some low stools of leather stretched over three, crossed legs.

Eight months pregnant, Merneith's belly looked strained to full capacity beneath her translucent white linen dress. Ebrium knew the pregnancy had been hard on her. For a time, there was a great fear that she might lose the child, though the last two months she had improved greatly. Merneith looked tired and worried, but relieved to see him. "Ebrium, thank the gods you are here."

Ebrium bowed on one knee to Merneith then stepped forward to place a light kiss on her upturned cheek. He gave her his most dazzling grin, hoping to coax a smile on to her harried face. "You are looking particularly stunning this morning, *Hem-etj*." Although she'd repeatedly asked him to call her by her name when they were in private, he still called her *Your Majesty*. He'd fallen into the habit of formal address during the months when her life was in danger and he and the rest of the Royal Guard were protecting her from her husband, the pharaoh Wadj, who died six months ago.

"How are you today, Hem-etj? I hope my friend here," he jerked his head towards Bey, "is taking care of you. If not, I'd be happy to remind him he's not the only man who would kill for a woman like you." Ebrium winked at Merneith and was rewarded with an upwards twisting of her lips.

Bey scoffed. "I would like to see you try." Ebrium turned to the large green-eyed man and clasped his forearm in greeting. "Brother." Ebrium and his oldest friend nodded good-naturedly at one another.

Merneith shifted on the bench, grimacing in discomfort. Ebrium didn't envy her carrying the extra weight of a baby in this heat. Bey moved to adjust the cushions behind her and Ebrium seated himself in a chair nearby, watching their display of domestic fidelity.

Merneith turned back to Ebrium, shaking her head wearily. "There is too much happening today. Did you pass Sekhemkare on his way out? He is the brother of the governor of the *Aneb-Hetch* district. He has come to stay in Thinis for a few weeks, managing some business affairs. I imagine you will run in to him at court soon enough. I would have introduced you, had I known you were outside when he left."

Ebrium and Bey exchanged a look over her head, and Ebrium could see that Bey had formed the same opinion of the man. Neither was much impressed by the governor's brother.

Just then the servant by the door announced a new arrival. When Ebrium heard the name called out he stiffened and turned his head with a jerk. *What in the name of the gods is going on here?* And then the entitled little woman who had toyed with him eight months ago stepped inside the tent.

Satsobek blinked as her eyes adjusted to the shade. Self-conscious in the darkness, she reached up a hand to smooth her chin-length black hair. Then she saw her cousin Merneith and gave a deep bow in her direction. *"Hem-etj."* *Your Majesty*, she addressed the pregnant queen.

"Satsobek, my dear. How have you been?" Merneith held out a hand to her, and Satsobek clasped it with both of hers. "Sekhrey Bey," Merneith addressed Bey by his formal title of Captain. "Allow me to introduce Satsobek, daughter of Sobek, and a distant cousin of mine. Satsobek, this is Sekhrey Bey." Satsobek bowed her head to the captain, who inclined his head and gave a smile, crinkling the skin around his bright green eyes.

"Nebet-i," *my lady*, Bey murmured. Satsobek had heard much about the man's exotic looks. Seeing him now, it would not surprise her at all if the queen had taken him as a lover, as was rumoured. He exuded a calm strength, despite the unsettling intensity of his green eyes.

Merneith looked past Satsobek to the right, a smile curling up the corners of her mouth. "And I believe you have already met Ebrium, Sekhrey Bey's man."

Satsobek's chest tightened. She turned to see the foreigner's massive frame sprawled out in a chair, knees spread wide as he rested with one elbow over the back of the chair in a posture of pure confidence and power. Even though he was sitting still, restless energy emanated from his tanned, moulded body. Like that of a stalking predator, lurking in the dappled shade of the tall papyrus reeds, stilled in mid-step, waiting for the moment to strike. Just like the tiger he'd saved her from.

She tore her eyes up to his, away from the thick ridges of his naked torso, and the large curved blade that hung from his hip off the side of the chair. He was looking sidelong up at her through impossibly long lashes, lashes so dark and thick they gave his unusual blue eyes the appearance of being lined with kohl. There was a coldness in them that made her think of the cold winds that blew over the desert at night.

The cold-eyed man hitched one eyebrow up a quarter of an inch and greeted her, "Nebet-i."

"*Wa-ew.*" *Soldier.* She returned his eyebrow, fighting to keep her face just as impassive as his, thrown off-balance that he had the nerve to be rude to her after what he'd done. *He is the one who rejected the messenger I sent to thank him for saving my life. Let him be as cold as the snow they say falls in the far north. It matters not to me.*

Merneith gestured to Satsobek to pull over a chair. "I am sorry to summon you to share bad news, Satsobek," the queen gave Satsobek an apologetic look. "But I called the both of you here because early this morning both the high priest and priestess of the Temple of Mehyt were found dead."

Horror washed over Satsobek. Despite the stifling heat of the day a chill ran across the surface of her skin. She put a hand up to cover her mouth as it dropped open. "No! Both?"

Merneith pursed her lips. "I am so sorry. I know you were close to them."

Satsobek closed her eyes, fighting back the tears that stung them. To say she was close with them was a complicated matter. When she was younger she'd spent most of her time in the Temple of Mehyt. Tiya, the high priestess, had taught Satsobek to read and write, and Satsobek spent countless hours sitting cross-legged on a woven papyri mat next to her mentor, learning to scratch out the symbols that made up their language. While not exactly a mother-figure, Tiya had been sympathetic to Satsobek's family situation, conscious of her father's disinterest. Tiya taught her to find peace in the quiet rituals of the temple - and sometimes the noisier ones as well, like the twice daily singing and dancing that took place during the goddess's meals. And Satsobek found a worthy purpose in documenting the daily worship of the goddess and the goings-on at the temple.

The high priest, Yuny, had been a benevolent fellow. It was he who had given Tiya permission to teach Satsobek to read, something almost unheard of for a girl to learn. Yuny had always reminded her of a friendly old goat, with his tightly curling grey hair and gentle, thin-lipped smile. Satsobek recalled the feeling of pride when Yuny once complimented her skill and swiftness in writing, as well as her usefulness in transcribing the letters and stories the other priestesses dictated.

Until recently, the hope that she might one day succeed Tiya as high priestess had deterred her father from pressing the issue of marriage. There was prestige to be had for him if she ascended the ranks. However, it had been over a year since she'd stepped foot inside the temple. Not since things had gone so terribly wrong with Inkaef.

Guilt filled her as she thought of how she had stopped going to the temple. She had been unable to explain to Tiya why she no longer felt comfortable in the sanctuary of the goddess, or why she no longer found the same peace in prayer she once had. She could only say that it no longer felt right.

After a moment, she looked up and cleared her throat. "I have not seen them for some time. How did they…" She couldn't finish the sentence.

Merneith shook her head, a mix of sympathy, sadness, and anger in her eyes. "They were murdered. Yuny," she turned to Ebrium to explain. "Yuny is the high priest of the *hwt* – the temple. He was beaten, we do not know by what instrument. He was found in the hallway outside his office. Tiya, the high priestess, had bruises around her neck. She was in the great room near the image of Mehyt."

Merneith looked from Satsobek to Ebrium. "I need the two of you to find who did this. I need two people I can trust. This was not just any common death. There was no robbery."

Satsobek shook her head. "I don't understand. Why would anyone want to murder Tiya and Yuny? They were both good people."

The men hesitated, apparently looking to Merneith for her approval. The queen nodded. "Satsobek has my absolute trust, and we must speak freely with her of these important matters. She lived here in the palace for a time after her mother passed away, and we were close, although she has not been to visit us much at court of late."

Satsobek's cheeks burned and she turned her head to hide her blush. To know she had the trust of a cousin she so admired was a great compliment. She was also blushing because one of the reasons she had been avoiding the court of late happened to be seated near her at that very moment, his penetrating lapis lazuli eyes boring into her.

Bey addressed Satsobek, his deep voice rumbling in impeccable, formal Kemeti. "There are several possible reasons for these murders. A few of them may have nothing to do with Tiya and Yuny at all. Whatever the reason, though, the repercussions for our queen are the same. This is not just a challenge to the authority of the temples. It is a challenge to the queen herself. There are already those who oppose her rule and think that, as a woman, she is incapable of ruling Kemet and acting as the conduit of the gods."

Shame swelled in Satsobek's breast. Her own father opposed the queen's rule while she supported Merneith with all her heart.

Bey continued, "Of course, there is the possibility this is a warning, a threat to her physical safety, and that of her unborn child." Satsobek wondered at the fierce expression that came over Bey's countenance. His lips narrowed, and the hands that rested on his thighs clenched into fists. *Could it be that the rumours are true? Could he really be the baby's father?* She wondered if she was being let into more than one confidence here.

The big man added, "We have increased security around the queen, of course, for the safety of her well-being." She caught the quick look and nod that passed between Bey and Ebrium, the silent communication of men who had known one another long enough and well enough to not need words.

Bey added, "But there are also rumours of rallying support for Anen, the governor of one of the northern districts. He is a distant cousin of the queen and with enough support, he may become a threat. If we do not find those responsible it will be considered a sign of the queen's inability to maintain *maat*, the balance of peace in Kemet. There are those who will use this to their advantage to discredit the queen. Especially with the harvest season coming to an end, and the Festival of the New Year approaching. We must find out who did this before rumours start."

Ebrium's leg bounced, emanating impatience and anger. "I've heard some of the villagers and soldiers here say if maat is disturbed there's a risk of dangerous floods, bad harvests, plagues of locusts, fire bolts from the sky." He waved a dismissive hand, "Whatever the nonsense, if they believe it, it doesn't bode well considering the upcoming harvest likely won't be large."

It was the first time she'd heard him speak at length. The timbre of his voice, his foreign accent, and his slang were so distracting it took her a moment to absorb the content of his speech. He spoke more like a commoner than a nobleman, unlike Sekhrey Bey. She was also shocked when she realized he had called maat, the order and balance of the living world that governed the daily lives of the people of Kemet, *nonsense*.

But she didn't have time to ponder Ebrium's religious inclinations as the reality of the situation began to sink in. She shook her head. "But I still do not understand. Surely the people would not revolt!"

Ebrium's appraisal of her made her feel as if she were a repulsive weevil infiltrating his grain storage. His tone was that of one speaking to an ignorant child and she chafed under the implication. "Much as they say they love their queen, people will support whoever they think will keep their bellies full." He shot Merneith an apologetic look and said in a softer voice, "Please forgive my bluntness, Hem-etj."

Merneith sighed, rubbing her hand in agitated circles over the mound of her abdomen. "No, Ebrium, you are right. You know better than most how difficult and delicate it can be to maneuver the political machinations here. If I am found wanting, if another is considered more…suitable…it would be far worse than just the deaths of the high priest and priestess. Kemet could fall into civil war and hundreds, thousands even, could die. If we lost, I would face exile. Possibly even execution. As does my child. As do those I hold close to me…"

Bey's lips had tightened to a thin line, but he reached out to place a hand over the queen's. "We will not let that happen. This is just as personal for Ebrium as it is for me." Once again Satsobek saw the men exchange a glance, a silent agreement indicative of their determination.

Merneith levelled her gaze on Satsobek. "So now you see why it is so important to me, to all of Kemet, that we find out who started all of this in the hwt of Mehyt."

Satsobek did see why it was so important. If the murderer, or murderers, weren't caught quickly the consequences could be staggering. There were plenty of men like her father who would happily turn against the queen, no matter what claims to divinity she might have as the daughter and wife of pharaohs. Ebrium might scoff, but the risk of displeasing the gods, and the potential for chaos to reign, was great. It would be a most serious transgression of maat if vengeance was not exacted for the deaths of two temple servants. Without retribution, chaos and disorder might well descend upon Kemet, which is precisely what would happen if the queen were unseated.

But Satsobek was still unclear what Merneith thought *she* of all people could do about it.

Ebrium had no clue why the queen had called in the nobleman's daughter. Merneith might trust Satsobek, but at the moment he certainly did not.

"With all due respect, Hem-etj," he addressed Merneith, "You know I'll not hesitate to do anything you ask of me, and I want to terminate whoever did this as much as anyone could. Any threat to you is as one to my own life and family. But I tend to be more effective at my job when ladies are not present."

Merneith snorted, her formal deportment slipping. "Nonsense. I have never known you to have a problem with *any* ladies." She obviously knew he was making excuses, though he wasn't sure if Bey had conveyed to her the details of his prior dealings with Satsobek.

She continued, routing any objections he might make. "Satsobek spent years as a priestess in the hwt. She is an incredibly skilled scribe, capable of reading any records the temple has been keeping. Satsobek is also familiar with the hwt and the people there. Especially Tiya and Yuny. I realize she might be an unconventional partner, but she knows people you do not, and I am confident that she will know the best way to approach them. She is the very best person I can think of to pair you with."

Ebrium's fist clenched. Like most people, he could neither read nor write in any language, whether it be his own or that of Kemet. He was well aware that his thick accent belied his foreign birth. He also spoke in the coarse dialect of the lower classes of Kemet rather than the refined language of the court, having learned to speak Kemeti from the militia soldiers he'd worked with. Those men were usually conscripted from the peasant classes, and were indentured labourers, farmers, and other commoners. Bey, an educated prince in their homeland, had once tried to teach Ebrium the formal language of Kemet. But Ebrium had little patience for such learning, or the niceties of the court for that matter. He preferred to be in motion.

While he recognized the utility of having someone who could read temple documents and gain access to the upper echelons of the temple elite, he wished it weren't *her*. Eight months ago he'd almost lost his arm saving her life. She had sent him a messenger thanking him and offering any assistance should his savaged arm prevent him from his duties, along with her services as a scribe. He had sent her messenger back, thanking her in turn for her concern and inquiring if he might see her at court in the near future. The messenger had returned to tell him that *her ladyship* had said it was not the place of a vagrant thief, and a foreigner at that, to inquire anything of her.

Despite his annoyance, it was no less than he'd expected. She was the daughter of a Kemeti nobleman and he was just "foreign scum" in their eyes. The queen had made Ebrium's position as an enforcer and investigator unofficial in order to avoid upsetting the well-born and wealthy who believed themselves entitled to higher-ranking positions than he. That hadn't prevented resentment amongst the noble ranks, though; particularly on the part of those he arrested and sent into exile, their property confiscated. Ebrium had every reason to believe Satsobek and her family were no different.

Satsobek opened her mouth to speak, but Merneith cut her off. "Your father might not be eager to spare you, but I will make your excuses for you. I am confident that you are capable of assisting Ebrium with this task, Satsobek, whatever doubts you may harbour to the contrary. Furthermore, Ebrium has been working for me the past several months to deal with the corruption amongst the nobility and temple benefactors. I cannot turn a blind eye, as Pharaoh Wadj did, to those who would line their treasuries while the servants and slaves starve. Not when the harvest season may be smaller than usual and there is a risk of insurrection. And Ebrium is particularly skilled at getting to the truth of matters."

Here Ebrium and Bey exchanged wry looks. By *skilled* they both knew Merneith meant that Ebrium was large and intimidating. The threat of being alone in a room with him – and his fists – was enough to get men talking.

"Also, I trust Ebrium to keep you safe while you both find out who did this. I need you to stop this person before they inflict any more damage." Here Merneith looked from Satsobek to Ebrium, and he wondered that she had the ability to make him feel like an unruly child in need of admonishment. *Wonderful,* he thought. *Now not only will I have a murderer to deal with, but I will have to babysit a spoiled little rich girl.*

Chapter 2 – The Temple of Mehyt

"Where are you going?" Satsobek demanded as she tried to keep up with Ebrium's long strides. The man walked so fast he kicked up a choking swirl of dust and sand behind him, the blade slung around his hip tapping lightly against the side of his thigh with each step. They'd left the queen's palace several minutes ago and yet he still hadn't spoken to her. He'd made his way out of the palace and into the network of narrow streets that lined the village, and Satsobek was forced to trail behind. She knew they were walking north towards the wealthier neighbourhood of the nobility and the temple, leaving behind the palace along the banks of the great river.

But instead of taking the main road, Ebrium wound them through streets unknown to her. Beige mud-brick huts lined the lane, tightly packed together and ringed by low retaining walls entangled with morning glory vines. Behind the walls chickens clucked, goats bleated, and the odd cow gave a low lament, stinking of livestock and baked manure mingled with jasmine flowers, while the chirruping rub of locusts echoed all around them. With the sun directly overhead she wished she had a palm leaf, or a head wrap, to protect her from its scorching rays.

Satsobek grew more furious by the minute. "This *will not* work if you do not tell me what your plan is." She warned Ebrium.

But he kept walking. Satsobek had had enough of being made to feel insignificant for one day. It had been a hard enough morning already. First she'd had to deal with her family trying to force her to marry. Then she'd learned about the murder of her mentor, Tiya. Now, the man she had once admired for saving her so heroically was behaving like the rudest donkey of a man she'd ever known.

Satsobek came to an abrupt halt on the thin avenue, confined on either side by the enclosure walls of various mud-brick homes. She crossed her arms over her chest. "Fine then. I suppose I will have to return to Queen Merneith and tell her that you refuse to work with me." It was the second time today she'd had to invoke the queen to get a man to listen to her.

Ebrium stopped, his back to her. The thick muscles of his naked, honey-coloured shoulders shifted as he took a deep breath. Sunlight glinted off the thin sheen of sweat along the columns of his back. A dragonfly fluttered past. She felt they were suspended in time, a heavy pause in the midst of an increasingly oppressive afternoon. A bead of moisture broke out between her breasts and rolled down along her belly as she held her breath, waiting for Ebrium to move, to speak, to do *something*. Scrutinizing the back of his head, a series of faint scars that criss-crossed his upper back and shoulders became visible.

She was about to give in to urge to step forward to study the markings more closely when Ebrium's shoulders relaxed. It seemed a great effort for him to look back over his shoulder, a dark expression in his azure eyes. She clenched her jaw and forced herself to glare back at him. She would not let him intimidate her.

In a languid voice laced with a thick accent, Ebrium said, "I am going to the hwt of Mehyt."

He was turning away again when Satsobek snorted. "Now was that so hard?" Although taken aback by the snarky tone in her own voice, she *was* angry. Angry at her father. Angry at whoever had killed Tiya and Yuny. And angry at this man who was also, for some reason, angry at her. He looked back over his shoulder at her, one eyebrow raised, and she stretched her lips in a sardonic smile. She had no idea why he took such offence to her, considering that *he* was the one who had ignored her messenger.

His lips tilted up and she couldn't be sure if it was a smile or a sneer. He said, "If you insist on following me, at least try to keep up." Then he turned and resumed his long strides.

"I… what?!" Forced to scurry once again, Satsobek didn't bother to hold back a string of insults muttered well under her breath. "*Follow* you? You arrogant son of a jackal-headed prostitute." After a moment she added for good measure, "donkey-breathed hippopotamus's ass."

Despite his irritation, Ebrium couldn't help but smile at the grumbled invectives he knew she hadn't intended him to hear. He'd been called many things over the years; bastard, peasant, thief, common, crude, the list went on. However, this was definitely the first time a woman had ever called him a donkey-breathed hippopotamus's ass. At least she was inventive.

A minute ago when she'd stood scowling at him, he'd had his first chance to really look at her. Defiant and fierce-looking, she reminded him of an angry little water nymph, the type sailors blamed for mischievous and unexplained happenings at sea. An image of her the first night he saw her came to mind. It was eight months ago at the queen's banquet and he and Bey had only recently joined the royal guard. She was seated across the palace courtyard as the sun set and the night sky deepened across the horizon. Her features fell short of striking, she was no great beauty, but there had been *something* that had drawn him to her.

It was his repeated glances her way that had enabled him to see the moment she was in danger when the handlers lost control of the two tigers. By coincidence, Bey had saved the queen that night from one tiger and he'd saved Satsobek from another. Of course, where things went after that were wildly different. Under other circumstance, under very, very different circumstances, Ebrium might view a woman like Satsobek as a challenge worth trying his hand at.

But not today, and not this woman. She'd made it abundantly clear after the banquet that she had no interest in him. And now the irritation of being hobbled with her was nothing compared to his ire at whoever had killed the priest and priestess. Anyone who threatened the queen's rule was, indirectly, threatening his family. At the age of seventeen, Ebrium left his hometown with his friend Bey in order to find work to support his mother and sister. After several years at sea, he and Bey took control of a small fleet which periodically raided wealthy merchant ships. Their situation was not as lucrative as many imagined and was, in fact, one of constant uncertainty. However, their reputation as fierce fighters and strong commanders preceded them. As a result, when some of their ships were dashed in a storm in the northern delta and subsequently captured by Kemeti militias, they were offered the choice between execution or secure, high-ranking positions and steady pay in the militias of the wealthiest region in the living world. With the decision an obvious one, they spent the next four years working their way through the military ranks, successfully distinguishing themselves. Once established, Ebrium was able to send for his mother and little sister.

Now, after a lifetime of poverty, subjugation, and uncertainty, Ebrium had managed to scrape together a measure of stability for his mother and sister here in Kemet. His mother, who'd worked herself into an early old-age just to help them survive, was able to relax. His sister was learning the proper manners of the court and spoke the language of Kemet much better than he did. She was now positioned to marry well. And Ebrium hadn't felt the sting of a whip on his back in over a decade. All this thanks to the distinction the queen had conferred on himself and his friend Bey in the last several months. If anything happened to damage the stability of Kemet, and Merneith's rule, he and his family were at risk. Never mind that Bey, the queen, and their unborn child were as good as family to him. The only thing that really mattered right now was finding whoever killed the temple priest and priestess and making sure they never saw the light of day again.

"Tell me about the hwt of Mehyt." Ebrium's question broke into Satsobek's thoughts after a few moments of silent walking. "Do you have any suspicions of who might have done this?"

After a moment's hesitation, she told him she'd just been contemplating that same question. She went on to explain that Tiya and Yuny had been selected as high priest and priestess over two decades ago by Queen Merneith's father, Pharaoh Djer. "In some places the high priests follow a hereditary line but here in Thinis they are appointed by the pharaoh. So it does not make sense that anyone would have done this for personal gain, as they could not be assured of being chosen as high priest or priestess. Whoever did this must have had another reason.

"The hwt employs two or three hundred people, some of whom I do not know. There are the full-time *hem-netjer* and *hemet-netjer*, the priests and priestesses who serve under Tiya and Yuny, as well as some who only serve a few days a week, or a month or so at a time. I know most of them, except for any who joined in the last year. Menkhaf is the man we are likely to deal with today, he is the second high priest under Yuny, and he manages the temple properties and inventories. Then there are all the servants and slaves beneath them who work in the hwt as well, cooking and cleaning and laundering and such. And of course the hwt has a vast expanse of land for farming and livestock, so there is a small village worth of common people that live within the hwt's grounds. But I have never dealt with any of them."

Ebrium cleared his throat and she looked up to see his cold blue eyes observing her through hooded lids. "By *common people* you mean…?"

Her face burned, conscious now that he might take her words as a slight of sorts. Of course she'd heard the rumours that in his northern homeland he'd been little more than the son of a gardener, albeit a gardener of the King's palace. Not a slave, but not much higher than one. In the days following their first encounter, she'd taken discreet means to find out about Ebrium. Not that it was difficult, as he and Sekhrey Bey had been the talk of every woman's circle in Thinis, and probably several other cities, for months after their dramatic arrival at the queen's court. Bey had saved the queen's life on more than one occasion and had almost died in an attempt to save the pharaoh from a group of vicious crocodiles. Since Ebrium was often by Bey's side, and his sister and mother lived in the queen's palace, he played a large part in these circulating stories.

"By *common people*," she chose her words carefully, "I meant labourers such as the farmers, builders, bakers, fishermen, beekeepers, and others who live and work on the hwt lands to supply food and goods. I… that is my duties did not extent to interacting with those people."

"And what did your duties extend to? Why were you there in the first place?"

Satsobek focused on the mud-brick houses they passed. They were leaving the smaller homes behind and moving into a more familiar neighbourhood. The houses were growing in size, as were their courtyards. Soon they would reach the temple grounds, situated as they were between the queen's palace and one of the wealthiest neighbourhoods in Thinis, the neighbourhood she lived in.

"My mother died giving birth to me, so my father sent my sister Amenia and I to live with an aunt in the palace, where I grew up alongside Merneith." Uncomfortable with this part of the story, she smoothed her hair down, tucking it behind her ears. "When I was ten, my aunt passed to the other world. Tiya, the high priestess, had been a friend and cousin of my mother's, and she offered to train us as priestesses, so we went to the hwt several days a week. My sister never really took to it, though. She was not interested in the quiet, the rituals, or the discipline."

"But you were?" Ebrium prompted, throwing her a sidelong look that she caught.

She nodded. "Yes. I…" Satsobek trailed off, remembering the calm, tranquil gloom of the temple, especially during the flood season, when the weather wasn't as hot or the days as long as they were now in the harvest season of *Shemu*. She'd felt that she was wanted and needed, doing something of value for others and for the goddess. Despite the horrible circumstances, she realized that once again she had a purpose and that she'd missed that feeling.

She finished shortly, "The other girls in the hwt were kind, and I had a purpose there in transcribing their letters and daily affairs. Tiya and Yuny were good to me, and it is my duty to find out what happened to them."

"Yet you stopped going to the hwt." Was he interrogating her? Satsobek turned her face up to him, narrowing her eyes to scrutinize him, but he stared ahead, a blank expression on his face.

"Yes," was her flat answer.

"Why?"

"Is this really necessary to know for our investigation?"

Ebrium lifted one shoulder in a lazy shrug. "Perhaps."

"Well I'm not involved if that is what you are trying to imply. I have not stepped foot in the temple for a year now." She glared up at him but he just kept walking, not bothering to look down at her.

In spite of himself the more Ebrium learned about the little woman the more curious he became. *Quiet, discipline, duty, kind.* These were not the favoured words of a selfish person, or one likely to be involved in a temple intrigue. He believed she was telling him the truth about her past with the temple, but also that she was holding something back about why she'd stopped going. Whether or not her reasons for leaving were relevant or not to their investigation remained to be seen.

By this time they had neared the entrance to the Temple of Mehyt. As Mehyt was one of the two most prominent goddesses of the city of Thinis, the temple grounds were large, stretching in a narrow rectangle west towards the desert, and encasing not only the large, multi-roomed temple but the servants' quarters, housing for many of the priests and priestesses, and several acres of farmland and livestock.

The actual temple structure sat near the lane, at the entrance to the temple lands, and was enclosed by five-foot high mud-brick walls. A long granite-tiled courtyard dotted with large potted myrrh trees imported from the south opened up before the temple. Through the courtyard, a pathway lined with lion-headed stone statues —

representations of the goddess – on limestone bases, led to the place of worship. At the end of the pathway stood the imposing temple, ringed with thick, etched columns that supported the overhanging flat roof.

Ebrium made to walk through the arched entrance of the temple's surrounding walls when Satsobek gasped out, "Wait!" He turned to look down at her as she ran her tongue over her full lips, drawing the bottom one in and indenting the soft, red pad of her lip with her little white teeth.

"Ebrium," Satsobek drew his attention upwards from her mouth. She squinted, the skin around her large brown eyes crinkling. "Have you ever *been* into a temple in Kemet?"

The question didn't surprise him. He hitched an eyebrow. "It's the same in my homeland as it is in yours. I lack the… what is the term? Ah, wait – the appropriate lineage." He didn't bother to conceal his scorn.

In both his homeland of Ebla and in Kemet only royalty, nobility, and servants of the temple entered the sanctuaries of the gods, either to work or to worship. Common people only saw the god of the temple when the god's icon was moved outside during festivals, or to visit other neighbouring gods from time to time. Sometimes they were allowed into the temple courtyard to leave offerings to the gods. Ebrium had never been allowed into a temple anywhere in his life. But that hadn't stopped him from sneaking in just once. It was a memory he preferred to forget.

Satsobek glanced back at the temple then said, "Perhaps it's best if you let me speak first when we are greeted."

As much as it chafed to admit, she was right. He made a sweeping, mock bow. "Lead the way, nebet-i. I am your servant to command."

Satsobek ignored Ebrium's taunt and moved past him. As they made their way down the pathway a man she recognized came to stand in the shadows of the temple's entranceway. Menkhaf had served directly under Yuny, and was the priest who managed the properties and inventories of the temple. He was short, only an inch or so taller than

Satsobek, and his full-length white robe did little to hide the paunch that jutted out in front of him. His bald pate was shiny with sweat and his large, wide-set eyes gave him a rather frog-like appearance.

He greeted them with a bow slightly lower than necessary, reminding Satsobek that she'd always found him to be a rather unctuous, awkward man. Satsobek inclined her head in greeting and introduced Ebrium and Menkhaf to one another. Although shy by nature, she pushed herself now to be more cordial. It was necessary to ensure the good-will of anyone who might be able to help them.

Her memory was passable, and she asked about Menkhaf's wife and sons before saying, "I imagine now that Yuny is gone," Satsobek turned to the priest, "you will be assuming his duties until the queen can determine who shall take his place."

An obsequious smile stretched Menkhaf's lips, and he bowed his head in acknowledgement. The subservient gesture wasn't necessary. Even if she were still working at the temple, he would rank above her.

Menkhaf gestured towards the entranceway. "Please, I am sure you are eager to conduct your investigation. Of course Tiya and Yuny have been removed to the mortuary temple where they can begin the rites of passage, so you will not see them here. But I have advised everyone that you would be coming and need to speak with them." He gave another deep bow and held his hands palm up as if supplicating them. "I have determined that you may be exempt from the cleansing stipulations generally required to enter the temple as the circumstances are... *unusual*... to say the least. You need only do the bare minimum today."

Satsobek noticed that Ebrium's lips thinned at Menkhaf's words and his jaw tightened. She took pity on him then. He couldn't be expected to know what to do. She inclined her head to indicate he follow her direction. A large stone basin filled with water stood near the doorway of the temple. Satsobek dipped her hands into it, cupping the water and rubbing it up over her arms to wash away the dust and dirt of the streets. The water was meant to cleanse and revitalize, and Satsobek took some comfort from the familiar ritual.

Ebrium followed suit, scooping water over his thick arms and across his chest and back. She bit down hard on her lip and looked away when he stood upright and beads of water dripped down between the ridges of his molded pectorals and the ridges of his shoulders. Following Menkhaf into the temple, Ebrium was so tall he had to duck his head entering in the doorway. The priest led them to a room with long, narrow windows cut into the mud-brick walls. The walls were brightly painted with scenes of the lion-headed Mehyt. It was empty except for a few chairs, a bench, and a low table.

Menkhaf left them to ensure the other priests and priestesses were in order for questioning. While they waited for his return, Satsobek's eyes turned to the frescos on the white-washed walls. When she was younger she used to trace her fingers over their lush, bright colours, imagining herself hiding within a rich garden full of vitality and peace. Without thinking, she reached out now and followed the lines of the beautiful green papyri reeds topped with soft fronds, running her hand along a cluster of pink and white lotus blossoms, stopping to hover over the yellow-red fruit of a sycamore tree. Her eyes roved over Anhur's golden, feathered headdress and blue and gold beaded jewellery, and Mehyt's feminine body and feline head.

Breathing in the still air of the temple, Satsobek waited for the familiar sense of peace and comfort to wash over her as it used to. Except it would no longer come. If she had felt unworthy after what happened with Inkaef a year ago, she felt even worse now that her mentor was dead. She did not deserve the peace of the sanctuary anymore. Her hand dropped from the painting to fall, lightly clenched, at her side.

When she was younger, she'd thought the story of Mehyt and Anhur had the makings of a great love story. Anhur had gone to the southern lands in search of a lion and found Mehyt, the lion-headed goddess. Capturing her, he brought her back to Kemet as his wife. Sometimes

Satsobek had gone so far as to imagine herself in Mehyt's place. After all, some said that Mehyt was like the moon who ran away from her father, Ra. She imagined that Mehyt might have gone willingly when Anhur offered to take her away and make her his wife. The gods were subject to domineering fathers, just as humans were. Perhaps Mehyt had found Anhur handsome, daring, and a means to escape her father. Satsobek understood the wish to be swept away, far from her father and family, to feel so desired by a man. *But that is nothing more than a childish dream. Such stories are reserved for the gods only.*

Life was never so idyllic. Tiya and Yuny, two good people, had been brutally murdered. No one came to save *them.* And no one would save her from being forced to marry a man she neither knew nor wanted. She couldn't even save herself from it. But at least she could try to find justice for the high priest and priestess and prevent Apep, the snake god of chaos, from descending upon Kemet.

She looked up and discovered that, instead of viewing the paintings, Ebrium was watching her. Satsobek ducked her head, letting her hair swing forward to cover her face, feeling she had somehow revealed something far too intimate. Thankfully, Menkhaf stepped back into the room just then, followed by a servant who arranged mugs of wine and sweet breads on a table for them.

Ebrium lost no time with pleasantries when the servant left. "Were you here last night when the priest and priestess were killed?"

"I? No." Menkhaf rubbed his palms together, and the movement of his fingers distracted Satsobek. The fluid turning of his hands was captivating. "No. I was at home, of course. Most of us leave the temple after the goddess's evening meal. Satsobek will tell you that. We do not stay here at night." He nodded at her for affirmation of her agreement.

Satsobek confirmed it, explaining to Ebrium that the servants of the temple fed the goddess twice daily. During these times singers and dancers, the *hnr,* performed for the goddess's pleasure. Once the goddess completed her meal, the priests and priestesses restored her to the tranquility of her cabinet, shutting the doors around her so that she could rest in silence.

Menkhaf's hands never stopped moving, turning over one another in endless, dry hand-washing. "Horrid business, all this," he interjected now and then. Under further questioning, Menkhaf confirmed that he'd been home all night, and that his manservant could verify it. "My wife and sons are usually home as well, but they are in the south visiting my wife's family." He also told them that, if it hadn't been for last night's horror, he wouldn't even be at the temple today, but preparing to leave Thinis to join his wife and sons for a two week stay.

Ebrium sat, adjusting his large body on the small chair. "Do you know any reason why someone might want to kill the high priest and priestess?"

Menkhaf moistened his lips and spoke barely above a whisper. "None at all, of course. Both were..." He licked his lips again, searching for words it seemed. "Both were good. So very good." His crooked teeth bared in an attempt at a smile, but he seemed to realize how inappropriate that was and stopped himself. "This is all such horrid business. Quite upsetting."

Ebrium's tone suggested only mild interest as he asked, "Do *you* feel unsafe here now? Do you think there's a chance of another attack?"

Menkhaf's eyes widened. "Another... Do you believe... No. Do you know something about these murderers? Why should they come back?"

"I don't know why *they* would have come in the first place. Do you?" Ebrium raised one eyebrow as he leaned back in a chair, resting one arm across the back of it. A tiger sitting across the room from them wouldn't be much more intimidating than Ebrium's cool demeanour.

She held her breath. Ebrium was skirting the bounds of propriety with his probing. The queen had told them to be discreet and respectful when questioning the priests and priestesses. They could not afford to rouse their ire at a time like this. The legitimacy of the queen's rule was, in part, indirectly dependent on the goodwill of the temples. It was within the priests' power to persuade the people that the queen was out of favour with the gods, should the temples choose to turn against her.

At the same time, she could see that Ebrium was rattling Menkhaf and that, if he were guilty, he might betray something. The man had always been nervous and graceless, but he seemed especially so now. Then again, she couldn't blame him given the circumstances.

"I?" Menkhaf's hands had stopped moving, forgotten as they clasped one another against his chest. "Nnn-no. I do not know. I do not think they should come back again."

One corner of Ebrium's mouth quirked up. "I don't think they *should* either. That does not mean they *will not*." Satsobek blinked, surprised by his quick grasp of the language and his emphasis on Menkhaf's assumption that there was more than one killer involved. His thick accent and peasant slang apparently covered a sharper mind than she'd given him credit for.

Ebrium dismissed the priest and they both turned their attention to questioning the stream of people that came over the course of the next few hours. They spoke with numerous servants of the temple, all of whom were visibly shaken. But nobody could suggest any possible motive for the deaths. Neither could anyone answer what the priest and priestess were doing in the temple at night. Both usually returned to their homes within the temple complex after completing their duties at the end of the day.

When the last of a long line of priests and priestesses had left the room, Satsobek took a deep pull from her mug of wine to firm her resolve and said, "There are two priestesses we still need to see. We must find Maketaten and Betrest. Maketaten was one of Tiya's pupils, like myself, and Betrest cultivates… information." *As well as lovers*, she thought, but that was hardly relevant at the moment.

They found the priestess Maketaten in the offering hall, just where Satsobek suspected she'd be. A smallish room at the back of the temple, the offering hall lay past the goddess's sanctuary which was the heart of the temple itself.

While the main statue of the goddess rested inside a cabinet in the sanctuary for most of the year, another statue remained in constant view on a raised platform in the offering hall. Here the priests and priestesses laid out the dozens of flowers, trinkets, and bits of food or drink that the common people left outside the temple walls in offering to the goddess. Each morning the offerings were gathered from outside and brought in here, that the goddess might hear some of the prayers of the people. Each night the lower priests and priestesses of the temple cleared away the offerings and redistributed them amongst the servants.

As Satsobek had predicted, Maketaten was in her accustomed prayer position. Dressed in a loose, long-sleeved robe and prostrate on her knees at the base of the goddess's platform, the priestess's neatly shaved forehead rested on the ground. The room was otherwise unoccupied and silent. Greasy cones of incense burned in bowls in the corners, while braided flax wicks resting in bowls of oil cast flickering shadows over the etched columns that held up the limestone roof.

Unwilling to enter the room without having completed the purification rituals usually required before entering into the goddess's presence, Satsobek gently cleared her throat from the doorway. Maketaten took her time pushing herself up to sit back on her heels and turning to look at them over her shoulder. Satsobek knew the action for what it was. Maketaten was making a point of showing how little deference she had for Satsobek. As if not joining the queue of other temple servants wasn't enough.

The priestess spoke in a slow, deliberate voice. "I have almost completed my devotions. I will join you in a moment."

"Please make sure you do." Satsobek was unable to keep the shortness from her voice.

They had just re-settled themselves in the room Menkhaf had cleared for their questioning when Maketaten joined them. A thin priestess the same age as Satsobek, Maketaten had always reminded Satsobek of a small black and orange hoopoe bird with its feathers slicked down. She kept her head shaved bald and wig-free, her narrow, rectangular pate accentuated by a long, thin nose and prominent, widely-spaced eyes. While she tried so hard to appear stern and solemn, more often than not she gave off the impression of being slightly outlandish.

"Maketaten," Satsobek greeted her, tilting her head. She would let the priestess choose the tone of their conversation. They hadn't parted on the best of terms, and for that Satsobek blamed Maketaten.

"Satsobek. It is *interesting* to see you back here. And with a man, no less." Maketaten seated herself without invitation, holding her loosely wrapped linen robe out to the sides as she did so to prevent wrinkling it beneath her. Once seated, she smoothed the fabric over her thighs and knees, sitting primly on the edge of her chair - straight as a temple column - and with her shoulders pushed back.

Satsobek cast Ebrium an apologetic glance. He returned her look with an amused glint in his deep blue eyes, his arched eyebrow letting her know that he'd already assessed Maketaten and discovered her nature. She introduced them and explained their purpose in the temple.

Maketaten lifted her head and sniffed, folding her hands neatly in her lap. In a voice tinged with fervour she said, "There is no higher purpose than to serve the goddess. If the great goddess Mehyt might find favour in it I would give my life to determine what happened to her two most devout servants."

Satsobek tried not to roll her eyes. She, too, would do whatever she could to help uncover Tiya and Yuny's murderer. But she wasn't doing it for the sake of winning the gods' favour, or personal accolades. She was doing it because Tiya, and even Yuny, had taken her in and given her a place for a time and they deserved peace in the afterlife. She was doing it because the queen, a woman she respected and admired, was at great risk and had asked for her assistance. Her homeland, Kemet, was in danger. A small part of her also knew that, if she was to be married soon, she might never have the chance to do anything of great use for anyone again.

Maketaten looked down at her hands as she flattened her dress again. "I suppose, in some way, you are doing the goddess's good works, even if it is only temporary." Although she phrased it as a compliment, Satsobek knew better. It was an insult, and a reminder that Maketaten hadn't supported Satsobek's decision to leave the temple.

Trying to arrange her face in a pleasant expression, Satsobek said, "Well then, perhaps you can tell us something helpful. Like what Tiya and Yuny were doing here late last night."

"Really, now," Maketaten kept her eyes down as spread her long, bony fingers spread out over her thighs, straining them wide. "How should I know? It is not as if I was privy to their private activities."

The bitterness in the woman's voice didn't surprise Satsobek. Maketaten had always been eager and ambitious. In the past, if something happened in the temple without her awareness, she would break down in tears of frustration for being left out or overlooked. A cold thread of fear snaked through Satsobek's belly. *Could Maketaten have been disappointed one too many times?*

When Satsobek asked if she knew of any arguments or dissatisfaction in the temple, she was sure Maketaten's back straightened even further, if that were possible, yet she denied knowledge of anything.

Satsobek thought her deliberately unhelpful, then wondered if she was judging the woman unfairly. Was she still angry with Maketaten? Hurt by the way things had ended between them? She pressed onward, asking Maketaten where she was the previous evening.

The other woman jerked her head to the side in a sharp, bird-like movement. "Here. Until after the goddess's evening meal. Then I walked along the Iteru for a time before returning home. It was a beautiful night."

Satsobek's brow furrowed. "Who did you walk with?"

Maketaten looked steadily at Satsobek, her face blank. "No one. I was alone."

Catching Ebrium's eye, he gave a casual shrug, as if to say it was her decision how to proceed. She didn't believe

Maketaten was telling her the whole truth, but she also had to take care not to push the priestess too much.

And yet her next question came out more aggressive than intended. "You did not have any reason to be upset with Tiya or Yuny, did you?"

Maketaten's chin lifted swiftly. "I do not think I need to justify that question with an answer." She stood, towering over Satsobek, and glared down at her. Then she ran her palms over her dress and once again her demeanour was calm though her voice was barbed as she said, "But I *do* hope this experience reminds you of the greater glory to be found in spending your days serving the gods, rather than the base pleasure of the flesh." She looked pointedly at Ebrium, as if his very maleness offended her. Then she turned and left the room.

Satsobek stared after her for a moment. Her heart thudded against her chest and her hands were shaky. Seeing Maketaten again upset her more than she cared to admit. She dug her nails into her palms until the sharp pain cleared her mind.

"Well *that* was interesting," Ebrium's tone was mild.

An unsteady laugh escaped her. "Maketaten is certainly that. But she is not capable of murder." She was surprised to discover she still felt a sense of loyalty to Maketaten. She didn't think the fanatical woman would understand why she'd left the temple, but they'd been friends once and it bothered Satsobek that she'd inadvertently hurt Maketaten.

"You are convinced of that?" Ebrium steepled his fingers. His cold blue eyes bored in to her.

"Not entirely," she admitted. "Yet I do not see that she has motive. She is not in a position to be next in line for high priestess. Most high priestesses come from families connected to the pharaoh, or at least high-ranking nobility. While she has always been ambitious, Maketaten's family is not well-positioned for her to be high priestess. Tiya would not have recommended her as a successor anyway. Maketaten's primary job is to mentor the younger priestesses in the rituals of worship, but she and Tiya often disagreed on matters pertaining to their training and such. Maketaten has a tendency to be… exacting, while Tïya's approach was more forgiving." *And Maketaten might be angry at Tïya for any of those reasons.*

Satsobek shook her head. "She is smart enough to make up a better alibi if she were involved. I can see her getting upset for a perceived wrong, but not enough to *kill* anyone. And she certainly isn't strong enough to overpower both the high priest and priestess on her own."

Ebrium nodded, "We'll see if anything else comes up. Perhaps there was someone else involved. And perhaps it's nothing." Then the corner of his mouth lifted in a mischievous smile. "You did something awful to upset her, didn't you? Did you turn that sharp little tongue of yours on her often?"

Satsobek ignored his taunt and said, "I suppose if you consider leaving the temple awful, then, yes." He cocked his head, waiting. She sighed and explained, "We were friends during the years I served in the temple. We were both priestesses of the type who dedicate ourselves solely to the goddess. We are… I mean I was, she still is… that is, the type who abstain from marriage and sexual relations in order to keep their bodies pure in perpetuity."

Her cheeks burned and she put the back of her hand to one, hoping to hide her blush. She continued, "Maketaten was different when we were younger, before we choose our path in the hwt. Sometimes she was even fun. Over time she became… well… as you see her now. When I told her I was leaving the temple, she said some unkind things."

Satsobek paused, remembering the accusations Maketaten had flung at her. While some of those things were cruel, others had the ring of truth. Satsobek *was* unfit to keep her vows. She *was* weak when it came to certain urges. Then again, she'd chosen the path of chastity, rather than that of a priestess who could take lovers or marry, to prevent her father from pushing a marriage on her and not out of complete devotion to the goddess. At the time, she'd been too young to realize the consequences of her decision.

She took a deep breath and said, "Maketaten told me she would never forgive me for leaving the service of Mehyt.

I believe she feels I betrayed not just the goddess, but her as well."

Ebrium leaned back and it was as if he had drawn a cool blue shade over his eyes, rendering his emotions unreadable. At the same time it seemed something restless stirred within his large, still body. He gave the impression of motion even though not a finger twitched.

"So why *did* you leave the temple?"

"I assure you it is not relevant."

"How do I know that if you won't tell me?"

"I suppose you'll just have to trust me." She said tartly.

"You're sure Tiya wouldn't recommend Maketaten to be high priestess?"

"Yes. I'm sure."

"So *who would* she have recommended?"

"Me." The word came out before Satsobek even realized it. His rapid fire questions had flustered her. Now she was left with her mouth forming an "o" of surprise that she'd revealed something she'd hardly even acknowledged to herself, never mind anyone else, in all her years at the temple.

On the other hand, it was almost worth it to see that she'd gotten a reaction from Ebrium. "You?" His tone was incredulous.

"Yes, me." She shifted in her seat, feeling both defiant and embarrassed.

"And yet you left? Is there something you'd like to tell me before we continue this investigation together?"

"No. I told you, it is in the past." There was no way she would discuss with him what she hadn't told even Tiya or Maketaten. "Come, we should find Betrest. She usually knows all the temple gossip, and if anyone can tell us about any grievances it will be her."

Upon inquiry they learned that Betrest's schedule had kept her out of the temple for over a week. They decided to first view the rooms where Tiya and Yuny had been found, as Betrest lived a short walk from the temple, though still within its vast grounds. So Satsobek led Ebrium back down the hall to the sanctuary chamber of the goddess – the room where Tiya's body was found in the early hours of the morning. On the way, they stopped in the hallway where Yuny was discovered, but being a narrow empty hallway, there was nothing to see.

Like the first chamber, the goddess's sanctuary had tall windows and walls painted with the image of the goddess, as well as her lover Anhur. Large enough to accommodate at least forty people, the sanctuary was almost devoid of objects aside from an assortment of small tables and stools clumped in one corner. Here the singers, dancers, priests, and priestesses gathered to entertain and feed the goddess.

The primary statue of Mehyt, the image believed to be invested with the spirit of the goddess herself, rested behind the doors of a tall, wooden cabinet against one wall. Twice a day the doors were opened to feed and entertain Mehyt and closed again to allow her to rest. The goddess stayed inside the sanctuary for most of the year. When she did leave, she was taken out in a procession to the courtyard, or the rooftop, to celebrate during festivals.

"What do you hope to find?" Satsobek asked Ebrium, watching him as he strode towards the corner of the room nearest the doorway. He walked the length of the room, scrutinizing the place where the wall met the granite tiled floor.

He answered in a gruff voice, "The servants were told not to sweep the floors this morning after they found the bodies. Perhaps the killer left something behind." Nodding, Satsobek swept a glance over the open expanse of the floor, searching for anything out of place or unusual. Ebrium circled the room, then came back to the cabinet of Mehyt and moved to pull open the doors.

"No!" Satsobek gasped. "You are impure." Ebrium's head jolted to look back over his shoulder at her. He blinked rapidly, and Satsobek saw his blue eyes darken and his face flush an ugly red. She took an involuntary step backwards, realizing he might interpret her words as an insult.

"Excuse me?" His voice was flat.

"I – I only meant that you have not performed a purification ritual, or abstained from…" her cheeks burned and she cleared her throat. "It is wrong for either of us to even be here in the goddess's sanctuary without having been cleansed, and – and you have not abstained from…" *Oh gods, why can I not say it?*

Ebrium's expression shifted from narrow-eyed irritation to mirth and she had to look away when the corners of his mouth turned upwards. "Sex?" He supplied.

She clenched her jaw and focused her eyes on Mehyt's cabinet, knowing Ebrium was laughing at her. "Yes. One should abstain for two weeks before entering into the goddess's presence."

"Ahh, and you assume I'm a man of great prowess?" She jerked her gaze back to him and caught his mocking, raised eyebrow. "You think me to be indecent then?"

Satsobek pushed herself to say something, *anything*, that would make up for exposing her embarrassment. "Oh, I have no doubt you are even more indecent than I could possibly imagine."

A reverberating sound, a chuckle, came from deep in his belly and she noticed a small dimple materialize on one cheek. "And yet," he gave her a cocky grin, "You *are* envisioning me being indecent, aren't you? So tell me, *nebet-i*, which of us is the impure one?"

Ebrium couldn't know it, but his remarks hit home. And while she would never admit it, there *had* been nights when she'd lain in bed, envisioning how Ebrium had thrown himself over her to protect her from the marauding tigers. Except that some nights he did more than just protect her…

Attempting to recover, Satsobek threw out a sharp quip. "Oh please. Your advances might beguile some poor fisherman's daughter or port-side prostitute, but such coarse references will not take you any closer to my bed."

His eyes had a roguish, knowing glint to them now. "No? But I didn't say *I* wanted to get closer to your bed. But perhaps one day *you* may find yourself trying to get into *mine*."

Satsobek's breath caught in her throat. She couldn't think of an angry retort to a comment that, sadly, held such a strong hint of truth.

Ebrium studied the angry, diminutive woman in front of him. Her mouth had parted in a small, plump oval when she'd huffed at his lewd comment. Her lips, he realized, were the same deep red colour of the sweet and tart pomegranates of his northern homeland. Many years had passed since he'd eaten one, and he had the urge to try and see if she tasted like fruit. To roll the velvety softness of her lips under his tongue, to delve deep into her warm mouth. Beneath her thin white linen dress, loosely belted at her waist with a gold chain, her body was softly curved and compact, her breasts small and pert. *A perfect little handful,* he thought before he could push away the image of her breasts filling the palms of his hands. He wondered what the oh-so-proper priestess would say if she knew what he was thinking right now.

She appeared to be preparing a sharp rejoinder, but just then he heard voices in the hallway and held up a hand in signal to silence her. Two young women were heading towards the sanctuary, discussing Tiya and Yuny's murders. He reached forward, enfolding Satsobek's waist with one arm and pulling her towards Mehyt's cabinet. Before she could protest, he yanked open one of the doors and tugged her in after him, closing the door and trapping the two of them inside.

Chapter 3 – Mehyt's Cabinet

With her compact body tucked in tight against his chest, Ebrium kept his arm wrapped around Satsobek's midriff. A thin line of light seeped through the doors in front of them. Neither moved as the young women, girls really he guessed by their voices, entered the room. He'd overheard them discussing the murders in the hallway. Despite the questioning most of the temple workers had undergone, they may have failed to share something of importance.

Satsobek strained to put space between them but he tightened his arm around her, tucking her in closer. If she suddenly broke free of him, she could fall right out of the cabinet, and there would be no good way to explain their situation. He tried to focus on what the girls were saying, but a few strands of Satsobek's hair brushed his collarbone, distracting him. The smell of cinnamon and cardamom and something sweet, like a freshly baked honey bun, wafted up from her. It made him want to run his tongue along the side of her neck, to take in her scent and taste her. Her chest expanded with each breath, his forearm so near to the underside of her breasts. *Just an inch or so away.*

After a few moments, with nowhere to go, Satsobek's supple, shapely body relaxed under his grip. Her soft curves seemed to fit more closely against him, the back of her head weighed more heavily against his shoulder, and the bottom of her breasts grazed his forearm. His groin stirred. If he wasn't so irritated by what she'd done eight months ago, he might've taken full advantage of the situation. If they were already lovers, he'd press his hardness against her behind and nip at her shoulders, running his thumbs over her nipples through her thin dress.

Ebrium heaved a silent breath, shifted his hips to avoid grazing her with his unruly body parts, and reminded himself why they were in the cabinet in the first place. He pushed aside the image of Satsobek gasping under his hands and forced himself to listen to the girls' hushed voices. He caught glimpses of them through the gap in the doors, and saw them moving the tables and chairs from the corner, preparing the sanctuary for the goddess's evening meal.

"Oh, it gives one chills being in here, doesn't it? In the same room where a murder took place just last night." The shorter of the two said in a tremulous voice.

"Don't be a ninny," snapped the other girl. "The high priestess's *ka* is gone with her body to the funerary temple. And it's plain there's no one here now."

"What do you think they were doing here so late at night?"

"Isn't it obvious?" Sniffed the second girl. "Think about it. Alone. At night. In the dark."

"No." The short one breathed out. "You don't really suppose they were having an affair?"

"Well I heard from one of the kitchen girls that she heard from one of the boys who works in the kitchen that this wasn't the first time Yuny and Tiya have been in the temple late at night."

The first girl made a tsk'ing noise with her tongue. "But Tiya has been married to her husband forever."

"Yet Yuny has never married."

The short one gasped. "Do you suppose they have been in love all these years, and that's why Yuny never married? Imagine if they had been meeting all this time, unable to declare their love openly for one another."

The second girl scoffed. "Why wouldn't they? Tiya could just divorce her husband and marry Yuny instead. It's not as if she dedicated her body to the goddess. You know not *all* the priestesses are chaste."

The girls' voices grew fainter as they moved down the length of the room, away from the cabinet. Ebrium strained to hear them, but missed a few sentences.

"Wait? What man did he see?" He heard the second girl ask after a few moments.

"I don't know. He only said the man was well-dressed and carried a *wass*."

"A *wass*? Who do you suppose that would be?" Ebrium's interest peaked. The elaborate, curved staffs were carried mainly by the gods, the pharaoh, or powerful noblemen. The word *wass* itself stood for power and domination. But the girls' voices faded to a murmur as they progressed about the room, moving small tables and stools around.

A few minutes passed as he and Satsobek waited motionless inside the cabinet. His mind wandered and he was again diverted by the delicate woman pressed against him. While they were questioning the priests and priestesses he'd found himself watching Satsobek. Her smooth, short hair reflected light like a polished sheet of black quartz. The strands that brushed his skin now felt as slick as they looked. Sable strands that would slide through his fingers like water if he plunged his hands into it. Cleverness flashed in her eyes and, when she wasn't being an angry shrew to him, she was quietly respectful of those they'd encountered. With ease she'd remembered their names and families, even those of the lower-ranking priestesses. In her kinder moments, her voice had a smoky tone that made him envision nights spent tangled up in bedsheets with her body moving beneath him.

Her abashed reaction to his mention of sex earlier had been intriguing. It made him question if, once she got comfortable with him, she'd be just as fiery in bed as she was when arguing with him. He wondered if she'd slap him if he tried to kiss her. He dipped his head and his chin grazed the side of her forehead. She jolted in his arms, twisting her face to look up at him, wide-eyed. A moment passed while his face hovered near hers, a moment in which their gaze locked and held, tension building with each short breath. And then her tongue darted out to moisten her lips and he almost groaned, watching the movement of the soft pomegranate-coloured pads of her lips. If she'd begged him to kiss her it couldn't be any more seductive than that artless little motion of her tongue.

But the very next moment, just as he'd been about to give in to temptation, he caught a glimpse of movement through the doors and he went still, tightening his arm around Satsobek in warning to do the same. The girls were moving back towards the cupboard and the topic of their discussion had shifted.

The tall girl said in a loud whisper, "And that man of the queen's that was in here today! I can't decide which one is more handsome, he or his friend, Sekhrey Bey. Just think if only half of the stories about them are true!"

"I couldn't even begin to imagine…" She trailed off wistfully, indicating she was *trying* to imagine.

The tall girl snickered. "Well they can certainly have their pick now! The goddess herself might have a hard time turning one of those pirates down."

"Oh! Ssshh, you cannot say things like that in here. What if the goddess heard you?" But the tone of her loud whisper belied that, while scandalized, the girl was smiling.

Ebrium wished he could see Satsobek's face. Her body had grown stiff again, and he suspected if he picked her up she would be about as pliable as a slab of granite.

The girls moved to the door and their voices faded down the hallway. Ebrium reached around Satsobek with his free hand to open the door. She put her slender hands on his forearm and pushed. Releasing her, she stumbled out, tripping and banging one knee on the ground before she could catch herself.

Ebrium stepped out and placed his big hands under her armpits, lifting her up and setting her on her feet. One hand slid down her side to rest at the top of her hip. He leaned down and whispered near her ear, "Alright there, nebet-i?"

Satsobek shook him off, avoiding looking at him. "I would be better if I had not been stuffed into a cabinet with you."

A brief and unfamiliar pang of disappointment nagged him. There'd been a moment when she'd felt yielding and luscious in his arms. Now she was back to being the prudish nobleman's daughter who'd sent him a thank you message then thrown it back in his face. So he gave her a smug smile and drawled, "Didn't you hear, nebet-i? Some women actually *do* find me pleasant to be around."

"Well then it is lucky for you that *somebody* does."

Ebrium took in the sarcastic twist of her lips and her hands fisted at her hips and chuckled in spite of his annoyance. Her angry look faded to a faint, embarrassed smile as if pleased with herself but too proud to show it. He thought she could be quite engaging if she wasn't so damned confusing, and if she learned to relax more often.

Self-conscious under Ebrium's gaze, Satsobek smoothed her hair down and tucked it behind her ears. She peeked up at him, watching the muscles in his back ripple as he turned towards the cabinet again, peering inside. His proximity in the cabinet had been... awkward. It was a year since she'd been that close to a man, and a lifetime before that. Although the temple was humid in the late afternoon heat, her body missed the searing warmth of his chest against her back, and his scent — something fresh that recalled the one time she'd seen the sandy, windswept beaches of the great northern sea — still swirled around her.

Despite his antagonistic behaviour towards her, the place that he'd held in her imagination these past several months was hard to forget. After all her fantasizing about the night he'd saved her, and what might happen if she saw him again, her body had a visceral reaction to his presence. For a moment there inside the cabinet she'd been sure he was about to kiss her. She'd even *wanted* him to. And how awful was that? Here, of all places, inside the goddess's sanctuary. She felt every bit the horrid, wanton woman Maketaten seemed to think she was.

With his broad back to her, he asked, "Who do you know that carries a *wass*? The pharaoh's dead. I don't know anyone else in Thinis with one, but I don't move in your circles often."

Satsobek shook her head and frowned. "Sorry?" His foreign intonation and casual slang caused her a moment's pause at the best of times, never mind when she was unsettled.

"The women. When we were in the cabinet." He looked back over his shoulder. "They said something about a man with a *wass*. You *were* paying attention, weren't you?" His raised eyebrow was suggestive, and the way his eyes raked her body made her breath catch in her throat.

"Oh! Yes." She cursed herself for giving him cause to suspect her feelings. As if he didn't have enough women falling over him. Clearing her throat, she said, "I *did* recognize one of the girls, she is a maidservant here and I believe we could convince her to talk to us further if needed. Otherwise, the governor of our region carries a *wass*, of course, but he lives further north and never visits. Each of the governors carries one. Some of the wealthier nobles who own great swaths of land also carry them. But mostly only for ceremonies, or banquets. I cannot think who might actually walk around with one."

Ebrium nodded as he studied the imposing, lion-headed goddess in the cabinet. Carved in smooth, black granite, the curves of her body were polished to a sleek shine. Satsobek watched Ebrium bend down and reach behind the goddess's feet. When he stood he turned something over in his hands. Satsobek stepped forward and plucked it from him.

"This belongs to Tiya. It is her Eye of Ra." She stared down at the necklace resting in her palm. Hanging from a beaded chain was one single eye made of gold, ivory, and red carnelian, with turquoise to create the impression of decorative kohl eye liner. "Why would her necklace be in there? Tiya always wore this. It is a symbol of Mehyt and is used for protection."

"Perhaps we're not the only ones who've been hiding in the cabinet."

"Tiya? But why would Tiya hide in there?" Ebrium was silent, head slanted and lips pressed together, as if waiting for her to figure something out. "Oh no." She whispered. "Oh gods. Tiya hid in the goddess's sanctuary and they must have found her here and killed her." She dropped the necklace and, palm pressed to her mouth, ran from the room.

Several minutes later Satsobek sat against the wall in the shade of the temple's porch. Her slender arms were wrapped around her drawn-up knees, her dress smoothed over her legs. Her eyes still stung, but at least they were dry now as Ebrium came through the temple door, carrying a painted mug.

She glanced up at him. "I just – I needed some air." Her hands shook slightly as she raked them through her thick black hair.

"Here," he said, handing her the mug. "Drink this. I got it from the temple's kitchen. It'll help quell your stomach."

"My stomach is fine."

He gave her a skeptical look and she realized he must have heard her retching in the small room next to the goddess's sanctuary. She capitulated and took a few sips from the mug. Cool, sweet, honey and carob juice. Her lips pursed in irritation when she realized that the tea was good and it *did* soothe her stomach.

Ebrium leaned against one of the porch's stone columns. The sun at his back cast long shadows over the golden crests of his powerful arms and chest. His thumbs were hooked into the top of his shenti, and he looked down at her. To avoid his penetrating eyes, she leaned her head back against the wall and closed her lids.

All day long she'd tried to repress thoughts of what Tiya and Yuny's murders would have been like. But when she saw Tiya's necklace she pictured what a horror the high priestess's last few minutes could have been. Alone, terrified, hiding inside the cabinet. And then that awful moment when the doors opened and she was discovered. Dropping her head onto her knees as a wave of nausea washed over, tears welled behind her lids. Maybe she wasn't fit to take part in this investigation after all. Maybe she was too emotional.

What right did she have to think she could be of any use? What if she simply wasn't smart enough or good enough?

Then she felt Ebrium's big, firm hand rest on her back. She jerked from his touch, angry at herself for letting him see her distress. She couldn't let the same self-doubts that had pushed her from the temple a year ago hinder her from doing all she could to help the queen, and the memories of Tiya and Yuny. She set her tea mug down and pushed herself up from the ground. "I'm fine." She said through clenched teeth. "What's next?"

If he was surprised by her reaction he didn't show it. Instead, he rolled his shoulders and looked out to the street. "It seems there's been a lot of nighttime activity in the temple lately. Maybe your friend Betrest or the priestess's husband can explain some of it." Ebrium jerked his head towards the gate. "Let's go pay Tiya's husband a visit first and see how he feels about his wife spending time in the temple in the middle of the night with the high priest."

Tiya's home lay on the temple grounds, just outside the walls that surrounded the temple proper and its storage buildings. However, they were just making their way into the network of large manor homes when they were met on the way by Betrest, a tall curvy woman with a braided black wig who, upon spotting them, rushed over and grabbed Satsobek's hands. Breathless, Betrest explained that as soon as she'd heard the news – and that Satsobek was involved in the investigation – she'd readied herself to come and see her old friend in case she was needed for anything.

Satsobek didn't even need to ask how Betrest had heard of the murders. Over the years Satsobek had learned the priestess was capable of plying the kitchen staff with choice ingredients, the maids with baubles, the male servants with pretty smiles, and her own parents with promises of good behaviour. No doubt someone or other from Betrest's network came to her as soon as anything noteworthy happened, well aware that tokens of appreciation would be immediate, or remembered and forthcoming. Betrest cultivated gossip not necessarily out of a spirit of meanness, but a desire to be well-informed about those around her coupled with a delight in dabbling in their affairs.

"Thank Mehyt it is you involved, Satsobek, we have missed you so much in the hwt. I'm sure it helped put the other girls at ease that you were there today." Betrest led them into a white-washed greeting room inside her family's manor. They settled into the greeting room, Satsobek and Betrest side by side on a bench and Ebrium in a chair nearby. Satsobek looked over her old friend. A few long, curly strands of hair were strategically pulled loose to frame Betrest's alluring face. Expertly applied kohl lined her eyes, making her green-flecked brown eyes stand out from her smooth, golden skin. Betrest was stunning, and everyone told her so. All the light in the room always shifted to her, leaving everybody else invisible as fleas on a bull's hide. Satsobek would never feel comfortable with all of that attention directed at her, but that didn't stop her from wondering what it might be like to have her beauty so admired. *Maybe just once or twice.*

Even as Satsobek thought it, Betrest turned her gaze to Ebrium, running her eyes down the length of him. He leaned back in his chair, and it served to emphasize the ridges of his abdomen. When he'd sat down, his shenti had fallen aside a little, revealing thick, muscled thighs as wide around as Satsobek's waist. As Betrest appraised him, one corner of his mouth curved up. When the priestess met his knowing gaze, Satsobek had to wonder if it were possible that beautiful people had a secret language all to themselves. As if they were aware of their physical compatibility, that their sexual relations would be spectacular, and that together they could produce a race of tall, beautiful children universally desired by all.

"I hardly know what to say that can help, but ask me anything you need." Betrest turned to Satsobek, her bosom heaving dramatically. She glanced at Ebrium each time her chest rose high. She had angled her upper body so that her profile caught the light, laid visible to Ebrium. Her shoulders, Satsobek thought, were thrown back just a little too far to be natural, and she wondered if Betrest's back hurt from the alluring, yet awkward, angle. A small part of her hoped it did.

On the way over, Satsobek and Ebrium had discussed how much to share with Betrest. Knowing Betrest as she did, Satsobek was in favour of asking her about Tiya and Yuny's supposed late night meetings. But Ebrium didn't trust the priestess – or apparently, Satsobek's recommendation of her – and had exacted her promise to only ask general questions.

So Satsobek asked, "Betrest, has there been anything unusual in the temple lately? Anyone dissatisfied, or angry with either Tiya or Yuny?"

"Nooo…" Betrest trailed off, looking thoughtful.

Ebrium leaned forward to catch the priestess's gaze. "Are you quite sure you haven't heard of any sort of unrest? Any little thing might be helpful."

The pretty woman cocked her head and pursed her lips in his direction. "Well… I did hear a rumour just the other day that Tiya and Yuny were seen inside the temple late at night. But I disregarded it because it came from a maid who overheard a priestess talking about it to another girl, and supposedly *she* heard it in turn from a kitchen boy. So really the chain of information seemed dubious at best."

Satsobek threw Ebrium a look that she hoped he'd interpret as *I told you so*. He shrugged one shoulder in response.

Continuing, Betrest said, "And it may not mean anything, but the farmers' rations have been reduced recently." Betrest lowered her voice and turned to Satsobek with a conspiratorial gleam in her eye, although she continued to flash sidelong looks at Ebrium through her lashes. "Of course there is little the farmers can do about it, but I know they are not happy. They fear it will only get worse if the harvest is small this year, which everyone thinks it will be. I have also heard some of the kitchen workers saying that even the offerings to Mehyt are less this season than last."

Satsobek pulled in a breath. "And if that happens then the goddess will have less to eat."

Betrest's eyes went wide and her voice was doleful. "And so, then, will we and *everyone* else who serves the temple." Satsobek knew Betrest well enough to know that her exaggerated expression was for effect, but it served a purpose also. Betrest was smarter than she let on to most people. She was hinting at rebellion, but wouldn't come right out and say it. Not in front of Ebrium, the queen's man.

Satsobek set that aside to think about later. She had one more question and she trusted Betrest to be discreet. After all, she knew many of Betrest's secrets. Secrets that the other woman would prefer her parents - and any potential husbands - not know about. "Betrest, do you know of any reason why Maketaten might lie about where she was last night?"

Betrest blinked, confusion furrowing her brow. "You do not think…" she made a turning motion with her hand, "do you?"

"No. I don't think she intentionally had anything to do with it." Satsobek hesitated and flicked a glance at Ebrium, a question in her eyes. He nodded, giving his silent agreement to tell Betrest the truth, so she continued, "But Maketaten said she was walking alone along the Iteru last night and I am not convinced she was telling the truth."

A twinkle appeared in the depths of Betrest's gaze. "My goodness, is that not just like her to keep some naughty little secret. I do not know what she was doing, but I most certainly intend to find out!"

Satsobek smiled. "And when you do, please tell me."

Chapter 4 – Ahmes

On their way across the temple grounds to seek out Tiya's husband, they passed several grain silos. Curious, Ebrium stopped in front of the tall, cylindrical brick buildings packed closely together. He and Satsobek stood on a lane lined by various buildings, mostly workshops for the temple artisans, potters, and sculptors. However, the work day had come to a close not long ago and many of the shops were now closed up, their workers likely gone to the neighbourhood of small huts located past the manor homes of the high ranking families such as Betrest's.

Only here and there did the faint ringing or thumping of a tool hitting stone or wood echo down the lane. The odd labourer or woman walked past them, casting suspicious or appreciative glances Ebrium's way before looking quizzically at Satsobek. Ebrium ignored them, as he'd learned to do after all these years in Kemet.

"Tell me about these," he cocked his head in the direction of the silos as he looked them over. Wide brick staircases wound up the sides of the structures, leading to narrow windows at the top where workers dumped buckets of grain into the building. Small wooden hatches were cut low into the sides of the silos, where the grain was collected as needed. "The temples collect most of Kemet's taxes. How are they administered here?"

Thanks to his recent investigations into local nobility, he had a good understanding of Kemet's tax system. However, although the temples had a large role to play in that structure, he'd yet to see the inside of a temple treasury or grain storage – the bulk of taxes being collected by the temples in the form of grain. Since food shortages could lead to an uprising, it was important that he familiarize himself with these matters if he wanted to have a hope of preventing any unrest.

Satsobek stepped towards the small, closed wooden door of one of the silos. "The temples act as a… a middle-man of sorts between the pharaoh, or Queen Merneith now, and the people."

She briefly explained that, while all the land of Kemet belonged to the pharaoh, the temples administered much of the farmland in the pharaoh's name. In some cases they leased the land out to farmers or estate owners, who in turn paid rents which were collected by the temple. In other cases, the temples had labourers and slaves who worked the land and were paid their wages in sacks of grain, bread, and beer, or a piece of the proceeds. Produce and goods made by temple labourers and craftsmen were shipped around the world. Once taxes were collected and wages paid, the temples gave an account of income to the pharaoh's vizier.

"Rather than handing all the taxes over to the pharaoh, the hwt stores them here, on the grounds." She tapped her fingers on the silo door. "Of course, just the grain is stored in here. The metals, beer and wine, cloth, and other things are stored in buildings nearer to the temple. It is why we have the high walls, to prevent thieves from sneaking in and stealing goods."

As soon as the words were out of her mouth he saw the blush creep up over her cinnamon-coloured skin. In a wry tone, he said, "Don't worry, nebet-i. The queen provides me with enough grain that you needn't fear for the safety of your hwt's wheat and barley supplies."

"I did not… that was not what I meant."

"Then why don't you move aside so I can look inside?" He stepped closer to her, placing one hand on the warm brick wall next to her head.

"What, now?" She shrank a little into the doorframe, as if fearing his nearness. He had the urge to move in even closer just to see her reaction. And perhaps take in her warm, inviting scent. While her friend Betrest was an attractive, seductive woman, Satsobek's appeal was more complex. She seemed to be completely unaware that she had the capability to be alluring, maybe even afraid of the possibility of enticing a man. She was very unlike most of the women he was familiar with, women who were well aware of their charms, wielding them to their advantage.

Leaning in, he dropped his voice and rasped near the shell of her ear, "I promise, you can watch me every second to make sure I don't steal anything." His face was almost close enough to brush her forehead with his own. He watched her pull in her full red lips and bite down on them.

She shook her head, keeping her wary eyes on him. "If the silo is full, we will not be able to push in the door. Then again, there might be nothing to see. Certainly some of the silos will be empty this time of year. The harvest has yet to begin, and most of the workers and slaves are supplied with grain throughout the year. There is probably nothing there…" Pressed flat against the door, she made rambling excuses as he reached across her and, placing one hand on the doorknob, pushed it open.

"Oh!" She gasped as she stumbled backwards into the now open doorway, but he caught her with one arm hooked around her lower back. And then, just like that, he spun her into the darkness of the silo next to him.

Satsobek blinked into the black expanse before her. A rectangle of light from the open doorway pooled at their feet. Beyond them stretched the emptiness of the tall silo. Only faint tendrils of light filtered in high above them through the windows, as the shutters were closed to help prevent dangerous pests like weevils, locusts, rats, and mice from getting in and eating all the grain.

The silo was not currently in use; otherwise the grain would have pooled around their feet, or made it impossible to open the door. It certainly smelled as though it had been emptied out some time ago, perhaps a month or more. Stale air sifted around them, mingling with the scent of old wheat and something more repulsive, possibly rat dropping. There was also a lighter, fresher scent, something salty and rich and pleasing. *Ebrium.* And that's when Satsobek felt the heat and weight of his arm around her, his big hand resting on the curve of her hip. Despite the stuffy heat of the silo, cold tendrils snaked across the surface of her skin while a knot tightened in her belly.

She shook him off and sniped, "Do you conduct all your investigations this way? Pushing and pulling people around into little dark spaces?"

He chuckled. "Only the ones involving prim little priestesses."

An exasperated noise escaped her. "Prim? Simply because I have *some* sense of propriety? Oh you are insufferable!" Every time she thought they might be on the verge of getting along, one or the other of them said something provoking and she was well aware that at least half the time it was her fault. But she couldn't seem to help herself. Gods forbid she allow herself to become one of those silly women who succumbed to his flirtations, likely to end up crushed like a sand flea beneath the weight of his callous indifference.

She pushed past him to move towards the door, but in doing so she stumbled over a stick on the ground. He reached out to steady her but she caught herself and dodged his attempts to help. Reaching down, she wrapped her fingers around the stick – which turned out to be the handle of a broom. With the broom in hand, she stood up and took a deep breath. "What are we doing in here anyway? Why are you wasting our time?"

He shuffled in the darkness near her, and the rectangle of light narrowed to a sliver as he pushed the door partway shut. Panic swelled up into her throat. An old memory, long forgotten, darted through her mind, spiking her fear and causing her to cling to the broom handle, seeking comfort in its smooth wooden pole.

Ebrium's voice was hushed as he said, "I didn't want our discussion to be overheard on the street. Tell me who manages all this. Who controls the farmers' wages, and the inventories?"

Setting aside her irritation, she fiddled with the broom handle as she explained that the temple employed several scribes who took stock of the wages and tax collection.

Scroll upon scroll of papyri, enough to fill hundreds of boxes, were housed in storerooms in the temple, documenting years' worth of inventories and taxes. This needed to be reported to the vizier, who in turn reported it to the queen.

"I believe it is Menkhaf who manages the inventories now," Satsobek mused. "He took over from Yuny three years ago, shortly after he came to the temple. If that is the case, he would be the one to keep the records of all the profits from the temple lands and trading, and he who determines the taxes that go to the queen."

"And what do you know of him?" The silo was so dark she could only see his shadowy profile. He was all broad shoulders and thick, wavy black hair.

"Menkhaf? He is certainly strange, but he has been that way since he first came to the temple. I suppose it is *possible* he might stand to gain from Yuny's death as he could be a contender for the next high priest now that Yuny is gone. But as I said before, he would not be the *only* one. I see no reason for the queen to choose him. Especially as he has no familial connection. She'd be more likely to choose someone known to be loyal to her."

"Do you know where he comes from?"

She shook her head. "Not exactly, but I think somewhere in the north, in the Aneb-Hetch sephat. Perhaps it was the capital city there, *Inbu-Hedj*? There is a large temple of Horus that he may have served in."

"Huh." Ebrium ran a hand over his jaw and she heard the rasping of a day's growth of dark stubble.

She stepped closer to him and queried, "Is there something else in *Inbu-Hedj*? I'm not very familiar with the city."

His voice was thoughtful as he said, "*Inbu-Hedj* is a strategic location. It's a major city, and a doorway between the northern and southern sephats along the trade route of the Iteru. Could it be that the priest has some scheme in place to discredit the queen and aid the northern governors? Perhaps the queen's cousin Anen in the north?"

He shook his head. "Those damned northern sephats have too much autonomy. It is too difficult for the queen," he held up a hand as if anticipating her protest in defence of Merneith, "or any *pharaoh* for that matter, to manage those regions from far away. Even with spies in the sephats it's difficult to know when they might rise up to seize control for themselves. Or shake loose from the queen's grip."

Satsobek frowned, "Is it really so bad? It has been over a hundred years since the queen's great-grandfather unified the Kemeti sephats." Clearly this was not a concern for her father, or else she would have heard more talk about it around the dinner table. Perhaps he even *wanted* it to happen, especially now that the queen was in power.

"Some are still almost entirely independent and don't like to pay taxes to the throne." He shrugged. "Others don't like to be governed at all. Let's hope we're in no immediate danger. If it's the northern sephats behind it, they could send Kemet into a bloody civil war."

"And that is why the queen is concerned about her cousin Anen." Satsobek murmured. It was a disturbing reminder that if they didn't find the temple killer the peace and prosperity of Kemet could be lost. She shook her head. "How do you know so much about all of this?"

The tone of his voice expressed mild incredulity. "Not all of us live the sheltered lives of the nobility, nebet-i. It is also *my job* to know these things in order to keep the queen, and Kemet, safe. I've spent years in the militias here, travelling up and down the Iteru and deep into the desert. Bey and I have informants throughout the militias, and in the sephats. And there are priests in many of the temples that are willing to throw their support in whichever direction the gold flows from." He paused and then asked in a voice devoid of his usual mockery, "Have you considered the possibility the queen didn't just choose me at random for this investigation?"

Feeling like a chastised child, she turned the subject back to his original question to hide her embarrassment. She couldn't deny that he was right. Despite the way her family treated her, she *had* been sheltered. It was only now that she was beginning to realize just how much.

She said, "I do not see how Menkhaf could be involved with Anen though. Menkhaf has been at the temple for just over three years. He was appointed by Pharaoh Wadj, long before he passed away. If he had intended some plan to aid Anen in seizing power, they have been waiting a long time to execute it."

Ebrium's breath came out in a frustrated puff and leftover kernels of wheat crunched under his feet as he paced in the darkness. "I don't know how it fits together. Perhaps it doesn't at all. It's a hindrance we're not allowed to search the priests' quarters, or question them too closely."

Just then Satsobek felt something brush past her ankle, and small claws scraped the side of her foot. "Oh gods!" She cried and kicked out, connecting with the furry body of a rat, sending it squeaking and scuttling across the floor. She smashed the broom down on the ground frantically. "Get back you little sons of bastards or I'll bash your dirty brains in!"

What followed was the sound of multiple clawed feet scratching the hardened earth of the silo's floor.

"Dammit dammit dammit," she muttered, backing away. "There are more of them."

Before she had a chance to protest, Ebrium was by her side, scooping her up into his arms and striding towards the door. He nudged it open with one foot, then kicked it closed behind them, setting Satsobek down by the silo wall and keeping an eye on the door.

She leaned against the warm wall, dropping the broom to wrap her arms around herself.

"Are you all right?" He looked down at her and, if she didn't know better, she'd swear there was concern in his blue eyes as he looked her over.

"I – I'm fine. I just... dammit I hate rats." She willed herself to stop shaking and slow her panting breath.

Laughter rumbled up from deep in his chest. "Well you certainly handled yourself admirably. I don't know how the rats fared but I believe you managed to beat that broom to death. And by the way, that was quite an impressive show of naughty language from the proper daughter of a nobleman." He winked at her and the smiling warmth in his gaze confused her already scrambled senses even more.

"I… what?" Looking down, she saw that several chunks of papyri reed bristles were missing from the broom, and those reeds that weren't missing were mostly broken in half or sticking out at odd angles. "Oh! Sorry." Why was she apologizing to *him* of all people? Gulping in air, she tried to collect herself. "It is only that…Amenia… my sister… when I was eight she locked me in a storage building. It was dark inside, and there were… there were rats. A lot of them. I was bitten several times before the groundskeeper heard me and opened the door."

"She locked you in with a rat's nest? On purpose?"

"I… she said she didn't mean to." Amenia had sworn to their aunt that it had been an accident, and that she hadn't known there were rats in the building. But then she'd smirked at Satsobek behind their aunt's back and, with her fingers shaped into curved paws and her front teeth bared, made a face in imitation of a rat's large teeth chewing.

Ebrium grunted and the squinting lines around his eyes belied his skepticism. "That's quite the sister you have."

Satsobek gave a shaky laugh. "You have no idea. But never mind that. I – I am fine now. And we have more important matters to attend to."

Any admiration and sympathy Ebrium had been inclined to show Satsobek dissipated on the way to Tiya's home.

"I have met Ahmes several times before." Satsobek contended when he suggested he should be the one to lead the questioning of Tiya's husband. "I know very well how to speak with him."

"You're too close to them both," he reasoned. "Have you even considered the possibility that he might be our primary suspect? What do *you* think the priest and priestess were doing late at night alone in the temple?"

Glaring at him, she said, "If you are implying what I think you are, you are wrong. Tiya was not like that."

"I am sorry to disappoint you, nebet-i, but most people *are* like that."

She scoffed. "Maybe *you are* but Tiya was not, so I suggest you try to keep your mind out of the sewage ditch in that regard. Tiya was faithful. She loved Ahmes. I know she did."

"Think what you like about me, but recognizing that someone else might be unfaithful doesn't necessarily make *me* false-hearted as well. Just observant. Most people have it in them to deceive or use others when it suits them. I'm sure you're not so innocent yourself, however much you might like to play at it." He stopped himself before he made any specific reference to her actions eight months ago, unwilling to give her the satisfaction of knowing she'd agitated him.

Glancing down at her, though, a thin tendril of guilt snaked through him. She'd stopped walking, a stricken look on her face. In fact, she looked mortified.

It made him feel every bit like a braying donkey. So far she *had* seemed to be a bit of an innocent. Most of the priestesses they'd questioned were genuinely pleased to see her, and she'd responded in kind. She'd also displayed admirable fortitude on more than one occasion already, what with discovering Tiya's necklace in the cabinet and then the rats. He'd let his own frustrations get the better of him and he'd taken them out on her.

Ebrium began walking along the lane again and she followed, looking ahead with her jaw clenched tight. Turning off the lane, they passed through the entrance to the date-palm lined courtyard of Tiya's mansion – a large mud-brick home with four columns holding up a granite slab overhang above the porch and doorway.

He tried to take the sting out of his voice as he asked, "You haven't seen the priestess in what, a year now? How do you *know* she wasn't involved with the priest?"

She scowled up at him. "Because *some* people are consistent in their behaviour." He got the sense she was talking about more than just Tiya, but by that point they were almost upon the doorstep of the home.

A servant informed them that Ahmes had left the house a short time ago, but was expected back any moment. He led Ebrium and Satsobek into a bright, spacious greeting room where they could await his return. The white-washed walls of the room were painted with pleasant, vibrant scenes of banquets set in lush gardens, and a mural of the great Iteru snaking its way past the royal palace of Thinis. Comfortable-looking, high-backed benches with thick cushions and several large wooden chairs were arranged in a semi-circle with small tables at intervals.

It was clear from the amount of effects in the room that Tiya and Ahmes were very wealthy. Most of Kemet's peasants went without chairs, tables, or even bed frames to sleep on. Most slept on woven reed mats on the floor. Good wood for furniture-making was hard to come by as the date palm and sycamore trees that grew along the Iteru were too coarse for cutting and polishing in long strips. Quality wood was imported from the north, from areas near his own homeland. Ebrium knew this well as he'd intercepted and raided many a merchant ship bearing cedar and pine destined for Kemet.

The servant indicated they sit and offered to send in cups of hibiscus blossom tea. Satsobek seated herself while Ebrium remained standing, pacing the room and looking out the narrow windows into the courtyard behind the house. While they waited for Ahmes he avoided looking at her. *That damnably obstinate little woman.* It irritated him that she'd somehow already judged him and found him wanting. He was used to people insulting him for his low birth, his foreignness, his past as a pirate and brigand. He'd expected it from her since the day he'd received her messenger eight months ago. But he *hadn't* expected it would bother him as much as it did.

After a few moments, a young woman with a shaved head and clothed in nothing but a shenti skirt came in bearing a tray of mugs and a bowl of fresh dates. She bowed shyly as she entered, and Ebrium caught her glancing his way as she laid the mugs and bowl out on a table.

He seized the opportunity she presented. "This must be a difficult time for you," he inclined his head to the girl, keeping his hands clasped behind his back in a non-threatening fashion. "Losing your mistress in such a way."

The girl looked up gratefully, and nodded. "It is, sir. Very difficult. The Great Lady was always very kind to all of us." She dropped her gaze demurely, but he saw how her scrutiny travelled up to the tattoo on his pectoral, then back down to rest on his abdomen.

He sucked in a breath, tightening his muscles to their best advantage before saying, "I'm sure your master must also be quite distraught." He could feel Satsobek watching him, the weight of her suspicion and disapproval weighing on his back like a sack of barley. So be it, let her mistrust him all she liked. She might not like his methods, but his motives were honest.

The maid's eyes slid down to the ground and she mumbled, "I… I am sure he is, sir."

"Of course," Ebrium stepped closer and lowered his voice to an intimate timbre, "if you have reason to believe otherwise, you would be doing the queen a great service by sharing that with us."

The girl reluctantly shook her head. "I… no, sir. I am sure my master must be very upset." She looked miserably down at the ground.

He took another step towards her and emphasized his lower-class drawl, hoping to set her at ease. "It's all right if you tell us. We'll make sure your master doesn't know who told us."

Still the girl hesitated. She flicked a glance over to Satsobek, and he held his breath. Would she trust him and give her assistance? His relief was almost visible when Satsobek nodded reassuringly at the girl. "We will not say a word. And you will be doing a great honour to the Great Lady's memory."

The girl's back straightened and she whispered hurriedly, "Ahmes and the Great Lady have not shared a room for some time now. I haven't been here very long, but I've heard the other servants and slaves talking and I know they weren't getting along. I don't know why."

Just then the sound of shuffling came from the doorway to the room, and a young man of about fifteen entered. His otherwise regular face was marked by a scar that slashed at an angle from his forehead over his right eyebrow and down along his cheek. With each step, his ankle-length white shenti flared out, exposing one foot turned out at an awkward angle, the likely cause of the pronounced limp in his step. Upon seeing him, the maid stepped back and quickly bowed herself out of the room. Ebrium was frustrated, hoping to get more information, but at least they'd gotten something.

Satsobek stood and strode towards the newcomer. Clasping the young man's hands, Satsobek exclaimed, "Seret! How are you?"

The young man flushed but kept his gaze levelled on Satsobek. "Nebet-i," he murmured. "I heard you were here and wanted to come say hello."

"Oh, Seret. I was so sorry to hear about Tiya."

Seret's lips tightened and his nostrils flared. "The Great Lady will be much missed. It is a great loss to us."

"Seret, this is Ebrium. He works with the queen under Sekhrey Bey." Satsobek placed a hand on Seret's thin shoulder. "Seret was found outside the temple gates when he was an infant. He lived there until a couple of years ago when Tiya took him into her home as a freed servant of sorts."

The young man gave an awkward bow, but when he straightened his shoulders were back and his chin high. His regard was steady as he said, "It is a pleasure to meet one of the queen's men, sir." *Strong, wary, and obstinate*, Ebrium judged, and liked him for it. Here was a boy who, like himself, should not have been allowed inside the temple but had somehow found a way in.

Satsobek took up the young man's hand and questioned him in a low tone. "Seret, I know how much Tiya meant to you. I know you have not been working in the hwt of late, but have you heard anything? Has everything been well here in the home?"

Seret's glance darted around the room, as if ensuring their privacy, then dipped his head towards Satsobek's. He was just opening his mouth to speak when Ebrium saw his eyes widen. A tall, gaunt man with a shaved head and a prominent nose entered the room, his sandals slapping against the tiled floor. The man turned with narrowed eyes to Seret, who took a step back from Satsobek, pulling his hand from her grasp to clench at his side. Ebrium could see defiance written on the younger man's face. He was sure the nobleman was about to snap something at Seret when Satsobek turned to face him. His look slipped from one of anger to a stretched smile.

Greeting the gaunt man, Satsobek took his outstretched hand. "Please accept my condolences, Ahmes. I was deeply saddened to hear about Tiya."

"Satsobek, my girl. It has been too long. I am sorry I was not here to greet you the moment you arrived. I am sure Tiya would be pleased you came to pay your respects." Despite the mention of his wife, the thin man hung on to Satsobek's hand, and his bloodshot eyes ran over her in a way that made Ebrium want to knock his lecherous orbs out of his head.

Seeming not to notice Ahmes's leering, Satsobek introduced them and told Ahmes they needed to ask him some questions. Ahmes gave Ebrium a cursory nod before inviting them to sit down. Ahmes looked pale beneath his olivine skin. He tapped the fingers of his right hand against his thigh as he looked out the window. "I only found out myself a few hours ago."

Satsobek placed a hand on his forearm. "How are you doing with all of this?"

"It has been a very difficult morning." The man murmured. His gaze travelled from Satsobek's face down to her neck and collarbones.

Clearing his throat loudly, Ebrium called the bald man's attention back to him. "Do you know what your wife was doing in the temple late last night?"

Ahmes looked down, pinching the bridge of his substantial nose, his pinky raised in a melodramatic gesture. "To be honest," he looked up, staring straight into Ebrium's eyes, "I have no idea. She was still at the temple when I went to sleep last night. I assumed she was working late. She is often busy in the days before the Festival of the New Year at the end of the harvest season."

"What time did you go to sleep?"

Ahmes looked out the window, tapping his leg again with his long, thin fingers. "A little after Ra moved the sun across the sky."

"Was it common for your wife to work that late?"

The man's eyes skimmed the room before settling on a tea mug on the table in front of him. "Sometimes. She dedicated almost all of her time to the goddess and the temple. But before the Festival of the New Year she is always busier, preparing for the festivities."

"Did you ever question what business she would have in the temple so late at night?"

Turning his palms upwards, Ahmes shrugged. "Who am I to question the needs of the gods?"

Ebrium held back a derisive snort. "And you were here all night?"

Ahmes's eyes bulged over his beaky nose. "Of course. I was sleeping. I was awoken by one of the servants at daybreak with the news of *my wife's murder.*" Ebrium could see he was becoming agitated with the line of questioning. *Perfect, let the lusty bastard sweat*, he thought.

"And if we questioned your servants they would all confirm that you were in your bed all night long?"

"Yes, of course. I was there alone. Question them if you like. They will tell you I was in bed. There was no one else there."

"And do you always sleep alone?"

"Do I what? What sort of a question is that?"

"Just a question." Ebrium shrugged one shoulder. "You said *of course* you were alone. Which indicated it was a matter of fact that you sleep alone."

"Well it is *not* a matter of fact." The man gave Ebrium a condescending look. "I do not understand what you are trying to get at, but I can assure you, you are looking in the wrong direction if you are trying to find out who killed my wife."

"Do you know any reason why someone would want to kill your wife?"

"No! Of course not!" Ahmes snapped. "Tiya never argued with anyone."

"Not even you?"

"I believe I have had enough of this *investigation* for one day." Ahmes stood abruptly. Ebrium and Satsobek had no choice but to follow. Ahmes turned to Satsobek and took her hand. "*You* will understand. I am greatly distressed today and this is all a bit much right now." He eyed Ebrium with distaste. "What did you say your name was again?"

Ebrium gave the man a smile that purposefully didn't reach his eyes. "Ebrium of the Queen's Royal Guard. Second-in-command under Sekhrey Bey."

Ahmes looked Ebrium over again, a faint sneer curving his thin lips. "Of course. I have heard of you. You're one of those Sumerians."

Ebrium's smile tightened. "Eblaiti, actually. It's north-west of Sumer. We don't even speak the same language. Although I do know enough Sumerian to take command of one of their merchant's ships at sea." Ebrium had no qualms about reminding the man that he wasn't one to be trifled with. He held Ahmes's gaze until the man was forced to turn back to Satsobek.

Ahmes said shortly, "Please do keep me informed about what you and the Sekhrey's man here," he jerked his head in Ebrium's direction without looking at him, "discover. For now, you must excuse me. I have much to attend to." With that the thin man turned and strode out of the room. Ebrium glanced around to see if the boy was still there, but he'd disappeared. He had little doubt that most of the servants would tell him whatever story their master told them to, but the boy seemed more likely to be honest and he appeared to have a liking for Satsobek. He'd find a way tonight or tomorrow to get the boy alone. It was better to do it away from Ahmes's presence anyway.

Once off the temple grounds and back on the dusty street, Satsobek turned on Ebrium. "What in the name of the gods do you think you are doing? Are you trying to raise the wrath of all the wealthy men of Kemet? You cannot talk like that to a man of the nobility. One whose wife was just murdered, no less."

Ebrium cocked an eyebrow at the woman staring up at him with her fists balled at her sides, reminding him again of a sea-nymph. "No?"

"No! That was reckless. Ahmes may be a suspect, and I admit circumstances are not in his favour, but the queen warned us to be delicate and yet here you are behaving like a water buffalo inside a glass bead workshop. Not that I should have expected anything different from *you*. And on that thought, must you attempt to seduce every woman you come across? I mean a poor young maid of all people?"

Ebrium drew his lips in, assuming a thoughtful expression. "Hmm. Well, I'm sorry, but you know it *can* be hard sometimes for us poor, uneducated *Sumerians* to know how to interact with the more refined people of your noble class."

Satsobek took a step closer to him, her face tipped back to glare up at him. "What is that supposed to mean?"

"Oh please, don't tell me you didn't notice how little your friend Ahmes thinks of people like me. He'd made his judgement before I even opened my mouth." *And let's not pretend you don't feel the same way.* His unsaid words hung in the air. Instead, he said, "Look, do you think you'd actually get any information from a man like that by being *nice* to him and tip-toing around civilities? If we did things your way we'd spend all day sipping tea and get nothing except tonight's dinner menu."

Her lips thinned and her eyes closed. He got the impression she was trying to master herself. *Good for her*, he admired her control even as he hoped he could goad her into a fight. Her voice was measured when she next spoke. "It is possible that Ahmes's rudeness was uncalled for. But by Ra, Ebrium, do you want to reinforce his beliefs by acting that way? Do you not ever get tired of proving people like him right?"

Ebrium shrugged. She might have a point but he had no intention of conceding it out loud. "What do I care what he thinks of me? I'm investigating a murder, not trying to make friends amongst the nobility."

"Did you ever stop to consider that doing the latter might facilitate the former?"

Rather than answer her astute question and continue that thread of the argument, he turned and continued walking along the narrow lane towards her home. White washed, mud-brick mansions lined the street, surrounded by chest-high stone walls. In the courtyards, date-palm tree branches swayed as a hot breeze puffed by. The sun was near to setting and his stomach rumbled. He had a lonely meal of plain, day-old bread and some heavy barley beer to look forward to. It wasn't exciting, but he was in no mood to prepare anything. And he certainly didn't intend to go back to the House of Iput tonight for dinner. Not after what happened last night, even though he'd sworn to himself – and Iput – that it wouldn't happen again…

Satsobek wondered at Ebrium's sudden shift in mood. She'd seen that cold blue wall go up over his eyes before he'd turned away. She hurried to keep up with his long strides as they walked north. "Very well then. Can we focus on what we learned from Ahmes?"

Ebrium pointed up a thumb from his fist and proceeded to count out points on his fingers. "Well, to start with he's not a kind man. It's obvious from the way he reacted to your friend Seret. Ahmes is hiding something. The maid told us they have been sleeping separately. Fine," he waved a dismissive hand, "maybe he snores too loudly, maybe she kicks, maybe there is another explanation. But when I asked whether he was at home last night, he was more concerned about proving he was in bed alone. That suggests that sometimes he's not alone, and if what the maid said *is* true, it's not likely to be Tiya in his bed. Also, he never asked us what we've found out about Tiya's death, or what path we're pursuing. Wouldn't he want to know what, if anything, we'd found? And finally, shouldn't a man care about his wife's whereabouts when she doesn't come home at night?

"So," Ebrium clapped his hands together and gave them a quick rub as if to say *that is it*. "If the man didn't actually kill his wife, he certainly knows something he doesn't want *us* to know. Perhaps this has all been a matter of jealousy rather than the trigger for an uprising. In which case, we may well have cause to thank the gods."

"Okay. But what about Tiya's necklace?"

"I don't know. Maybe Ahmes caught them in the midst of something and she tried to run from him. It's also possible that your cranky friend Maketaten is somehow involved. Or the jumpy little priest, Menkhaf."

Ebrium stopped walking and Satsobek watched as he gazed off into the distance. To the east, unseen behind the city of Thinis, the great Iteru flowed. To the west, undulating mountains of desert sand rose up in the distance, their tops just visible above the mansions' roofs. Ra was pushing the sun towards the desert now, casting long rays of dying sunlight over the city.

The streets in the northern part of the city were mostly empty this time of day. Servants were making meals while nobles were napping or preparing for dinner. They kept their voices low, but few were around to overhear them. Those men that passed only gave Ebrium a cursory glance, or a less-than-polite one, before hurrying on their way. Satsobek realized that he must draw attention everywhere he went. If she were him she wouldn't be able to stand it. It was enough that her family was constantly criticizing her, never mind strangers on the street judging her all day long.

"So what do we do next?" Satsobek turned her face up to him.

"Tomorrow I want to speak with your friend Seret. It seems like he might be willing to tell us if he's seen or heard anything of use. And perhaps we lean on the priest some more. If we're still at a loss, we go see the bodies."

The thought of seeing Tiya and Yuny's bodies sent a shudder through her. She wrapped her arms around herself and rubbed her biceps. "Very well. I also think I should go through some of Tiya and Yuny's scrolls. Tiya kept meticulous notes on everything that occurred at the hwt. If anything unusual happened, she would probably have recorded it."

Ebrium acquiesced and took up walking again.

"But where are you going now?" She asked. They were moving deeper into the neighbourhood north of the palace and the temple and her father's manor was now within view, just up the street.

"Walking you home before I return to the village."

"Why?"

"The queen has tasked me with protecting you. I know you don't think it, but I'm fairly good at my job, nebet-i. And right now that includes escorting you through the streets. I will, however, stop short of your home as I imagine your family wouldn't like to see you with me."

Still confused, she spoke before censuring herself. "But why are you going to the village? Are you still living there? I thought the queen had given you a mansion in the north neighbourhood near the temple?"

His look turned to one of mild amusement. "So you've been making your own investigation into *me*, now, have you?"

Her cheeks burned and she hoped that the glow from the setting sun would cover any blush. "Hardly. One just...well it was hard *not* to hear about how you and Sekhrey Bey saved the queen when you first joined the royal guard. Back when that Sumerian prince tried to have her kidnapped."

"Hmmm. If you say so." Ebrium's eyebrow cocked in a mocking fashion.

"I do, thank you very much." She was beginning to understand why the queen credited him with skills of interrogation. She'd heard rumours Ebrium wasn't seen around the new home, but assumed he was just too busy to spend much time there. It hadn't occurred to her that he might not even be living there. And if he wasn't, *why* wasn't he? It was common knowledge that his mother and sister moved to the queen's palace months ago, around the same time the queen gifted him the new home. Was it possible he was living with someone else? And why did she even care?

The setting sun in the desert off to the west cut lazy streaks of reddish-gold light through the hot, dusty air that floated around them. Satsobek scrubbed a hand over her arm. She felt grimy and self-conscious thanks to the sand and dust that had accumulated on her sticky skin during all their walking about in the heat of the day.

Ebrium's eyes flicked off over her shoulder, surveying the neighbourhood where many of the noblemen lived and she watched as he rubbed the back of his neck with one rough hand. The low sun cast deep shadows along the ridges of his muscled abdomen. Shadows so deep she wanted to reach out and run her finger along their crevices, tracing the lines between light and dark that traversed his naked torso. As he massaged his neck the muscles in his arms and chest shifted and rippled. Satsobek wondered what it would be like to have those strong, thick hands kneading her shoulders, her calves, up her thighs… She tore her eyes away before he caught her staring.

Too late. Ebrium's mouth curved upwards. He was merciless, staring her down with that infernal regard of his until she bit the inside of her cheek hard. There was a heat in his eyes that was at complete odds with the cold stare he used to intimidate people. She wasn't sure which look made her more uncomfortable.

He snorted softly. "Look, I'll send someone tomorrow morning to escort you to the manor and we'll see if we can go talk to Seret without Ahmes around."

Now it was Satsobek's turn to put *him* on the spot. "To your new manor? Not to the village?" Why was he being evasive about his living circumstances?

"Have you ever even *been* in the village?" She opened her mouth to protest but he must have seen the flush creeping back into her cheeks. Of course she hadn't. She was a proper nobleman's daughter, *a prim little priestess*, he'd called her.

Shaking his head a little, he said, "Right. I'll send someone for you in the morning. And now, if you'll excuse me, *nebet-i*," he gave her a mock bow, "this lowly soldier has to go prepare his evening meal. I believe even a sheltered noblewoman can find her way home safely from here."

Before she could form a sharp retort, she was left watching his back stride down the empty lane, still wondering why he was sleeping in the village instead of his new home.

Satsobek turned to face her home, a white-washed mansion with four columns on the front porch propping up a section of the granite slab roof. It was only one house away, but she needed a moment to compose herself. She needed time to sit and put things in order, and to deal with her guilt and sadness over Tiya and Yuny's passing. The midday meal she'd shared with her family earlier that day seemed weeks in the past.

Satsobek's heart stopped in fear. She remembered her father's demand that she be home for dinner. *By the gods! He will kill me.*

That got her moving, even though she dreaded seeing Sobek. He was serious about marrying her off soon. And she would have no choice. Tiya would have taken her back into the temple, but of course that was no longer an option. She wasn't sure who the next high priestess would be. Regardless, she didn't think she would ever be able to set foot in the temple again without thinking of the murders. She could hardly beg the queen for assistance when the queen had more than enough troubles to manage. Besides, her father hated the queen enough that if Satsobek fled to her for help he would do everything in his power to bring the wrath of the nobles down on her. The queen couldn't just go about interfering in the family affairs of noblemen.

As Satsobek neared the front steps she heard a scuffling noise behind her and her heart jumped.

She whirled around to look but Ra had pushed the sun below the desert and now only a few dying glimmers of light burned on the horizon. Her eyes scanned the murky shadows of the street. *Oh gods, what if whoever killed Tiya and Yuny followed us?* Why hadn't she seriously considered that before? Her throat constricted with an agonizing paralysis.

All was silent. Satsobek struggled to draw in breath against the heat and the thumping pain of her heart. She took a step back, ready to run up the steps to her door

Shuffling sounded to her right and she squinted. "Hello?" she croaked.

"Nebet-i?" A man's voice called out. A white shenti materialized, catching a ray of light and glowing in the darkness. Satsobek's breath finally heaved in and out as Seret's scarred face appeared a few feet from her.

"Oh, Seret! Thank the gods. What in the name of Ra are you doing following me like that? I almost died of fear here in the street!"

"I am sorry, nebet-i. I've been following you since you left the house."

Satsobek could see the anxiety on his face and dread gripped her again. "Seret, what is it? What is the matter?"

Seret pursed his lips. "I didn't know if I could trust the soldier, nebet-i. I don't know anymore who I can trust. But I know that you loved the Great Lady, and that you must want to help her now so she can move into the afterlife in peace."

"Yes, of course I want to help Tiya. And you can trust Ebrium. I know he is a little rough, but he has the queen's trust, and he is a good man." *At least, I think he can be trusted to do good.* "But tell me, what has happened?"

Seret glanced behind him before stepping closer and lowering his voice. "Earlier today I overheard Ahmes sending a messenger to a man. I think his name was something like Hark, or Haerk, or Herk?" Satsobek nodded for him to continue.

"When Ahmes heard about Tiya he insisted the man meet with him. Then, just after you left, the messenger came back with an arrangement for them to meet late tonight at the House of Iput."

Satsobek drew in a sharp breath. She'd heard servants murmuring of the House of Iput, a tavern where men from the village went to drink, gamble on board games, and find women to sleep with. Her sister had also once made a joke about the types of women who worked there. It was not the type of place a man of Ahmes' stature would frequent. Noblemen had their own places of disrepute to go to.

"Seret, do you think Ahmes had something to do with Tiya's death?"

"I don't know for sure, nebet-i. But I do know that he was not truthful when he told you they never fought." The young man fingered the scar on his cheek - an unconscious gesture Satsobek knew he had always done. "He and Tiya fought quite a lot last year. The past six months they have not been speaking at all. They were sleeping in separate quarters."

"Do you know what they were fighting about?"

Seret shook his head. "I couldn't always hear their words, only that they were angry. I didn't want to stand near the door like the other servants sometimes try to do." He chewed on his bottom lip. "I only listened today because I thought Ahmes was acting strange about the Great Lady's passing. He hasn't cried, or been sad at all. Instead, he has seemed... worried, or afraid, perhaps?"

"It was very brave of you to come tell me this, Seret. Now I need you to do something else for me. Do you think you can find Ebrium's house in the village?"

He shrugged. "Everyone knows who he is. I'll ask around. It won't be hard to find him."

"Good. Please go now as quick as you can and tell him exactly what you told me. He will know what to do."

Seret nodded. "Of course, nebet-i. Anything that will help."

Satsobek looked out into gloom. Specks of light - burning flax wicks resting in bowls of oil - flickered in the windows of the homes lining the street. She searched for anyone who might be lurking in the shadows.

"Seret," she pressed his hand. "Do be careful. Until we catch whoever did this we must all try to stay safe." Then she turned and, with a quickened pace, mounted the steps to her front door. She was going to be very late for dinner and she wasn't sure whose wrath she was more concerned about, her father's or a potential killer's.

Chapter 5 – Sekhemkare

An anxious female servant met Satsobek at the door.

"Nebet-i," The young maid greeted her. Two years younger, but taller and broader than Satsobek, Sadeh had lively eyes and a round olivine face speckled with dark-brown freckles. "Your father has asked that as soon as you arrive I fix your hair and make-up, and dress you."

Satsobek followed Sadeh down the hallway to her room.

"Why in the name of Ra would he ask you to do that? Is there someone else here tonight?" Anxiety gnawed at her belly, wondering if her father had already set about procuring her a husband.

"Indeed there is. He's up on the rooftop with your father and sister." Sadeh opened the door to Satsobek's room. All four walls of the room were white-washed and unadorned. On the far end of the room was a narrow bed. A thin, stuffed mattress rested on top of a plain, raised wooden frame. White linen sheets encased the mattress, and white linen hung from the ceiling around the bed to keep out the bugs at night. A tall cabinet stood to the left, next to a square window cut at eye-level into the wall. On the right was a table. The top was obscured by the medley of pots, jars, and bowls that made up a woman's toilette. Tucked into the table was a low stool - a triangle of leather stretched over three criss-crossed wooden legs. Sadeh reached for the stool and pulled it out. She poured some water from a jug into an empty bowl and dropped in a strip of linen.

"Who is it? Why does my father concern himself with my appearance?" Satsobek allowed Sadeh to tug her dusty day robe over her head, leaving her naked. Sadeh was clearly in a hurry. Like most of the servants the girl was afraid of Sobek, Satsobek's father, and since Satsobek was late the maid likely feared the repercussions would rain down on both their heads.

"His name is Sekhemkare." As was the custom with their pronunciation, Sadeh rolled the *r* and dragged out the syllables of the name, pronouncing it *Sssek-hemm-karrr-ay*.

The girl set about forcibly scrubbing the dirt from Satsobek's body with the strip of wet linen. Usually she bathed in a large stone tub filled with warmed water and scented oils. But given how late she was this would have to do. She bit back a low grunt of pain as Sadeh nearly scraped the skin of her thighs off.

Sadeh continued. "He is the brother of a governor, and we believe your father wants to make a favourable impression. The man is involved in trade somehow, and perhaps there is an alliance to be made."

Satsobek went rigid. By "we" Sadeh meant the servants. Sadeh and Satsobek had become close since the girl came to the house a few years ago. Sadeh kept Satsobek informed of the things the servants overheard. It was how Satsobek had first known that her father was not as wealthy as he once was. Or as he now pretended to be.

It did not surprise her that her father wanted to conduct business with the brother of a governor. What concerned her was that this time it might involve her.

Satsobek compressed her lips and hauled in a breath. She asked, "What is this man like? How long has he been here?"

Sadeh answered as she grabbed the white linen wrap she had laid out on the bed earlier. "He is handsome, fit for a man his age."

"His age? How old is he?" Satsobek twisted to look at Sadeh, who put a hand on her shoulder and turned her back around. It would be foolish to hope her father would choose a desirable young man as her husband. However, she had hoped he would at least choose one not so old as to be her grandfather, like her sister Amenia's husband. *Then again*, a horrid little voice whispered in her head, *if he were old he might not be able to force himself on you for long*. She shivered. Both at the thought of some strange man climbing on top of her and at the evil wish for the man to become impotent. Or to even just simply die.

"Of course," Sadeh waggled one eyebrow at her, "Sekhemkare is not quite the same as the man I hear you've been working with today. The kitchen is all abuzz with how you were all over the temple grounds today with Ebrium, Sekhrey Bey's man. I expect to hear all about it later when you have time. I promise on my little brother's left hand I will not tell a soul. I hear he made quite an impression on the temple girls." Sadeh tilted her head side to side in a suggestive fashion, widening her eyes comically.

Not only did Sadeh keep Satsobek informed of what went on in her own home, but she'd also been one of Satsobek's primary sources of information about Ebrium after he'd saved her life. The maid moved in the servants' circles, went to the market, and stayed up to date on all the court gossip. She'd been the one to help Satsobek secure a private messenger to send Ebrium that botched thank you message.

Thinking of the temple girls talking about Ebrium caused Satsobek's hand to fist against her side. "There is not much to tell. Ebrium is maddening and arrogant."

"No doubt. And with plenty of right and reason to be. He has the queen's favour, and the favours of all the women he could ask for." Wrapping the fabric around Satsobek's waist, Sadeh tied it up over Satsobek's right shoulder, leaving one breast bare.

"Pfft." Satsobek scoffed, a tightness closing in around her chest. "Not *all* of them." There was no way she would admit that she might be one of those women.

Sadeh ignored that, obviously knowing better considering how many questions Satsobek had asked about Ebrium over the months. Instead, the girl said, "The governor's brother has been here for a little while now. Your sister has been doing her best to entertain him. As has your father's concubine."

Although Sadeh said it with a straight face, Satsobek caught the note of humour in the girl's voice, and responded wryly. "I bet they have been."

Amenia had no chance of divorcing her husband and re-marrying. Their father would never allow it. Not with the ensuing scandal, or the loss of Amenia's husband's shipping contacts. But that wouldn't stop Amenia from trying to conquer their dinner guest in some other way. Satsobek also had no doubt Kiya, her father's concubine, would overthrow her father in the span of a heart's beat if she thought a lover as high-ranking as this Sekhemkare was within her reach.

Satsobek let Sadeh push her down onto the stool. Sadeh hurriedly brushed green malachite over her eyelids and touched up the lines of black kohl around her eyes. She smudged red ochre powder on Satsobek's cheeks and lips, then rubbed cardamom-scented oil over Satsobek's neck, chest, breast, and arms before securing a gold disc around her throat.

The metal felt cool and heavy against her chest, resting just above her breasts. For some reason it reminded Satsobek of the cool blue of Ebrium's eyes when she'd first met his gaze in the queen's tent. She recalled his hard, muscled chest and groin pressed against her inside Mehyt's cabinet. His thick, strong arm wrapped around her. His heady scent - fresh, salty, and masculine - had enveloped her inside the cupboard. And then when he'd carried her out from the silo her face had been so close to his, her nose near his neck, the heat of his skin burning against hers. Now she could almost smell him in the air, as if his scent still clung to her despite Sadeh's treatments. She shivered as something like desire flashed through her body.

That is, it *could* be desire if the man was not so infuriating. She bit her lip, worrying at it. A man like Ebrium would never be satisfied with one woman, and she knew from experience she couldn't be trusted to have trysts, like Betrest or her sister. Her emotions were too fragile to stand physical intimacy without reciprocating feelings. And gods forbid she ever fall in love with a man like Ebrium. There could be no more dangerous fate for her emotional well-being.

She flinched as Sadeh roughly raked a comb through her hair, scratching her scalp.

"Really, Sadeh, if my father cannot present me to this governor's brother without such a production perhaps it is best if I dined in my own room tonight." Satsobek knew it was a futile protestation. Sadeh proved it by ignoring her completely. Instead, the girl muttered something about not having time to do anything else with Satsobek's hair. Much to Satsobek's relief Sadeh finally pulled back, comb in hand, with all the flourish and bravado of a man winning a sprinting race.

Sadeh ushered Satsobek towards the door. She whispered in a fierce voice. "Your father says it is imperative that you make a good impression, and that you behave yourself."

"I – what?" Satsobek jerked her head around to glare at Sadeh, who only pushed against her back and flapped a hand at the door. With the dread in the pit of her belly growing, she muttered to herself, "Oh, I will give him a good impression alright. A fantastic one. He will be absolutely charmed by me, just like all the other men are."

Satsobek climbed the steps to the rooftop of her father's house. The tightness in her chest grew more painful with each step. She smelled burning incense and heard the muted sound of music long before she reached the top of the stairs. She distinguished the tones of a lute, a hand drum, and a harp. Her father must have deemed their guest worthy of hiring a group of *hnr* - musicians and dancers.

When she finally stepped on to the solid slab of the roof, she took a moment to catch her breath. She had always found pleasure in watching the sun set over Thinis from atop her father's house. The last vestiges of the sun's rays had dropped below the desert to the west, leaving only a navy blue line on the horizon that blended up into the blue-black night of the sky above. Stars twinkled overhead, along with a bright crescent moon partly obscured by clouds.

Looking out to the south, Satsobek could just make out the outlines of the Temple of Mehyt and the queen's palace.

Past that was the village, nothing but a dark mass against the night sky. *Ebrium lives somewhere in that mass.* Somewhere in a village she had never been. *Unless, of course, Seret does not find him.* She stopped, shocked at the thought. She could not seriously be considering going to the village, to the House of Iput. That would be absurd. And dangerous. Very dangerous.

No, she assured herself. *Seret will find him. He has to.*

All around the rooftop, braided flax wicks floated in bowls of oil, their small, flickering orange flames casting deep shadows in the darkness. By their light, she made her way towards the tent where her family sat, their bodies silhouetted against the night. The tent flaps were rolled up to allow any passing breeze to blow through. The air was still so hot however, that moisture prickled her skin, threatening to roll a trail of sweat down between her breasts. To the right, a little ways from the tent, the musicians played softly, half-shrouded in gloom.

As she neared the tent her father caught sight of her. "There she is! My *sat*." *My daughter*, he called her. "Please forgive her lateness, Sekhemkare. She is sometimes still like an impetuous child, in need of a strong hand to guide her."

Satsobek's belly tightened into a hard, sharp stone. Her father was drunk. When he was drunk he became both demonstrative and jeering, sometimes within the same breath, swinging wildly from one to the other with the speed and dexterity of a small, trained monkey.

A few steps more brought Satsobek close enough to see Sekhemkare for the first time. He sat next to her father on a plush cushion on one side of the low table that rested on a large reed mat. The women sat on the other. Glowing oil wicks ringed the tent and were set on the long table, their glow emphasizing the lines and crevices of each of their faces.

Sadeh was right. Sekhemkare was not unattractive. He had broad shoulders and a narrow waist. His head was bald, save for a side-lock that he wore in a long braid on the right side of his head. His cheekbones were high and sharp, set below eyes that sported prominent lids lined in kohl.

However, something about his eyes, or the way they reflected the glimmer from the oil wicks, brought to mind a crocodile floating along the great Iteru, made lazy by the heat of the sun and a recent feast.

Sekhemkare looked to be in his early to mid-thirties, and she wondered if he still had all his teeth. Although some of the people of Kemet lived as old as seventy, or even eighty, to reach fifty was considered an accomplishment. To keep all of one's teeth at his age was even rarer still. Unlike many of the wealthy men of Kemet, who considered a round paunch a sign of wealth and prosperity, Sekhemkare was fit, his body molded and firm. She couldn't help but wonder what Ebrium would look like at Sekhemkare's age, and concluded he was the type of man to remain strong and chiseled for all his days. Despite his reckless attitude he struck her as a disciplined man, one used to austerity. If he weren't, he wouldn't have been able to work his way through Kemet's military ranks to stand by the queen's side.

Satsobek pushed aside those useless thoughts and acknowledged Sekhemkare with a slight deferential bow of her head. "*Em hotep, tayi neb.*" *Greetings in peace, my lord.*

"*Em hotep, nebet-i.* It is a pleasure to meet you." Sekhemkare nodded back. He was cordial, as expected from one of his station. But his eyes were bored as they raked over her, resting briefly on her bared breast before returning to the plate of baked fish on the table. As if they held more interest for him than she did. It was not unexpected. In spite of Sadeh's ministrations Satsobek knew that her looks did not appeal to many men. Nor did she particularly want Sekhemkare to find her tempting.

Regardless, though, to be so easily dismissed was still mortifying to a woman's pride.

Ebrium's words from earlier played back in her head. *I didn't say I wanted to get closer to your bed. But perhaps one day you may find yourself trying to get into mine.* Although he'd teased her, there'd been a heat in his eyes, something like interest, hadn't there? Yet later he'd called her a prim priestess. The man was a paradox.

Satsobek seated herself across the table from Sekhemkare and grabbed a honey roll from the table. The horror of the temple murders – along with the fear of her father's anger – crushed her appetite, but she needed something to keep her hands busy. Looking around, it was obvious that her father had outdone himself with the evening meal, ordering dishes that even some of the wealthiest households ate only rarely. Roasted water fowl, grilled fish, a platter of lettuces and vegetables, bowls of nuts, dates, and grapes, and a plate of sweet honey cakes covered the table. A jug of wine and a jug of thick barley beer rested in the centre of it all. Like most noble families, they owned two sets of dishes, simple ones for everyday use and a set of elaborate, hand-painted ones. Her father had laid out the ornate ones.

"You see, Sekhemkare, my little *sat* can be very… *demure*." Taking a bite of lettuce and chewing, her father waved the remaining piece for emphasis. "She needs a firm hand to keep her aware of her duties, but most of the time she hardly says a word." Satsobek doubted his descriptions of her were helping her father's cause. So far he had essentially described her as quiet, simple, and childish. Of course if that appealed to Sekhemkare then she would most certainly not make him a suitable wife.

Sekhemkare stretched his lips in a polite smile. Satsobek saw him wince as he did so, as if in pain. Before she could say anything her sister Amenia, dressed in a thin, see-through robe that accented her rounded curves, leaned towards the governor's brother. Amenia's smoothly braided wig, strung through with beads of red carnelian stone and draped in thin gold chains, sat high atop her head. Red carnelian beaded earrings swung from her ears, and a matching necklace with multiple strings around her throat. On her wrists, two wide gold cuffs glistened.

Amenia's ochre-reddened lips tilted in a suggestive smile. "Perhaps tayi neb does not care for demure, though? Perhaps he prefers a woman who is bold?"

Their father waved his half-gnawed lettuce leaf again. "Oh my little *sat* can be that, too, sometimes! Sometimes she is downright impertinent."

Sekhemkare ignored her father and turned to Amenia. His face was arranged in a pleasant expression, but rather than looking at her eyes, his gaze rested somewhere around her throat. He seemed to have as little interest in Amenia as he did in Satsobek. If he wasn't so obviously (and rather rudely) bored by them all, Satsobek would have been embarrassed for him and for their awkward situation. Her father was clearly trying to throw her at him, while her sister tried to seduce him. For once, the only family member Satsobek was not ashamed of was her father's concubine, who had so far been silent.

And then she wasn't. Although her voice was hushed, it thrummed with an eagerness that Satsobek found repulsive. Some people revelled in titillating gossip, no matter what the subject, finding pleasure in others' distress. As if to match her enthusiasm, Kiya's bare breasts wobbled as her shoulders shook slightly. "What do you think of this awful business with the hwt, tayi neb? Is it not just the most shocking matter?"

When he answered, Sekhemkare's voice was smooth, low, with a soft rumble in it. Some might consider it pleasant, but knowing her father's intent she found it unsettling listening to this strange man who might, one day, be her husband. "Of course. I have heard that the people take it as a sign of the gods' displeasure with our queen."

"Pfft, the queen." Her father scoffed. He'd moved on to waving his mug of wine around. "Of course the gods are displeased. There ought to be a grown pharaoh on the throne, not a woman with a babe in the womb." Satsobek wished it were possible to kick her father "by accident" under the table. But now that the conversation had turned she feared bringing any attention to herself, or what she had been doing with Ebrium all day.

Sekhemkare spoke in a slow even voice, as if measuring his words. "There have been so many fears this year for the harvest. While the crops are growing, it is not yet enough. If there is dissatisfaction and starvation amongst the masses, I fear that a woman may be too soft-hearted to keep them in their place. A firm hand is needed with those *common* sorts of people. Particularly if that woman is to sit on the throne for the next fifteen years until the next pharaoh comes of age. And then there is the question of what will happen if the babe is a girl. Will the queen then step down and allow a strong man to take her place? Perhaps her cousin Anen, who may have a closer ear to the gods? Or will she do something else utterly unheard of, like pass the throne on to her daughter?"

Satsobek's father roared with laughter and Kiya and Amenia twittered. Satsobek's hand tightened around the honey roll. She wanted to throw it at Sekhemkare's head, envisioning it bouncing off the bald side of his pate, but instead squished it into a hard ball of dough in her palm. *Those common sorts of people.* People like her servant, Sadeh. And Seret, who was risking himself to betray Ahmes and help the queen. *People like Ebrium.* She frowned.

Ebrium might be arrogant, but she did not think him cruel, or even unfeeling. His arrogance was unlike Sekhemkare's smugness. Ebrium's attitude was more cockiness, laced with a brash humour that, looking back over the day, made her smile to herself more than once. She sensed that he was also bitter and angry. Not without good reason. From what she had seen today alone, he was often treated crudely based on things beyond his control – such as the station of his birth and the location of it.

She found herself strongly disliking the governor's brother, even hoping he might have an accident on his way down the stairs tonight. She wished impotence upon him.

Amenia leaned forward, her breasts straining against her dress. "Oh, tayi neb, you are so funny. The queen could not possibly pass on the throne to a little girl. But what a funny picture that would be. I can see it painted on the palace walls now. The gods bestowing the *nemes* crown of the pharaoh on a barefoot, naked little girl."

Sekhemkare smiled and took a sip of his wine, but winced again and put a hand to his jaw. Satsobek was about to take the opportunity to turn the conversation when her father cut her off.

"My little *sat* here is close with the queen, though. Was even called to her this morning." His hand was full of grapes and this time, when he waved it for emphasis, a few grapes fell from his greedy palm and rolled across the reed mats. "Seems she has some skill of value because she used to work in the hwt." Satsobek couldn't figure out if his voice was proud or mocking. His mood was turning and she was afraid where this conversation might lead.

Sekhemkare was suddenly alert, scrutinizing Satsobek with a sharp, attentive look he had bestowed on no one else tonight. She shuddered. His eyes were like a crocodile with prey in its sights. When he blinked she half-expected to see the third, translucent inner eyelid that protected the reptiles' eyes underwater sliding across from the inside corner of his dark orbs to the outer.

He drawled in his deep voice. "Is that so? What skill would that be?"

Everyone's attention turned to her now. Amenia and Kiya sat completely still, looking at her. Her father gobbled some grapes from his palm, watching her over his fist. She forced a light laugh, hoping to downplay her involvement and change the subject. "Oh, truly it is not so much. She asked if I might speak with some of the ladies of the temple. I used to worship amongst them and I learned to write there. But in truth, I have not been to the temple in a year, nor have I seen the high priest or priestess in that time. So," she shrugged nonchalantly, "I do not know that I can be of much use."

Sekhemkare's gaze remained steady. "Do you know something of who is involved?"

Amenia broke in. "Yes, *Satsi*, tell us what you know." For the third time tonight Satsobek wished violence upon someone. If she'd had something of use to lob at Amenia's head, she just might do it.

Instead, Satsobek shook her head and chose her words carefully. "Truly, there do not seem to be answers. It is as you said, tayi neb. Some people believe the gods are displeased with the queen, and brought this down upon her as a warning. Everyone is, naturally, quite distressed."

"Well," Amenia smirked at her, looking well-pleased with herself. "I heard from Tawaret that you were seen in the hwt of Mehyt with one of those foreign pirates. Tawaret heard it from her maid Reputneb, who heard it from one of the kitchen girls in the hwt. They say everyone was talking about *you* and the queen's man."

It hurt her heart that the deaths of two of her friends were being bantered around the dinner table like common gossip. And the way Amenia mentioned her and Ebrium's involvement made it all sound so sordid. Her father cut in, preventing her from defending herself.

The way his knuckles tightened around his mug, and the ugly red flush that crept into his dark cheeks caused her belly to harden. "The queen is letting one of those foreign bastards investigate?"

Sekhemkare's smooth voice cut through the tension, his face a mask of bored disinterest. "I have heard something of these pirates the queen is keeping about her. Which one is it?"

Satsobek was almost thankful, as Sekhemkare's question diverted her father's anger, reminding him that he had a guest to pander to. She addressed the man, "Actually, Pharaoh Wadj brought the sailors to court, not the queen. It was he who stationed them in the royal guard."

Sobek snorted, "So now they are sailors? The men are *thieves*." Satsobek's father, a merchant, had lost ships to pirates in the past. He'd raged for days when the pharaoh brought the former pirates to court, but that was conveniently forgotten once the queen announced her regency. All blame for the brigands' presence transferred to her instead.

Their guest leaned back on his elbow, stroking his chin with long fingers. "How *exactly* did these foreigners end up in the guard again? We hear things up north, of course, but sometimes rumour is not the same as reality."

The story of how Ebrium and Bey had come to Kemet was well known to most women — it was a favourite for miles around. While many Kemeti noblemen disliked the foreigners, their wives and daughters were titillated by the thought of being captured by a group of dangerous – yet extremely handsome – men. Although Kiya and Amenia spoke of the pirates with distaste *now*, they had shared in the chatter willingly enough when the men first came to court.

Satsobek had even briefly harboured the suspicion that Amenia was jealous after Ebrium saved her from the tiger attack. Amenia had made some snide comments about having a disgusting, low-born foreigner's hands all over her, and how Satsobek was *dirty* now as a result. It had struck her as odd because Satsobek was sure she'd seen Amenia's gaze following Ebrium the night of the banquet.

More than happy to jump in and share gossip, Amenia and Kiya proceeded to relate all they knew about the queen's royal guardsmen. Given her previous personal interest in Ebrium, it was a story Satsobek was well-familiar with. After their capture at sea, and years in the Kemeti militias, the crew eventually came to the pharaoh's attention and, shortly before he died in a hippopotamus hunt, Pharaoh Wadj made Bey Captain of the Royal Guard, allowing Bey to bring some of his men along with him. Ebrium, of course, was one of those men.

Kiya's breasts jiggled as she said, "Of course everyone knows now that Bey was a prince back in Ebla, so I can see why the queen would let him keep his position. But this Ebrium…" her breasts shimmied faster, "why his parents were just servants in Bey's household. They say his father was a gardener, and his mother some kind of common maid."

Ironic of Kiya to judge, thought Satsobek, *considering her own origins remain dubious.*

Kiya continued, "But the queen *did* take his mother and sister into the palace to live with her a few months back. They became close when the queen had to flee Thinis in the middle of the night. You know, back when the Sumerian prince tried to have her kidnapped. Ebrium brought his mother and sister to attend to the queen while they were away. A few months back the queen also honoured Ebrium with a manor."

Satsobek wondered at the sense of fullness that sparked in her chest – was it perhaps a small glow of pride? How was that possible? Ebrium was nothing like she'd imagined him these past few months. She had no business feeling proud of him, or protective. And yet that's precisely what she felt when her sister added to the story.

Amenia's looped braids swung about her ears as she leaned forward and said in a loud whisper, "He arrested one of the noblemen who lived nearby, Addaya, for withholding taxes. They exiled Addaya and the queen gave the pirate his manor." As if it was a secret. As if the entire noble class hadn't talked about it for weeks. The men were mostly on the side of Addaya, saying that everyone lied a little bit about how much revenue they collected from their fields, while some women whispered that it served him right for being a lecherous old man.

Sekhemkare smirked. "It sounds to me as if this Ebrium's thieving ways continue still. He managed to steal the house from right under a nobleman's nose." Kiya and Amenia tittered and her father pounded a fist on the table in agreement. "Damned right, you are." He spluttered.

Perhaps it was because everyone seemed to have forgotten a rather important service Ebrium had provided that compelled Satsobek to speak. Apparently she had yet to come to terms with the fact that her own life was valued so little by these people around her – her own wretched family.

"Well, Ebrium *did* save my life from a tiger a few months back, so I suppose he deserves *some* small measure of thanks." If anyone missed the sarcasm in her voice they'd have to be well into their mugs of wine. She was brash in bringing up the contentious issue between her and her father. They'd argued about sending Ebrium a message of thanks afterwards. Her father won, as usual, refusing to acknowledge such a base-born man who, he said, was simply doing his job. But that hadn't stopped her from sending a secret message anyway. The same one that Ebrium had scorned.

Yet she defended him still, knowing something of what it felt like to be so little appreciated. "I have also heard that Ebrium took to pirating in order to support his mother and sister. When they settled here in Thinis, he sent for them so they could join him. And besides, if Addaya was lying about his revenues and not paying the proper amount of taxes, is that not a form of stealing from the queen? Is it really so different how one goes about the matter – either pirating or lying – when the end result is a theft of wealth? It is all a violation of *maat*, is it not? Or is it because Ebrium is of a lower caste that makes it a more heinous crime?"

Silence – hot and smothering – fell heavy over the tent as all eyes turned to her. Her father's face flushed that menacing shade of red, his eyes flashing a warning. "What did you just say?"

Satsobek blinked, sucking in her lips and biting down hard on them. What in the name of the gods *had* she said? She should have thought before speaking and drawing so much attention to herself.

Once again Sekhemkare came to her rescue. His reptilian eyes stayed on her, but he addressed her wrathful father. "I believe your little sat is something of a philosopher, Sobek. It is rare to meet a woman who feels inclined to argue the finer points of morality. In my experience most women do not bother to concern themselves with where or how they acquire their wealth as long as someone acquires it for them."

Sekhemkare watched her over the edge of his mug as he sipped some wine. She saw him wince again as he set the mug down and seized her chance to turn the subject. She asked him, "Are you in pain, *tayi neb*? Is there something wrong? May I fetch you something?"

"It is nothing, really, just a pain in my tooth." *Well, that settles it,* she thought, *if he has all his teeth now, he likely won't have them all for long.* He continued, a grim smile replacing his stern look. "But I have found a remedy. If you would call for some hot water, I may make myself some tea for the pain."

Satsobek gestured for a servant to bring some heated water. Her father leaned forward. His eyes, although clouded with drink, were shrewd. "Ah, and what is this? Have you some new medicine from the north, perhaps?"

"In fact, I have." A note of triumph snuck into Sekhemkare's voice as he untied a small leather sac from the belt that held up his shenti. "A little something I had shipped from Sumer."

A servant hurried up the steps with a jug of warm water and a mug and placed both before Sekhemkare. Sekhemkare poured the water into his mug as he explained in his silky voice. "A few years back I heard rumours of a flower grown in Sumer that is said to relieve pain. It is said to be quite a pretty flower, actually. Bright red. Even more so than ochre. The plant produces a pod that seeps a liquid. This liquid is then dried and becomes quite sticky. When it is consumed it can be quite helpful in relieving bodily pain."

Satsobek watched, fascinated, as he pinched off a very small amount of the sticky brown resin and dropped it into the mug of hot water. He dipped his little finger into the mug and twirled the water around, dissolving the powder. "Within a few minutes," he continued, "the effects will begin to be felt. It is also," he paused to take a sip, "supremely relaxing."

He took a deep breath and, as he released it, his body seemed to loosen. He gave a lazy smile and Satsobek felt as if she were somehow watching an erotic, private moment. Sekhemkare turned his gaze on her, staring beneath half-shuttered lids in a way that unsettled her. She wished he would go back to being bored by her.

Impatient to know more, Satsobek's father asked, "How did you obtain this medicine? I have not heard of it."

Sekhemkare finally turned from his sluggish scrutiny of her and she breathed a sigh of relief. He spoke to her father. "The Sumerians call it *hul gil*. It means 'the plant of joy'. I have only recently obtained it through some of my contacts in Sumer, and only in a small amount. I wanted to test it myself first. If all goes well, however, I think it could be quite useful for us here in Kemet." Sekhemkare's eyes drooped as he smiled. He swayed just a little, as if moving to the low strains of the musicians. His behaviour made her uneasy, but no one else seemed to notice.

Satsobek's father continued to press Sekhemkare for information regarding the hul gil, and the man offered it up readily. Satsobek was sure her father would try to find a way to insinuate himself into the trade. While the men talked she shrank back from the table into the shadows, her presence forgotten. Leaning back on the cushions to peer at the night sky, she searched for the easily identifiable cluster of stars known as Hathor.

The other constellation she could always find was The Foreleg of Seth. The seven stars were said to be the leg of Seth in his bull shape. At one point during their long struggle for dominance over Kemet, Seth turned himself into a bull and used his foreleg to stomp on his brother Osiris. In turn, Osiris tore away Seth's leg and removed it to his domain in the sky.

The brothers' battle for domination of Kemet was not a happy story. Seth was unwilling to concede defeat time and again despite Osiris's triumphs. He had even gone so far as to kill his brother and cut his body into pieces, dispersing them throughout Kemet. It was no surprise, then, that Seth was associated with violence, chaos, and the absence of *maat*, the peace and order of the world.

When she was younger and had first heard the story of Seth and Osiris she thought of herself and her sister Amenia. Although she'd tried not to, she couldn't help but cast Amenia as Seth. Amenia had always been relentless in her taunting of Satsobek. Satsobek often questioned how often they'd have come to blows if they'd been boys instead of girls.

She worried at the inside of her lip, wondering again if Seret had found Ebrium. She couldn't recall if she'd told Seret to send word to inform her of his progress. Enough time had elapsed that he should have found the big Eblaiti man, but there'd been no word to let her know.

The conversation amongst her family and Sekhemkare only reinforced her need to find the temple killer. She had to help her cousin, her queen, before the situation got out of control. If the killer were found and brought to justice swiftly, there could be a way to spin it to prove just how *efficient* the queen was as a ruler. A little voice in her head also noted that it would prove just how efficient Ebrium was at bringing about justice and preserving the maat of Kemet. People would have no choice but to respect him then.

It was not as if Ebrium could blame her for not going to the House of Iput tonight. The queen would never expect her to risk her reputation, or her safety, in such a way. Yet Satsobek couldn't help thinking that if she were a man there would be nothing to stop her. Perhaps even if she were a woman of the lower classes it would not be so inconceivable. Ebrium had already made it clear he felt saddled with her, a woman. And one of her class, no less. While he could not find fault with her not going, it could give him just one more reason to dislike her.

Prim little priestess indeed. He had no idea. If she was prudish now, it was only because she'd been heedless in the past and suffered for it. But reckless or not, if she didn't find a way to ensure someone was at the House of Iput tonight to catch Ahmose, they might miss their chance to stop a killer.

Satsobek shifted on her cushion, trying to let the blood flow back to her numb legs and bottom. Could she go to the village on her own? Perhaps if she could bribe one of the male servants to take her to the House of Iput…

She was still asking herself that question two hours later as two servants helped Sekhemkare to his feet. Although his stance was wobbly Sekhemkare's eyes sharpened as he looked at her. "Nebet-i, *senebti.*" *Be well,* he wished her. "May Seth be with you." His voice was smooth. *Smooth as the Iteru on a calm night,* she thought. She shivered as she envisioned the surface of the snaking river - black, glossy, and depthless on a moonless night.

She crossed her arms over her chest, chilled despite the heat. Although his farewell could be considered as a blessing, to ask Seth to protect her from his own chaos, it was the second time tonight the dangerous god had come to her attention. Her lingering feelings of dread were enough to cause her to make up her mind. She could not let chaos win over Kemet.

"Senebti, tayi neb." *Be well, my lord.* She nodded to Sekhemkare and watched his back fade into the darkness as the two men helped him down the stairs and out into the street. She noticed that the clouds were closing in over the sky, blotting out the crest of the moon and the stars. Soon there would be little light in the village.

Satsobek wished her father, sister, and Kiya a quick goodnight, claiming exhaustion from the day of walking in the heat. Her excuse cut off any hope the other women had of gossiping about Sekhemkare. She knew they would spend a good amount of time tomorrow, and the next few days, dwelling on every moment of the evening and she would inevitably be sucked in to the conversation sooner or later.

But not tonight. Tonight she had more important things to do.

Chapter 6 – In the House of Iput

"Hello, darlings. I did not expect to see you all back here tonight." Ebrium tensed as Iput's gaze raked over him, a mocking smile playing on the corner of her lips. One perfectly plucked and re-drawn eyebrow was raised in a silent question, asking if he were in the mood to banter.

He was not. He had no interest in their usual game, but circumstances left him no choice but to come back far sooner than he'd intended. After dropping Satsobek off by her house, he'd thought better of leaving her alone on the street and waited in the shadows to ensure she made it inside safely. He'd seen Seret approach her, and intercepted the boy after Satsobek ran up her stairs. Seret told Ebrium what had transpired and so Ebrium arranged for Batr and Makae – fellow guardsmen and trusted old friends – to join him at the House of Iput to root out Ahmes's secrets.

"Ah Iput, who can resist your charms?" Batr placed a hand over his heart and gave a deep bow. The tall man's braided hair swung forward and back, causing the shadows of the House of Iput to deepen further around his dark face. Iput's lips curled upwards in the expected response, but her eyes flicked to Ebrium.

A series of images from last night clashed in his mind. Iput's hands on his bare chest. Iput removing her wig and running her palms over her smooth pate. Iput's pendulous breasts above him, her legs, the silver armbands circling her biceps. The clattering of her bracelets. The nauseating scent of her incense and too-strong perfume.

The widow of a traveling merchant, Iput had always been the one to brew the beer her husband sold in the village markets along the great Iteru. Once he was gone, she'd scraped together some wealth and chosen one of the few professions available to a lone woman – running a tavern. Iput didn't engage in the same business as the girls who worked for her, but took lovers where and when she chose. She had a strong business sense and an ability to charm customers while keeping them under control, refusing to let anyone impose their will on her.

Ebrium shook his head, hauling in a deep breath of stale, tavern air. He raked his big hands through his wavy black hair and tried to rid himself of the distaste he felt. His aversion was not for Iput, for she was not to be held accountable. No, it was distaste for his own weakness. For continuing to return to Iput's bed when he'd told himself – and her – he would not do so any longer. Particularly when she kept telling him he owed her nothing and that, although she thoroughly enjoyed his occasional company, she had no interest in tying herself to any one man ever again. Not that he wanted to tie her to him. Not at all. He simply wanted to stop waking up in her bed every now and then after those nights when the silence in his hut grew deafening.

Instead of rising to her mocking challenge, Ebrium glanced around the dark tavern. Men sat on cushions on the floor around low tables. Some were playing the board game senet, while others sat and drank. Screens made of dyed purple and blue linen were stretched across wooden poles, separating the tables. Here and there women wearing robes wrapped in various states of nudity sat with the men, or served bowls of beer and wine. The tavern was dimly lit by wicks of braided flax floating in bowls of oil. Ahmes was nowhere in sight, and he hoped they'd arrived in time to catch the priestess's husband.

It was hard to see past the dark room, but Ebrium was well aware of what lay beyond the tavern. The House of Iput had several rooms behind the main one, equipped with beds for the girls who worked, and lived, in the House of Iput. Iput took good care of her girls, and there was more than one stern-looking man stationed around the tavern to ensure that no one, either in the tavern or the back rooms, got out of hand.

Ebrium turned his attention back to the tall, imposing woman in front of him. He lowered his voice so he would not be overheard. "We're looking for someone. His name may be Hark, or Haerk? I believe him to be a man for hire." Iput would know what he meant. Although the House of Iput was one of the finer men's taverns in the village, it was still a place where men met to engage in the type of business not suited to daylight hours.

"Ahhh, I know the man." Iput scanned the room before shaking her head. "A gambler. He isn't here now, but he comes in once in a while and stays all night, playing senet and twenty squares. Poor man never does very well, and often loses more grain than he makes. Do you want me to tell him you're looking for him?"

"Gods, no!" Ebrium glanced around to make sure he hadn't attracted attention. Not that it mattered much if he were noticed, as he was known to frequent Iput's and his presence here wouldn't be deemed unusual by any of the regulars. He just preferred discretion in this particular business. Leaning towards Iput, he said, "No, I don't want him to know we're looking for him at all. He's supposed to be meeting with another man here tonight and I need to know what they talk about."

The older woman tapped a finger – the nail stained a reddish-brown by henna – to her lips and glanced around the room again. "I can help you with that. I have two empty tables right now that are side by side. I can seat you there, and if your fellow comes in I can put him next to you. But I tell you what, darling, I can't keep that table empty all night. I'll keep it open as long as I can but if it fills up in here I'll have to use it."

Ebrium's eyes narrowed. Although never unkind, Iput was a businesswoman before all else, something that he both admired and was irritated by. "It's the queen's business, Iput. If I have to, I'll pay you for the loss."

Her well-drawn eyebrows rose. "In that case, darling, never mind. If I can be of some service to our dear queen, I ought to be. I do, after all, like to support a woman in a position of power." She winked and indicated a table at the back of the dark tavern. "Haerk is a little man," she held a hand at nose-level, "with a scar over his eye. I'll bring him to the table next to you if he comes in."

Ebrium gave her a description of Ahmes, too, just in case he arrived first. Then he, Batr, and Makae made their way over to the table on the other side of the screen. Ebrium's size, looks, and tattoo made him stand out in any crowd. Batr and Makae, twin brothers of the Libu tribe to the west of Kemet, usually attracted their fair share of attention as well. The men were tall, lean, and fierce-looking with long, braided hair and tattooed cheeks and legs. Tonight Ebrium wore a long-sleeved tunic that covered his tattoos, but there was little else he could do to disguise himself. He hoped that a dark tavern, a screen, and a tunic would be enough to prevent Ahmes from spotting him right away. Luckily, the table Iput directed them to happened to be in the darkest corner of the tavern, and had only the empty table on one side, and nothing on the other. They were not likely to be easily seen, or overheard.

The three foreign men settled themselves on cushions, ordering bowls of Iput's strong barley beer. To pass the time, they set up a round of senet. Each of two players had five carved stone pieces that they had to move across the board in a snaking fashion. Their goal was to get all their pieces off the board before the other, hampered (or aided) by the toss of a set of sticks. While they played, they discussed in low voices the progress of the investigation. Ebrium had filled them in on the days' highlights and the brothers in turn told him about their day. It had come to their attention that a group of men had gone into the village market earlier that day and callously announced the murders of the high priest and priestess.

Batr shook his head, "We were walking through the market and some of the women were practically in hysterics over the deaths."

"Son of a jackal's ass," Ebrium swore. "As if we really need someone stirring things up right now. What with the likelihood of a bad harvest season looming and the rumours that the queen's unborn child doesn't belong to the pharaoh. People are already afraid."

Makae, a quiet and often serious man unlike his brother who was the older of the two by seven minutes, cleared his throat. "It gets worse. They insinuated the gods allowed it to happen because they were displeased with Kemet for letting a woman rule, that it's a violation of maat."

Batr described the five men, "Fardu the merchant told me he didn't recognize any of them. One of them was a bit taller than average, wearing some gold earrings and such. He stood out there in the village market all dressed up like that. As if he didn't care he'd stand out in the crowd. The rest were average age, average height, nothing remarkable except that they looked strong enough."

Ebrium's eyes followed the movement of the pieces on the board as the brothers moved them around based on the toss of a handful of notched sticks. Makae moved the last of his five carved pieces along the board towards the end point, beating Batr who snorted in disgust.

"I assume you went looking for them?" Ebrium asked, setting up the next game to play against Makae.

"Mmm," Makae nodded. "We didn't find them, obviously, but we *did* meet a merchant who sold the men some bread. He noticed their strange accent while they were talking and asked where they were from. They said they were from up north, in the Aneb-Hetch sephat."

Blowing out a puff of air, Ebrium frowned. "That's the third time today that sephat has come up. This morning, when I went to the queen, she and Bey were meeting with the brother of the governor of Aneb-Hetch. There's a priest in the hwt, one who manages the finances, who's also from Aneb-Hetch. And now these men."

Makae tossed the sticks and moved his piece forward three spots, overtaking one of Ebrium's. He tossed the sticks again and placed a piece two spots forward. Then he asked, "And you suspect these men might all be connected?"

Ebrium shook his head. "I don't know. Aneb-Hetch isn't exactly a small sephat. There are several villages and a couple of large cities. These men may all be from different cities and have never met. What would a governor's brother, a priest, and five thugs all have in common?" Only half-engaged in the game, he moved forward two spaces. Too late, he realized he could have taken a piece off the board and swore.

Makae gave him a knowing smile and Batr chuckled then said, "If the brother and the priest are from the same city it's probable they'd meet. They'd see one another at court often."

Makae waved a hand. "That's *if* they are even from the same city."

Running his hands through his thick black hair, Ebrium tugged at it to clear his head. The day had been too full already. "Somehow those men knew of the murders before any announcement was made. Maybe they're aligned with the queen's distant cousin who has claims to the throne. Maybe he's testing the waters to see if he can garner enough support for a rebellion. It wouldn't be so difficult to incite a rebellion right now, given the unrest over the harvest season. Wages at the hwt have already been cut in anticipation of the low harvest. It's possible the murders were a result of tension over wages, perpetrated by some angry farmers or other workers."

He blew out a deep breath and shook his head. "Which leads us to the nervous, jumpy little priest. Menkhaf is in control of the hwt's economic affairs. He may or may not stand to gain something by the high priest's death. I don't know his ambitions, but if he wanted to become the high priest, he may now be poised to do so."

Batr raised an eyebrow. "But what were the high priest and priestess doing in the hwt at night in the first place? Clandestine meetings are rarely innocent." His eyes twinkled. "I should know, I've had a few myself." His twin brother rolled his eyes.

"What?" Batr threw his hands up in supplication. "It is not as if any of you here are strangers to unusual locations. You recall the time we brought those women on to the ship in the port of Piraeus. Remember how they asked to see the kitchen for a late night snack?"

Makae gave a thin smile. "Would that I could forget that blonde one. She had the strangest appetite."

A deep laugh boomed from Batr. Ebrium grunted and shook his head. "There are some things best forgotten indeed." A year ago he would have had no problem laughing at the memory. Lately, however, the ridiculous exploits of his youth had begun to seem just that – ridiculous.

It didn't help that he had to be more careful now that he was under the watchful gaze of the queen's court, and that his actions would reflect on the queen's reputation. Not to mention now that his mother and sister had joined him in Thinis they were much more likely to hear about his activities than when he'd been sailing on a distant sea. Despite being gnarled and old, his mother wouldn't hesitate to take her walking stick to his head if she discovered even a quarter of the things he'd done back in his brigand days. Furthermore, sooner or later he'd have to assist his sister in obtaining an advantageous marriage. Sleeping with the sisters, daughters, and wives of men who could help him with that would not be conducive to his best interests in the long-term.

Daughters of the nobility like Satsobek. The thought wandered into his head unbidden. Entangling himself with such a high-ranking woman could prove very complicated – a woman once destined to be high priestess, no less. Too educated and high-born to be entertained by him for any length of time. Yet lately the unschooled daughters of other soldiers and villagers he'd met held little interest for him. They treated him as if catching him was like hauling in a prized merchant ship, loaded with the riches of Kemet. His newly elevated position and wealth blinded them to all else, and they simpered and flirted in a tiresome fashion. Satsobek, on the other hand, didn't seem the type to be the least bit dazzled by such corporeal things, going so far as to downplay her importance to the other priestesses of the temple. Yet at the same time he was certain he unsettled her. *Complicated indeed.*

He tugged at his hair again before pulling the subject back to the present. "Hopefully tonight we'll discover something useful about the appetites of the priestess's husband. He seems off, not like a grieving man. Perhaps tonight we'll learn why." Ebrium tossed the sticks and moved a piece forward five spaces, overtaking Makae's. He took another turn and moved one of his pieces off the board. He now had three pieces left while Makae had four.

Makae took his turn and removed a piece from the game. Now they were tied.

"Speaking of clandestine meetings," the corners of Batr's lips twisted upwards, "the woman the queen has paired you with, isn't she the one you saved some time back? What's she like? I've heard she's… quiet and a bit unusual."

Ebrium was in the middle of tossing his sticks, but looked up at Batr with narrowed eyes. Batr was not known for his subtlety. Then again, neither was he. "Already had time to ask around about her, did you?" Batr shrugged in response and Ebrium snorted. "Well, she might be unusual, yes. But not at all quiet. Difficult and stubborn, with a sharp tongue. Good luck to the man paired to marry her one day."

In spite of what he'd said, his body recalled the feel of Satsobek's pert behind snugged up against him inside the cupboard of Mehyt earlier that day. The softness of her skin as he'd held her in his arms and carried her out of the grain silo. The provocative sweep of her straight black hair on his chest. *What would it be like to go to sleep and wake up next to that each day?* To be able to tease her and watch that angry little frown crease her brow, to hear her funny quips in response… To smell her cinnamon-honey scent each morning, to be enveloped by that perfume. Better yet, to be enveloped by that compact body of hers…

Ebrium cut his thoughts short. She'd made her feelings clear when she'd sent her messenger eight months ago, reminding him of his place. And she hadn't argued with him when he'd left her near her house today, citing that her family would not want to see them together. *Best to focus on the task at hand and be rid of the woman as soon as possible.*

Makae's voice cut through his thoughts. "You still haven't moved a piece."

"What's that?" Ebrium looked up.

Makae raised an eyebrow, and Batr smirked. "You tossed the sticks a few minutes ago but haven't moved your piece. You've just been staring at the board."

Ebrium swore and Batr roared with laughter. "By the gods, man! Have you finally met your match?"

"What in the name of Dagon does that mean?" Ebrium growled.

Batr grinned, clearly enjoying Ebrium's discomfort. "It means that you've never described a woman as *difficult* before. I've never once known you to have a problem where women are concerned." His words echoed Merneith's from earlier that morning.

Makae added, "Unless their fathers are also concerned, that is."

Sarcasm tinged Ebrium's voice as he said, "Well then, let's just say that her father would be very, very concerned."

Batr's lips quirked up. "That's never stopped you before. You've always found a way to get what you want."

Refusing to let Batr bait him, Ebrium grimaced. "I never said I wanted her. So let it go." Out of the corner of his eye he saw the brothers exchange knowing looks and he pointedly chose to ignore them.

The men were on their second bowls of beer some time later when Batr gave a low whistle. "Did Iput get a new girl?"

Ebrium was focused on the senet board, contemplating how best to box Makae's remaining pieces in. "I don't think so. Why?"

"That pretty little one that just walked in. Poor thing looks like she's never stepped foot in a tavern before."

Ebrium almost choked. Without laying eyes on her, he *knew* who Makae was talking about. He looked towards the door, his eyes skittering over the faces of customers and girls until they settled on the one face that had no business being there. It took him a second to register what he was seeing, masquerading as she was in a tall braided wig, more make-up than she'd worn during the day, and plain jewellery, but once his voice was working again he swore aloud. "Son of a jackal's ass." He was angry. No. *Furious.*

He was already rising when Batr asked, "Who is it?"

Ebrium gritted his teeth. "*Her.*"

"The woman you've been complaining about? I had no idea she was such a sweet-looking thing. Listen, friend, if you need help handling her, I'd be more than happy to…"

But Ebrium cut him off before he could finish. "And I'd be happy to put my foot up your ass." He scowled, not wanting Batr anywhere near her. Batr was far too charming. And the last thing he needed was more complications on his hands.

Batr threw his hands into the air, palms up, chuckling. "Well then, go deal with her. We'll stay here in case your man shows up. This is no place for a nobleman's daughter." Ebrium was thinking just that as he strode across the room. He was also thinking of forcibly carrying said nobleman's daughter out of the tavern and dumping her on her sweet little rump in the street. He should have known better than to assume she would stay home, he should have tied her to a post inside the queen's palace for the night.

Satsobek had yet to spot him. Her eyes were wide as she scanned the dark tavern. She was making a valiant effort to cover it up, but he discerned her anxiety in the way she licked her lips, biting down on the soft lower one while twisting her dress in her hands. A dress that was wrapped around one shoulder, placing one small, perfectly rounded breast on display. That outfit, coupled with the innocent apprehension on her face, was bound to draw the attention of every man in the room. *Like jackals to a helpless baby rabbit.*

He was there, hand on her elbow, at the same moment that her eyes adjusted to the darkness and she recognized him. Her large, kohl-rimmed eyes looked up to him, full of relief. He had a flash of admiration for her as he comprehended what an unfamiliar world the tavern would be to a sheltered nobleman's daughter who'd never even been into the village, never mind a place like the House of Iput. That aside, however, with her wig and jewellery she certainly looked the part of a woman who belonged here. Which only served to stir his anger. It was unlikely she'd be recognized here, but it wouldn't help her reputation one bit if she were. To add to his irritation, he found he didn't want any other man here running their lecherous orbs over her and taking a notion to try and buy her for the night.

To prevent just such a thing from happening he did the first thing that came to mind, the one thing that seemed to come naturally to him when he was with Satsobek. He started a fight.

"Dammit woman, didn't I tell you to leave me alone?" Ebrium growled loud enough to pique the interest of the men nearby. Which is exactly what he wanted. They were watching her already through lascivious, hooded lids, so best to give them a show.

"Wh-what?" She blinked at him. "Are you drunk?"

"Come now, stop playing silly. I told you it was over between us. You need to stop following me around. You have no business here." He slid a big hand down to her hip and squeezed it, giving her a slight nod. With her brow furrowed in confusion, Satsobek glanced past his shoulder. He saw understanding dawn on her face and she tipped her face back to his, transforming her expression into a sexy, wide-eyed pout that almost knocked him out of his sandals.

Pitching her voice into a lower-class accent, she whined, "I'm sorry, please don't be mad. I just had to see you. I've missed you so much." She ran her delicate fingers up over his arms and shoulders, lacing them behind his neck.

He'd wanted her to play along, but he hadn't expected her to do it so readily, or so well, and it took him a moment to recover before he could manage to respond. "I've missed you, too, honey, but you have to stop being so jealous all the time. A man needs to get out and breathe once in a while."

A glance over his shoulder told Ebrium the watchful men were losing interest in the lovers' quarrel as the couple were, apparently, on the verge of reconciliation rather than a noisy – and much more entertaining - spat. But still he wanted Satsobek out of sight, so he maneuvered her behind an unoccupied screen near the door, partially shielding them from the entranceway. He rested his forearm on the wall next to her head and brought his cheek close to hers, pretending to nuzzle her neck while taking in her alluring scent. All the blood was making its way south from his head and damn if he didn't wish the rest of the tavern would just disappear into the underworld. The way her hands skimmed his neck and shoulders was maddening, and the vision of her as a wanton seductress was more than appealing at the moment. He wanted to push her against the wall and have his way with her. The very thought of some other man here trying it fueled his anger.

"This is no place for you," he admonished her in a harsh whisper. "It's dangerous and if you're recognized it'll ruin your reputation. And Ahmes *will* recognize you, even with all this." He gestured to the tall, black braids piled atop her head and the red beaded earrings and necklace that emphasized her delectable, cinnamon-coloured skin. Skin he very much wanted to lick and taste.

Irritation blossomed in her eyes as she turned her face to his, almost bumping noses. "I didn't know if Seret found you or not."

"So you decided to stroll on over to the village *by yourself* in the middle of the night?" Though incredulous, he could have kicked himself for not sending Seret back to her, that *damnably stubborn little woman*. He scraped the fingers of his free hand through his hair, tugging on it to prevent himself from steering her right out of the tavern. Or kissing her. Or both. "By the gods, woman, do you even *know* where you are?"

Satsobek faltered and she chewed the inside of her lip. "I…I have heard of the House of Iput. I am not so very sheltered…"

Ebrium sighed. He almost felt sorry for her discomfort. *Almost.* "Who escorted you here? I can't take you back home now. Ahmes and Haerk have yet to arrive." He gave a quick look over his shoulder to affirm that neither man had appeared while he'd been occupied with Satsobek.

He cursed when he saw two men seated at the table on the other side of the screen from Batr and Makae. In the darkness he couldn't make out their faces, or if either was the man Iput had described as Haerk. He hoped Iput hadn't gone back on her word and seated someone else there. Somehow, he'd have to deal with Satsobek *and* this unexpected hitch.

With his ardour dissipating, he sniped at Satsobek. "You know, it would be wonderful if you didn't make my job more difficult. I have enough to do without having to manage your willful little behind at every turn."

"I can assure you, *waew*," she flung out the word *soldier* like it was an insult, "I am quite capable of taking care of myself. I am hardly the spoiled child you think me."

He was about to toss out a refutation when the front door swung open and Ahmes walked in. Ebrium had a split second to think before the man's eyes would adjust to the light in the room. Moving fast, Ebrium covered her with his bulk and did what now seemed the second most natural thing to do when he was with Satsobek. He kissed her.

Satsobek gasped at the same moment Ebrium took her mouth in a ravaging blast of heat. Bold and carnal, his kiss caused the skin that had prickled with cold fear minutes before to now race with searing warmth, hardening her nipples and clenching the intimate space between her legs.

With his fingers digging into her hips, he pressed his body against hers. Her hands splayed over his chest, smoothed over his skin, solid as marble, her slender fingers barely making their way over the muscles that strained under his white tunic. After the initial shock of contact, her mouth became soft, pliable, responding with a will of its own. She'd craved this moment so many times in the last eight months that her reaction was almost inevitable. A desperate need to feel his naked skin against her own rose up in her as the fabric of his tunic rubbed against her one exposed nipple in an excruciatingly pleasurable parody of a caress.

But then he pulled away, looking down at her with surprise in his eyes. Her lips were still open as she panted for breath, trying to quell her desire. Her eyes flicked past Ebrium, and that's when she saw Ahmes making his way through the room, towards the back. *Of course. I'm such a fool,* she thought, realizing he hadn't kissed her because he wanted to, but because he *had* to. To hide them both from Ahmes. Just like how he'd started a lover's spat to avoid attracting more attention to her arrival.

Pulling herself together, she decided if he could be mercenary so could she. She watched Ahmes jerk his head in a meaningful gesture to a man in the back of the tavern, turn and, with the man now at his heels, stride back past them and out the door.

Satsobek ducked out from under Erbium's arm and, before he could stop her, slipped out the door into the night.

Ebrium caught up with the reckless woman as she was peering around the mud-brick corner of the House of Iput. The midnight air was hot and, aside from the chirping of crickets and locusts and the odd braying donkey, silent enough that he was able to discern the slapping of sandals alongside the building. He tapped Satsobek's shoulder and indicated that she follow him around the opposite side of the tavern to the back of the building. Attached to the side of the tavern was a brew house where Iput prepared the thick barley beer she served inside and sold in the market. This brew house had a back entrance, with a doorway just deep enough for them to tuck themselves into. Whether Ahmes and Haerk went behind the building, or alongside, from the doorway there was a good chance they'd be able to overhear them without being seen.

Once there, he stole under the arch and pulled Satsobek in front of him so that they were pressed chest to chest. With her tall, braided wig and her back to the outside, it would be difficult to recognize her, and the wig offered him camouflage to hide his face behind as well. She tipped her face up to him and glared as he took advantage of the situation and ran his big hands over her back, but he pursed his lips to encourage silence as a man's voice, Ahmes's he thought, reached his ears.

"Haerk, you fool! What have you done?"

"Me? I didn't do anything." Haerk's voice was a low squeak.

"Do not lie to me, you braying donkey. I wanted you to *watch* my wife, not *kill* her." Ebrium exchanged a speaking glance with Satsobek. Perhaps Ahmes wasn't their killer after all.

"I did watch her. I never touched her. I'm not stupid."

"I doubt that. But if you did not kill her, then who did?"

"I don't know." The man almost wailed in his anxiety. "I truly don't. I had nothing to do with her death. I swear on Ra and Ptah and Ammit and…"

"Shut up, *alase*." Ahmes called Haerk an ass. "I do not care how many gods you swear to. You were supposed to be watching my wife *last night*. If you were, you would have seen who killed her."

Ebrium was straining to hear the men when Satsobek turned her face in the direction of the voices, listening closely. As she did so, her wig brushed his face, tickling his nose. He pushed it aside, but a few stubborn strands continued to stick out and irritate his nostrils from time to time. Between the hairs and the strong perfume that scented the wig, his nose itched and he had to hold his breath a few times to avoid sniffling.

Haerk insisted he hadn't seen who Tiya was with last night. "I – I only saw the front entranceway where she entered."

"Was Yuny with her?"

"When they entered, yes, yes he was. But I saw no one else."

There was a pause. Then Ahmes said, "I was questioned by one of the queen's foreign dogs this morning. If he comes sniffing around, you had better hold your tongue, Haerk, or I will tell him that you went after Tiya of your own volition. I will tell him I hired you to watch her, but that you tried to bribe her for money in exchange for information about me, and when she refused, you murdered her."

"What?! No! You can't do that."

"I can, and I will. Unless you hold your tongue and act like you and I never met. Believe me, Haerk, I am a better liar than you. I have had the whole duration of my marriage to practice, and that is almost longer than you have been alive. I also have friends far more powerful than you."

And that's when Ebrium sneezed. Satsobek's wig muffled the noise, but not by much. He and Satsobek both held their breaths, rigid as two planks on a pier.

"What was that?" Ahmes hissed.

Satsobek saved them by doing the unexpected. She giggled. Loudly. In her high-pitched, lower class voice she teased, "Oh, honey, you couldn't afford for me to do *that* for you. But I bet we can come to some kind of agreement on the other thing you wanted."

Haerk grunted from around the corner and said dismissively, "'S nothing. Just one of Iput's girls probably trying to make a little extra by not paying Iput for the room. They bring men back here sometimes."

"Never mind," Ahmes growled. "We're done here anyway. Just keep your mouth shut, Haerk, or I will make sure they look to you next."

Ebrium waited until they heard the sounds of the men's sandals fade before he released Satsobek. His body felt the loss of her warmth and softness, and he was aware of the dim desire to pull her back against him. Despite her small stature, she fit well against him. If it weren't for her wig, he'd easily be able to rest his chin on the top of her head, tucking her into his arms.

"Come on," she whispered, jerking her head in the direction of the tavern. "Maybe we can find out something else if they haven't left yet."

Once back inside, Satsobek could see that Haerk had returned to his companion at the table in the back of the room. She took two steps into the tavern before Ebrium gripped her elbow and led her back to the privacy screen, and the empty table, near the door.

"You're not going over there," he growled. "Those men are dangerous. You've done enough. Stay here," he pointed at a pile of cushions in the corner. "Sit down, keep hidden, and wait for me. And *do not*, under any circumstance, go anywhere." His face had turned hard, his words clipped. He was a military man, after all. He expected her to follow his orders.

Already turning away, Ebrium left her no time to respond. Her stomach did a flip and she stumbled over the cushions to hide and wait, her thoughts in turmoil.

Ebrium made his way to the back of the tavern where Batr and Makae were still waiting for him. After exchanging a meaningful look with the brothers, he proceeded to loudly and, in a belligerent, drunken voice, challenge them to a round of senet while at the same time berating them for being cowards. Thankfully, Batr and Makae also remembered what Iput had said about Haerk being a gambler, and played their parts well. They refused to play him, citing that, as friends, they felt bad for always winning his profits and it wouldn't be kind of them to take advantage of him when he was too deep into his bowl of beer.

So Ebrium turned to the next table, where Haerk sat with a large fellow with a face like an angry bull. Haerk, on the other hand, was a small man with narrow sloped shoulders. His head was shaved bald save for a thick chunk on the left side that was braided and looped around itself. Aside from the scar over his eyebrow, his features were unremarkable. The only noticeable thing about him was his eyes. They shifted constantly, never still in one spot, even as he looked up at

"Hey there, friend," Ebrium addressed the small man. Haerk had clearly overheard his conversation, and the calculating gleam in his eye was obvious.

"You look familiar. You're the queen's man, aren't you?" Haerk asked hesitantly. Ebrium could see the man was nervous about betting with a guardsman, but no doubt knew there was a good profit to be had from a high-ranking drunk.

"Mmm hmm. One of 'em." Ebrium swayed a little and gave Haerk a bleary grin, letting his accent thicken to slur his words. "But don't trouble yourself with that, friend. Nothing wrong with a little wager on a game between friends, is there? My buddies here," he jerked his head towards the privacy screen behind Haerk's back, indicating where Batr and Makae were seated, "won't play me anymore. I win too much, you know what I mean? But maybe you'd like to try a turn or two on the senet board?"

"By all means! I'm not very good myself, perhaps we could start off with a small wager?" Smiling to himself, Ebrium agreed. Haerk wasn't totally stupid; he wanted to see if he could beat Ebrium before he bet too much. What Haerk didn't know was that, although he'd been losing to Makae earlier, the both of them had spent countless hours at sea with little to do to entertain themselves except gamble, fight, and tell stories. Even with only half his attention, Ebrium was a better player than most, and he intended to give Haerk his full attention.

He maintained his drunken act, calling for another round of beer for the men and, after a few minutes, Batr and Makae joined them. Ebrium lost the first two games, sacrificing a small sack of grain. The men were having a rather raucous time when Ebrium's luck miraculously began to change. Within a very short period of time, he'd beaten Haerk to the point where the man had nothing left to lose, and had even borrowed from his friend in an attempt to recover his losses.

"How about one more game?" Haerk asked feverishly. "Just give me the chance to win something back. I – I have kids to feed, you know."

Batr snorted. "Perhaps you should've thought about that before you spent all your grain on senet."

"Tell you what," Ebrium laid his hands out on the table, palms up, in a gesture of good-will. "I could use something else instead."

Haerk must have noticed that Ebrium's voice had suddenly become clear and sober, and he shrank back a little, his eyes darting for an escape route. Unfortunately for him, he was seated with Ebrium on one side, his dull buddy on the other, and Batr and Makae on either end of the table. There was nowhere to go.

The small man licked his lips nervously. "What do you need?"

"A man named Ahmes hired you to watch his wife." It wasn't a question, but Haerk took it as such.

"What? No. I…I don't know what you're talking about."

"Of course you do. I want to know why."

Haerk shifted on his cushion, looking uncomfortable. His eyes flitted from Ebrium, seated cross-legged with his elbows on the table and his fingers laced together, a vision of menacing calmness, to the brothers who sat with arms crossed and eyes narrowed. Ebrium saw Haerk's friend tighten his grip on his bowl of beer, tensing as if to strike the nearest head – which would be Makae's – with it, but Batr made a *tsk tsk* noise and shook his head.

"Watch yourself, friend. You're outnumbered, and frankly you look a bit too slow to keep up with us." The man glared at Batr but slowly put his bowl back on the table.

"Come now, Haerk," Ebrium tilted his head. "I already know he plans to frame you for the murders, so there's no reason not to tell us what you were doing. I promise, you can have your grain back tonight, along with the sack you won from me early on, if you tell me what I need to know."

"But I didn't *do* anything!"

"Of course not. It's not like you *killed* Tiya and Yuny, right?"

"No! I would never!"

"Of course you wouldn't. That's why I'm asking you what you *were* doing. Now we can do this here, right now, while you're sipping a bowl of Iput's beer and watching the beautiful ladies pass by, or we can do this tomorrow, after I've tied you to a stake in the *hnrt* – the prison – had you flogged, and perhaps, if you persist, cut your nose and ears off. Now tell me, which way do you prefer?"

Haerk paled and for once his eyes stilled as he stared at Ebrium. Ebrium stretched his lips again in an unpleasant smile to let Haerk know he was serious.

Haerk's shoulders dropped and he hunched over his bowl of beer.

"Ahmes hired me. Wanted me to watch his wife at night when she went to the temple. They'd been fighting. For months." The words tumbled from the man. "He said he thought she was having an affair with Yuny."

"And was she?" Ebrium pressed Haerk.

The man wagged his head and scoffed. "No. There was no affair. Never was. I snuck inside the temple after Tiya a couple of times and it was clear they weren't doing anything. Just talking."

"About what?"

"I don't know. They'd meet in Yuny's office and I could never get close enough to hear them. But I could see that they never touched, never looked at each other, nothing like lovers do."

"So what did you see last night?"

Haerk sucked his lips in and looked away. His eyes jumped around the tavern.

"Haerk, what did you see?"

"I didn't see anything."

"Why not?"

"I never hung around to watch them very long and I… well I stopped watching Tiya a couple of weeks ago."

Ebrium sat back and blinked. "What do you mean?"

Haerk lifted his narrow, bony shoulders in a sigh, exhaling noisily. "I knew they weren't having an affair," Haerk looked down and fiddled with his shenti, "but I told Ahmes I couldn't tell for sure. I've been…ah… gambling a bit of late and I've been a little short of funds and I…ah… well Ahmes was paying me with gold."

So the man was lying to Ahmes and taking his money. Well Ebrium didn't care that Ahmes was being taken in by Haerk, but he did want to know everything Haerk had seen in the short time he'd been watching Tiya and Yuny.

He pumped him for information for a few more minutes. In the end, he learned that, on one occasion, Haerk had seen another man arrive, a short, stout man. Another time Yuny had gone to the house of a man named Imhotep late in the evening after meeting with Tiya. Haerk learned that Imhotep was a *ḥmww*, a carpenter / furniture-maker who lived on the temple property.

Ebrium made a mental note to drop in on Imhotep the *ḥmww* tomorrow. Finished with Haerk, Ebrium stood up, stretching long limbs and muscles that had stiffened from sitting so much throughout the evening. He happened to glance over to the corner near the front door – the same corner he'd left Satsobek in some time before. When he didn't see her he felt something like fear twist in his gut. If that damnable woman had taken it into her head to leave he'd be sure to tie her down next time he wanted her to stay somewhere. He quickly scanned the room, looking for her tall wig and dark, round face.

What he saw made him bolt across the tavern.

Satsobek sat in the corner, squinting against the darkness and following Ebrium's shadowy figure. Her mind whirled with all that had happened in such a short time. From time to time, her fingers brushed her lips absently. She'd been more relieved than she cared to admit when Ebrium appeared at her side moments after she stepped into the House of Iput. She'd been terrified on the way over. After retiring for bed, she'd had to bribe Sadeh, her maid, to help her style an old wig and prepare her makeup, then to find a servant boy to guide her through the village. When she'd walked in the door she'd been almost as frightened as the night Ebrium saved her from that tiger. The men and women here were of a sort that she'd never encountered. They had a rough look to them, one of hunger, of fierceness, of desperation. Their looks spoke of a life she didn't understand. *Yet.*

In that one petrifying moment Satsobek saw what her life might be like if she defied her father and left his house. She could well end up in a place like this, selling her body to the dregs of society for the sake of mere survival. The thought made her blood freeze and her skin crawl. When

Ebrium materialized out of the gloom she'd almost cried with relief. She would have done her best to uncover what Ahmes was doing if Ebrium hadn't been there, but *by the gods* it was good to see him.

And then he'd kissed her and they'd pretended to be lovers.

Her lips still tingled from his kiss, setting off an ache deep in her belly that was both thrilling and painful. Thrilling because, despite how hurt and angry she was by his rejection eight months ago, there was no denying her body, worse still her heart, responded to him in a way it had never done for anyone else. Yet the throbbing want she felt was tinged with sadness, knowing that Ebrium didn't want her. Had never wanted her. Even if he did, there was no possibility of them being together. Her father had made his feelings about Ebrium abundantly clear tonight during their discussion with Sekhemkare, as he had the night Ebrium saved her life.

Trying to set her conflicting thoughts aside, she focused on mulling over what they'd learned from Ahmes and Haerk's conversation. But that only occupied her mind for so long, looping around as it did trying to find a new suspect, as she was now fairly certain Ahmes hadn't killed Tiya and Yuny.

After what seemed like hours of hiding in the darkness, Satsobek was stiff, thirsty, restless, irritated that she'd been cut out of the investigation, and in desperate need of the ladies' facilities. Ebrium had told her to stay put, but by the gods he hadn't told her to wait until she was middle-aged and half-starved. She watched some of the women in the tavern until she determined where the ladies went to relieve themselves, and slipped out of the corner to do the same.

It was a small room with a locking door on the same side of the tavern she'd been sitting in. She was surprised to see it in such neat, clean order, with torches on the walls to light the space. The low, wooden seat with a hole in it was reasonably comfortable, a bowl of scented water for washing one's hands rested on a wooden stool, with a polished bronze disc that served as a mirror hanging above it, enabling her to check that her hair was still well-tucked under her wig. So far she was no worse for wear despite her escapades in and around the tavern.

When she re-entered the main room, she discerned that Ebrium was still sitting with Haerk, and decided that she was sick of waiting. Her recent success at play-acting emboldened her, and she resolved to go over there and resume her and Ebrium's "relationship". Or pretend to be one of Iput's girls, trying to pick up a customer.

She was just making her way towards their table when a hand closed around her wrist, pulling her up short.

"Hello, darling." A voice crooned from behind her, and she was tugged unceremoniously down, banging her rump on the hard floor beneath a thin cushion.

Satsobek thrashed amongst the cushions for purchase, at the same time twisting to see her attacker. Somewhere in his mid-thirties, the man was lanky and leanly muscular. He had loose, greasy hair and smelled unwashed. Like a man who had spent several days in the heat of the sun, sweating, without bathing. Another man sat cross-legged on the other side of the table, leering in amusement at her struggles.

"Excuse me…" Satsobek started to say as she made to stand up and move away, but the lanky man grabbed her wrist again in a hard grip.

"No need to leave, sweet thing. I've had my eye on you for a while now." He grinned, revealing more than a few gaps in his teeth. Those that were left were grey and moldy-looking. Deftly, he yanked her closer so that she was sitting in his lap.

"I am sorry, but you must have me mistaken," Satsobek again tried to pull away from him. She didn't want to cause a scene and attract more attention. She didn't want Ebrium to have due cause to berate her foolishness for coming here, and she didn't want to ruin their chances of getting information from Haerk.

"No, I don't think I'm confused at all. I saw you kissing that big bastard earlier, so don't play coy with me, girl. If you're willing to fool around with foreign filth like him then you can't have any problems with a good Kemeti man like me." The man ran his thick tongue over his lips. "You look new to this, sweet thing, but don't be shy. Why don't we take this into one of the rooms in back and I'll show you how things are done? My friend here is willing to go second, since I saw you first."

Mounting panic threatened to burst from her chest in a scream. She squirmed like mad, kicking out and breaking free long enough to stand, but he jumped up with her and seized both her biceps in a painful hold. He pulled her towards him and she leaned away, pushing against his chest with the palms of her hands.

She tilted her head back, looking around wildly for something to hit him with. Her eyes lighted on a mug of beer that must have rolled under the table. She was about to try and drop to the ground and grab it when suddenly she heard the man spluttering and his grip loosened.

"The lady isn't interested in what you have to show her, *friend*," Ebrium snarled, looking at her over the man's greasy head. The throat attached to that head was, at present, being throttled in the crook of Ebrium's arm. The man's eyes bulged as he scrabbled at Ebrium's thick forearm in a futile attempt to get free. The angry gleam in Ebrium's narrowed eyes was visible even in the murky room. His lips were tightened in a thin line, as if the slightest provocation was all that was needed for him to tighten his arm enough to end the man's life.

Satsobek heard the other man at the table stand swiftly, coming to his friend's aid.

"Let him go," the man's voice was a low threat.

"Nah," Ebrium's lips stretched in a grim smile, and Satsobek got the distinct impression he might enjoy hurting both men, and was more than capable of the task, too. "I don't think I will."

At the same time, however, two tall men with their hair in long, thin braids came up behind Ebrium, the same men that had been sitting with Ebrium throughout the evening. "Everything alright here, Ebrium?" One of them asked casually, looking from Satsobek to the man in Ebrium's grasp.

Ebrium relaxed his hold and the greasy man coughed, gasping for breath. Ebrium dropped his arm, rubbing the knuckles of one hand with the other. "I don't know." He looked at Satsobek, cocking his head and asking her, "Is it?"

"I…I am fine, thank you. He – uh – he took me by surprise." She glanced over her shoulder for the lanky man's friend, but he seemed to have slipped away.

The lanky man rubbed his throat, looking at her in disgust. "By surprise? What's the surprise? She's a whore, ain't she? It's her job…"

But he didn't get to finish his sentence. Ebrium's fist connected with his face, and the man's nose exploded in a spray of blood, some of which spattered onto Satsobek's bare arm. She flinched and took a step back as the man screeched and reached for his nose.

One of Ebrium's companions swore under his breath and his braids swung around his chin as he shook his head. He addressed the broken-nosed man. "No one to blame but yourself for that one, friend. You asked for it." He turned to Satsobek and gave a slight bow. "Batr, at your service. And this is my brother, Makae." He gestured to the other man who, she realized now, looked almost exactly like Batr.

"Nebet-i," Makae murmured as he inclined his head in a small, deferential bow.

Can this day get any more surreal? Satsobek had to blink a couple of times to make sure she was not having some bizarre nightmare. How on earth had she ended up in a seedy tavern in the village in the middle of the night, mistaken for a prostitute, with a strange man's blood on her arm? And now these soldiers were introducing themselves as if they had just met at the queen's court. Beside her, the broken-nosed man groaned and sat down on the cushions, clutching his bleeding nose.

"I… hello." She drew in an unsteady breath.

The corners of Batr's mouth lifted in a knowing smile as he cast a sly glance at Ebrium. Ebrium seemed about to speak, but was interrupted by a stately, middle-aged woman who appeared next to them.

"Ebrium, darling," the woman said in a smooth, low voice. "You know I don't allow outside girls to operate in my establishment."

Taking in the woman's elaborate, braided hair, and confident carriage, Satsobek realized this must be Iput. At the same moment she apprehended that the woman was speaking with Ebrium on very familiar terms.

Ebrium's jaw tightened. "She is *not* operating here."

"Come, let us discuss this a little more privately," Iput indicated the dark corner by the door, away from the prying eyes of the patrons who'd been focusing on them the last few minutes. With any luck, they might think the lovers' quarrel had simply culminated in a bout of jealous fighting. Iput craned her neck, making eye contact with one of the guards that patrolled the room. He moved forward to pick up the bleeding man and Makae helped him drag the man towards the door.

Once in the privacy of the corner, Satsobek felt compelled to explain herself. She drew herself up to her full height, trying to pretend she wasn't a good several inches shorter than everyone else around her. She'd played a lower-class woman already tonight, now she could play a woman of self-assurance, one not at all unsettled by the evening's extraordinary events. "My apologies, I didn't mean to intrude in your establishment. However, I came here to see Ebrium on a matter pertaining to the queen. I realize that is not what it looks like, but things took an unexpected turn or two. I beg you to believe I am not at all here for *business* of any other kind."

Ebrium blinked at her, and the corners of his lips twitched. Iput narrowed her eyes, scrutinizing Satsobek, and in response she lifted her chin and held the woman's gaze. Finally Iput nodded and her face softened. With her long lashes and high cheekbones, it was obvious the woman had once been a great beauty. Whatever her age or her lifestyle, she'd kept herself well.

"Well," Iput said with a faint smile, "I am a great supporter of our dear queen. And she has done well to recognize the value of keeping men such as Ebrium and Sekhrey Bey by her side, as well as these two fine brothers." Iput gestured to Batr and Makae, where they were hanging back a ways. Iput then rested a hand on Ebrium's forearm in a familiar gesture. Satsobek chewed the inside of her lip, biting down hard.

"Ebrium," Iput inclined her head towards the door the bleeding man had been carried out of, "is there a good reason for assaulting one of my customers? You know it will be bad for business if word gets around that one of the queen's men assails my patrons for pleasure."

"He mistook the lady here for one of your girls. Had she been one, he still would have deserved what happened." That Ebrium moved his arm out of Iput's grasp didn't escape Satsobek's notice.

Iput flicked a glance back at Satsobek, her lips curling upwards. "Well, I cannot blame him for trying, I suppose. She is small, attractive in her own way, and has that young, innocent look that some men quite like. She could do very well here. Is she interested in a new line of work? I would, naturally, expect seventy percent of her profits but would be happy to pay you a finder's fee."

Satsobek was too surprised by the bizarre, off-hand compliment to formulate a response, but Ebrium's face was already darkening. "No."

"Pity. I'm sure she'd be quite popular. Her body is fresh, she is well-spoken, and I suspect she's something of a wit. Did you know that men pay extra for a woman who speaks like a lady? They're a rarity, and it makes the men feel more powerful."

"Iput." There was a note of warning in Ebrium's voice.

"Hold on, darling." Iput put up a hand to him and leaned in closer to Satsobek, studying her. "Yes, an unconventional beauty." She gave a wink that, given their closeness, only Satsobek would be able to see, and asked, "Are you sure you are not interested in working for me, little one? I take good care of my girls. You'd be safer here than anywhere else in Thinis. I provide room and board and, as you have just seen, there is abundant security to watch over you." She gave a meaningful look in Ebrium's direction.

The din of the tavern made it difficult to know for sure, but Satsobek thought she heard Ebrium growl. That her interaction with Iput might irritate Ebrium intrigued her, so she said graciously, "Thank you, your offer is very kind. If I ever find myself in such circumstances that would warrant my seeking a profession of sorts I will be sure to consider you first."

Iput threw her head back and laughed. "Oh, you would do well here indeed, little one. I could use a diplomatic girl like you." Iput smiled, a conspiratory gleam in her eyes.

"Enough, Iput." Ebrium's face was tight, his arms crossed tight across his chest. "We need to leave."

Iput placed a hand on his forearm again, her face suddenly serious. "May I speak with you a moment before you go? Just one quick moment."

Ebrium flicked his gaze to Satsobek, clenching his jaw. Satsobek gave him a haughty look, desperately wanting to appear as if this were all perfectly normal. *Yes, of course this is normal. It so happens that almost every day I am offered the opportunity to prostitute myself in a tavern after being assaulted by a drunken commoner.* All joking aside, she didn't want to think about the real possibility that this might be her only option should she refuse her father's pressure to marry.

"Don't move. I'll only be a minute." Ebrium ordered in clipped tones. He and Iput took several steps to the side and, while she couldn't overhear them, the way they spoke to one another belied an intimacy that was almost painful for her to observe. Their eyes flitted her way and she wondered if they were discussing her. Neither seemed upset, though, and in fact at one point Ebrium's brow cleared in an expression of relief. Then he turned to the two brothers who were surveying the room and said something. He bid goodbye to Iput and gestured for Satsobek to follow him. Batr and Makae bowed to her in unison.

As Satsobek began to move, Iput stopped her with a hand on her forearm – the same familiar gesture she'd used with Ebrium. The older woman leaned in and Satsobek was overwhelmed by the smell of incense and scented oils. The look on her face was not unfriendly as she said in a low voice, "Do not let him put you off, he's not as rough as he seems."

Satsobek pulled back, stuttering. "He is not – I am not – it is not what you may think."

"Oh no, little one." Iput's voice was gentle. "I saw everything that happened tonight, from the moment you first walked in the door. Believe me, it is *precisely* as I think. He is a good man, one of the very best. He just does not always believe himself to be so. If he could be made to see it, he would be most worthy."

Satsobek blinked in confusion. Iput took her shoulders and turned her towards the door, waggling her fingers goodbye with one eyebrow cocked in amusement. Satsobek followed Ebrium out into the black, stifling hot night.

Chapter 8 – Disclosures

As Ebrium led Satsobek away from the House of Iput, his mood was even darker than it had been when he'd left the tavern that morning. It was hard to believe not even a full day had passed. He'd had little sleep, his head still ached, and he was unsatisfied with the course of the investigation. Although he was sure the priestess's husband was hiding something, Ebrium didn't think he was their murderer.

Furthermore, he'd experienced a variety of emotions he'd rather not deal with. *Ever.* The way that Satsobek responded to his hasty kiss in the tavern was entirely unexpected. If he'd had time to consider it, he would have anticipated resistance, perhaps even a slap across the face. Never would he have predicted that she'd respond so passionately; her lithe little body pressing against his, her hands sliding over his arms, her lips parting, so soft and yielding. And yes, her mouth had been even sweeter than he'd expected it to be. He'd had a hard time tearing himself away and putting her out of his mind while he dealt with Ahmes and Haerk. Of course, the murderous rage he'd felt towards the man who assaulted her didn't help matters.

And then there was Iput. Her last words still rung in his ears, repeating her old refrain. "Come now, Ebrium," she'd said. "Don't you think it time you took a wife you could bring to your mother and sister? I can't give you a family. Nor would I want to even if I were not almost past childbearing. I've been twice married, and that was more than enough. I'll not subjugate myself to any man's will again, even a man such as you. It is only that you have been lonely since your mother and sister moved out, and I have become familiar."

He'd tried to protest that last point, but she shook her head. "*You are a good man*, Ebrium. But you're not in love with me, nor I with you. I could never look at you the way a young girl looks when she is in love with a man. Not like that little one over there was looking at you." She inclined her head towards Satsobek. "Strange as it sounds, you deserve to experience that sort of love and I am no longer so full of idiotic naivety as to be able to provide it. You needn't feel any obligation to me and you'll get none from me."

Ebrium was privately relieved at such an easy disentanglement. He'd never stayed in one place long enough to find himself in the type of situation he had with Iput. The women he'd been with over the years knew he'd likely be gone in the morning, shipping out of whatever port city they happened to be in. Any fantasies of him those women had afterwards had been of their own devising. He'd never made them promises.

Iput's comment about Satsobek had surprised him, though. Of course he'd seen the desire in Satsobek's eyes after he'd kissed her, but she'd made her feelings about him clear repeatedly. But what Iput didn't know was that whatever physical attraction the nobleman's daughter might have for him was no doubt tempered by her notions of class superiority.

Something solid and scratchy hit his shoulder, startling him out of his musing. Turning, he saw a broken sandal laying on the dusty ground and Satsobek glaring at him, fists clenched at her sides. One foot was bare, balanced daintily on tip toe on the ground, weight shifted to her shod foot.

His eyebrows shot up. "What's your problem now?"

"You have not yet told me what happened with Haerk. And my sandal has broken," she gritted out through clenched teeth.

"So you threw it at me?" The corners of his lips crept up in an incredulous, mocking grin. "I am a soldier, nebet-i, not a *tbw*, a sandal-maker. Am I somehow to blame for your broken sandal?"

"No. But I scraped my foot and I asked you to wait a moment. My feet are unaccustomed to walking bare and I needed to fix my sandal. But *of course* you chose to ignore me once again."

Ebrium snorted. "I do not *choose* to ignore you, nebet-i, but put simply, my thoughts don't revolve solely around you. There are more important things on my mind than your sandals." He knew he'd taken the teasing a little too far the moment the words were out of his mouth, especially since his thoughts *were* revolving around her to some extent, but it was too late.

Satsobek gasped, recovering quickly enough to snipe back, "Truly? I had not imagined there was much of import on your mind at all."

Ebrium's temper flared and he spoke before measuring his words. "Why? Because I'm low-born? It might be true I don't have your learning, nebet-i. I don't read. But believe me when I say that even one such as I can have more serious problems than the privileged daughter of an affluent nobleman."

Satsobek's face slackened, and Ebrium felt a flash of regret. He *had* been too harsh. He knew better than to indulge in resentment, but lately his temper had been resting too close to the surface. He'd heard too many insults in the past few months about his birth and background, and too many unspoken words of frustration had built up between them. Her comment was the piece of straw that broke the donkey's back.

Satsobek choked out through a quavering voice, "Why do you *hate* me so? What did *I* do to you? I never called you any such names, yet you keep repeating them as if I had flung them at you."

This was too much for him, and his voice turned cold. "Come now, let's not avoid this any longer. Eight months ago you had your messenger warn me away, saying that one such as me should not dare to inquire after you. I don't know what little game you were playing at, but I presume that the reason *you* sent a messenger instead of your father is because he couldn't even bring himself to thank me. But let me guess, you thought it amusing to play around with a soldier, and a foreigner at that. Afterwards you realized it might ruin your chances at a good marriage to have any hint of indecency, and that your esteemed father would be angered. Am I correct, nebet-i?"

Ebrium felt an immense sense of satisfaction at having finally got things out into the open, even as guilt crept in for venting his anger on her.

Satsobek stared at him, wide-eyed, her mouth forming into a small "o" as her brow furrowed. She shook her head slowly. "I do not know of what you speak, but the messenger *you* sent told *me* that you had no need of my assistance, that it was unwanted. I never said what you accuse me of. As for not daring to upset my *esteemed* father and worrying about my *chances* at marriage," her voice hardened with anger, "you, *wa-ew*, are a jackal's *ass*," she hissed the last word out. "You know nothing of which you speak."

"Oh please, don't try to tell me you are not the beloved daughter. *You bear his name.* A man doesn't name his child after himself for no reason."

Her bitter laughter caught him by surprise. "Except that my father is not the one who named me." Her eyes were flinty and defiant as she said, "My mother died in childbirth and my father didn't care enough to name me at all. The servants knew not what to call me, so they referred to me as daughter of Sobek. *Sat-sobek.* You are right, in part, about my father. He didn't wish to thank you due to his dislike of foreigners. Especially foreign pirates who threaten his ships. But it is also partly because he does not care much whether I live or die.

"My father considers me as little more than a commodity. More often than not, I am merely a troublesome liability. Our position and lineage is, by far, better than our coffers, as my father has a penchant for good food, wine, and decoration, as does his favoured concubine."

Satsobek was running out of breath, he heard it in her gasped words, but she was relentless in her tirade. "And as for my supposed marriage chances, it would make my life much easier if I could do away with that particular expectation. Perhaps I should make *more* of an attempt to be seen here at Iput's with you after all. It might destroy my reputation beyond repair."

Ebrium cocked his head as he took a moment to absorb what she'd said. He couldn't fathom a man who cared so little for his own offspring, and a daughter no less. Nor did he understand her desire to render herself unmarriageable. He had to question if he had understood her correctly. She spoke so quickly that his mind raced to follow her in Kemeti, his language skills stretched to their limit.

But she didn't give him much time to formulate an answer before continuing. "So if the only reasons you have for disliking me so much are that you *think* I sent you a rude message and that I am, supposedly, rich and spoiled, let us dispel these notions now for the fallacies they are. I admit I disliked you initially because you sent me an ill-mannered message. Now I am willing to believe there was some mistake, and can dislike you on the grounds of your unpleasant personality instead."

Ebrium blinked as he translated her rant. Then he caught her meaning, threw his head back and burst out laughing. "Well done, nebet-i. How quickly you dismiss my suppositions. We should've had this conversation this morning. It might've saved us much hostility."

Ebrium levelled his blue gaze on her and she had the sensation that she was rocking. As if she were on a ship on the Iteru, or perhaps even on the great northern sea. She felt light-headed now that everything was in the open. *Well, not quite everything.* She had just told him she disliked him when she was well aware that was not true. He infuriated her, without a doubt, but it wasn't because she didn't like him. It was because she wanted *him* to like *her*, yet everything had gone so horridly wrong between them and she feared it was irreparable.

But their exchange was cut off by a sneering voice that came from the shadows behind her.

"Is this Sumerian mongrel bothering you, dear lady? If so, please do allow my men and I to escort you elsewhere."

Satsobek whirled around, even as Ebrium stepped in front of her. *Too late*, she realized, her heart speeding as the sound of footsteps closed in around them. Several men appeared out of the gloom. One of them was the man that had grabbed her back in the House of Iput. From the group a hawk-nosed man with sharp features stepped forward. He appraised her and she shivered at the cold light that flickered in his eyes. On instinct, she stepped closer to Ebrium and he put a hand across her midsection, tucking her further behind his back.

The man craned his neck and smirked at her. "I have it on good authority that this disreputable Sumerian has been making trouble across the village tonight, including assaulting innocent tavern patrons like my friend here," he gestured to the bloody-nosed man who had grabbed her back in Iput's, and she recognized his companion amongst the group, "in their attempts to make legitimate business transactions. We are just visiting your lovely little town and my friends were looking for a spot of fun. No doubt, my lady, you do not want this foreign scum interfering with your commerce. Come, let us take you somewhere more *comfortable* than this street so you may continue your good work."

Even as fear crawled across her skin Satsobek wondered at being mistaken for a prostitute *once again*. A hysterical laugh caught in her throat, and a strangled noise escaped her.

Ebrium rested his hand on the hilt of the wide, curved blade that hung from his hip. His voice was a menacing growl. "Eblaiti, not Sumerian. I'll thank you to remember it. And she is not a whore. I'm going to assume you were the assholes in the market today who blamed the hwt murders on the queen's rule, and I'm charging you with treason. You are, of course, also wanted for questioning in connection with the murder of the high priest and priestess."

Satsobek blinked, wondering what he was talking about, setting her questions aside for later. *If* they survived long enough for her to ask, that is…

The hawk-faced man scoffed. "You do not expect that we are so unwise as to meekly follow you to the hnrt? Not when there are many of us and only one of you."

And with that, Satsobek was plucked up by a strong pair of hands and pulled away. She cried out, but Ebrium was already fending off a man who had run at him with a dagger, and he could do little more than turn in her direction.

Her response was all panic and instinct. Hardly thinking, she knew one thing for certain, if these men got a hold of her they wouldn't hesitate to do the worst things imaginable. She flailed wildly, kicking, squirming, and lashing out in a frenzy of limbs and gnashing teeth. Neither strong nor skilled, as the man struggled to pin her arms to her sides she still managed to get her nails into his forearm and dig in, making him curse and loosen his grasp. She wriggled enough to turn in his clutches and drive her knee upwards between his legs. She felt his soft, tender parts crumple satisfyingly against her kneecap, and the man shrieked, dropping to the ground.

His cry caught the attention of the others, and Ebrium took the advantage to lash out with his knife, slashing the bloody-nosed man in front of him. The man dropped to the ground, a wide gash opening up across his abdomen. The look of shock on his face was so exaggerated, it recalled a play she'd once seen in which one of the many deaths of Osiris was enacted. It was too theatrical to possibly be real. Yet the blood pouring from his belly indicated otherwise.

A man came up behind Ebrium and wrapped a forearm around his neck, hampering his movement. But it was an awkward grip as Ebrium was the taller and more agile of the two. At the same time, another man with a knife advanced on him, slashing out while Ebrium twisted in the first man's grip to avoid the knife. Satsobek cast around for something to stop them. Finding nothing, she threw herself at the advancing man, catching hold of the forearm of his knife-hand with both her hands.

"Get back!" Ebrium thundered, even as his assailant shook Satsobek off his arm. The man then shot his arm out, cuffing her across the face with his elbow. Her head snapped back and she hit the ground with enough force to scrape her shoulder against the rough sand. Her wig flew off her head, the combs holding it in place painfully torn out. Ebrium managed to pry off the man around his neck, but now stood facing two circling opponents.

Forgotten for the moment, Satsobek curled her hands into the sand, scrabbling to get a handful of grit. She thought of how sometimes the wind blew silt up into the air, and the servants had to cover the windows with sheets of linen, lest the sand fly into their eyes and up their noses. As the men circled one another, thrusting and dodging, Satsobek crouched and crept towards them. One man neared her and she flew up to cast her handful of sand into his eyes.

"Argh!" The man started, stopping his attack to rub at his eyes. Ebrium swung out and punched the blinded man, knocking him to the ground, before turning to engage the one with the dagger. As Satsobek watched, the two men's shadows blended and separated as they lashed out at one another.

Then she heard the pounding of feet and whirled. Her heart thumped as she feared more men were approaching. An unusual clicking noise reached her ears and, even in the midst of the confusion, she strained to discern its origin. Two familiar figures appeared. Batr and Makae, the twins from the tavern. The clicking had been the beads braided into their hair. Satsobek gasped in relief. She called out for them to help Ebrium, that there were more men somewhere to beware of.

With the twins' arrival, Satsobek lost the thread of events. Dazed, she couldn't seem to tear her eyes from the bloody-nosed man with the slashed abdomen, as she saw him wheeze and bleed out his last breath. She kept replaying the slash of Ebrium's blade, and the almost comical expression on the now-dead man's face. Her legs weakened, and she apprehended that she might be on the verge of fainting for the first time in her life.

Chapter 9 – A Hut in the Village

When the sand finally settled around their feet, Ebrium was able to better assess what they were left with. Batr and Makae held two men in arms. One of them, the man that Satsobek had temporarily blinded, the other was the man Ebrium had been fighting when Batr and Makae arrived on the scene. The man who'd assaulted Satsobek back in the House of Iput lay in the sand, his belly split open. Another was dead nearby, killed when Batr and Makae arrived. The hawk-faced man who'd started all this was nowhere to be seen.

Despite rather persistent questioning, the two men in custody were not answering questions. *Yet*. Ebrium would see to them later, after they'd spent a night in the *hnrt*, the small prison complex on the outskirts of the village. The hnrt was where petty thieves, disgraced state officials, deserters from the militias, and others awaited trials or lived out their sentences in a state of penury and forced labour. If they still weren't willing to talk… well, he'd have to be more *persuasive*.

Satsobek stood nearby, her arms wrapped around herself. She was trembling, despite the heat that still clung in the night air. When he spoke her name she turned her wide gaze on him, but her glassy eyes indicated she was having difficulty focusing.

Makae stepped towards her. "Nebet-i?" He asked in a soft voice. She hunched in further and Ebrium swore he heard her teeth chatter. Makae shook his head. "Poor thing. It's been a rough night on her, eh? What with Iput's and now this."

"But she fought like a little desert *miu* – a wildcat. You should have seen her, she'd put most men to shame."

Admiration crept into Ebrium's voice as he knelt in front of Satsobek, scanning her exposed skin for cuts. His calloused hands skimmed the smooth surface of the back of her arms, rubbing gently to comfort her. Blood oozed from her scratched shoulder, and some had dried on the edge of her lip. If it had been his sister Akshaka in her place, as stalwart as she was, she'd be hysterical.

Without another thought, Ebrium scooped the woman into his arms, nestling her little body against his chest. He turned to the brothers and spoke in a brisk voice. "Right. I need you to take these bastards to the hnrt and give them two of our *finest* rooms." Ebrium took no pleasure as the captive men's eyes widened in fear. "Send someone to remove those bodies. I'll take care of the woman."

Batr lifted an eyebrow. "Taking her home like that? I doubt her father will thank you for it."

"No. To my hut near here first to get her cleaned up."

Batr lifted both eyebrows and an amused expression came over his face. Ebrium glared at him. "I *will* take her home right afterwards."

Batr held up his hands. "Of course you will!" Ebrium didn't miss the sarcasm in his voice.

"Off with you both," he growled. Satsobek reached out a shaky hand and murmured, "But my sandal…"

"Forget it." Ebrium clipped as he turned from the group of men and strode off into the night.

Satsobek's teeth chattered for a time. However, she came back to herself as Ebrium took them through the few short blocks to his hut. He'd uttered some soothing words, telling her to take deep breaths and calm herself. She tried to, but each breath brought in a wave of his warm spicy scent, mingling with the salty, masculine scent of fresh sweat worked up from fending off a group of men bent on rape and murder.

His scent reminded her of the time her father had taken her and her sister north, to the great sea. She'd loved the crisp smell of the sea and the feel of the soft warm sand under her bare feet. Not like the hard-packed sand of the city of Thinis, pressed by thousands of feet for hundreds of years. The sand of the beach was laved over daily, sifted, sorted, made clean and new. Satsobek had wanted to wade out into the great sea and let herself be carried away, washed off to some foreign shore, enveloped in that clean salty air.

Now each breath only made her want to cling more tightly to the firmly muscled torso she was pressed against. Ebrium's skin was all hard ridges beneath his torn linen tunic. Her one bare breast was mashed against his chest, and each long stride he took shifted her slightly against him. His voice rumbled from his chest straight into her ear, resting as it was against the hollow of his shoulder.

The assault on her senses was an exquisite, yet painful, pleasure. No matter what Iput might insinuate, men as powerful, attractive, and eligible as Ebrium were not interested in the flat-chested, fish-lipped, headstrong daughters of extravagant nobles who happened to hate foreigners and the queen they served. Excusing her lapse of reason by blaming circumstances, however, she allowed herself to forget all that and accept the comfort afforded by his nearness. She breathed in his salty essence and wrapped an arm around his neck, entwining her fingers into the black curls at the base of his skull, and closed her eyes. She let herself wonder what it would feel like to be able to do this every night for the rest of her life.

A few minutes, later Satsobek sat alone, perched on a long, wide bench up against a wall inside Ebrium's hut. She gripped the edge of the thin, reed-filled mattress beneath her, looking around the main greeting room. She'd never been inside a commoner's house in the village before and, despite her lingering shock from the night's events, she looked around in curiosity.

Shadows flickered around the close space from the braided wicks resting in bowls of flax oil which Ebrium lit when they first arrived. He'd left her to fetch some water and clean strips of linen to clean her cuts. The woven papyrus mats that covered the dirt floor sounded unusually loud, crackling beneath his feet as he moved about the hut. Or maybe it was just the silence of the village at such a late hour that amplified the noise.

The greeting room was only slightly larger than one of the bedrooms in the servants' quarters of her father's house. It contained a bench, two simple carved chairs, a stool, and a couple of small tables on which the oil wicks rested. There was a narrow window cut into the wall on the opposite side of the room.

The hut was surprisingly clean, free of clutter, the reed mats recently swept. Satsobek wondered at this as Ebrium's sister and mother now lived in the palace. She felt a pang in her chest as she envisioned Ebrium sweeping his floor before laying out a simple, solitary evening meal of mashed barley and lentils. *It would be very lonely.* Everyone she knew lived with large extended families and multitudes of servants and slaves. Solitary living was rare in Kemet, especially so amongst the nobility. For the first time in her life she was in a building with only one other person in it. The oddness of it added to the surreal quality of the evening.

Ebrium returned to hand her a small bowl full of wine. "Drink it. Slowly." He said gruffly, before returning again with large bowls of water. He also laid out a neatly folded, clean, white linen dress and a pair of his sister's sandals for her. His tunic had been ripped during the fray, and he pulled it off now, tossing it over a chair.

Satsobek almost dropped the bowl of wine in her hands. She couldn't take her eyes from the ridges of his abdomen as they rippled and shifted. The lambent light pitched shadows across his chest, playing across his skin and casting it in a golden hue. The ebony tattoo that circled his arm, shoulder, and pectoral almost blended into the darkness, the rest of him emerging from the gloom like a fantastic dream. A foreigner unlike any man she'd ever known. She wanted to be back in his arms, running her hands over that bare skin, pressing her lips to his like she had in the House of Iput, letting him take her mouth in another bruising, urgent kiss.

The glow from the oil wicks caught on something she hadn't noticed before – three shining, white streaks cut across the thick black lines of the tattoo on his right bicep. Scars, she realized, from the tiger that had swiped at him when he'd thrown himself over her that night at the banquet. She shivered. How strange it was that each time they were together they faced the threat of death, and each time he'd saved her.

Ebrium knelt beside her, the bowls of water arranged nearby. His nearness set her heart pounding in anticipation of his touch as he dipped a linen strip into the water and squeezed it out.

She stammered out, "I-I should do it. Let me clean my shoulder. I should not... I should not even be here."

His face turned up to hers and, even in the dim light of the oil wicks, she saw the amusement dancing in his eyes. "No?" He asked.

"No. I-I should not be... that is, if I were found out... alone here with you..." She felt foolish for saying it, and put the back of her hand against her burning cheek to cool it. She tried to pull some semblance of defence back around herself. His touch made her long for something she knew she'd never have. That longing for love and comfort led her astray once before. And she'd been hurt so badly it almost ruined her. She couldn't permit herself to be so irrational again. What she wanted did not exist in her world. Especially not with a man like Ebrium. A man who could have almost any woman he wanted.

Ebrium surprised her by giving a small hoot of laughter, shaking his head. "Nebet-i, you snuck out in the middle of the night to follow a foreign brigand to a tavern where men drink, whore, and gamble. How many times were you mistaken for a prostitute tonight? And *now* you're concerned with propriety?" He gave a soft chuckle. "You might be just a little bit too late, nebet-i."

"Just let me do it," she heard the plea in her own voice as she reached for the damp fabric, trying to tug it from his hand. He was too quick, though, and enfolded her fingers, trapping them in his. His grip was gentle but firm, brokering no argument. She raised her eyes to his, on a level with her own face as he knelt beside her. There was a light in his eyes which, on a man other than this hardened soldier who had teased her relentlessly, she might take for tenderness.

The corner of his lip quirked up, and he shook his head again. "I admire your determination. I really do. But you can let it go now. I imagine this day hasn't been easy for you. Two of your friends were murdered. You're covered in blood, most of which is not your own. You've been assaulted more than once, and you watched me kill a man or two. While I'm accustomed to these things now, I *do* remember what it was like the first time I saw a man die. Let it go and let me take care of this for you."

Although they were said with kindness, his words slammed like a hammer through the mud-brick wall of her defences. *Let it go and let me take care of this for you.* She released her grasp on the linen strip. Both of her hands flew to her mouth as she drew in a shaky breath that turned into a ragged sob. Sickness rose in her belly again at the thought of Tiya and Yuny lying dead in the temple. And then what those men had threatened to do to her tonight. If Ebrium hadn't been there, she might have ended up just like Tiya.

Her body shook uncontrollably, chilled straight through. It was more than just the images of the evening assaulting her senses that caused the silent sobs to rack her body. Although those were upsetting enough. Nobody had ever offered to take care of anything for her. Not her father, her sister, or even the aunt who had raised her and passed away when Satsobek was ten years old.

"There you go." Ebrium moved up on to the bench beside her and, with an arm around her shoulders, pulled her to his chest, tucking her face against his warmth. His lips brushed the top of her head in the most tender gesture she'd ever known, and the shock of it made her weep even harder. "Have a good cry. It's better to get it out as soon as possible. And then if you really need to, you may hit me with a pillow, or call me the worst names you can think of. Like the son of a jackal-headed prostitute, or…what was the other one? Ah, a donkey-breathed hippopotamus's ass."

Satsobek gasped and with a hand on the smooth ridges of chest, pushed herself back to look up at him. But his eyes were twinkling and, absurdly, that beautiful dimple dented his right cheek. Despite the pain in her chest and the tears that still fell, she began to laugh.

"How did you… How do you…?" She tried to ask through gulps of air. How did he know that she needed to both cry and laugh? How did he know that she was on the verge of becoming hysterical?

He grinned and his straight white teeth glowed in the light of the oil wicks. "Like I said, I know what you're feeling." She doubted that, since her feelings made her want to cry, scream, laugh, and, most of all, bury herself in his arms. Ebrium continued though. "I also have a little sister. And when she's angry with me for not allowing her to do something, or for making fun of her, it's best to let her get a bit angry, hit me a few times with something soft, and then make her laugh." He winked, and the dimple dipped in his cheek. "It seems to be cleansing."

Satsobek blinked at him, surprised to find such insight and thoughtfulness in the man who had tormented her all day. Although by now she shouldn't be taken aback by anything he said. And she realized there had been little signs of his kindness all day long, ones she'd been unwilling to admit, like rubbing her back after she'd been sick. Like carrying her out of the silo, and concerning himself with her reputation at the House of Iput. She also realized that, for a split second, she was jealous of Ebrium's sister. Jealous that this girl had someone in her life who actually thought about making her feel better. Jealous that that someone was Ebrium.

He saw her confusion and his brow furrowed. "I used the right word in your language, didn't I? Cleansing, like when you sweep the dirt from your house and arrange the furniture in a pleasing way, or like purifying yourself to enter the temple. It's the same thing with your feelings when you cry or laugh very hard."

"I – no, you are right. I just…"

"Ahhh, I see. You didn't think I'd understand something like that? Or that I would care how my sister felt?" He made a tsk'ing noise. "I thought we'd moved past that by now, nebet-i." His tone was joking, but he withdrew from her and moved off the bench to kneel by her side again. He dipped the linen strip back into the water, squeezing it dry; his face was stony, his blue eyes hard.

"No, I – that is not it." She missed the heat of his body, his nearness, and grasped for an explanation, not wanting him to know that he was, in fact, partly correct. Iput's words echoed in her head, *He is a good man. He just does not always believe himself to be so.* It must be horribly frustrating to have people always insulting him for being foreign and low-born, two things not of his own doing.

She said, "I was thinking that if a typical day with you is anything like today, your sister must be upset quite a lot."

The cold light in his eyes softened. "Well, that is certainly true. She isn't afraid to tell me when she is, either. She's not unlike you in that regard."

Satsobek relaxed a little at the sight of his dimple. "Your sister is lucky to have you, then." He glanced up at her with a carefully neutral expression on his face, as if gauging the honesty of her compliment, but he quickly looked down again. She pushed on. "You also mentioned entering the temple, and I recalled that you looked angry when I asked earlier if you had been inside one before." She'd scrambled to divert him, but realized too late that mentioning such a thing would not ease his mood.

Ebrium searched Satsobek's face. She was so easy to read, her emotions always showed on her face. It was obvious she was trying to cover whatever she'd been thinking, but he decided not to press her. She'd dealt with enough for one day. And his own words rung in his head. Perhaps it was time he let go of certain things, too. He'd buried memories of his early years when he left Ebla almost eleven years ago. Since there was nothing to be done with them, he'd put those scenes from his early years aside and moved on. But lately, with the constant reminders of his origins, those memories and the feelings associated with them had been coming back.

Ebrium focused on gently wiping away the spattered blood on Satsobek's arm. He tried very, very hard to ignore the small brown, delectable nipples that rested so pertly atop her soft, rounded breasts, the one so visible outside of her one-shouldered wrap. One of his hands encircled her wrist, drawing her arm out straight so he could wipe it down. His groin tightened as he envisioned holding that wrist over her head and pressing her against the wall, covering her body with his and taking her mouth in his, thrusting up into her and letting her moans fill his head, forcing out old memories.

He'd been wrong about Satsobek being like a water nymph. He'd told Batr and Makae she fought like a wild desert cat, and she had. Although small, desert cats were known to eat poisonous snakes, and rodents almost as large as themselves. Satsobek had attacked a sizeable man with a knife to help protect him, and taken another one down. She was loyal and responsive to any small act of kindness, and *by the gods* if she didn't kiss with a passion that sent flames of lust straight to his groin.

He imagined if she were under him she would not be silent or indifferent. The tension that had been coursing between them throughout the day was like that of two cats in heat - circling, tangling, and stepping back to arch their backs and circle again.

But he'd also seen her vulnerable, wide-eyed, and scared. While on the one hand, he wanted to bury himself inside her, he also wanted to fold her in his arms and stroke away her fears. And he wanted to hurt the men who had hurt her. He wasn't surprised to discover that this included her father, a man who didn't even have the decency to name his own child.

He forced himself to look at the wall behind her and cleared his throat. "As you've no doubt heard, Sekhrey Bey's father was king of Ebla for many years. I assume you've heard my family worked in the king's palace?"

Satsobek nodded, the cock of her head indicating she was listening intently. He looked away and began to dab at the cut on her shoulder, trying to clean as much sand and dirt from it as possible. "My father oversaw some of the gardens in the king's properties. My mother was a serving lady. I grew up in the palace, that's how Bey and I became friends. There weren't any other children for him to play with on the grounds except his older brother, and he wasn't exactly a kind playmate.

"When I was seven I began working with my father in the gardens. That year there was a drought. No rain for months. The crops were failing. My father was anxious for his job. My parents fought all the time." Ebrium squeezed water from the linen strip. He didn't look up at Satsobek. If there was disgust, pity, or horror on her face, he didn't want to see it.

"I wanted to help my family. So I snuck into the hwt of Hadad. Hadad is our god of storms and rain. In Ebla the people believe without Hadad there will be drought, starvation, and chaos. Like here in Kemet, the common people of Ebla aren't allowed to enter the hwt, only the nobles, priests, and servants of the gods. I decided it wouldn't be enough just to leave an offering for Hadad outside the hwt walls. Everyone does this, and the gods don't answer their prayers. I was young, and stupid. I thought Hadad might listen to me if I went inside and prayed to him directly." He shook his head, contemptuous of his naivety.

"I wanted Hadad to bring the rains to help protect my father's job. But I got lost in the hwt and was caught by one of the priests before I even made it to the icon. The priest beat me, then dragged me through the street back to the palace where he told my father. To appease the priest, my father beat me some more. They told me I had to learn my place."

Ebrium shrugged. "That night, instead of praying for Hadad to come and bring rain, I prayed for Mot, the god of death, to take both Hadad and the priest." Ebrium prepared a dry strip of linen to wrap around Satsobek's scraped shoulder. A bitter smile twisted his lips. "So to answer your earlier question, yes, I *have* been inside a hwt before. It didn't go well."

He still didn't meet her eyes as he leaned in close to her to tie the linen strip over her shoulder. His fingers brushed her skin and, despite the metallic scent of blood and hot sand that clung to the air around them, she still smelled of cinnamon and honey.

Ebrium spoke in a soft voice, almost to himself. "But the gods don't listen to one such as me. Perhaps there wasn't anything I could have done as a child to help the people I care about. But as a grown man, there is. Tonight, a man connected to the temple murders slipped through my fingers. If I catch him again, I intend to kill him."

Satsobek wondered if his story was the reason for the long white scars she'd noticed on his back – scars that indicated he'd been whipped. Most slaves and servants were whipped at some point, but rarely hard enough to break the skin, or leave marks like those on Ebrium's back.

Her heart ached for this big man who was so much more complicated than she'd ever envisioned. In all her fantasies of him she'd pictured him as strong, charming, heroic, confident, and *perfect*. He had been godlike in her imagination. Too perfect and lofty to bother with someone like her. His rejection of her messenger had been almost excusable given how untouchable he seemed. Blaming him was almost as absurd as blaming Ra for not responding to her prayers. The gods – and Ebrium – had more important things to worry about than Satsobek.

This morning, however, he'd smashed through that vision when he'd been so rude to her. Over the course of the day her impression of him had been slowly rebuilt into a much more *human* man. He was, in fact, many of the things she'd first imagined. He *was* charming, strong, and heroic. But he was also flawed; temperamental, bitter, and self-doubting. In that way he was not so unlike herself. And he had just shared a memory that clearly still held all the pain of a fresh wound. That kind of disclosure deserved a response.

Satsobek reached out and stroked the thick lines of the scars on his right bicep. Ebrium froze, but she continued fingering the raised bumps along his tattoo, a forest of creatures both mythical and real. A griffin chased a ram, while an eagle soared over a twisted lion with a tongue as long as its own body, and curling black lines entwined around and through them all.

She spoke in a low voice, focusing on the tattoos and scars lest she lose her nerve. "I am truly sorry about what happened with the messenger. It is true that my father did not want to thank you. He does not like foreigners and he is a merchant. His ships have been raided, and he blames you and Sekhrey Bey. But you *did* deserve to be thanked, and I wanted you to know that *I* at least appreciated you saving my life."

She took a deep breath and forced herself to look up into his eyes. His expression was wary. He'd just finished tying the linen on her shoulder and one big hand still cupped the back of her upper arm. His heady scent enveloped her like a soft caress, his face mere inches from hers. His sun-bronzed, muscular chest rose and fell with each breath.

He didn't move, and she looked back down at her hand, resting her fingers on his thick forearm. "I do not know who intercepted the messenger. If my father did it he would have said something to me, I am sure of it. Perhaps it was my sister or my father's concubine. Or perhaps the messenger was in error. But…"

Doubt flitted through her, making her hesitate. She was putting her feelings dangerously out in the open. But after what he'd told her he had a right to know.

She said, "I do not think it was a mistake to thank you. And I have thought of you, of it, every day since. My life is not of much value, I have done little to merit it, but it meant something to me that you thought it worth saving. If you had not been there, maybe the gods would not have seen fit to help me. Even if you were only doing your job and do not care at all for me…" she trailed off because she'd run out of words to express herself, and because she couldn't tell him what else she was feeling.

His fingers tightened around her arm, and she raised her eyes to his, afraid he'd still be wearing that stony, wary look. Instead, warmth gleamed in the cerulean depths of his eyes. Keeping one hand on her arm, he dipped a strip of linen in a bowl of water, squeezed it, and dabbed at a spot of crusted blood at the corner of her mouth. It had split when the man with the knife had hit her and knocked her to the ground. She flinched when the cloth touched her swollen lip. He murmured an apology.

When he had daubed her lip a few more times he put aside the linen strip and pulled her to her feet. Satsobek stared at him, bewildered. With his hands wrapped over her biceps, he maneuvered her around the bench and table. She let him walk her backwards until suddenly her shoulders bumped against the brick wall. Her breath came in shallow bursts, her heart pounding so hard she could feel the blood thrumming through her. Although the night was still hot and sticky, goose bumps ran across the surface of her skin, tightening her nipples.

Ebrium's blue eyes captured hers and kept her on her feet. He ran his hands up from her arms to cup her chin; the calloused pads of his fingers and palms were gently abrasive on her neck and jawline, an erotic sensation. His thumbs grazed her cheeks as he tilted her face up, exposing her neck. She was light-headed, faint, terrified, aching, tingling all over, and utterly mesmerized.

He dropped one hand down to her hip and leaned towards her, nudging his cheek against hers. His breath tickled her neck. She was quite sure that her heart was on the verge of stopping, or maybe bursting, and she was barely breathing. His scent overwhelmed her and she could almost taste him on her tongue.

The length of his body pressed along her, hard, thick, and hot. The light stubble on his cheek rasped against her jaw as he brought his lips to hover over the shell of her ear. His voice was husky as he whispered, "It was not a mistake."

Satsobek shuddered beneath him. She was on the verge of losing control of her limbs, like she was being swept away in the rushing waters of the cataracts of the Iteru. If she didn't get out of the water now, she was in danger of being battered against the rocks and torn apart like a fragile, thatched reed boat. But in that moment, she didn't care.

He murmured against her neck, his lips so, so close to her skin she was desperate to feel their touch. "I was watching you that night at the banquet."

Shocked, she pulled to the side in order to see him better. "You are mocking me." Hurt and anger rose in her, and something stupidly like hope.

His eyes were fierce and direct. "I assure you, nebet-i, I'm not. You sat between two other women that night. Your hair was down and simple, as it is now, except you had red beads braided into parts of it." He rubbed a strand of her hair between his fingers before hooking it behind her ear, catching her chin in his palm as he did so.

Satsobek held still, struck dumb. She'd been sitting with Betrest and another friend of theirs that night. She'd actually been sitting next to the utterly beautiful Betrest and yet for some reason, he'd noticed *her* and remembered how she wore her hair. It took her breath away to think he'd singled her out.

She knew not who moved first, but suddenly his lips were against hers, crushing in their intensity. And she was pressing back, need surging up in her breast. She kissed him with the pent-up energy of a full day's worth of tension, eight months of longing, and a lifetime's worth of need. Her hands were everywhere, running over his hard flank, his back, shoulders, chest, any piece of flesh she could touch she wanted to feel under her fingertips. She wanted to know every scar, every muscled ridge, every rib and vertebrae. She wanted to dig her nails into him and never let go.

When his hands moved to cup her breasts, almost completely encasing them in his large, rough palms, she moaned into his lips. And a second later she gasped as his thumbs brushed over her nipples. She had to tear her mouth from his to draw breath, panting while he skillfully manipulated the peaks of her breasts between his fingers. He nipped at her neck, licking and kissing along her collarbone, causing her whole body to quiver in pleasurable anguish.

Sweat beaded on her brow, and it wasn't just from the stifling heat of the windless night.

She threaded her hands up into his thick, wavy black hair. The base of his neck was moist, and she moved to press her lips to it, savouring the salty taste of his skin. He groaned against her neck and swore softly. He pulled back to look down at her, and she took the opportunity to spread her hands over the massive expanse of his chest and kiss along his clavicle then down the centre of his chest, between his pectorals.

"By the gods, woman," he growled. Then he planted his hands on her shoulders and pushed her back against the wall. He moved away and Satsobek suffered a twinge of loss and bewilderment. But he was only blowing out the oil wicks, throwing the hut into blinding darkness. It took her eyes a moment to adjust, and she glanced towards the window, realizing that their every move would have been visible through the small opening in the wall.

Now, with a few stars reflecting off the sand-coloured huts nearby, she could just make out Ebrium's bulk stalking back towards her. And then he was covering her again with his body, taking her mouth in a kiss that obliterated any feelings of trepidation, stoking the inferno that spread through her core and made her pant for more. He reached for the hem of her dress, hiking it up her thighs, skimming her legs with his hands, pushing the fabric up and exposing the length of one leg. Then she felt his rigid arousal pressing against her leg and quelled a little. She wasn't yet familiar enough with a man's organ to not be a little frightened. Of course she had seen them before. Servants and men in the fields often worked naked. But not with erections. And surely not ones that were as sizeable, powerful, and unabashed as the one now crushed up to her thigh, so obvious through the thin fabric of his shenti.

As far as her time with Inkaef was concerned, their rare, late night meetings consisted of much awkward and over-eager fumbling, concluding in a rather rapid and dissatisfying fashion for her. Suddenly, she was afraid and self-conscious that Ebrium would find her inadequate, inexperienced. And yet too headstrong and demanding. She couldn't go through what had happened with Inkaef all over again. How could she ever be intimate with Ebrium and not hope for more?

Ebrium must have sensed her hesitation, as he pulled back to look down at her, his eyes narrowing in a question. She tried to speak, but didn't even know what to say. "I... that is... I have not..." she licked her lips and tried again. "I am not..."

But before she found the words Ebrium blew out a deep breath and dropped his forehead against the wall near her. He swore and Satsobek stiffened, worried she'd upset him somehow. His hands rested on the wall on either side of her shoulders, caging her in although his face angled away from hers. His shoulders heaved as he laboured for breath.

"I'm sorry, Ebrium." Acutely feeling the loss of contact with his body, she placed a tentative hand on the rippling muscles of his arm.

He flinched and she pulled back. But he surprised her by turning and catching her wrist, trapped her curled hand against his chest. "No, it's not your fault. I should've known better. I'm an ass."

Never had she expected to hear such an admission from him, unused as she was to others' apologies. It struck her that he must really blame himself. As if he'd done something wrong by desiring her. Splaying her imprisoned hand over the solid strength of his expansive chest, she murmured, "No. I wanted you to. I *want* you to. I just need more time for *that*."

Ebrium searched Satsobek's face for the truth of her words and found it there. Relief made him grin wickedly and say, "How about something else instead?" Still holding her hand against his chest – he liked the way it burned against his skin – he tipped his head to her upturned face and brushed her lips in an achingly tender caress. Then a feather-soft kiss on the corner of her mouth, over her cheek, the tip of her nose, making her smile sweetly with her eyes closed, working his way to one delicate ear, which he tucked her hair behind so he could flick his tongue along the side of her neck.

Her whimpers were intoxicating. Ebrium luxuriated in her little noises of need as he swiped a thumb across the tip of her exposed breast, appreciating the moment when her back arced towards him, pressing her breast into his palm. It filled him with a craving to feel her wet warmth around his fingers, and to make her climax. He needed to know that he could do that to her, for her, and to hear her cry out his name when it happened.

He slid a hand down her hip, over the curves of her body. This time, before he bunched his fist into her dress, he whispered, "Don't worry, not *that*." Smiling reassuringly as her eyes widened in trepidation.

Her hips lifted away from the wall, towards him, allowing him to push the folds of her dress higher up her thighs, up to her waist. Keeping his lips pressed to hers, he hooked her knee over his forearm and splayed his hand on the wall for support, holding her upright on one leg, stretching her open for him. With his free hand, he reached down and played his fingers along the soft skin of her inner thighs, through the silky thatch of her hidden curls.

Satsobek gasped into his mouth. "Oh, gods, Ebrium, I..." but whatever she might have said was cut off when he slid one finger along the plush folds of her sex. She yelped in shock then swore. Ebrium chuckled, loving the erotic sound of such words on her sweet, ripe lips, and loving that it was him that put them there.

"Ebrium. By Ra and all the gods. You will... drive me... mad," she gritted out between breaths.

He smiled as he trailed his lips along her neck. "Then I will have accomplished the desire dearest to my heart, nebet-i, because you've been driving me mad. All. Day. Long." He accented the words with little nips to her neck and collarbone.

"Is this punishment then?" But she was rocking against his hand, making it clear that, if she thought it to be so, it was sweet punishment indeed.

"Are you complaining?" He smiled against her neck.

"No, I – ah dammit!" She swore again and fell back to whimpering as he circled the slick nub of her sex with his thumb. The musky scent of her desire filled his nostrils and Ebrium's own want almost overwhelmed him. She was slick and swollen and he wanted so badly to bury himself in her. But he held back. He might not be a nobleman's son, but he knew better than most men how to pleasure a woman. It was a petty, selfish conceit, but he wanted her to know at least that much about him.

He parted her soft folds with one finger and sought her moist opening. Her eyes snapped open and her mouth formed into an engaging "o" as he pressed into her. She was hot, lush, and so very, very tight. His cock pulsed in response, hopeful in anticipation of nestling itself against her. He ignored it and bore up into her soft, liquid heat, but he couldn't prevent a guttural growl from escaping his throat as she clenched around him.

She clutched his shoulders, her weight unsteady. Her thighs quivered around his hand. He gently thrust his finger back and forth into her, continuing to circle her sensitive peak with his thumb. Her breath came in sobs and her nails dug into his flesh. If he had to pay with his blood to make her finish in his hand, he'd happily bleed out right now.

"Ebrium, I… oh by Ra…I cannot…" She was attempting to practice restraint, trying to master her emotions and reactions. He'd seen her do it all day long. But now he wanted her to give control to him, and to forget the terrible events of the day.

"It's okay, little *miu*," *little cat*, he called her. "It's alright. Do what you need to do."

But she held on, tensing, tightening, trying to hold back. So he worked another finger in between her slick lips and plunged into her. She cried out, and he released the leg that was wrapped around his arm so that he could tangle his fingers into her thick hair and cup her head. She clung to him and buried her face in his shoulder. He urged her on as she shuddered, knowing she would peak soon. When she finally climaxed she gasped his name, pitching her hips against him, her muscles clenching around his fingers. It was one of the most satisfying moments of his life and he hadn't even gotten deep inside her yet.

Never in her life had Satsobek lost control like that, and she remained in a state of thoughtless awe for more than a few moments. Her body was weightless, propped up in the protective circle of Ebrium's tattooed arm. Like a jar of date syrup left in the sun too long, tipped over, spilling out in a soft, syrupy mass of sticky matter, as though she could somehow blend into the broad expanse of Ebrium's chest.

His fingers had slowed their movement, finally sliding out to simply cup her in the palm of his hand. Her breath was erratic, alternating between deep gulps of air and shallow pants. She tried to focus on regulating her air flow, but with each breath she drew in Ebrium's warm scent, and that only served to stoke the inferno re-building in her core. The hand that wasn't holding her upright was now making slow, soothing circles over her back.

Satsobek realized with some embarrassment that she still clutched Ebrium's hard biceps, and that she'd perhaps acted with a bit too much abandon. Still shaky with amazement and release, she said, "I'm sorry," though her voice was muffled by his neck.

He chuckled, and the sound reverberated through his chest and into her ear. "For what this time? Don't worry, I won't arrest you for having a good time. It's not a crime." When she didn't answer right away, he said, "You *did* have a good time, didn't you?" She marveled at the hesitation in his voice.

She pulled back to look at his face. Ebrium, of all people, was actually biting his lower lip, a small furrow of worry between his brows. Smiling, Satsobek stroked her fingertips along his jaw, enjoying the sensation of his stubble rasping against her skin. "Yes, I had a *very* good time."

"And no need to do *that* tonight." He waggled one suggestive eyebrow, coaxing a laugh from her, the first one she'd shared with him all day. "Now perhaps we should finish getting you cleaned up and I'll take you home. The sun will be up soon."

Chapter 10 – The Villa

Ebrium scrubbed his hands over his face then ran them up through his thick black hair. He was not interested in whether the colours of the bench cushions would match those of the curtains. He didn't care which side of the room the chairs were placed, nor which rooms were to be allotted for which servants, and he certainly didn't need more than one cook. In fact, this was the first time he'd ever even had a cook. Or any servant, for that matter. *And what am I to do with them anyway?* He was a man of simple needs and this was all too ridiculous and complicated. No wonder it had taken him so long to move.

He'd forgotten that he had promised his mother and sister he would be here, in the new manor, this morning. Luckily he'd chosen to spend the night there, and was there to greet them. He'd been too tired to walk all the way back to his hut in the village after taking Satsobek home last night and regardless, he'd arranged to meet her here this morning to continue their investigation.

He sprawled out on one of the wide benches that rested, for now, in an alluring beam of golden sunlight streaming through a window in the spacious greeting room. The room was to the right of the main entranceway and sunlight bounced off the white-washed mud-brick walls, setting a warm glow bouncing around the room. Nearby, his sister and mother prattled on in Eblaite, the language of their northern homeland. From time to time his little sister, Akshaka, would stop to direct a furniture-laden servant in the language of Kemet. Some men brought furniture in, while others took it out.

Ebrium was exhausted and just wanted to take a nap while he waited for Satsobek to arrive. He'd slept little after taking her home. Despite having left his house in favour with one another for once, an awkward silence had hung between them on their way back to her father's house. There seemed nothing to say, or at least no way to say it. He still felt like a bastard. Although he'd believed her to be the insulated daughter of a nobleman he hadn't stopped to think just how far-reaching her lack of experience might be. It never occurred to him that Satsobek might be *untouched*. He'd forgotten she'd been a chaste priestess of the temple not so long ago. And there he was, treating her like a common woman, or worse, like a woman from the House of Iput.

Not that he regretted what they'd done. It was easy to conjure up the feel of Satsobek in his arms, her weight against his chest, the smell of cinnamon and honey, her breasts in his palms. Any one of these was enough to inspire an agonizing – yet pleasurable – tautness in his groin, a craving for more of her. He could never regret her gasping out his name as she came against his hand. There'd been a special intimacy between them of a sort he'd never shared with any other woman.

But thank the gods she'd put a stop to things before he'd gotten carried away and taken it too far too fast for her. He wondered if he was really so depraved that he simply assumed *everyone* to be as base as he was? Perhaps the insults flung at him lately had some truth in them. Perhaps he'd been spending too much time consorting with the lowest dregs of society. For many years he'd passed his days with brigands and vagrants, and sleeping in filthy port cities. Now he occupied his days investigating and arresting some of the foulest and most corrupt of the nobility. He'd known for a while that unless he wanted to spend the rest of his life jumping in and out of the beds of women like Iput, he needed to change some things in his life. He just hadn't realized, until Satsobek, how drastic those changes needed to be.

He'd felt juvenile watching her sneak around the side of her father's house, slipping into the kitchen door. Sneaking around like that was not something a grown man did. A man tasked with the safety of the queen and the peace of Kemet, no less. But the thought of a nobleman's daughter sleeping in a tiny hut in the village with a man who antagonized half the nobles he encountered was laughable. It's not like he could have asked her to stay. She wouldn't appreciate the resulting scandal, and his own mother would not be pleased.

For years he'd lived from moment to moment, just trying to survive. But not anymore. It was no longer his entire life that was unstable; *he* was the unstable factor now. Yes, the temple murders could throw Kemet into chaos, but once he solved that problem – and he *would* solve it, one way or another – he could get on with putting his life in order. No more nights at Iput's – or any other damned tavern for that matter. Perhaps it was even time he tried being nice to other members of the nobility. Sooner or later his little sister would need to make a match. And what of him? If he changed his circumstances, would he be more likely to consider marriage?

More images of last night rose to mind. The artless way Satsobek laid her hand on his arm and thanked him for saving her. Her sweet kisses, the way she brushed his jaw with the back of her hand, her fingernails digging into his shoulders – thank Dagon the marks had faded – her inner muscles contracting around his fingers. *By the gods*, he thought, *I'm going straight to the underworld for thinking of this with my mother and sister in the room*. He shook his head, dragging his hands through his hair and tucking them behind his head. He closed his eyes and pulled in a deep breath.

Unfortunately, that's precisely when his sister caught sight of him laid out on the bench.

"Ebrium!" His eyes snapped open to find Akshaka glaring at him. Her dark blue eyes, so like his, flashed as she thrust her fists on her hips and hunched her shoulders at him. *Uh oh. Here we go.* He steeled himself, not wanting to arouse her suspicion. His little sister was far too perceptive, and there was no way he could even begin to tell her what was going on with him.

He threw a hand up to arrest her, while he laid the other one out over his eyes in a gesture of exhaustion. "Mercy, sister! All of these decisions have thoroughly worn me out. Take pity on your poor brother. You know how little I know about domestic matters." He peeked out at her between two fingers but tried to maintain a pitiable expression.

Akshaka stepped towards him, her long-lashed eyelids narrowed, lips tightening. She wagged a finger at him. "You mean how little you *care* about domestic matters. But you *should* care. The queen has given you this estate and since you are impossible to live with you will be here all alone. If you do not pay attention, how in the name of Dagon will you manage a household of servants by yourself?"

"Oh ho ho! Now *I* am the impossible one? You're lucky the queen is pregnant and has no time to notice how obstinate and thorny a companion you really are. If she sends you back I think this time it'll be *you* sleeping in the common room, rather than me."

Akshaka advanced towards him, sweeping up a pillow from the bench and whacking Ebrium on the arm. "You big oaf! You're supposed to be pleased with the queen's gift! It's been six months now. Are you not tired of making your own breakfast, washing your own shenti, and sweeping the floor yourself? Or wait," a suspicious look came over her face and she raised an eyebrow. "Oh gods! Ebrium! Are you not cleaning your hut or shentis? Eeeeww!"

Jumping up, he pulled his little sister to his bare chest in a bear hug. She shrieked and kicked her legs out. "Get away from me you smelly, dirty man!"

He clutched her lightly in his arms, chuckling out a warning, "Careful, little sister. Even though you're a queen's lady now I can still toss you down and tickle you just as easily as when you were a little girl."

"No," she breathed in horror. "You wouldn't dare."

Ebrium laughed mischievously, but released her. She took another swipe of her pillow at him and the elaborately braided loops of her long black hair swayed as she jumped away and glared at him, though a smile played on the corners of her lips. She hunched, pillow in hand, waiting for him to make his next move.

Ebrium grinned even as he felt a flash of sadness. As crazy as they sometimes drove him, he missed living with his sister and mother. He'd left Ebla when Akshaka was only four, and had been away from his family for ten years by the time his ship was captured off the coast of Kemet. The two women made the treacherous journey to Kemet almost two years ago, and lived with him for a year before catching the queen's notice. He was proud that they'd gained Merneith's favour, and that she'd invited them to live at the palace with her. And at first he thought he'd like the quiet of having his own space all to himself. But lately he'd been finding the silence oppressive and dark. Yet the estate the queen had gifted him felt too large, too open. He was accustomed to small spaces: the overcrowded servants' quarters he'd grown up in; the tiny, shared cabins of the pirate ships he used to sail; and the cramped rooms in portside inns and places of ill-repute.

In a strange contradiction, he was afraid that his large, clumsy body would break something if given too much room to move about in a house of this size. This was not something, however, that he was going to admit to his little sister – or anyone else – when they asked why he had yet to move into his new home.

Akshaka still circled Ebrium, throwing out a jab with her pillow from time to time. "Ebrium, when are you going to find yourself a woman? Bey has Merneith, and look how happy they are!" Akshaka was amongst the small group of close friends who knew the true nature of the queen's relationship with Bey.

Ebrium grabbed a pillow for himself and thumped Akshaka on the arm. "Do you have another queen up your sleeve, little sister? If so, I might consider it."

"Pffft." She panted, glaring at him, "I heard from the palace servants that Merneith has paired you with that lady you saved when the tigers broke loose. Satsobek, right? She sent a messenger to thank you. Don't shake your head at me! I remember, I was there. Since then I've heard nothing from you about any women." She feigned a jab at his side, but he spun away.

Ebrium's mood, lightened somewhat by his sister's taunting, grew dark again. "What makes you think I want to find a woman, anyway?" He avoided answering her question.

"Because you've been crankier of late. And you live alone and…" here she tried to distract him with her free hand and managed to thwack his side with the pillow. "…and I think that you're becoming morose."

"Morose? What does that mean?" Her grasp of the Kemeti language was better than his now that she lived at court, and he was proud of her for it. But if she was insulting him he'd like to know it.

"Morose. It means that you are even worse than usual. You are *ill-tempered…*" she swiped but he dodged, "*depressing*," he twisted to avoid a side hit, "and like a grumpy old man."

Indignant, Ebrium stood up tall, his hands dropping to his sides. "What in the name of the underworld is that supposed to mean?"

THWACK. She cracked him upside the head with her pillow and his ears rung with the blow. He put up a hand. "Enough!" He tossed his pillow onto the bench, shaking his head. "You almost knocked my head clean off. Besides, I may be too *morose* to continue with these games. Perhaps I should just lie down and wait for death to overtake me."

Akshaka stuck her tongue out at him, but relinquished her pillow, muttering, "It's true, though. You're not nearly as much fun as you used to be. You've been more sullen of late and you know mother is anxious for you to start making babies. She tells me every day how she longs for you to settle down and start a family. *Every. Single. Day.* Ebrium. Every day!"

Ebrium snorted. He knew very well how much his mother would like grandchildren.

His sister added, "And I heard Satsobek is a very smart woman, that before she left the hwt of Mehyt there was talk that she could be the next high priestess one day. Just think, you could make brilliant babies with her. When you're not being morose I've heard that some women find you rather charming." She winked. "Perhaps there is hope for you with her."

Ebrium wasn't sure what surprised him more – that he felt a glow of pleasure blossom in his chest at the thought of Satsobek bearing his children, or that for once, his sister had bestowed a compliment on him, albeit a rather back-handed one.

Just then they were interrupted by someone clearing their throat, and brother and sister both turned towards the door. Ebrium's muscles turned to stone when he saw Satsobek standing in the doorway.

Earlier that morning Satsobek was deep in the midst of a confusing dream-memory that happened to involve a tattooed man with beautiful, penetrating blue eyes and thick black hair. She and Ebrium were in the greeting room of a large manor with white-washed walls. Golden sunlight streamed through a window nearby, and he had her up against a wall. His rigid arousal rubbed her thigh and his stubble scratched at her cheek. He whispered that he was Anhur, Mehyt's consort and saviour, and he'd come to take her away from her father. But first, he told her, she'd have to take off her head – in her dream she had a lion's head like that of the goddess Mehyt – in order for him to kiss her. He refused to kiss her if he was in danger of being eaten.

Sadeh, her maid, came running into the unfamiliar room and grabbed her hand, trying to drag her away from the Ebrium–Anhur god. The girl was babbling something about a strange, tattooed man at the door, sent by Ebrium. Satsobek assumed Sadeh was a part of her dream and told her to go find her a sharp knife. It was imperative that she cut her head off in order to get her kiss.

Sadeh took her by the shoulders and shook her. Satsobek's eyes snapped open and her maid's face came into sharp focus, mere inches from her own. "Sadeh," she groused, "I *told* you to go get your own tattooed foreigner. I am busy with mine."

The girl blinked in confusion then gave a hearty laugh. "Wake up, nebet-i. There is no man here for you to be busy with. Only me."

Satsobek came to her senses and swore as she looked around, realizing she was in her own room and that she was, indeed, alone except for her maid. She wished she could go back to that warm, delicious place in her dream where Ebrium wanted her and what she needed to do to have him was clear. Well, even if it meant cutting off her own head…

Giving her a knowing smile, her stalwart maid shook her head. "No, nebet-i, it is not *that* tattooed man at the door. It is another one. He says Ebrium sent him to escort you. His name is Makae. I believe he is one of those twins that came to Kemet with Sekhrey Bey and Ebrium."

Satsobek took a moment to process this, and then last night came flooding back to her. "Oh gods, I have overslept! Quickly, Sadeh, help me get ready! I never meant to fall asleep." By the time she'd removed her make-up and bathed herself after her return in the early morning hours, the sun was lighting the sky. Since she was due to meet Ebrium again shortly, she'd just sat on the edge of her bed to think over the events of the day. She must have fallen asleep at some point.

Sadeh made quick work of Satsobek's morning routine and within a few minutes she met Makae in the kitchen, where the servants had taken him to wait. It was not lost on Satsobek that her father had obviously not wanted him in their home, or else Makae would have been directed to the greeting room. Satsobek grabbed a few honey buns from the kitchen and told Makae she was ready to go.

On the way to Ebrium's, Makae told Satsobek what they'd gathered from Haerk's meeting with Ahmes last night at Iput's. He also explained that the men that had assaulted her last night were wanted for questioning, having announced the deaths of the high priest and priestess earlier yesterday and blaming it on the gods' disfavour with the queen. Despite the fierceness of his high cheekbones and nearly-black eyes, Makae struck her as a quiet, introspective man, and she found herself liking his calm presence.

They'd almost reached Ebrium's when they ran into Betrest, on her way to the Temple of Mehyt. The beautiful woman greeted them and Satsobek introduced her to Makae. Betrest gave Makae a suspiciously demure smile before asking Satsobek to step aside to talk. Their conversation was brief. Betrest had discreetly discovered where Maketaten *really* was the night of the temple murders.

With all that had happened since yesterday afternoon, Satsobek had almost forgotten that she's asked Betrest to look into Maketaten's story. Betrest told her that the bird-like woman *had* been seen walking along the great Iteru on her own, just as she said. However, she'd also been seen leaving the Widow Inhapi's hut.

"Widow Inhapi?" Satsobek's brow furrowed. "The woman who used to tell our fortunes and sold us charms to ward off evil? Why would Maketaten go to her? She used to make fun of us all the time for visiting her." Widow Inhapi was known for her *heka* – her magical abilities. As young priestesses, Satsobek and some of the other girls used to visit her, sometimes for simple things like curing common colds, or skin blemishes, and other times for things like love potions, or dream readings. She wondered what Inhapi would make of her lion-headed Mehyt and Ebrium-Anhur god dream.

"Yes, that Inhapi," Betrest nodded emphatically, her eyes wide. Her voice dropped low as she tilted her head towards Satsobek's. "I don't know what her purpose was there, but isn't it odd that she used to scorn us, and yet she went herself the night Tiya and Yuny died?"

Satsobek blew out a long slow breath, trying to determine where this fit into the murders. "It's strange," she hesitated. "But I don't understand it yet. Betrest, please don't tell anyone of this. I'll speak with Maketaten and find out what she was doing. Until then, I *need* you to keep this to yourself."

"Of course," Betrest grinned. "But you must promise to tell me all about it as soon as possible. Wait a moment," she still held Satsobek's hand, and tugged her back as she was turning to leave. "Tell me, darling, are any of those men of the queen's guard free? I'm particularly interested in that stunning man you had with you yesterday – the one that saved you from the tiger. There is not a single Kemeti man that size, and doesn't it make you wonder if he is built that big *all over?*" She waggled one eyebrow in a comically suggestive fashion.

Or it would be comical if Satsobek didn't have the urge to tear that eyebrow off her friend's face. She opened her mouth, then snapped it shut. "He is… it's complicated, I think."

Betrest's eyes grew to the size of the full moon as she watched the blush creep across Satsobek's face. She gasped. "Satsobek! You've been hiding something from me. Oh, this is too much. You must tell me. Right now!"

"Betrest, I can't. I have work to do. Besides, there is really nothing to tell."

"Liar. I cannot believe it!" But Betrest grinned with delight, almost hopping from foot to foot in her excitement, until she glanced towards Makae and sobered. "Fine," her voice was a furious whisper, "I'll wait until you have solved this horrible thing, but I know you're lying and I am absolutely thrilled. Not about the lying, but about the sex. There must be amazing sex. I want to hear all about it. It's about time you did it again."

Betrest was the only person who really knew about what had happened between her and Inkaef, and that reminder coupled with Betrest's harassment – especially with Makae so nearby – was enough to mortify Satsobek. She blushed harder and mumbled something about the lack of sex and the need to leave immediately.

Betrest shook her head. "Now I *know* you are lying. No woman could be alone in a room with that man and *not* have sex with him. Ugh, now I'm jealous. Off with you then. Go have your wonderful foreign sex with that beautiful man." Her brief pout turned into a barely contained smile and she whispered, "I want all the wicked details and I will get them out of you one way or another."

Satsobek sighed, knowing there was no point in trying to argue with Betrest. Besides, she didn't have the time.

"We'll talk later, Betrest. I promise. And thank you for your help."

"Anytime, darling. I miss you at the hwt every day." Betrest waggled her fingers and threw Makae one last half-smirk. Satsobek shook her head and snorted, even as her heart warmed at her friend's words.

A few short minutes later, Makae bowed to her in the courtyard of Ebrium's new home as two men carried a large bench past them. Makae took his leave, saying, "It has been a pleasure, nebet-i. Ebrium is inside waiting for you."

"Thank you, Makae." She inclined her head and watched him stride away. She turned to look over the house that used to belong to Addaya, the lecherous nobleman. The mansion was beautiful on the outside, white-washed to reflect the heat of the sun and keep the bricks cool. It shone in the morning sunlight. Addaya had spared no expense in building it. A small courtyard lay between the street and the main entrance, and tall doum palm trees lined the inside of the walls, offering comfortable shade. Following a brick pathway through the sand and up two steps was a granite slab and the main door. There, an overhang was upheld by granite columns and several tall, narrow windows were cut into the wall. The large wooden front door stood partially open.

Satsobek took the steps and stood in front of the door. She knocked, but no one came. The sound of laughter drifted out, so she pushed open the door and stepped inside. The main entrance was mostly empty except for a jumble of chairs and benches in one corner. Hearing noises to her right, she made her way to the door there.

She didn't mean to listen in, but she could make out the voices from the moment she'd stepped in the door. A young woman berated Ebrium for waiting so long to move, and Satsobek couldn't suppress her surprise at how the woman easily made fun of him for living alone, and the good-natured way in which he joked back with her. It was so unlike the irritable, grouchy Ebrium she'd come to know.

There was something so relaxed, so comfortable, even loving, in the way the two interacted that Satsobek could hardly believe this was the same man who had been so remote last night on the way home. He'd barely spoken two words to her on the way back to her father's house. Before she'd fallen asleep, she'd sat on her bed replaying every detail of the time spent in his hut. She'd ached when she recalled how safe and protected she'd felt in his arms, how he had obliterated the worst visions from that terrible day, and made her feel more peace than she'd ever experienced in her quiet hours inside the tranquility of the Temple of Mehyt.

She'd also had several minutes' worth of gut-wrenching doubts. *Had he changed his mind, or realized his mistake?* When he'd dropped her off he'd given her a detached bow and told her to sleep well. When Inkaef had told her he'd made a mistake being with her, she thought her world might end. She knew better now, she'd survive, just as she had once before, but it still hurt horribly to think Ebrium might not feel the same way she did.

Listening to them now, Satsobek couldn't believe a brother and sister could be as candid with one another as Ebrium and his sister. She heard him refer kindly to the girl as "little sister." It was so unlike her relationship with her own sister that she found herself wishing she'd had a brother like him. It wasn't even *what* he said, but *the way* he said it. There was warmth and laughter in his voice, something she yearned to hear when someone, *anyone*, talked to her. Surely if there'd been someone in her life who cared so deeply for her, she wouldn't have made the stupid mistake she had with Inkaef.

When the girl questioned Ebrium about her, she drew nearer the doorway, heart pounding, wanting to know his response. Did he want children? Could it ever be possible he might want them with her? She quickly changed her mind about listening in, afraid to hear his answer and afraid to get caught sneaking around his house. She stepped into the doorway and cleared her throat.

Akshaka appraised Satsobek before turning to Ebrium with one deliberately raised, expectant eyebrow. He stopped himself from rolling his eyes and growling at her to cut it out. He knew full well his little sister planned to interrogate him later. And Akshaka was just as tenacious, if not more so, as he when it came to getting answers. On the other side of the room, his mother had looked up from her conversation and was making her way over, leaning on a carved walking stick.

Ebrium sighed and gestured at Satsobek before running a hand through his hair. "Little sister, this is Satsobek, daughter of Sobek. Satsobek, this is Akshaka, my sister. And this," he reached out a hand to his mother, who had neared them, "is Ishara, my mother. Satsobek is assisting me in a matter concerning the queen."

Akshaka bowed, as was customary for a girl of her class to acknowledge the daughter of a nobleman. "*Em hotep*," she murmured the greeting, *in peace*. Ishara, as an elderly woman, dipped her head in respect. Ebrium held his breath for a moment as he wondered how Satsobek would react to meeting his mother and sister. He didn't even stop to wonder why he cared.

"Em hotep," Satsobek smiled at the wizened older woman. Ebrium's mother was small, even smaller than Satsobek, hunched and wrinkled, with skin the colour of a hazelnut shell. She looked nothing like her tall, fair-skinned, blue-eyed children. There was something in the woman's dark eyes that drew Satsobek to her. She had a kind look, and a calm presence.

Then Satsobek turned to Akshaka, and the girl pulled herself up to full height, several inches taller than Satsobek. Satsobek glanced between Akshaka and Ebrium and thought that, although Ebrium's skin was darker, sun-bronzed from years at sea and soldiering, the two looked very much alike. They had a similar energy to them, as if something restive stalked beneath their smooth exterior. Akshaka was not masculine like her brother - although she was not exactly delicate - but there was an appealing quality in both brother and sister's features. Or it would be appealing if Ebrium's eyes had the same inquisitive kindness in them that his sister's did. Instead, his eyes were once again guarded and watchful.

She turned to Ebrium's sister. "I am very pleased to meet you, Akshaka. I hear you have become close friends with my cousin Penebui." Satsobek was distantly related to Penebui, another cousin of the queen who lived at the palace.

Satsobek felt a pang of jealousy when the girl smiled. Akshaka was actually painfully beautiful, with her fair skin, thick black braids, and unusual blue eyes. Satsobek was conscious of all the injustices of being short, dark, small, flat-chested, fish-lipped, and all the other things she knew herself to be.

"Penebui is my dearest friend," Akshaka spoke with enthusiasm. "She has helped me so much to improve my language skills. But I have heard that you can read and write? I stand in awe of you. I would so dearly love to understand how to do this, it looks so very difficult. Some time I hope you will tell me all about how a woman can become so educated."

Satsobek was overwhelmed by the girl's open friendliness, dispelling any ill-will she might have had. She couldn't help but grin at the younger girl's eagerness. "And I would love some time to hear all about your home country, and your journey to Kemet. I have only ever been as far as the shore of the great northern sea once for a brief stay. You and your mother must be terribly brave to make the long journey here."

One corner of Akshaka's mouth lifted in a knowing smile. "But I believe my brother would be much better suited to tell you about travelling. He has, after all, been almost *everywhere*. And he is *far* braver than I."

Satsobek almost choked as her eyes flicked from Akshaka to Ishara, and then Ebrium. Ishara had a gentle smile on her face as she looked up at her massive son. Ebrium, on the other hand, was clenching his jaw and glaring out the window.

Ebrium was saved from throttling his little sister when his mother stepped forward and laid one gnarled hand on Satsobek's forearm. She gestured towards several rolls of fabric heaped on a table nearby and asked in her broken Kemeti, "Nebet-i, you have more experience than my daughter or I. If it's not too much trouble, we would appreciate any assistance from a lady such as yourself. Do you not think the curtains should match the bench cushions? Perhaps the pale yellow? Which colour do you prefer?"

It was horrible of him to want to clamp a hand around his own mother's mouth, but *by Dagon* would they please stop insinuating themselves into the situation? He'd known it would be awkward having Satsobek in his home with his mother and sister there, but he hadn't anticipated them being quite so desperate to see him with a woman.

He cleared his throat and growled, "Thank you very much, mother, but she's not here to decorate. And for the last time, I don't care what damned colours the cushions are." He pushed the last words through clenched teeth.

His mother's eyes widened in his direction and he knew he was in trouble. She pointed one knobbly index finger at him and waggled it. She didn't even need to say what she was thinking. He knew it. She'd taught him better than to speak like that. He sighed, chastised, and nodded. "Excuse me, mother, my apologies."

Ishara raised an eyebrow and cocked her head. He pursed his lips. *Damn the gods*, she was going to make him apologize to Satsobek, too.

He narrowed his eyes and turned to Satsobek. "Please excuse my language, nebet-i. My mother raised me to speak better in the presence of ladies. Now dear mother and sister, you must excuse us. Although the colour of the benches is *truly* of the utmost importance, we have other matters to attend to."

He placed a hand in the small of Satsobek's back and began to steer her out of the room. She turned back and called out, "It was lovely meeting you both, and the pale yellow is beautiful. And I agree about the cushions."

Ishara nodded and said, "Do come back again, dear, if you have the time. We could use your assistance." Akshaka called out just as they were leaving the room, "Please help him to find a manservant! He needs one and won't listen to me."

Ebrium didn't remove his hand from her back until they'd passed beyond the shady trees and to the other side of the gate, onto the dusty street. She tried very hard not to laugh at the dark look in his eyes when he finally stopped a little ways down the street.

He glared at her and she could no longer contain the grin that broke out across her face. Despite all the awkwardness of last night, seeing Ebrium with his mother and sister had been enlightening. Like last night when he'd told her about sneaking in to the temple in Ebla, she felt she'd stepped beyond the exterior he maintained and caught a glimpse of the man who'd risked his own life to save her eight months ago. She had to admit, this good-natured and kind-hearted side of him was utterly endearing.

"Your mother and sister are very sweet, and I do hope they go with the pale yellow fabric for you. I think it suits your cheerful disposition." She teased him, emboldened after witnessing his browbeating at the hands of a young girl and an old woman.

He snorted, but actually seemed relieved, as if she'd somehow eased his apprehensions. "Do you? You should see my sister when she's angry. She's hardly sweet then. More likely to rip a man's face off than worry about the colour of his cushions."

There was an awkward pause as their eyes met. The sky was cloudless, and the sun beat down on them. Satsobek's skin prickled with perspiration, and her head felt warm. She wondered if she were to reach up and run her hands through Ebrium's black hair if it would be as hot as her own. If he would flinch, or if he would look at her with the same intensity he had right before he'd kissed her.

Ebrium licked his lips and looked away. "About last night..." he began.

"No, I should..." Satsobek didn't know what *she should*, but she spoke anyway. Was he upset he hadn't gotten satisfaction? In her experience men didn't give pleasure without expecting it in return. She couldn't tell him *why* she'd stopped him last night. Or could she? Perhaps his own background would render him more understanding...

"No, you should not. I was wrong." His lips compressed, his jaw clenched. "You had a difficult day and I took advantage of it. You deserve better than that. I promise it won't happen again."

Deserve better than what? She wondered. Better than for him to make her feel desirable? To take her to the peak of pleasure in mere moments and then stroke her hair while she climaxed around his fingers? There were much worse things for a man to do. She didn't want him thinking he was to blame, or that she hadn't invited his attentions.

She tried to explain. "Ebrium, you did not take advantage..." But he cut her off. "No. You're the unmarried daughter of a relation of the queen's. I should know better than to attempt to dishonour you. *I was wrong.*" He pronounced it as though he'd made a final judgement and would bear no argument. "Now let's go visit Tiya's husband and see what he has to say for himself."

Chapter 11 – Clandestine Affairs

Ebrium was staunchly trying *not* to think about why it had pleased him so much that Satsobek was so kind to his mother and sister, when she slipped her fingers into the crook of his elbow and tugged, pulling him up short.

"I think that's Ahmes," she whispered, pointing up the street past the house they were walking towards. A tall figure, bald except for a braided side-lock, was striding up the lane away from the house, his back to them. "Should we follow him?"

Ahmes was so pre-occupied that he never once turned to see the two figures trailing behind him at a distance. It wasn't a long journey, as they followed him into the village on the temple grounds, near the grain silos and workshops they'd passed yesterday. Ahmes stopped in front of an average-sized hut and Ebrium and Satsobek slipped into the narrow space between two workshops on the other side of the street. Ebrium let Satsobek cut in front of him, being the shorter of the two. Although the morning was rapidly warming as the sun climbed overhead, he liked the feel of her warm shoulders against his chest when he leaned forward to peer over her head and around the corner.

Ahmes opened the door to the hut and stepped inside, but within a moment was repelled backwards, his arms pin-wheeling for balance.

"Get out!" A woman's voice shrieked from within the darkened doorway. Ebrium craned his neck but couldn't catch a glimpse of the woman's face.

"Shhh, Neferu, darling, please listen…" Ahmes held his hands out, palms up, glancing around him in trepidation.

The woman cut him off. "I will not *shhhh*, Ahmes! I have kept quiet for months and I'm not doing it anymore! I told you yesterday to stay away from me! I'm done here."

"*Please* Neferu, lower your voice. I need to talk to you."

"No. No talking. I don't know what you've done, Ahmes, but I want no part of it."

"I?! I didn't *do* anything." Ahmes's voice was a furious whisper. "You know I didn't. With all that I've given you… I have nothing left, Neferu. If you're going back to your brother's home you don't need all of it anymore…"

"Really? You want me to give back the wealth you gave me to take care of *our* child? After everything you've done, trying to get rid of me, and now your wife is dead?" The woman's voice was verging on hysteria, and Ebrium could see Ahmes cringe and whip his head around. Lucky for him the street was a narrow sideway, and not busy. The woman continued her tirade. "Well you can consider that paltry sum you gave me as payment for what you've done. Stay away from me, or I'll go to the authorities, Ahmes, I swear to Ra I will. And then you'll be in for it!"

With that the woman slammed the door, leaving Ahmes standing on the doorstep. Slowly, he turned. As he did so, Satsobek and Ebrium both flattened themselves against the wall, holding their breath.

And that's when an angry voice shouted at them, "Hey! What're you two doing, sneaking around out there under my window?"

It cost Ebrium a small sack of grain, and a polite and apologetic speech from Satsobek, to silence the angry potter's wife. By that time Ahmes was long gone, and they had no way of knowing if they'd been seen. They had no choice but to hope he'd returned to his manor and catch him there.

When they did just that, Ahmes's eyes bulged at the sight of Satsobek and Ebrium on his doorstep. "I'm sorry.

I'm just on my way out. I have no time to talk this morning." He clipped.

"No time to talk about your murdered wife?" Ebrium inclined his head, out of patience with the man's arrogance. "You don't think that looks suspicious at all, do you?"

Ahmes bristled. "Why should it? I did nothing wrong. I loved my wife." Ahmes turned to Satsobek in appeal. "You know I did. I am sorry, but if you will please come back later I will have more leisure to speak with you."

He began to close the door but Ebrium put a hand out to stop it, his voice a menacing growl. "I think you can make the time, unless you want me to arrest you on the spot."

"Arrest me? For what? I was home when Tiya was killed."

"So you say. But I met your friend Haerk last night at the House of Iput and he told me some things I'd like to ask you about."

"That fool?" Ahmes spoke with disdain, but Ebrium detected a note of fear in his voice. "If he did anything to my wife, I beg you to punish him to the fullest extent. In fact, I believe it is quite possible he *was* involved. I should have thought of it yesterday."

Satsobek stepped closer, under the protection of Ebrium's out-stretched arm. Her voice was quiet, but Ebrium could hear the simmering anger lurking within. "We also just saw you arguing with a woman about a baby in the village. So you had best talk to us now. I am confident whatever other matters you have to attend to can wait, else you'll be much later if we have to take you to the *hnrt* for questioning." Surprise and a healthy amount of pride swelled in Ebrium's breast as he looked down at the top of the fierce little woman's head. Perhaps he was having an influence on her after all.

Satsobek's threat was effective. Ahmes shoulders slumped as he stepped back, opening the door to allow them in.

It took almost two hours, but they were able to tease out all the sordid details of Ahmes's story. When it all came out, Satsobek had very little sympathy left for the man, and felt even worse for her dear old mentor.

Tiya was planning to divorce him, Ahmes told them. Being of the same bloodline as the royal family, Tiya was very wealthy when she married Ahmes twenty years ago, and her father negotiated a marriage contract that strongly favoured her. Under the terms of the contract she was to be Ahmes's primary wife, he was allowed no others without her consent. She would also retain all her properties in the event of a divorce – and she was free to initiate a divorce if she so chose. One year ago Tiya discovered that Ahmes was keeping a concubine in another house and threatened to divorce him. He'd begged her not to go.

Ebrium pressed this point, asking why he'd wanted her to stay if he had another woman.

Slouched deep in his chair, Ahmes admitted it was for practical reasons. "If she left, I'd lose all the tax revenue from her properties. I would have nothing left but this house and a few small properties. I convinced her I would amend my ways."

And he had, at least to all outward appearances. Although Tiya decided to stay, they slept separately and fought regularly. In the meantime, Ahmes continued to see his concubine. He'd just moved her to a new location where his visits were less frequent and more furtive.

"But, uh…" Ahmes licked his lips, flicked a glance at Satsobek, then stared down at his hands in his lap, mumbling. "Two months ago the woman, my er…"

"Lady friend?" Ebrium supplied helpfully, a smirk plastered across his face.

"Er, yes. She showed up here, at my home." He paused, heaving a breath. "Pregnant. Demanding *things* I cannot give, wanting me to set aside Tiya and marry her instead. If Tiya discovered the pregnancy, I would be ruined."

"So you had Haerk follow her?" Satsobek leaned forward. *Poor Tiya*, she thought. How heartbreaking to discover her husband had been deceiving her. Of course it happened. Men kept concubines and sometimes, if they were very wealthy and high-born, they had two or more true wives. But such relationships were generally not a secret and the women found a way to strike a balance with one another. Sometimes the primary wife consented to it for various reasons, to have extra help in the home or caring for children, if she was unable to bear children herself, or if she no longer chose to satisfy her husband's desires.

Satsobek also knew that it was a source of sadness for Tiya that she couldn't bear children. She'd lost several in miscarriages, until it was determined too dangerous for her to keep trying. To have a secret concubine provide what she couldn't would have been especially painful for Tiya, had she lived to learn of it.

"Yes, I had her followed." Ahmes pulled himself upright in his chair. "Tiya had been out late several nights in the temple. I thought perhaps she had decided to get back at me, and was having an affair with Yuny. The gods know they spent enough time together."

"And you hoped to catch her." Ebrium prodded him along.

Ahmes nodded. "Yes. If I could catch her in adultery, I would have grounds to initiate a divorce, and would likely retain more of the properties in the end."

"But aren't you better off now that she's dead?" Ebrium's voice was deadly calm. "After all, now you stand to gain everything. Did you know Haerk wasn't watching her anymore? That he was taking your money and gambling it away? Did you think you could set him up for the murder and then walk away with everything?"

"What?" Ahmes sat up tall, gripping the arms of his chair. "Haerk was… that bastard! He didn't watch her then?" He slouched back down, speaking more to himself. "I should have known. He kept saying he needed more time. To get closer." Ahmes looked up sharply. "I didn't know Haerk had stopped watching her, I swear to Ra. Even last night, I thought he was just lazy and not watching her close enough.

"But it never crossed my mind to kill my wife. I could never do that. Until last night, I assumed Haerk had done something to her, perhaps to blackmail me, or her. I don't know. But when I saw him last night I realized he was too stupid and cowardly to do such a thing."

"But you stand to gain from Tiya's death now." Ebrium's eyes narrowed. Satsobek looked between the two men, trying to determine if Ahmes was being honest with them.

"No." Ahmes gave a bitter chuckle. "No. I may be even worse off now than before. Worse than if we had divorced months ago. I had to sell all my own properties just to quiet that wretched, scheming woman. I paid her a large sum of wealth to leave town so that Tiya would never learn of it, but she wouldn't go. *Now* she's saying she'll go live with her brother. With Tiya gone, it's possible that under the terms of our marriage contract the properties revert back to her family, as we had no children to inherit them.

"That is where I was going when you arrived. To meet with the official who was holding our marriage contract for safekeeping. So no. I would never have killed Tiya. My concubine is leaving me, my wife is gone, and I am left with absolutely nothing. Knowing her family, I'll be out on the doorstep begging before the Festival of the New Year. I cannot help you more than that. I don't know who killed Tiya, but whoever it is, they have absolutely *ruined* me in the process. If you find her killer, please oblige me by cutting their nose and ears off before you execute them."

Satsobek almost felt bad for Ahmes. Or at least, she might have, if he'd shown the least bit of remorse for Tiya's death, and a little less concern for his own state of affairs.

Satsobek and Ebrium made their way back through the temple complex towards the smaller huts at the far end of the temple lands, in the same direction of the village workshops and the hut of Ahmes's concubine. Around them, the large mansions of the upper echelons of the temple hierarchy faded to crowded huts separated by small yards with low, mud-brick walls. Chickens and goats nibbled here and there on thin, low-growing shrubs.

Having dismissed Ahmes as a suspect, they moved on to share their latest discoveries. Satsobek told Ebrium about Maketaten's visit to the widow who sold potions and fortunes, and Ebrium recounted how Haerk had seen the high priest visiting Imhotep the hmww – the furniture-maker – in the middle of the night. They were on their way to the man's house now. Satsobek was frustrated, feeling thwarted at every turn. There were too many suspects and nothing firm to indicate who killed Tiya and Yuny. She hoped Imhotep had something useful to offer.

Ebrium knocked on the warped, wood-plank door of a spacious mud-brick hut, larger than many of the others nearby. The size of his home indicated the carpenter's elevated status amongst the common residents of the temple properties. There was no answer to the first knock, and Ebrium knocked again. Satsobek peered around them and, in doing so, glanced in the narrow window cut into the wall near the door.

"Oh!" She gasped, "Ebrium, look!" The devastation of Imhotep's hut was apparent, even with a limited view through the window into the darkened greeting room. Intricately carved cedar chair legs, polished to a glossy red sheen, lay on the ground, smashed off their seats as if they'd been battered against the wall. A table rested on its side and fine bits of painted pottery, shattered in hundreds of pieces, littered the floor.

"Stay here, keep a lookout," Ebrium warned her as he slid his long blade out, holding it at the ready as he pushed open the door. Satsobek stood on tiptoe, watching him pick his way through the bits of pottery shards to the back rooms of the hut. She glanced frequently over her shoulder to make sure no one came up from behind and surprised her.

After several agonizing minutes, Ebrium returned, shaking his head. "There's no one here."

Back out on the street, Satsobek stopped a man and a young boy who were walking by, asking them if they knew

Imhotep the carpenter, and where they might find him. The man was clearly a labourer of some sort, given the deep-set wrinkles around his eyes from squinting against the sun and the rough, cracked lines in the strong hand that settled on the boy's shoulder, inset as they were with dirt that no amount of scrubbing could vanquish. He looked pointedly at the blade hanging from Ebrium's hip, and then over the fine linen of Satsobek's dress.

Ebrium untied another sack of grain from his shenti and passed it the man with a reassuring smile. "We don't want any trouble with the man. My uh – wife and I are looking to have some furniture made for our new home. She's… she *was* a priestess in the hwt here, and Imhotep has a reputation." Satsobek was too startled by Ebrium's story to do anything but blink at the man and give his son a plastered-on smile. Last night she'd been Ebrium's whore. Today she'd progressed to his wife. She couldn't begin to guess what tomorrow would bring.

The labourer hefted the sack of grain in his hand, testing the weight, before slipping it onto his shenti ties and giving a quick nod. "Got a workshop over on the next street," the man jerked his thumb over his shoulder to indicate the lane of shops near the silo they'd been in yesterday. "Has a sign with a wooden chair painted on it. Saw him there not long ago."

A few minutes later, they were standing in front of the closed door of a small shop front. Ebrium knocked and a shuffling noise came from within. The door opened to reveal a very handsome man with high, well-defined cheekbones, luminous eyes rimmed by thick black lashes, and full lips a deep shade of pink. Clad in a long-sleeved, full-length robe of unbleached linen, he was slender and tall, only a few inches short of Ebrium's towering mass. A white scarf loosely wrapped around his head covered his hair.

She was so taken in by his attractive features that it took her a moment to realize he was not, in fact, a young man. He was more likely to be in his early forties. Not at all a young man for Kemet. He had a dark line of stubble along his jaw and his eyes were rimmed in red, puffy flesh.

"Yes?" The man's wary gaze shifted between Ebrium and Satsobek.

Satsobek stepped forward. "You are Imhotep? The temple hmww?"

The man nodded, his suspicious look intensifying. Satsobek introduced herself as cousin to the queen, a former priestess of the Temple of Mehyt, and Ebrium as one of the queen's men. "We need to speak with you about what happened to the high priest and priestess. And about what happened to your hut."

"Yes," his face had gone pale and resignation crept into his voice. "I suppose you do."

As the workshop afforded little in the way of seating, Imhotep led them on to the small rooftop, where they arranged themselves on woven papyri reed mats under the shade of a large white linen canopy.

"I was away from my home last night," Imhotep began. His hands twisted in his lap, pulling at the fabric of his robe with long, fine fingers. *An artist's hands.* She thought of the furniture she'd seen in his hut, and how heartbreaking it must be to have one's workmanship smashed to bits like that.

Imhotep went on to explain that when he returned home, in the early hours of the morning, he found his hut had been vandalized. Nothing stolen that he could see, but almost every stick of furniture, every piece of pottery, every icon of the gods, had been destroyed.

"Do you know why? Does it have something to do with Yuny?" Ebrium asked in an even tone unlike his usual gruff interrogation.

"I – I do not know for sure." Imhotep turned his reddened eyes off into the distance. "But I do not think I am safe there anymore. I came here to try to sort things out, to figure out why this happened."

"Imhotep," Satsobek reached out and laid a hand on his arm. Making physical contact with a strange man, particularly one of a lower class, was not something Satsobek was familiar with. But Imhotep brought out the urge to be kind. "We know Yuny came to visit you late in the evenings. What was your relationship with him? Do you know something about Tiya and Yuny's deaths?"

Imhotep turned his wide eyes to her, then flicked them over to Ebrium and back again. "Yuny was... that is, he has been *distracted* lately. I know there have been some problems with the labourers. I've been working on a project, helping in the architectural plans for building some new homes on the north side of the temple property. I have heard some of the workers complaining that the wages are not enough, that they cannot feed their families. Quietly, mind you. They do not speak much aloud for fear of upsetting the goddess, but they are...*unsettled*, I suppose.

"I mentioned it to Yuny about two months ago. He said he would speak with Menkhaf, to see if there was something that could be done. He is...*was*... always very considerate of the workers."

Ebrium cleared his throat. "Perhaps it is time you told us the nature of your relationship with Yuny. As far as I'm aware, furniture-makers are not in the habit of discussing the well-being of labourers with the high priest, are they?" His tone was not unkind, but it was insistent.

Imhotep nodded, his head down. "We were... he was..." Imhotep appeared to search for words.

"You were lovers." Ebrium spoke the three words as a neutral statement.

Imhotep started. He turned to Ebrium, his eyes clear and sharp for the first time since they'd arrived. "How did you know?"

Satsobek was wondering the same thing. Although something in her had wanted to reach out and hug Imhotep, it had never occurred to her that it was because she instinctively recognized the mourning of a lover. She had heard of such men, of course, but only in whispers. How Ebrium would have deduced it so quickly was a mystery to her.

A mystery he quickly resolved when he said, "I've lived many years at sea, frequented some of the worst taverns in even worse port cities, and spent months on campaign in the desert. I've seen far stranger things than two men spending time together. When you've known men desperate enough to consider interfering with a flea-bitten donkey..." he shrugged one massive shoulder, "you are less inclined to judge where someone else finds their pleasures."

Imhotep blinked at Ebrium then laughed softly. Satsobek marveled that he managed to put Imhotep at his ease when she'd foolishly been at a loss for words. In comparison to the life he'd experienced, she really was just a sheltered woman who knew little about the world outside her neighbourhood.

Ebrium urged Imhotep to continue talking. "Do you think your relationship had anything to do with what happened to Tiya and Yuny, or to your house? Who knew about you two?"

"Well," Imhotep gave a wisp of a smile, "it is not as though Yuny had to choose between myself and a donkey. We had a... mutual respect for one another. We met when I first came to work at the temple, eighteen years ago. I was working with another architect building an expansion here - some new workspaces for the priests. I designed a desk and chairs for Yuny's workspace. After that he hired me to design some furniture for his home. He imported wood from Palestine so I could carve new chairs and a bed for him. And I was enamoured of him, of course. He was older than I, and had such presence."

Satsobek understood what he meant. Yuny had been a powerful man, and he carried himself as such. High priest of the Temple of Mehyt was no minor position. He controlled large swaths of land, presided over hundreds of people and, sometimes, had the ear of the pharaoh. He'd come to the position through family connections, as was the way, but he always ensured that the people who worked in and around the temple did not go hungry. Now she wondered if Yuny's relationship with Imhotep had opened Yuny's eyes to the suffering of other people. Not unlike the way the last two days with Ebrium had made her more aware of the lives of the lower classes.

Imhotep's voice grew strained again. "We saw each other as often as we could without raising suspicion. We were as close as we could be, I suppose, given the circumstances. But as for who did this, I don't know. I didn't think anyone knew about us. We've been so careful, and it has been so long. He was always concerned that someone might find out and use it against one of us somehow. That it might ruin my reputation and I would be driven out, or that it would affect him and people would respect him less, that he would lose influence in the court."

Imhotep drew himself up, straightening his back. "I know only that Yuny had been under great stress lately. He was more nervous, more cautious about our meetings. He visited less often, and would not stay as long. When I asked him what was wrong, he laughed and said it was nothing. At first I thought perhaps he was tiring of me, that he had found someone else. So I pressed him about it the last time I saw him, five nights ago. He said that it was nothing to worry about, that it would all be over soon. He said he was taking care of something and it would be done with by the Festival of the New Year. That's all I know."

Imhotep hesitated, flicking a glance between her and Ebrium. Ebrium tilted his head. "If you're concerned for your safety, I can arrange for you to leave Thinis. At least until we can determine who did this."

The carpenter gave Ebrium a grateful smile. "Thank you, although it's not necessary. I was already packing what little I have left when you came. I intend to leave tonight. I have a brother in the north I thought to visit for a time. I cannot say for certain that what happened to my home is related to Yuny's death, but I believe it is not safe here for me right now. I believe if I were home last night when these midnight visitors arrived, I would not be sitting here with you right now."

Ebrium nodded in approval. "You're wise to leave. But you mentioned you were out last night when your house was destroyed. Where were you?"

Satsobek thought she could detect a blush creep into the golden skin of Imhotep's cheeks. "Here, in my workshop. These past few weeks I'd been working on an icon of Mehyt for Yuny, as a gift. I wanted to finish it last night before I left town. In exchange for a small piece of gold I was able to…*convince* the embalmer this morning to include the icon when he wraps Yuny's linens, so that it might be buried with him. So that he may have a piece of me with him always and know that, if I could join him, I would."

Satsobek knew what he meant, and her heart went out to this man. Ebrium, however, looked at her with furrowed brows, a question in his eyes. She tried to explain as succinctly as she could, struggling to put into words the mysteries of the religious beliefs of Kemet. In death, the gods differentiated between souls. Only the *ka,* or eternal life force, of the wealthy and those deemed useful were able to attempt the arduous journey to the heavenly fields of the afterlife, *Sekhet-Aaru.* Yuny, as a high priest from a noble family, would be wrapped in linen, then placed in a stone sarcophagi and buried beneath the ground. His tomb would be filled with objects he might need in the afterlife, such as jugs of food, wine, beer, furniture, and jewellery.

Once the rituals and burial were completed, Yuny's ka would travel to the underworld where he would meet with Osiris, god of the afterlife and the dead. From there, he'd have to complete a multitude of difficult tasks and overcome obstacles. If successful, his life force would pass through the peaceful reed fields of Sekhet-Aaru in the sky, near the eastern horizon where the sun rises.

On the other hand, the ka of a man such as Imhotep would have little claim to the afterlife. His was not of a high rank, and while carpenters planned and built the great temples and furniture of the gods, it was those who commissioned the works that were deemed worthy. The wealthy received funerary processions, professional mourners, a proper burial, and the chance to travel to the paradise of Sekhet-Aaru.

Satsobek felt bad for Imhotep. At least when they were alive Imhotep and Yuny could *see* one another. Once dead, Imhotep's ka would slip away, probably to rest in the darkness and gloom of the commoner's afterlife. His body would simply be buried under the desert sand and forgotten.

Ebrium gave a bitter chuckle. "It's not so different from Ebla. Although for us only the king has the chance to be received by the gods. The rest of us are consigned to eat dust and thirst for all time."

Satsobek and Imhotep stared at him. Satsobek spoke without thinking. "What a sad concept. Is there no hope?"

His blue eyes twinkled with dark humour as he turned his gaze on her. "Indeed. Some believe that, instead of swallowing dust, we wallow in dark, filthy muck, never to see a spot of light or comfort again. I suppose that's better than eternal thirst. That's why, nebet-i, I try not to waste my time worrying what others think of my actions. Our time here above ground is short and the afterlife is long, lonely, and inescapable."

His words brought to mind the way the oil wicks had flickered on his naked chest last night inside his hut, casting him in shadow. As if they were half in this world and half in another. Despite the heat and the damp sweat that prickled her skin, cold shivers ran over her arms and chest. She could die at any time, never knowing what it was to be intimate with a man who truly desired her.

They were preparing themselves to leave when Imhotep stopped her. "You worked in the temple for years. Did you know Yuny well?"

Satsobek could feel Ebrium turn his inquisitive eyes on her and it made her nervous. She nodded and said, "Well enough. He was always good to me."

"Please, tell me what you knew of him." Imhotep licked his lips. "I know it is not my place to ask. It is only that I have not been able to speak with anyone about him. I... Please... I just need to hear something of him from someone who knew him." Imhotep crossed his arms and rubbed his biceps. "I will forever have to keep our relationship secret. I would just like to speak of him once before I leave Thinis behind, and before they take Yuny away."

He referred to Yuny's funeral procession, where his family, the queen, professional mourners, priests and priestesses, musicians and dancers would all make their way to the burial along with him. As a simple commoner with no known connection to Yuny, Imhotep would be unable to watch them bury the man he had loved for eighteen years.

"I… yes. Of course." One of her earliest memories of Yuny came to mind, and she shared it amongst a few others. Yuny was bending over one of her papyrus scrolls, smiling, and she could smell the incense from the goddess's sanctuary clinging to his robes. Yuny's close-cropped, curly grey hair and kohl-rimmed eyes had made him seem like a friendly grandfather goat, setting a young Satsobek at ease in an unfamiliar setting.

She told Imhotep how she had come to the temple, and how Yuny had encouraged her studies, and enabled her to learn to read and write. So unlike her own father, Yuny always had an aura of serenity and benevolence about him, yet he was a man who knew how to command respect and obedience.

When she was finished, Imhotep smiled at her, and his own eyes shimmered. "Thank you. Truly, you have been too kind to share this with me. Yuny is certainly worthy and I am sure his ka will rest in the fields of paradise for eternity. And you," he clasped her fingers in his hand, "speak with such joy of your work, and you have the hands of an artist. I hope you return to your writing soon."

With that, Ebrium and Satsobek took their leave of the lonely furniture-maker. Ebrium gave the man the location of his home, in case he thought of anything else. Satsobek noticed that he gave Imhotep directions to his new mansion, rather than his hut in the village. Somehow, it made her feel safer knowing that he would be sleeping nearby tonight, rather than on the other end of the city.

Ebrium carried a tray laden with bowls of food and mugs of wine down the narrow hallway of the temple. Rather pleased with himself, he looked forward to seeing Satsobek's face when he placed the food in front of her and told her his news.

After leaving the furniture-maker's they'd come to the temple and then separated. Leaving Satsobek to sift through Tiya's papyri for any useful notes, Ebrium went looking for Menkhaf. When he learned the priest was gone for the day, he'd taken the opportunity to search for the boy who was said to have seen late-night visitors to the temple.

He neared the scroll room where he'd parted from Satsobek almost two hours ago. As he approached he could see her through the doorway, sitting on a chair behind a table, papyri scrolls spread out around her. He stood back and watched her for a moment. Hunched over, her dark hair tucked behind her ears, light streamed through the white curtains on the wall beside her, illuminating her cinnamon-coloured cheeks with an amber glow. She was absorbed in her work, running a finger along the lines on a scroll. Her lips moved, whispering to herself, as she went.

He admired her cleverness. Reading and writing were two things the vast majority of people never had the opportunity, or inclination, to learn. Bey used to teach Ebrium some of the things he learned from his instructors, but at seven years old Ebrium was put to work helping his father in the gardens. He'd had little time to devote to scratching out symbols on stones, and it hadn't seemed the least bit relevant for the life he'd been destined for, that of a simple labourer.

Satsobek had told him that she enjoyed the quiet discipline of the temple and he believed her now. Yesterday he'd observed the look of longing in her eyes as she traced her fingers over the paintings on the temple wall. She missed that life, but for some reason she'd left it. He wanted to know why.

Despite her appreciation of tranquility, she was a woman of great passion. That much was evident last night in his hut. Thinking of that and seeing her in an unguarded moment like this made him want to push her up against the wall here, now, in this temple, gods and priests be damned. In his vision, she was no longer an innocent. In his imagination, his head dipped into the curve of her neck, inhaling the cardamom and cinnamon scent of her skin, nuzzling her glossy hair, brushing the shell of her ear with his lips, trailing down along the fine hairs of her neck, just barely skimming her collarbone. His hand would find its way under her dress to graze at the soft, moist folds of her sex. He wanted to make her come in his hand like she had last night, her nails digging into his shoulders, taking her gasps into his mouth and swallowing them whole.

He could see it all. One hand pinning her arms up over her head, her legs locked around his hips as he cupped her bottom with his free hand, grating her back against the sun-heated wall as he thrust up into her. He wanted to turn her impish, sarcastic insults into pleading moans, to make her pant and clutch at him and whimper his name.

She was more complex than any woman he'd ever known. She was a dichotomous combination of innocence and edification, vulnerability and fierce determination, along with a sarcastic sense of humour to match his own. Listening to her repeat her story to Imhotep earlier today, he'd come to realize just how strong she was. Not only was her father the type of man to not care for his child, but she'd lost her mother before even knowing her, then the aunt who raised her, and now Tiya and Yuny, two people who had cared for her. He understood why she was so determined to find their killer. She appreciated any shred of kindness she'd received over the years.

If he ever thought to take a wife, he would want her to be like Satsobek.

By the gods he was hard. He'd had no relief after last night's escapade, and he felt foolish standing in the hallway of a temple, a tray of food in his hands, and an erection sticking straight up in front of him, tenting his shenti. He snorted at the absurd image he must now make. *This is why they don't allow people like me in these places.*

Yet this time when he thought of his boyish expulsion from the temple he found he was no longer bitter. In fact, it made him think of Satsobek and what had happened between them last night. He marveled that a memory that had once made him so angry could now actually make him hard, thanks to its immediate association with Satsobek climaxing in the palm of his hand.

He stepped back into the shadows for a moment to master himself, leaning against the wall and taking deep breaths, thinking of every unsexy thing he could muster. He couldn't marry Satsobek. Never mind that he'd never really considered marriage a possibility. To her or anyone else. Her father would never allow it, and he could hardly steal off with her. In the past, when he had fewer people to worry about and he was more impulsive, he wouldn't have hesitated to take what he wanted if she were willing. But now, such actions would have painful repercussions on his family, Bey, and the queen. He couldn't do that to them after all they'd done for him.

Never mind that he had no idea how Satsobek felt. He could see the desire in her eyes when she looked at him, in spite of her little snipes. He'd had enough women look at him that way to know it. *But that is temporary.* Sooner or later she'd realize she lusted for an uneducated, peasant foreigner and that a marriage between them would likely alienate her from the high circles she was familiar with. She belonged in a place like this temple. A place he was only tolerated in because of the queen's orders.

Why in the name of the gods am I even contemplating marriage in the first place? Because he was intrigued by a women? No. This would pass. *It has to.*

Such reasoning had the necessary effect of cooling his ardour and he was finally able to enter the scroll room and face the cause of his discomfort. The mud-brick walls of the priestess's workspace were white-washed and painted like most of the other temple walls. On the wall to the left of the door was a large image of the lion-headed goddess sitting side by side with her lover, Anhur, in a boat on the great Iteru. To the right, several tall, narrow windows were cut into the wall and covered by white linen curtains that hung almost to the floor, blocking out the worst of the afternoon's blazing sun.

Tiya's large table took up the bulk of the room. In one corner behind the table a tall cluster of potted papyrus grew in the cheerful sunlight streaming through the curtains. Satsobek looked small behind the desk, dwarfed by the rolls of papyri. Behind her rose stacked rows of carved wooden boxes – boxes for storing papyri.

Ebrium set the tray on the edge of the table and Satsobek looked up, startled, her big brown eyes wide. The confused look on her face shifted to embarrassment, obviously self-conscious about her lack of awareness when reading. He thought it utterly adorable and had to remind himself, and his stiffening man parts, that it didn't matter how endearing she might be.

She gave him a tentative smile. "I see you have been making yourself comfortable here."

He chuckled. "We haven't eaten in hours, and the kitchen ladies insisted on feeding us. I couldn't say no."

The lines of her face crinkled in good humour. Then, quickly, as if she hadn't meant him to see it, her eyes traveled up his arms, over his chest and back to his face. When her glance met his, she blushed and dropped her gaze to the food. Ebrium's groin tightened, knowing she was probably remembering last night in his hut. *By Dagon, how is a man supposed to ignore that look and everything it hints at?*

He grabbed a handful of figs from the tray and pulled over a chair from nearby, seating himself on the opposite side of the table from her, a little ways away. From this angle he was able to hide any unruly body parts and get them under control before she caught him standing in front of her like a horny donkey, his cock waggling in her face. Before he frightened her again like he had last night, pushing too quickly for things she wasn't ready for.

"Any luck with the priestess's documents?" He asked, popping a fig into his mouth.

She shook her head, blowing out a loud sigh. "Not yet, but I am still hopeful. I've been working through them in order, starting from four months ago. Mostly they are accounts of the comings and goings of the goddess. Days when she was taken out of the cabinet to be moved to the roof of the temple for festivals and other special days. A schedule of her feedings. Were you successful in your search?"

While she nibbled on a chunk of fresh barley bread and a few leaves of lettuce, he told her how he had spent most of the last two hours chatting with the kitchen staff, regaling them with stories of his travels. In that time, he was able to question some of them about who might have been working an evening or early morning shift, and who might have seen the participants of a clandestine meeting in the late hours of the night. By a stroke of luck, one of the other men told Ebrium they knew of a boy who had witnessed just such a meeting.

The boy, Ebrium learned, hadn't been to work for the past two days, but Ebrium did get the location of his home. He intended for them to pay the boy a visit as soon as Satsobek was finished with the documents.

"That is wonderful news." He liked to see her smile, her small white teeth shining bright in contrast to her warm, dark skin. "I'll try to hurry through these scrolls so that we may leave soon."

He let her continue working while he ate and sipped his wine. Once finished his meal, though, there was little to occupy him. When he turned to watch Satsobek work, his mind naturally wandered to thinking about what it might be like to lift her up, to place her rounded rump on the table, scattering the scrolls, and stepping between her legs. He'd push her dress up around her hips and kneel before her, running his hands up her smooth thighs and inhaling her warm, spicy scent. He wanted so badly to press his lips to the soft curls of her sex, to taste the liquid centre of her being. And then, once she'd come in his mouth, to thrust himself into her, stroking in and out until he had finally sated the ridiculous and impractical carnal feelings he'd been having about her.

The ache in his groin called him back to reality, and he bit the inside of his cheek. Hard. He sat, bouncing his knee and looking around the room, trying to avoid staring at her in case his mind returned to his lewd delusions. Once he was safely able to, he stood and paced the room, trying not to think about the sexy woman murmuring to herself behind the table. He assured himself that he was most definitely *not* going to let himself get too close to her again.

Satsobek became aware of Ebrium's scent swirling around her. His hand brushed her shoulder as he gripped the back of her chair, and she jumped at the contact. She bit her lip and tried to keep her face immobile. Nonetheless, she glanced up at his face as he bent forward to look at the hieroglyphics painted on the long papyrus scroll.

His deep, thickly accented voice was gruff as he asked, "Still nothing?" A slight frown creased his forehead as he studied the hieroglyphics. His face was so near to hers, near enough she could almost graze his jaw with her lips.

She tore her eyes away, shook her head and gave what she knew her sister would call a less-than-lady-like snort of exasperation. "I have gone through everything from the last few months now, and nothing of note seems to have occurred. Nothing except the schedule of the daily feeding of Mehyt, which of the women were employed to sing and dance this month, which priestesses cleaned the rooms on which days."

She pulled a scroll from the middle of the stack and gestured to it. "The only thing I do not understand is this one. It is a list of days, but they appear to be random, and next to them are only a series of letters and numbers.

Nothing more. No explanation." Not knowing what it meant troubled her.

Ebrium ran a hand through his thick, wavy hair, dragging it back from his face as he sat back in the chair he'd pulled over, and gazed at the scroll in her hand. The muscles of his biceps bulged as he leaned back and Satsobek's mouth went dry. The space between her legs throbbed and, suddenly light-headed, she was thankful she was already sitting.

Ebrium sat forward abruptly and squinted at the symbols on the papyrus. All of his restless energy seemed to be harnessed for once, focused on the scrolls. Satsobek was struck by a thought. *Was he trying to read?* Was it a sensitive issue for him? Having been punished for entering a temple as a boy and growing up with an educated, wealthy friend like Bey?

Softening her tone, she ran a finger over one of the symbols, a kneeling man with outstretched arms next to a club of sorts. "See here? This represents a servant. But this one," she ran her hand over another image, the same kneeling man but this time paired with the outline of an ax. "This one is a hmww, like Imhotep."

Keeping his eyes on the scrolls, Ebrium shifted and his knee almost touched hers. The very pores of her skin seemed to lean towards him in the hopes of accidentally brushing his knee, or making *any* sort of contact. She was so far gone that the small voice in the back of her head warning her from touching Ebrium was just that - a very small voice.

He lifted his gaze from the scroll up to her face. A lock of wavy black hair had fallen over his forehead and she was once again struck by the contrast of his dark hair, tanned light skin, and shocking blue eyes. He was mesmerizing when he looked at her like that. The air in the room was so still and thick with tension it was like breathing through scorching hot sand. Her will ebbed away, stripping her common sense until she was left in a dream-like state where only she and the frighteningly beautiful man beside her existed. Nothing else mattered.

And then his lips crushed hers. His strong fingers cupped her neck, drawing her to him, and she responded by running her hands over his powerful chest. He tasted like wine and spiced nuts. Delicious and warm. His kiss was demanding, possessive, and raw. She would never have believed two days ago, even yesterday, that a man like him could kiss her with such heat and *pure want*. But there was no denying that he was kissing her with more passion than she'd ever hoped to inspire in a man.

Their kiss deepened as she opened up to him, letting her defences and excuses slip away. His hand slid down her arm to her hip, his fingers kneading the soft flesh of her thigh. She ached to feel more of him, to have the intimacy they'd had last night, to have his fingers on her, in her, and more. Her hand dropped to the curve where the hard shaft of his thigh met his abdomen. Yes, she was afraid of the bulging ridge between his legs, but she very much wanted to overcome that. She just needed a little bit of courage.

A throat cleared in the doorway and Satsobek's heart skipped in her chest. Ebrium tore away from her and she whipped her head around.

There, in the doorway, stood Maketaten, a stricken look on her bird-like face.

"Oh, gods," Satsobek groaned, jumping up. "Maketaten, please, it is not as you think…" But of course it was. The only good thing was that at least the table had hidden their lower halves, and Maketaten wouldn't have seen Ebrium's hand nearing her breast, or the direction her own hand was traveling in.

Maketaten lifted her nose in the air. "While I suspected you had not the fortitude required to devote yourself fully to the goddess I never would have imagined that you would behave with so little respect in her temple. And in the very spot where our dear priestess used to work and worship." Her voice was icy, yet smug.

Satsobek stepped around the desk, reaching out to the angry woman. "Maketaten, please, you don't understand."

"No. You are correct. I don't understand. I don't understand how someone could be so callous, disrespectful, and *deceitful.*" Maketaten hissed the last words and Satsobek felt like she'd been punched in the chest. Maketaten's barely suppressed rage knocked the breath out of her. She'd had no idea the woman was so hateful. Before she could stop her, Maketaten whirled around and stormed out of sight.

Satsobek turned to Ebrium, dazed, her palm pressed to her aching chest. She fought back tears of outrage and shame. He stood and reached out to her, gently drawing her into the protective circle of his arms, tucking her head against his shoulder. Satsobek felt weak. Not just from Maketaten's outburst, but now from Ebrium's tenderness. How very good it felt to be simply held, to have someone to comfort her. She couldn't recall the last time anyone had hugged her. And certainly no one had ever done it like this.

She pushed off his chest. "No," she shook her head. "I cannot."

He tried to pull her back. "Nebet-i, *Satsobek*," he used her name for the first time. "It's ok. Give yourself a minute and we can go catch her. We need to talk to her anyway about what she was doing the night of the murderers. She's just being nasty. Clearly the woman has issues." He reached up and hooked her hair behind her ears, cupping her chin.

"No," she twisted from his grip, taking a step away from him and holding out a hand to ward him off. "She's right. We should never have done this here. We should never have done it at all. And I can't rely on you." He looked pained, as if she had insulted him, and she rushed to explain. "I'm sorry. I didn't mean that I can't trust you…"

He cut her off, "No, of course not. I understand." His eyes had resumed that cold, closed expression again.

"No, really, that is not it –" but he stopped her again and said coolly, "But that's precisely it, isn't it? Because I'm just an unreliable, untrustworthy commoner. Come, take that scroll you found and let's go. There's nothing else for us here." He started towards the door without looking back at her.

Satsobek's anger flared. He had ordered her to "come" as if he expected her to obey. Furthermore, he hadn't even given her a chance to explain. *Must he be so damnably sensitive?*

She hadn't meant that she *could not* rely on him for support, only that she *should not*. If she did, she might get used to it, and then where would she be?

Without thinking, she grabbed the nearest solid thing within reach, a fig from the tray of food, and flung it at his back. The little purple fruit hit him square between the shoulder blades, bouncing off and rolling across the floor.

He turned to face her, nostrils flaring and eyes flashing. He strode towards her, a stormy look on his face. On instinct, Satsobek reached for something else to ward him off. Her groping fingers found another fig. She raised her hand to throw it, but he was quicker and caught her wrist easily, suspending her arm in mid-air. The motion pulled her a step towards him so that their bodies were mere inches apart.

"By Dagon, woman, is it never safe to turn one's back on you?" He growled.

She tried to control her voice. "Not when you have behaved like a jackal's ass."

"I? You are the most difficult, temperamental female I have ever been cursed with knowing."

"Ha! I'm the temperamental one? *You* are more sensitive than any woman *I* have ever known. If you get the merest hint that someone is insulting you, you pounce on them like you want to tear their throat out. I would have expected a great big pirate who spends his days chasing down traitors and thieves to be a little less delicate." She mimicked a large man rocking from side to side with his arms ballooning out around him.

"And I would not have expected anything less from a brat of the nobility."

Her lips parted in a gasp. Silence hung in the air as she stared at him in shock. Silence so loud it almost deafened her ears. That last shot had hurt. The malicious tone of his voice was worse than the words themselves. She ignored the look on his face, one that suggested he was just as stricken by his words as she was.

She shook her hand from his grip, dropping the fig on the table. She rubbed her wrist as she stepped carefully around the table away from him. His hold hadn't been hard, but the burn from his comment seared through her as a physical pain. She collected the scroll, along with her composure.

She avoided his gaze until the last possible moment. Then she steeled herself and spoke in a low voice. "Not everyone is out to hurt you, you know. You are not the only one who has been made to feel bad for who they are, and for things they cannot control. Most people, at some point in their lives, have been hurt. In the long run, though, it is not the injury that matters but how you live with it afterwards. If you let it continue to affect you then it will always be there. It's like a mosquito bite that always itches, and bleeds every time you scratch it. But if you stop scratching and treat the bite, eventually it stops itching, and then it heals." She shrugged. "The more you pick at it, opening it again each time, the more likely it is to leave a scar.

"And unlike some others you are actually lucky." She was warming up to her argument now. Her first few words had been soft, almost sympathetic. But the more she thought about what he'd said, the angrier she became. "You have a mother and a sister who very clearly care for you. You have friends who you can trust. Friends like Bey and Batr and Makae and the queen that will stand by you and respect your decisions. *Some* people, yes not everyone, but *some people* at least, admire your accomplishments. They know who you are."

Her voice became like a running bull, picking up speed and force as she spoke. "And unlike some people *you* have control over your own life. You have traveled the world. *You* get to choose where you will sleep tonight and whether or not you will sleep alone. *You* get to choose whether or not to go to the tavern for dinner. *You* get to choose if you will stay in Kemet or sail away elsewhere. And sooner or later, *you* get to choose who you marry. *You* are not in danger of being sold like a piece of livestock so that your father can continue to buy his concubine jewellery."

She was heaving in breaths now, ignoring the hot tears spilling out on to her cheeks, while she fought a painful lump in her throat. "So please, next time you think to insult me for my birth, remember that I have *never* insulted you for yours," she stabbed her finger towards the ground for emphasis, "and that while I might have grown up wealthy I have *nothing* of my own and no control over anything in my life. So I am sorry, but I don't feel much sympathy for you any longer. In terms of who has the more wretched life, I believe I win.

"These last two days have been the only time in ages that I have been able to do anything of value, or use, for someone else. And even then, I have failed because we have not found the killer yet, have we?" She knew her voice was becoming shrill, and that she should stop, but she couldn't help herself. The words just kept tumbling out of her. "We have failed because I've been too busy thinking about you! I didn't mean I do not consider you trustworthy or dependable, only that it really doesn't matter whether I do or not, does it? Because when this is over I can't ever see you again. So please, let us just finish this all and get on with our lives."

With that, she stormed past him out of the room, leaving him to follow, or not, as he pleased. She no longer cared.

Chapter 13 – Visitors in the Night

Ebrium held on to the edges of the large stone basin and submerged his head under the water. He held his breath for as long as he could, squeezing his eyes shut and swishing his head from side to side. When his lungs began to scream for air he flipped his head up, letting the water spray up and around him before settling to roll down his naked back and chest in cool rivulets.

He was kneeling in front of the basin in the centre of his manor's lavatory, a room with granite-tiled floors and white-washed walls. Scenes of a banquet were painted on one wall and a hunt on the opposite one. A sizable basin for washing hair and clothing stood next to an even larger tub used to immerse one's whole body in. In the far corner was a toilet, a low seat of wooden planks with a hole carved in the middle and a ceramic bowl underneath to be emptied out by servants. It was the first time he had made use of a lavatory of such grandeur, aside from the times he'd been on duty at the queen's palace.

He bathed himself in the dark, a small sliver of moonlight from a narrow window reflecting off the white walls and illuminating the room with a bluish-silver glow. The gloom suited his mood better. Earlier he had used the kitchen behind his new home for the first time. He'd made himself a plain dinner from some barley and lentils he'd found in the little storage space under the flooring of the building and eaten that in the dark as well.

Ebrium hauled in a breath and dunked his head into the water again.

By Dagon, he felt like a bastard. He didn't know what was wrong with him, or why he'd said what he did to Satsobek. When she'd said she couldn't rely on him he'd felt all the injustice of his position, of his frustration and desire for her, and of all the prejudices that had been leveled against him over the years.

It wasn't her fault. All the things she'd said about her situation, he'd been thinking not long before when he'd watched her from the hallway of the temple. And yet when he'd thought she had insulted him, it all slipped away in a haze of anger. He'd followed her out of the temple to try and explain himself, but he'd done a terrible job of it. She'd refused to listen, insisting they let it go and focus on finding the killer instead.

They'd gone to find Maketaten but, like Satsobek, the angry bird-woman didn't want to speak with Ebrium present. He'd been irritated enough to threaten to arrest her, almost causing another scene in the temple. In the end he'd no choice but to leave the women alone in a room. When Satsobek finally emerged some time later, it was obvious from her reddened eyes that she'd been crying. Emphatic, however, that nothing was wrong; she told him Maketaten's visit to the fortune-teller had nothing to do with the murders. He was doubtful, but Satsobek was adamant, telling him that she'd worked things out with Maketaten and was positive the fanatical woman wasn't involved.

They'd finished the day together with a journey back to the homes of the temple servants to find the kitchen boy. Unfortunately, they learned the boy left town two days ago to visit a sick relative in the north, unlikely to return for another week or two. Ebrium escorted Satsobek home in the same awkward silence as he had the night before.

He flipped his head out of the water again, shaking it in disgust and spraying water around the room. *Awkward silence* was not something he was familiar with when it came to women, well-acquainted as he was with all manners of sounds that women made, from chatter and scolding to flirtation and pleasure-filled moaning. But it seemed that silence was a sound all its own, unlike any other. It weighed heavy on him. It buzzed in his ears, pregnant with possibilities and tension. He'd never realized that the absence of sound from a woman could be so disconcerting.

But of all the sounds that a woman could make awkward silence was now his least favorite.

After escorting Satsobek home, he'd gone to the mortuary tomb to view Tiya and Yuny's bodies. He hadn't told her he was going out of concern that she'd want to come, and he didn't think she needed the trauma of viewing their bodies. He wanted to see if there was any indication what had been used to kill Yuny. The man had been beaten. Ebrium wanted to know with what.

The mortuary priests had let him into the dark temple, lit only by narrow windows and oil wicks. In a deep chamber, Tiya and Yuny lay on separate tables, their corpses covered by linen sheets. They'd been washed, and the process of the death rites begun. It would be another day or so before the preparations for mummification began. Tiya's body held no new revelations, except that he saw the marks around her neck where someone's fingers had held her in a tight grip. Tight enough, according to the priests who were attending, to crush her windpipe.

Yuny's body, on the other hand, showed peculiar bruising. Greenish-purple marks over his back, chest, and the side of his face, about the length of a small hand, curving at a sharp angle. To measure the bruises, and to determine what could have made such a mark, he cupped his hand and held it to the bruises. Whatever it was had been narrow, angled, hard, with odd markings along one edge. He had no idea what it could be.

From the mortuary temple, he went to update Merneith and Bey on the investigation, wretched that they were no closer to finding the killer than they'd been yesterday morning. Merneith had chewed on her lip and rubbed her ever-growing belly, but assured him she trusted he was doing his best and would find the man soon. Bey, dear friend that he was, had clapped him on the back and told him to clean himself up, that he looked like he'd been dredged through the underworld and back.

Ebrium plunged his head under the water again. This time, he opened his eyes to peer into the murky depths of the basin. When he finally flipped his head up he listened hard, thinking he'd heard a noise. *There.* A pounding. Someone was pounding on his door in the middle of the night. Alone in the house, he still hadn't hired any servants, not having truly moved in yet.

Ebrium grabbed his shenti off the floor to wrap around his nakedness as he jogged to the front of his house. Few people knew where he was staying tonight, and only one person – one damnably persistent little woman – had a habit of following him. And she had no business whatsoever being out at this time of night. Just in case, though, he snatched his knife from the bench near the door where he'd left it earlier that evening.

When he pulled open the door, his suspicions were confirmed.

On his doorstep stood Satsobek, propping a young man up against his doorframe. Despite all his good intentions, Ebrium couldn't help himself when he thundered, "By the gods, woman, what have you done this time?!"

Earlier that evening Satsobek returned home utterly exhausted. Her emotional outburst in the temple had served to both embarrass her and set her resolve. She'd let herself get too attached to Ebrium. She'd become distracted. Her talk with Maketaten had helped to clarify some of her thoughts and feelings. Unfortunately, it also intensified her feelings of guilt and inadequacy.

Satsobek and Ebrium had caught up with Maketaten in the hallway near the goddess's sanctuary. Maketaten, refusing to speak in Ebrium's "corrupting" presence, agreed finally to talk alone with her. After another round of apologies and useless explanations on her part, she decided that it was time to flip things around to Maketaten, and demanded an explanation for her deception. Maketaten hedged and delayed, trying to avoid telling the truth. But Satsobek finally warned the woman that Ebrium wasn't just blustering when he threated to arrest her. He wouldn't hesitate to haul the woman to the hnrt for questioning.

Normally so composed, Maketaten's hands alternately bunched the fabric of her dress in her lap then smoothed it out over her thighs. "Yes." Her voice was a whisper. "I went to the fortune-teller. I wanted a potion, or a charm, or a spell. Whatever she could offer. I – I was just so tired. I couldn't deal with it anymore."

"Deal with what? Maketaten, you must tell me." Satsobek's breath had stopped in her throat. Had Maketaten finally lost her control and let her anger and fanaticism get the better of her?

Spine still straight as a marble column, Maketaten rocked slightly as she said, "I – I have worked *so hard* and all I wanted was for her to like me. To see me as more of a friend, and an equal."

"Who, Maketaten? Do you mean Tiya?"

She nodded, her thin face twisting with emotion. "I know she thought I was *reliable*, but I always felt she had some small measure of disdain for me. I know how the other girls feel about me. They laugh behind my back sometimes, they think I'm stuck-up, and don't know how to have fun. But I *do*. Or at least I did. Once. Do you remember? We used to be friends. I was not always so awful to be around, was I?"

"I…," Satsobek paused, at a loss for words. She'd never expected to see Maketaten like this. But she *did* remember, and so she said, "No." She took Maketaten's hand. "You were never awful. Only in the last few years you have become… *hard*, and perhaps sometimes a bit judgemental." It was a massive understatement, but Satsobek didn't want the woman to get angry and stop talking.

Maketaten looked down at their clasped hands. "Sometimes I wish I could be the way I used to be. I don't know what happened. I was so hurt when you left the temple. I was jealous, you know. Tiya treated you like a daughter, and everyone knew she was grooming you to be the next high priestess. And even though I wished so much that it could be me and not you…" she gave Satsobek a half-hearted apologetic look. Tears filled her eyes and, given Maketaten's mournful tone, they began to prickle at

Satsobek's lids, too. "I was still happy for you, Satsobek, because I just *knew* that you would be a better high priestess than I. But then you left, and I was so angry. You had the chance I always wanted and you threw it away. And you didn't even tell me why."

Maketaten's free hand clenched around the fabric pooling in her lap, pulling it up into her fist and twisting it. "I got a friendship charm from the fortune-teller because I wanted Tiya to like me. It was just to be a little bit of powder in her drink, to make her look upon me favourably. That was all. But I swear I had nothing to do with her death. I would have never wished it on either of them."

Satsobek nodded. She believed Maketaten, and tightened her grip on her fingers. "Maketaten, I had no idea you felt that way. I'm so sorry you were so hurt when I left the temple. I… I made a mistake with a man and I felt inadequate, that I was no longer deserving of the goddess's favour, or anyone else's. I realized that the life of a celibate priestess was not the right path for me. But I *do* miss the temple terribly, and everyone here. I'm sorry I wasn't a better friend, and that I didn't see what you were going through."

The other woman slid her hand out from Satsobek's. A trace of her lofty airs returned as she lifted her nose and said, "I still do not condone whatever it is you were doing with *that man* in Tiya's room." Her posture softened somewhat – a fraction of an inch, perhaps. "But Tiya's death has pressed me to reconsider some things. I realize that perhaps, *sometimes,* I have been too hard… that things might go better if I were to try not to be so….*critical.* Do you suppose that others have sensed that in me, and stayed away because of it?"

Satsobek smiled at Maketaten's attempt at insight. It was better than nothing. "I do believe it is possible, Maketaten. People have a tendency to avoid those who are negative and judgemental. In the past I did notice that the young priestesses blossomed under you when you encouraged them and complimented them, but pulled away when you chastised them. Too much negativity can bring one's energy low and dampen the spirits, whereas praise can motivate and inspire. And I, for one, have missed the old you. We *did* have some good times together."

Although her back was still rigid, Maketaten's thin lips spread in a faint smile as she swiped a tear from her cheek. "We did. And I hope that, perhaps, we could try to again."

"I would like that."

As she was preparing to leave Maketaten laid a hand on her arm. The woman appeared to wrestle with herself for a moment before she said, "Some of the priestesses have expressed their concern that there will be no female scribe to read and write for them now that Tiya is gone. They've asked about you, and if you intend to return. They've missed you. If you were to come back – not as a celibate priestess, of course, but in another capacity – I for one would be willing to support that decision."

"Thank you, Maketaten." Common civility enabled her to speak through her shock. "That's very generous of you. I have much on my mind at present, but I will certainly give it my full consideration once this situation is over."

This was just one more thing in her life to wrestle with. She'd fled the temple out of guilt and shame and childish emotion, but now she realized staying away might be selfish. If she truly wanted to honour Tiya, shouldn't she make the most of the advantages Tiya had given her and share her abilities with these women? She ought to write down their stories, their letters, their desires, and read them others' in turn. Just as Tiya had trained her to do.

Odd as it was, her truce with Maketaten and the possibility of a return to the temple she missed were positive things born from her awkward situation with Ebrium. For that at least she supposed she should be thankful. But it also served to re-inforce her conviction that she had to check herself around him. Their relationship was too complicated, infuriating, heated, destructive, and all too temporary. It made it impossible for her to think rationally about the other things happening in her life. As soon as they caught the temple killer, and this was all over, she would have to forget him. She'd try to forget that a man had ever made her feel desirable, elated, and furious all at the same time. She would go back to her quiet, isolated life.

Except that there was a good chance she wouldn't be allowed to do that. Sekhemkare, the governor's brother, was already at her father's house when she returned home. Again, her servant Sadeh went through the rushed ritual of bathing her, rubbing oils into her skin, re-applying her makeup, and fixing her hair. Satsobek knew there was no point in trying to argue.

Satsobek sat through another uncomfortable dinner with her family and Sekhemkare. This time the older man showed her more attention, asking her about the investigation and her relationship to the queen, as well as Ebrium and Bey. She tried to avoid his questions about the progress they were making and if they had any suspects. She didn't think it right to share Imhotep and Yuny's secret romance, and she grieved too much for Tiya's memory to disrespect it by her sharing how her husband had humiliated her with another woman.

Twice Sekhemkare indulged in his Sumerian *hul gil* tea, although she saw him for a much shorter period of time this evening. Both times his eyes took on a glazed appearance and he seemed much more relaxed. The effects appeared to wear off after about an hour, after which he appeared more alert, more anxious, and he glanced at her more often.

Although he was much more amiable, attentive, and considerate during their second encounter, she found herself hoping that the pain in his tooth was getting worse. Perhaps it would cause all his teeth to fall out. With any luck, he might be unable to eat at all and would starve to death before she was forced to marry him. She prayed to Mehyt and Ra and Hathor that he would not ask her father for her.

After dinner her father dismissed Satsobek, her sister, and his concubine so that the two men could speak alone. Satsobek was forced to endure an hour or so of gossip from Kiya and Amenia. Satsobek was exhausted from lack of sleep and walking back and forth in the sun all day, but knew that it would less painful to indulge the other women than to try to escape to her room. Since she'd left early that morning they'd had no chance to discuss Sekhemkare's visits with her and were anxious to do so. Clearly they'd already formed their opinions of him.

The women sat inside the main greeting room of the home, sprawled out on reed mats and large cushions on the floor, oil wicks casting flickering shadows across their faces. Kiya sat up, straightening her legs out in front of her and flexing her toes. "You know, a woman could hardly do much better than the brother of the governor of the Aneb-Hetch sephat, Satsi. He is very powerful, and I don't doubt there are many women who have tried to catch him."

Satsobek pursed her lips. "I don't doubt that, either. But then one must wonder why he has not yet married. Why wait until he is in danger of losing his teeth?"

"Pfft." Amenia scoffed. "Really. Most men lose some teeth, as will you one day, *Satsi*. Father has lost a couple, as has my own husband. Do you really think you are better than any of us? That you will find a man with perfect teeth for all his life?"

Satsobek furrowed her brows. "I did not say that. Only one must wonder why he has not married already, if he could choose whomever he wanted."

Kiya shimmied her shoulders, sending her bare breasts swaying. "Mmm, perhaps he was waiting for the right arrangement. Is he not handsome as well? I think he is quite attractive."

Amenia smirked. "Yes. I would not turn him from my bed either. He looks quite… virile, if you ask me."

Satsobek was incredulous, and snorted. "He looks unwell, if you ask me."

Amenia turned sharp eyes on her. "Why?" She sneered. "Because he does not look like the queen's Sumerian? That *low-born foreigner* you have been running all around Thinis with? Please, you know very well father would never let you marry a man like that. And you should know better than to even think it."

Anger welled up in Satsobek's throat. "First off, he is *not* Sumerian, he is Eblaiti. Why does nobody understand the difference? And what do you mean by 'a man like that'? A man who has worked hard to support his family? One who has worked to merit his position, and not simply born in to it? One who is kind to those beneath him, and who supports a woman in power?"

She'd been angry at Ebrium before, but hearing him insulted raised all her protective instincts. She hauled in a furious breath, realizing she had already revealed far too much to her sister and Kiya. She tried to temper the damage, saying, "Besides, I never said anything about him. Why bother to bring him up now?"

Amenia gave her a satisfied grin, a malicious gleam in her eye. "Because if you were not thinking of him you would see that Sekhemkare is better than any other man you could possibly get. And if he offers for you, you had better be pleased about it because it is unlikely anyone else ever will. As I recall, even your precious *Sumerian* didn't respond to you after you sent him that secret message behind our father's back. He must not be very happy to be paired with you now."

Satsobek rose. Her hands were shaking she was so angry. She regretted ever telling her sister about the messenger situation. She'd been upset after it happened and needed someone to talk to. Amenia had seen her distress and coaxed the story out of her. Now, she wondered again if Amenia had been involved in the mix-up somehow.

She threw out her next words in her wrath. "You know, sister, if I didn't know any better, I would think that you're jealous. Because I don't recall that there were men lining up outside the door when father decided it was time to marry you off. But then, perhaps if you had made yourself – what was it you said to me yesterday morning? Ah yes – *a little more agreeable*, you wouldn't have had to marry a toothless old man who prefers sleeping with his slaves over you."

With that parting shot Satsobek spun around and left the room.

She made her way back to her bedroom, pressing the palm of her hand to her mouth, feeling awful about what she'd said to Amenia. She knew better than to let her sister rile her like that, but the things she'd said about Ebrium were intolerable. Yes he was difficult, arrogant, mulish, and sensitive, but he was admirable in so many ways. She hated him. But perhaps she was also falling in love with him - maybe just a little bit. Perhaps she had been half in love with him for the last eight months, but the real man was so much more than the fantasy she'd created.

She slammed her bedroom door behind her and flung herself onto her bed. So far today she'd argued with Maketaten, Ebrium, *and* her sister. Each time she'd felt worse and worse about herself. She blamed herself as much as she blamed everyone else – she had to learn to control her temper or else she would have no one left in her life. On the other hand, she wished that the people she *did* have in her life were not always so provoking. She let loose her frustration in a flood of tears that was at once throat-tearing, painful, and cathartic. Eventually, she exhausted herself and fell asleep.

Sometime much later, in the middle of the night, she was awoken by a soft call near her window.

"Nebet-i? Are you awake?" There was a pause and then again, "Nebet-i? Please, are you there?"

In her sleep-addled state her first thought was that the temple killer had followed her home. She sat straight up, terrified, unable to see anything past the white linen sheets draped around her bed to keep out the bugs. Fear cleared her head, though, and she realized that a killer was unlikely to address her politely from her courtyard.

She pushed aside the curtains and moved to the window, peering out into the night. "By the gods! Seret!" Her voice was low, but forceful as she chastised the boy who Tiya had taken into the temple as an infant. "Next time you wake a woman in the night, or sneak up on them on an empty street, you really ought to identify yourself, lest you cause the poor woman's heart to stop. Or she hits you. What in the name of Ra are you doing here? What's happened?" Panic gripped her. "Did something happen to Ebrium?"

"No, lady. I'm sorry to frighten you. I've come to say goodbye. I'm leaving Thinis." As her eyes adjusted to the darkness, she realized he seemed to be standing awkwardly, as if in pain.

"Seret, what happened? Never mind, wait just a moment; I'll come out to you. Stay there and be quiet."

Satsobek was not unfamiliar with sneaking out of her house. She had done so on several occasions last year to meet Inkaef. She knew how to get around the servants' quarters and her father's rooms. Within a few minutes she was standing outside in the silvery moonlight with Seret. When he told her why he was leaving, she knew she couldn't let him go. He was in no shape to travel anywhere, and there was only one place she could think to take him.

"Ebrium, please, help..." but she was too late. With Seret propped against the doorframe of Ebrium's house while she pounded on the door, she'd been trying to hold him steady with only one arm around his waist. Seret was too weak to stand on his own after the short walk over, and slid down the doorframe, pulling Satsobek off-balance. Ebrium dropped his knife and grabbed for Seret. As he did so, the shenti Ebrium had tied in haste slid low on hips, revealing a trail of dark curls on his lower abdomen.

The thin young man was lifted easily into Ebrium's arms. "What happened?" Ebrium's voice was gruff.

Her anxiety for Seret made it easier to ignore Ebrium's near nakedness. Servants, both male and female, often worked without even a shenti on. She had seen it countless times before. She just hadn't seen *Ebrium* naked. And she suspected that Ebrium naked in the pale moonlight would be a powerful, frightening, glorious thing.

He was also wet. Water dripped from his black hair onto his chest, rolling over the curves of his muscled body. Suddenly aware of the dampness that had formed between her breasts from half-dragging Seret through the neighbourhood, she shifted and cleared her throat.

"Ahmes." Her voice was a whisper. The shock of seeing the blood seeping through the back of Seret's white robe, a dark stain in the moonlight, still weighed on her chest. "Ahmes whipped him. He discovered it was Seret that told us about his meeting with Haerk at the House of Iput. Seret wanted to run away. I – I couldn't let him go like that. I thought you could help him. That you might know what to do."

Ebrium gave an angry, animalistic growl and then strode through the house with Seret in his arms. Half an hour later, Seret was laid out on his belly on a bed in one of the extra rooms, his wounds washed and wrapped. They left him alone to sleep and moved through the house to the entranceway. Ebrium brought Satsobek a mug of wine while she seated herself on a bench near a window. She held onto the mug, shaking her head. People were whipped. That was nothing new. It happened to almost every slave and servant over the course of their servitude. Ebrium had scars on his back, too. But Seret's wounds were extreme. Ahmes must have taken out all his aggression on the poor boy.

She turned to look at Ebrium, his profile dark as the moonlight streamed in the window behind him. He had been so good with Seret. He'd talked to the boy while he bathed the lashes on his back, telling stories of times when he had been whipped. But he'd actually made light of them, trying to make Seret laugh. He told them about the time he punched a nobleman's son in the street. Ebrium was carrying a sack of manure from a nearby farmer's over to the palace garden, helping his father. He'd been young then, still small, and the sack was too heavy for him. It hung over his shoulder, and as it began to slip he lost his balance and fell. The sack opened, spilling manure onto the street - and over the bare feet - of this boy who happened to be standing nearby with his friends.

The boy taunted Ebrium, calling him a stupid slave. So Ebrium knocked the boy down, thereby breaking his nose. He'd refused to apologize and – in the retelling – joked about how the boy had cried like a girl and run to his father. Ebrium was whipped for his insubordination. Yet he made Seret laugh by saying that the pain of the whipping was temporary, but that his punch had permanently damaged the other boy's nose. The nose healed crooked, and was perpetually running. For years afterwards people called him "snot-nose" behind his back. Few other boys tried to cross Ebrium after that.

Satsobek didn't think the story was particularly funny and the moral was dubious at best, but it seemed to make Seret feel better. Considering how bitter Ebrium had been last night when he'd related how he was kicked out of the temple as a boy, it must have taken a great effort on his part to joke about his past for Seret's sake.

She told him just that when he sat down next to her. He brushed off her comments, but she was insistent. "It meant so much to him that you tried to make him laugh, I could see that. It is very good of you to help him. It means a lot to him. And it means a lot to me. It was difficult for him growing up, not knowing who his parents were. He's not a slave, he's a free servant, but he hasn't always been treated well by others." She took a deep breath and then blurted out, "I'm sorry for my outburst in the temple. I shouldn't have said the things I did. It was wrong of me."

He gave a soft snort and raked a hand through his thick hair. He gazed out the window. "No, nebet-i. It was I who was in the wrong. I should never have insulted you." He turned to look at her, his gaze searching her face. "You've been very brave throughout this. I suspect you've had your own battles to face." He chuckled. "And if the way you fight off a group of men is any indication of the way you've faced your past, I'd say that you handle yourself admirably."

Everything about this situation was wrong. Her being in his vast manor in the middle of the night, alone, drinking wine, the beautiful soft moonlight streaming in the window. It was all too perfect and wrong in so many ways. She was so painfully aware of his nearness, the fine hairs on her arm rose in anticipation of the merest hint of a touch from him.

"Ebrium," she paused to lick her lips. "About that kiss…"

Ebrium held up a hand to stop her. "I should never have kissed you in the hwt today." He studied Satsobek's shadowy face. He hadn't lit any oil wicks since she'd arrived, not even being sure where his mother and sister had placed them. Her pupils were huge in the darkness, and she was angled towards him in such a way that emphasized her petite curves. He wanted to reach out and seize the rounded arch of her hip. To rip her dress off, lay her out on the bench, grip her thighs around his ears, and make her beg for forgiveness for every sin she'd ever committed, and then commit a few more.

She'd risked her reputation by sneaking out to come to his home of all places, all for the sake of helping an orphaned servant. And that act spoke volumes more than any collection of papyri ever could about the nature of her heart. She was obstinate and temperamental, but those same qualities also made her brave, loyal, smart, and incredibly sexy.

His voice was husky when he spoke. "I won't lie, though. You drive me mad and you're impossible most of the time, but gods help me I do want you. So you must stop looking at me like that with those damnable eyes of yours or I'll have no choice but to utterly ruin you here on this bench."

Her eyes registered surprise, followed by a glow of pleasure. "Ebrium," she bit down on her bottom lip and he fixated on her mouth, and those sweet red lips. He wondered what it would be like to have them wrapped around his shaft. He wouldn't last long, he knew it.

"Ebrium, you would not be…erm…ruining me."

He blinked. "Pardon?"

She blew out a deep breath. Her hands twisted in her lap. "I am not exactly *untouched*. It's why I left the temple."

He held his breath, fists clenched. Gods if someone had touched her against her will he'd kill them. He'd tear all their limbs from their body and send the bits on a trip around the world, dooming them to an afterlife of ceaseless searching. Just like Seth did to his brother Osiris.

She continued. "About a year and a half ago, I was at a banquet at a neighbouring home and met a man named Inkaef, the son of a nobleman, recently returned from several years in the north." She went on to tell him that Inkaef had paid her more attention than any man ever before. He'd complimented her and taken the time to speak with her, asking her questions about herself. His attentions continued, they saw one another often at court, and she thought she'd fallen in love. He asked her to meet him secretly so they could spend more time together. She snuck out of her house at night and eventually, he convinced her to make love to him. He'd said that he was planning to take a wife, and that he wanted her to be his.

Ebrium made a choked noise in his throat at the thought of a man manipulating an innocent in such a way. Certainly he'd charmed more than his share of women, but none of them had been unwilling, and none were inexperienced. The lowest sort of men conned innocent women into bed with broken promises of marriage and love.

Satsobek shrugged. "Of course I should have known better. I think in some way I *did* know. But I *wanted* it to be true, so I believed him. Later, I realized that I wasn't really in love with Inkaef. It was just so nice to feel desirable, I confused the emotions. I wanted to *be* wanted. But regardless, I didn't feel that I could continue at the temple after what happened. I was supposed to abstain from relations with men. I could have become a regular priestess, but it didn't feel right any longer. And then, after a couple of months, he told me his father had found him a wife. The fourteen year-old daughter of a governor in the north. Unlike me, he said, she was quiet and acquiesced to his opinions. She had none of her own, after all. He said she was not so *shameless* in her behaviour." She looked up at him, nibbling on her full lip again in that way that made his shaft stiffen.

Ebrium's voice with thick as he said, "That man's a fool then. I quite like you when you're shameless." He let his eyes trail over her, roaming down to the soft curves of her breasts. "In fact, I'd like to see you that way more often. Preferably with less clothing on."

Her breath caught before she rushed on. "I'm telling you so that you do not blame yourself for last night, or today. I might have been naïve once, but I am not so innocent any longer. Marriage does not always follow desire, nor does desire follow marriage. Sometimes it *cannot*. But that does not mean that one's yearnings can't be gratified."

Although Ebrium's grasp of the Kemeti language was not always perfect, a man would have to be thicker than stone not to recognize her implications. Especially when coupled with the invitation her upturned face presented. Her moist red lips were parted, and there was an artless, naked question in her eyes, as if she were afraid he might reject her now that he knew her history.

Ebrium was not thicker than stone, and he was in no position to judge.

He gripped her slender hips with his large, rough hands, sliding her across the bench and up onto his lap. Her rump ground up against his hardness and she gasped in surprise even as he crushed his mouth against hers. Her whole body leaned into him, deepening the kiss with her urgency. Delicate fingers ran over his shoulders and threaded into the thick hair at the nape of his neck, tugging on his locks and urging him on. His wide hands circled her waist, almost enclosing it, seizing her tightly before making their way up her sides to cup the outer curves of her breasts.

Satsobek moaned and arched towards him, offering up her soft mounds to his touch. He grazed her hard brown nubs with his thumbs and raw need raged through him when she gasped in response. He wanted her under him, *needed* her under him. Knowing that she was not a virgin, that he wouldn't be the one to take her innocence, was a relief. She still might not be up to the task of slaking his desires, but he wouldn't have to be quite as careful.

And then she surprised him.

She slipped off the bench, down onto her knees between his legs, and placed her hands on his thick, corded thighs. Her eyes, dark liquid pools churning with apprehension and determination, peered up at him. With agonizing slowness, she slid her small, soft hands up his taut muscles, gliding his shenti up along with them, keeping her eyes locked on his. Every nerve in his body froze. Was she really about to do what he thought? His breath choked in his throat and he feared his rigid shaft might explode from anticipation alone.

He dropped a hand to her shoulder, clutching her and pushing her back at the same time, preparing for a phenomenal effort of self-control. "Satsobek, you don't have to…" But at that moment her tentative fingers brushed the base of his cock, and his head dropped back to bang against the wall behind him. A curse escaped him, but no more words of protest made their way to his lips.

Nervousness gave way to curiosity, followed by amazement, as she caressed the soft skin of Ebrium's shaft. Smooth and delicate, it reminded her of the petals of an iris flower. A remarkable contrast given how thick, hot, and hard he was beneath the fine layer of skin. It was something exquisite to behold. Powerful and almost graceful, yet sheathed in a fragile casing. The very opposite of Ebrium himself.

She wrapped a hand around it, testing the weight and firmness of him. He groaned and she pulled away, afraid she'd hurt him. He opened his eyes but didn't take his head from the wall. Instead, he reached down and took her hand in his, placing it back over his length, guiding her to help her gauge pressure and motion. Soon he let her develop her own rhythm, and he curled his fingers back over her shoulder.

His jaw was slack, eyes half-closed and made lazy with pleasure. He looked provocative, yet vulnerable. Although his breath was ragged, his usual predatory restlessness was subdued; the tension his body held now was different. Not the stillness of a stalking hunter, or a man with an overactive mind. It was the muscle tautness experienced before the rush of relief. It gave her a sense of power, and tenderness, to know that she had brought that on him.

He was so beautiful leaning back against the wall, illuminated by nothing but the soft bluish-silver light of the night sky. His drowsy eyes were watching her as if she were the most fascinating, desirable thing he'd ever seen. She wanted that to be true far more than she was willing to admit.

When she took him into her mouth Ebrium couldn't suppress a growl. The sensations were so strong it was agonizing. The torment of her breath on his shaft, her tongue twirling over his sensitive head, her hand around him, it was almost too much. Watching her watch him as she wrapped her soft, plump lips around his unyielding maleness was the most sensual thing he'd ever seen.

Satsobek was not the most skilled woman he'd ever had. He was fairly certain she'd never done this before. Despite that, the sensations were more powerful than anything he'd experienced with another woman. Knowing that she wanted this as much as he did – and he wanted her more than he'd ever wanted a woman – was a potent aphrodisiac. This was more intimate – *they* were more intimate – than any other coupling he'd known.

His grip tightened on her shoulder. He forced the words out in panting rasps. "Satsobek. If you don't... Stop... I can't... Control it... Soon..." But her mischievous black eyes just glinted as she slid her warm, moist mouth further over him. He swore again as he grabbed the edge of the bench with his free hand to keep from wrenching her arm out of its socket.

The pressure mounted inside him to an unbearably pleasurable torment. He tried to push her back, but the wicked woman refused to release her hold and only gave him a sweet smile around his shaft. The tension twisted in his gut until he had no choice but to let go and let her have her way with him.

Satsobek was quite pleased with herself as she watched Ebrium's eyelids flutter, his head thumping against the wall again. Waves shuddered through his body and he clung to her shoulder as if hanging on for his life, but she didn't mind the crushing grip, relishing that she could do this to him. A guttural curse escaped him and, when he was finished, she crept up onto the bench next to him. His head lolled over to look at her even as he raised a heavy arm to wrap around her shoulders and draw her against him.

She curled up along his side. The space between her thighs was throbbing and moist. Her body craved release, but she was quite happy to bask in this moment, knowing that she gave him the same pleasure he'd given her last night. She felt powerful, reckless, and something else. *Liberated.* As if all the things she'd feared about being with a man again disappeared. As if she could become anyone she wanted to be. She could even just be herself.

He chuckled at her smug smile. "You look just like a little miu, like a little cat that's just stolen itself a water fowl from the kitchen."

"And you look like a giant one that's about to take a long nap."

"A nap? By the gods, no. There will be no napping here. Just give me a minute or two until I can use my legs again and then you'll see. For once your smart little mouth has disabled me, woman." He gave her a lazy grin. "If you want to throw something at me again now is your chance."

"Truly? Is that all it takes to weaken a man? I will remember that in the future if I should come across another one as difficult as you."

"By Dagon you will not." He growled. Even in his relaxed state his body stiffened.

Was it possible he was jealous? She shivered at the thought, and heat rushed through her, tightening her core and making her shift closer against him. Her breasts mashed against his chest, her nipples so hard they hurt. Her body yearned to feel all of him against all of her. He must have sensed it, for all at once he scooped her up and tossed her over his shoulder like a sack of barley.

She pushed herself off his back, trying to twist around to see the back of his head. His jaw was tight, and her heart sped up. "Where are you taking me?"

"Someplace where there will be no napping."

A minute later, Ebrium cast Satsobek lightly onto his bed. She bounced once, laughing at his fierceness. He'd lain in the bed for the first time the night before, and he was as yet unaccustomed to such a luxurious piece of furniture – one far larger and softer than any bed he'd ever shared with a woman. A thick, rag-stuffed mattress, set on a carved wooden bedframe, and covered in soft white linen sheets. It even had a stuffed pillow on which to lay one's head. A far cry from the narrow, itchy, reed-stuffed mats belonging to the taverns and fishmonger's daughters he was accustomed to spending the nights with.

The contrast of Satsobek's cinnamon-coloured skin and onyx-black hair on this big white bed, *his* bed, was one of the most beautiful things he'd ever seen. Like she belonged there. *What might it be like to see such a sight every night? To wake each morning beside a woman who roused every passion within, both good and bad.*

She rolled on to her side and reached out for his shenti. Her deft hands made quick work of the ties, letting the fabric flutter to pool at the floor around his feet. He stood naked before her, his manhood jutting out in front of him. It had taken all of five minutes for him to be ready for her again.

He knew what she wanted, but he had to be sure before he went any further. "Satsobek, you know I can't promise you anything after this night."

Her mouth quirked up. "And I have nothing to offer you."

It was an exchange he'd had with dozens of women before without a twinge of his conscience. For some reason with Satsobek it didn't feel right. She wasn't like the other women he'd known. Could there be some way to change things, if one were truly so inclined?

But once again, she erased his thoughts. This time by shimmying her dress up over her head, leaving her skin bare in the pale moonlight. His breath caught at the inviting sight of her stretched out on his bed. He took his time drinking it in, her delicate feet with their toes arched into the bed, pushing her knees up and together in modesty, the soft curls of her sex, the curve of her hips into her flat belly, leading up to her gently mounding breasts. Her eyes were pools of shimmering darkness, nervous but resolute.

She reached out and took his large hand in her small one, drawing him down next to her. He kept his eyes on hers as she ran her fingers over his collarbones, skimming over his sturdy shoulders, then up over the strong column of his neck and into the hair at the back of his head.

He caught her wrist and trapped it above her head. Moving over her, he nuzzled her, inhaling the sweet fragrance of her hair, her graceful neck, the space between her breasts. Her back bowed beneath him, her body seeking his mouth. He trailed his lips over the soft skin of her slight shoulders, moving down to hover at the tops of her breasts. He flicked his eyes up to her face when she whimpered, squirming beneath him with her eyes closed, her teeth pressed into her lower lip. The nails of her one free hand were digging in to his shoulder as she tried to push him towards the hardened, copper-coloured tips of her nipples. He paused, relishing the moment and curious to see what she would do.

Satsobek's eyes snapped open in frustration, looking down at Ebrium's upturned face. A languid smirk lifted the corners of his lips.

"What is it?" Her voice sounded like a protest in her ears.

"I was just thinking of what I warned you about yesterday."

Impatience crept in as she rubbed her thighs together to give herself some relief from the aching heat pooling between them. "The details fail to come to mind. Perhaps you could remind me some other time?" She ground out, thinking he must be far crueller than she'd ever given him credit for to stop to chat at a time like this.

"I warned you that you might find yourself trying to crawl in to my bed. I believe this is proof that I was right."

She scoffed and tried to wiggle from his grip. "Congratulations. You win." He grinned and she hated that his cocky, dimpled smile had the ability to set her skin on fire. "If that's what this has been about then please let me go and I promise that you will never have the satisfaction of saying I tried to make my way into your bed again." She smacked his shoulder with her free hand, the other still trapped over her head.

He chuckled, his breath a soft caress over her breasts. "No, that's never what this has been about. But I won't lie and say I haven't thought about having you under me like this." He placed a kiss in the space between her breasts. "I've also thought about having you up against the wall," he punctuated each of his sentences with kisses around her nipple, never quite touching it. "Laid out on a table." "Bent over a couch." "In the bathtub, with you on top of me."

Satsobek went from hating him to hating herself when her body lifted up towards him of its own volition with each kiss. He was still smiling as his lips wrapped around one of her hardened peaks, the moist heat of his mouth sending a spike of pleasure through her whole body, causing her to cry out.

In the span of a few seconds her hand shifted from pushing at him to nearly ripping his hair out. He suckled at first one, then the other breast, working her rigid peaks until she was mindless with desperate need. He moved between her parted knees and began rubbing the hot, thick ridge of his erection against the slippery centre of her desire. Her hips moved against him in rhythm, extending up to meet his agonizingly slow cadence.

His lips were against the shell of her ear now. "Do you still want to leave?" His husky voice cut through her haze of pleasure.

"Mmmm?" She didn't know what he was talking about, his words not making sense to her pleasure-drunk brain.

"I asked if you'd still like to leave. A minute ago you told me to let you go." He was still whispering in her ear, his words a direct contrast to the wicked effect the tone of his voice was having on her molten core.

She swore, causing him to laugh softly against her neck. "You know," she twisted to glare at him, "I like you much better when you are silent."

She could *hear* that insufferable, sexy smile in his voice as he nuzzled her ear and murmured, "And I like you much better when you are shameless, swearing, and crying out."

In that instant she shifted and, unintentionally, the slick warmth of her depths lined up with the head of his shaft. He reared up, holding perfectly still, blinking down at her. All trace of his teasing was replaced by tension. She could feel it in his taut arms, and see it in the clench of his jaw, the flare of his nostrils. He was waiting to see what she would do.

He'd let go of her wrist, his fists now depressing the mattress on either side of her chest. Her tongue darted out to moisten her lips as she ran her hands up his powerful biceps. She gave a wry smile, looking over this beautiful man that drove her so mad. Then she began to move.

Satsobek raised her hips to meet him, nudging him with the liquid warmth of her sex, and Ebrium nearly lost control right then. He resisted the urge to grab her hips and drive into her with reckless abandon. Instead, he lowered himself and kissed her, letting the tip of his manhood nestle against her.

Despite his banter, he wanted this to be special. *She* was special. The fiery little woman could take his teasing and throw it back at him. He'd never had this much fun with a woman in bed before, and her reactions to his touch satisfied every ounce of his male pride. They'd shared one another's confidences, and although they'd only known each other a short time, he'd trusted her with more knowledge about himself than he'd shared with men he'd battled alongside for years. He wanted this to be exceptional for her.

And so he changed the tone of their play by kissing her slow, soft, and sensuous. He took the time to taste her lips, to stoke the fires of their passions to the highest possible peak. When she was writhing beneath him, pushing her hot core against him, he deepened the kiss, taking her mouth and claiming it with his. And then he pressed forward.

Satsobek gasped as Ebrium entered her. He moved at a gentle pace, letting her adjust to the thickness of him filling her before moving deeper. She clung to his massive back, panting against him. Although there was a small measure of pain - he was large and she was out of practice - he felt so strong, so powerful, and so *right* that she thought she could be satisfied with just this, this half-measure of him. She wanted more, of course, but if there was nothing else the moment he penetrated her depths was pure ecstasy and she could live with just that feeling alone.

When she was ready, she raised her pelvis to take more of him, and he took her meaning. Soon she was completely full with a feeling more profound than anything she'd ever known. As if by entering her Ebrium had brought some revelation with him, some absolute truth of which the particulars mattered not.

When Ebrium drew back Satsobek wrapped her calves around his thighs, pinning herself to him. She ran her hands over his sculpted hips and rear, reveling in the feel of the potent muscles bunching and pistoning beneath her palms as he thrust forward into her over and over again. She was hardly aware of what she was doing as she kissed his shoulders, neck, jaw, and lips.

Her body thrummed with sensations. The manly smell of his clean skin, the feel of him buried deep inside her, the ragged sound of his breath, the taste of him, it all enveloped her. It was when he lifted his face to hers, though, that the pleasure tightened within her, drawing to a point. He was looking at her with something like tender reverence. It was such an honest expression that, although he didn't say a word, she believed that he truly felt something for her.

That belief was enough to send her over the edge of pleasure. She cried out as the tension building within her body suddenly rose up in a crescendo and crashed over her. Waves of bliss ripped through her, shaking her body and vibrating her limbs, leaving her dazed and weakened.

Sensing she had reached her zenith, Ebrium sped up, his thrusts deeper and more forceful. When she regained her wit, she urged him on with her gasps and utterings. Sweat sprung to the surface of their skin as they strained against one another. His breath rasped against her neck and she entwined her hands into his now-damp hair. Another climax rocked her body at the same moment he uttered a hoarse cry and pulled from her, spilling wet warmth onto the sheet between her thighs. She hung onto him until the last shivers wracked their bodies and he collapsed over her, moving his big body to the side so as not to crush her.

As she rolled on to her side to face him he reached out to tuck a lock of her hair behind her ear, eliciting a smile from her at the familiar gesture. Catching his hand, she placed her lips against his palm. Noting the way his pupils widened as she licked his skin, she continued roaming her mouth over his large, calloused hand. She took his index finger into her mouth, licking the length of it before sucking it past her lips. Heat flared again in her pelvis, and she knew that she wanted even more of him.

The lines around his eyes crinkled. "By the gods woman, you are insatiable. If I had met you ten years ago you would be in serious trouble. But I am not the puppy I used to be."

"Mmmm," she smiled around his finger, nipping it. "I can still try, though, can't I?"

Ebrium pushed himself up on one elbow to watch her. Even if the entire Sumerian army burst through his door at that moment, he would have been unable to take his eyes off her plump mouth, bruised a deep red from their rough kissing, as she moved it over his finger. She was mesmerizing in her seduction. No, she was definitely not as innocent as he'd thought. She might, in fact, be completely nefarious. "You're not even going to give my heart time to return to its regular measure, are you?"

She shook her head slowly, keeping her lips wrapped around his finger and her wide, wicked eyes locked on his.

"Well then, nebet-i, I wish for nothing more than your success."

This time it took him all of fifteen minutes to be ready for her. There was no way he could help himself – not that he wanted to – when she rolled on top of him and began exploring his body with her delicate fingers and her sweet mouth. When she ground her pelvis against him he dug his fingers into her soft hips and, positioning her over him, drove up into her. His hands roved her body as she rocked against him.

Having spent himself twice already, and the initial urgency of their lovemaking sated, he was able to take his time now. He measured his thrusts, holding her in place to check her urgent pitching in order to torment her and prolong the pleasure, sucking the tight, dusky peaks of her breasts, and holding her close to him, basking in the feeling of her naked body against his, in his arms, and the sound of her soft moans in his ear.

If he didn't know better, he might think he was falling in love.

A while later, she knew not when, Satsobek lay curled in the crook of Ebrium's arm, trying not to doze. Sooner or later she'd have to make her way home, sometime before dawn. However, getting up seemed an impossible task, as she was so thoroughly spent and so perfectly content. Idly, she tested her strength by reaching out to trace the tattoo over Ebrium's chest.

He looked down at her hand and he gave a self-effacing snort. "Bey and I got them when we were younger. They're supposed to help your family identify your spirit, as you say here, your *ka*, in the afterlife."

"You had them done in Ebla?"

"No. It's not common in our homeland. This was done by a sailor from the very far north. In their belief system you might be lucky enough to find your family and friends in the afterlife. It's a more hopeful idea than that of my homeland, where we eat dust for eternity, or yours, where a man like me might just disappear, or have my heart eaten out by Ammit."

"When did you leave home? Bey was a prince, how did you both turn to pirating?"

"With all your investigative efforts to find me out, you haven't heard this already?"

She glared at him though there was a smile playing on her lips, and he capitulated. "Since my sister came to Thinis she's told more than a few people." His smile was indulgent and exasperated. "I believe she thinks she's garnering sympathy for us, when we'd both just prefer to let it lie."

"Please, if you don't mind. I'd like to hear it from you."

Ebrium sighed. It was not a story that he himself had ever told. He tried to relate it as quickly as possible rather than dwell on old memories. "As I told you yesterday, my father was a gardener in the royal house. Bey and I grew up friends, being of the same age in the same household. His family never forbade us and he was never condescending about his position. When we were around fifteen or so Bey's father, the King of Ebla, died. Bey's older brother tried to seize power. In Ebla the title isn't hereditary. Rulers are voted in by the local nobles. So Bey's brother's attempt to steal the throne went against all precedent. Of course the nobles ousted him from power, and he ended up spending all the family's wealth on gambling, whores, and drink. He lost the family home. Bey was in school, but his brother refused to pay any longer, so he had to quit and find work to support himself and his mother."

Ebrium gave a casual shrug, pressing down the bitterness that rose in his throat. "My father died around the same time. My family and I had no choice but to leave Bey's home, the home I grew up in. Bey and I both tried to work around town for a time, but people didn't trust Bey because of his brother and his background. They didn't think he'd work hard, or be reliable. They assumed he'd think the work beneath him. Because he and I were close I was also shunned. My own mother tried to work but it was difficult. You see my sister was still very young and in need of care. It's amazing how people will turn on you when you no longer have something they want, particularly those of the noble class." He held up a hand, palm up, to cut off any protest. "No offense, little miu, but in my experience those with the most to give are generally the least willing to share it when one of their own is in need."

"I can understand why you might feel that way." Her fingers played over his chest in small, idle circles, and he decided she was lucky he'd utterly spent himself, or else he'd flip her over and take her again, and she'd never hear the rest of this story. It wasn't one he liked to dwell on.

He dropped his head back on the pillow, focusing on the ceiling, and said, "Then Bey's mother fell ill. Neither of us could afford to pay for a healer. We sought work outside our town, but she passed away before we could make enough to help her. After that we decided to leave Ebla and go elsewhere, some place we were unknown. So we took to the seas. Eventually, we were able to command our own ship, and then a few more. We sent whatever we could home to my mother and sister."

Satsobek rested her hand near his heart, and he could feel his own pulse mingling with hers. "Why did you choose pirating?"

He snorted. "We didn't exactly *choose* it. We happened to get work on a ship that we later discovered was manned by brigands. We made a good profit and no one was hurt." He shook his head. "You don't understand. Half the time when we sent goods to my mother she didn't receive them. Sometimes the messengers stole from us. Sometimes they were killed, or robbed themselves. Sometimes they just disappeared. The distances they had to travel were great, and could take weeks or months to cross.

"I lived in fear for over a decade that my mother or my sister might die like Bey's mother had, and I wouldn't know for months, if at all. Or that I'd die and they'd be destitute. It wasn't until we settled here in Kemet that I was able to send for them. I hadn't seen them since my sister Akshaka was a babe. Now she's almost ready for marriage. Thanks to Bey's brother and the *great benevolence* of the nobility, I missed over ten years with my family." He shook his head, the old anger tensing his limbs.

Satsobek fought back the tears prickling her eyes. No wonder he was bitter about the way some people spoke to him. But she didn't want to focus on the sadness in his story; she wanted him to be happy. A man so incredibly kind and strong and brave deserved admiration. Her voice was only a little wistful as she said, "But you're all here together now, and they're lucky to have you to care for them. Bey is lucky to have a friend as loyal as you. Not many would stand by someone if it caused them such strife."

He placed a finger under her chin and tilted her head up to look her full in the face, his eyes serious and probing. "Bey is my family just as much as my mother and sister are. He stood by me when other boys would make fun of him for having a servant like me as a friend. My family has grown here. Merneith and their baby are a part of it now. A man should love his family enough to do anything to protect them, even if that means he has to protect them from himself. He should never leave them or risk their harm without good cause. That is why I *will* find this killer and protect my family."

Satsobek ducked her head, afraid he would see the tears welling in her eyes. His words made her think of how her father had sent her away to live in the palace after she was born, and how little concern he had for her well-being. She didn't want thoughts of him – or Sekhemkare – to ruin her few stolen moments of happiness.

Ebrium stroked Satsobek's arm, taking comfort in the presence of her warm, soft body nestled against him. He wanted to ask her if there weren't some way to make this night happen again. Her father might not like him, but Ebrium was no longer just the poor son of a gardener. While not of noble birth, he was now closer to the queen than most other men in Kemet. It could be so easy. She could stay tonight and send for her things in the morning. After all, if she moved in with him they'd be as good as married. That was all the peasants did. No ceremony necessary, just the consent of their parents. In their case, because there was wealth involved, all that would be left was to have a marriage contract drawn up with her father.

For a few moments, he forgot that he'd never envisioned himself as a married man. He was on the verge of formulating his question when a noise froze the words in his throat.

Satsobek heard the sound at the same time and they both sat up together.

Someone was banging on his door, and the one person he'd expect it to be was already in bed next to him.

Chapter 14 – More Papyri

Of all the people Ebrium imagined might arrive at his house in the early hours of the morning, the lover of the high priest of the Temple of Mehyt was last on his list of possibilities.

In fact, Imhotep the carpenter wouldn't even make it on the list if Ebrium had had the time to think of it. Which he hadn't. He tumbled out of bed, ordering Satsobek to get dressed and stay hidden in his bedroom while wrapping his shenti around his waist and grabbing his curved blade. But he slipped the knife into his belt when he saw Imhotep standing alone on his doorstep.

"By the gods, man, what in the name of Ra are you doing here? I thought you'd left town?" Imhotep held several beige papyrus scrolls, nervously passing them between his hands. Behind the carpenter, the front lot of the manor was cast in deep shadow thanks to the date palms that lined the courtyard. Beyond that the skyline on the eastern horizon had gone from midnight blue to a lighter shade of azurite. Ebrium had to get Satsobek home soon, before the sun came up, before she was missed.

"May I come in? I have something to show you." Imhotep's fine features were emphasized by the thin light and Ebrium sensed his urgency.

He opened the door wider to let the man in and closed it behind him. It was then that Satsobek came padding across the floor from his bedroom, and his jaw tightened, ready to chastise her. Although dressed, she was barefoot, and had the look of a woman who had been thoroughly ravished. Hair mussed and well-kissed lips riper than sweet, deep red plums, coupled with the unhurried air of a languid feline.

Ebrium suddenly wished Imhotep and this whole business of the temple murders to the bottom of the great river so that he could scoop the little woman up and prove to them both that he had the energy for another round in his bed. While he didn't have much fear that Imhotep would divulge their secret – after all, they held one of his – he was seized with an irrational fit of jealousy that Imhotep had seen Satsobek looking this magnificently beddable. The fact that the man was more likely to be interested in *him* than Satsobek didn't make Ebrium covet her any less.

Imhotep looked between the two of them, one perfectly sculpted brow arched, but he didn't seem surprised. Before Ebrium could order Satsobek to the back of the house, she moved in front of him.

"What is it, Imhotep? What do you have there?"

"Scrolls, nebet-i," he held them out to her. "Stolen from the priest Menkhaf's work room. I can only read a little bit, but as soon as I saw them, I thought they might be important. I came right over to give them to the queen's man here." He nodded his head towards Ebrium.

Satsobek took the scrolls to a bench situated near a window in the entranceway and unrolled them. Ebrium asked Imhotep how he'd acquired them. Imhotep's strong, slender fingers reached up to adjust the white scarf that he wore wrapped over his head.

"After you left today I thought about everything. I remembered how upset Yuny was when I told him the workers and slaves were having their wages and rations cut. He said he would speak with Menkhaf about the temple resources, but he never mentioned it again and nothing changed."

Satsobek nodded and turned up her face. "Yes. Ebrium, you remember. You wanted to see the grain silo after Betrest told us about the workers being upset." Ebrium dipped his head in acknowledgement.

Inhotep hurried on. "Well I realized that it was around that time that Yuny became distant and nervous. My first thought was to find Menkhaf's records of the temple's inventory. I had a vague hunch that if I could find them and bring them to the woman here," he gestured to Satsobek, "that she might see something. It just didn't feel right, and I've never liked Menkhaf.

"So I snuck into the temple tonight. I searched Menkhaf's desk. I can read enough to get the sense of something, though I don't know all the symbols. But I couldn't find his papyri anywhere. There was not one out in view at all. It was strange."

Ebrium wondered if the gods did sometimes answer prayers. He'd been aggravated when the queen ordered him not to search the priests' quarters but, blessedly, Imhotep had done what he could not.

The carpenter continued. "Then I remembered something from many years ago. As you may recall, I told you when I first met Yuny I was involved in expanding the priests' rooms in the temple. At the time some of the rooms had hollow spaces behind the brickworks. This was in the same space in each room, partway up the south-facing wall. At one time, long ago, the spaces were used to house icons of the goddess, but this custom has faded.

"During the construction, some of the spaces were bricked up at the priests' requests. Very few are aware of this, but they were not actually sealed completely. We simply supplied the bricks that they could use to cover the hole in the wall. Most left the holes open in order to store things, like papyri, or bowls of incense. But if they choose to put the bricks in place, it would look just like a part of the wall and no one would ever know there was a space behind them. Some chose to use them as a private, invisible cupboard of sorts.

"I noticed that Menkhaf's wall was bricked over. So I found the space and pulled the bricks out. That's when I found his accounts."

Satsobek interrupted him. "Two accounts."

Both men turned to her. "Two accounts." She repeated in an excited voice. "I need more light to be sure, but I believe these are two different copies of the same account. Please, Ebrium, we need more light."

It was several minutes before Ebrium could unearth the oil, wicks, and bowls to provide the necessary light. In the process, he stubbed his toe in the darkened kitchen behind his manor and spilt flax oil all over his shenti and leg. When he made his way back to the hall, still muttering curses to himself, he found Satsobek and Imhotep squatting side by side, legs almost touching, heads bent together as they squinted over the scrolls.

Again that unfamiliar jealousy rose in his chest and he had the urge to grab the back of Imhotep's robe and cast him out the door. Deciding this was not the best course of action, he chose instead to arrange the oil wicks on tables near the bench. It took him another few minutes to strike a spark with the flint he had brought from the kitchen, but finally there was light. Ironically, by the time Ebrium managed to bring light into the room the first rays of the morning sun brightened the eastern horizon.

"Satsobek," he crouched near her, wanting to breathe in her scent once more. He glanced at Imhotep but it was too late to worry about propriety. "I don't want you to stop, but the sun is rising. We must get you home."

She waved him off without looking at him. "It's fine. My father never wakens early. He was up late last night drinking with some new business partner. I would not expect him to be out of bed before midday."

He placed his hands on her shoulders, forcing her to turn and look at him. "Satsobek, I know you want to find Tiya and Yuny's killer, but you can't risk yourself. If you're found out for being here with me, and now with Imhotep, there will be consequences. I don't know what your father will do, but given what you've told me, he won't be pleased." While he'd wanted to ask her to stay before, now wasn't the time to have such a discussion. He wasn't even sure it was a good idea anymore.

She made an exasperated noise. "It's fine, Ebrium. Do you want to discover what is in these accounts and find the killer or not? If so, then please just let me finish this." Her dismissal was apparent as she leaned back towards the scrolls, and Imhotep.

Irritated, he stood and ran his hands through his hair. Of course he wanted to find the temple killer. Hadn't he made that clear already tonight? That it was for the sake of protecting his family? There was no sense in pushing his point now, though, and no sense in trying to force her to let him take her home. She was too stubborn and it would only lead to another argument.

He paced the floor for several minutes while Satsobek and Imhotep compared documents. His big hands clenched and unclenched, as if the action alone would help him feel less useless and annoyed.

Satsobek leaned back on her heels and Ebrium stopped his restless motions. She placed a dainty hand on Imhotep's shoulder. "Imhotep, do you see? This confirms it. Two different renderings of the tax assessments and inventories. The dates on both documents reference when the accountings were taken, but on this one here," she pointed to the scroll on the right. "The inventory revenues are larger. Here, see, it says that there were one hundred sacks of barley and eighty sacks of wheat taken as taxes from the grain farmers last month.

"But on this one here," she moved her finger over the scroll to on left, "it says that there were only eighty sacks of barley and sixty sacks of wheat. That is an entire twenty sacks missing from each item. It's similar with others as well, like corn and dates. I can't be sure unless I check the document we took from Tiya's workspace today, but I believe that the dates on these accounts match the dates that Tiya had written down. I didn't know what they meant at the time, but perhaps they have something to do with these accounts."

Ebrium swore as the implications dawned on him. This would be a most delicate matter to deal with. And Ebrium was not a delicate man.

She looked from Imhotep to Ebrium. "But I don't understand why Menkhaf would need two accounts? And why would they differ?"

Her question was a reminder that, passionate enthusiasm in the bedroom aside, Satsobek was a fundamentally sheltered, innocent woman with a trusting nature. Imhotep raised an eyebrow at Ebrium, indicating that he also saw it and was waiting for Ebrium to tell her.

Ebrium stepped to her and, hooking a hand under her elbow, drew her up to her feet. "Satsobek, we need to get you home and I need to go find Menkhaf right now. He's obviously been stealing from the temple. He's been keeping two records, one for himself, and one to show Yuny and anyone else that asked. The differences between the accounts are probably the amounts that he was skimming from the tax revenues. Yuny likely discovered it somehow, and Menkhaf killed him to cover it up."

Her eyes widened as she gasped. "But why were he and Tiya in the temple late at night?"

"Who knows? What matters right now is finding Menkhaf and getting you out of here."

Ebrium started to guide her towards the door, but she wrested her arm from his gentle grasp. "Wait. I want to go with you when you arrest him."

"No." His voice brokered no argument.

"Why not? I should be there. I want to ask him some questions."

"Later. It's not safe for you now. The man may have killed two people. You *will not* make a third." He ushered her towards the door, ignoring her protests.

Satsobek had no time to say a proper goodbye. She'd been arguing with Ebrium on the way back to her house, and then suddenly they were there. There was no way to make him take her with them to arrest Menkhaf, and no way to discuss what had happened between them before Imhotep arrived. She anticipated that perhaps in a few hours, late afternoon at the latest, she might be able to see him again, though. The memory of the things they'd done left her shivering, aching for more and knowing that, no matter what, she'd very likely find herself stealing off to see him again tonight if she could.

The eastern horizon was a fiery colour and the sun's rays stretched across the sandy earth when Satsobek parted from Ebrium and Imhotep in the shadows of a building across the street from her home. She left them knowing they were watching her make her way safely on to her father's property. From there she hurried around to the back door of the house near the kitchen to sneak in. She opened the door, her mind filled with hopes that Menkhaf would be caught and all would be uncovered.

The last thing she expected to see when her eyes adjusted to the still dark room of her house was her father sitting on a chair, holding a mug of wine, waiting for her to walk in the door.

Menkhaf's servants were bewildered when four large, foreign men appeared on the doorstep in the early hours of the morning. They were even more confused when, upon obeying Ebrium's missive that the queen required Menkhaf's immediate presence, they went to wake their master and found him gone. Swearing that they had no idea when or where he could have left, Ebrium believed them, and was at a loss.

He'd roused Bey and the queen from sleep in order to obtain Merneith's confirmation that he could search the priest's rooms and make an arrest if necessary. Bey insisted on coming, and they'd picked up Batr and Makae as well, just in case. The four of them stood in front of Menkhaf's house, debating whether or not to search the temple and the grounds, or seek some other means of finding the priest.

That is until Ebrium remembered something Menkhaf himself had let slip the other day. The priest had told Ebrium and Satsobek that his wife and children were in the south, visiting family, and that he'd intended to join them. The murders had prevented him from leaving Thinis.

The docks were only a short jog from the temple grounds, and it was there they caught Menkhaf attempting to make his escape. The priest, rising early in his anxiety, had gone to the temple and discovered his documents missing. Unbeknownst to his servants, he returned home to pack a small sack of valuable goods – a few pieces of jewellery and chunks of gold, before heading to the docks.

Luckily for Ebrium, Menkhaf's escape was delayed when the anxious little man, in his haste, tripped and twisted his ankle. They found him limping along the waterfront, trying to commission some sleepy fishermen to give him passage south. Menkhaf's flight attempt sealed his fate, and was nearly confirmation enough of his guilt – if not for the murders, at the very least for his theft.

Accordingly, they escorted Menkhaf straight to the *hnrt*, the prison complex on the southern outskirts of town. Ebrium sat the rotund priest on an uncomfortable stool in a little room inside the prison. At first Menkhaf's eyes flitted around the room, taking everything in. Ebrium recognized the behaviour as that of a cornered animal, one hoping to find any means of escape.

The only light in the room came from a small window set high in the wall. Batr and Makae stood on either side of the heavy wood door, arms crossed, faces impassive. Ebrium pulled up another stool across from the man, and Bey added his impressive presence to an already intimidating trio. The four large men nearly filled the room, taking up all the space, the light, and the air, leaving little for Menkhaf. The former seamen were used to tight spaces, stale air, and discomfort. Menkhaf was not.

Once he realized there was nowhere to go, the little bald man appeared resigned to his fate, hunching down over his paunch. Between his knees his restless hands turned over each other in that endless hand-washing motion he had. Ebrium and Bey, on the other hand, leaned back and stretched their long legs out in front of him, taking their time and questioning at their ease.

Ebrium had anticipated excuses from the priest. He'd expected the man to whine and snivel. Men like him always did. Men who had enjoyed every comfort in life, privileged men who had come to wealth and power through familial connections, men who scoffed at men like Ebrium – these types of men always broke down when deprived of their comforts and fragile sense of power.

Menkhaf was no exception, except that he didn't even try to deny wrong-doing.

The priest gave up information willingly. They didn't even need to tell him they'd found the falsified accounts. All they had to do was imply they knew about the theft and the priest was quick to talk. Menkhaf confessed to stealing from the temple for well over two years. At first it was only a few sacks of grain here and there, a bag of dates or dried figs. Then, as it became apparent that no one had noticed, it grew each time taxes and rents were collected. Menkhaf even added to their case against him by offering up the information that he was also watering down the expensive honey that some wealthier patrons donated as an offering to the goddess, stealing barrels worth of it and selling it for gold.

"And let me guess," Ebrium drawled, feeling no sympathy for the priest's discomfort. "You got greedy, and decided to cut the workers' wages so you could have a little something extra for yourself."

The man nodded, running an unsteady hand over his bald pate. "Yes. Yes I decided to do that. I – ah – that is – at first it was because my wife wanted a new gold necklace, you see."

"No. I don't." Ebrium answered although the priest's comment was more statement than question. "Depriving poor slaves, workers, and their families of food and wages so that your wife can have a new gold necklace is *not* something I comprehend. Perhaps there is a language barrier between you and I." Ebrium's eyes narrowed, and the priest compressed his lips. His eyes didn't meet Ebrium's, and he began to rock back and forth on his stool.

Bey, seated next to Ebrium, leaned forward. His green eyes flashed. "And then the priest came to you when the workers started to complain about their wages."

Menkhaf licked his lips, flicking his eyes between Bey and Ebrium. His head bobbed again. "Yes. That's right. He demanded to see the accounting. I showed him the papyrus I had been keeping."

Ebrium crossed his ankles out in front of him. "So how did Yuny discover what you were up to?"

Menkhaf shrugged. "He didn't believe me about the accounts. He began keeping his own accounts of the harvests and inventories. He knew that I had been stealing."

"And why didn't he report you then?"

The little priest's thin lips spread in the barest trace of a smile, as if he was pleased with himself. "He couldn't."

"Why not?"

"Because I was having him watched."

Ebrium's eyebrows rose, although he tried to school his face to remain impassive. The little priest was smarter than he'd expected. He'd been looking for something to use to blackmail the high priest in case his deception was uncovered. The priest showed forethought, indicating that he was more thorough than the average greedy thief. Ebrium wondered how long he'd been planning to steal from the temple.

Menkhaf continued speaking, unprompted. "I knew about his lover, that furniture-maker. I threatened to expose him and the man if he turned me over to the queen. I convinced him that I could ruin him *and* his lover. I told him if he were exposed no one would believe him about my stealing, but would think he was just trying to seek his revenge against me."

Ebrium and Bey exchanged a knowing glance. So this was why Yuny had remained silent about the theft, and probably why he'd included Tiya, the high priestess, in the scheme.

With more questioning, they learned that Menkhaf had forced the high priest to go along with his thievery. They met regularly – late at night – to tally the inventories. Menkhaf claimed that Yuny threatened him at their last meeting two days ago, saying he wanted the theft to stop or else he himself would go to the queen and report it, regardless of the consequences. According to Menkhaf, there was a struggle and Menkhaf hit the high priest, knocking him to the ground. In the process, the high priest cried out, but hit his head and fell unconscious. That's when Menkhaf heard a noise in the goddess's sanctuary and discovered Tiya in the cabinet. He'd had no choice but to kill the woman as well. A noise in the hallway, which Menkhaf took to be a servant arriving early for work, caused him to flee before he could do anything with the bodies.

Ebrium and Bey questioned the priest for hours, and still something didn't fit right. Ebrium brought up Sekhemkare, the governor's brother that had seemed so suspicious, as well as the men that had attacked him and Satsobek the day before. But Menkhaf adamantly denied any knowledge of the other men, although he did admit to sending some men to Imhotep's hut to scare him.

Although Ebrium and the other men weren't entirely satisfied with Menkhaf's story, in the end they had no choice but to leave Menkhaf to his fate. Unable to use the sort of force they might have with a man of lesser rank than priest, they had to accept the extent of their questioning abilities. Without a doubt the priest's family would be sentenced to remain in exile in the lands south of Kemet, never to return. All that remained was for a judge to determine the priest's punishment. Considering his confession, it was only a matter of deciding in which manner, and when, he would be executed.

Ebrium looked forward to at least a few hours of uninterrupted sleep, and then he and Satsobek had much to discuss.

Eight days later Ebrium remained dissatisfied.

It was late in the evening as he wove through the crowd milling about the courtyard of the queen's palace. Around the massive yard at various intervals, flax wicks burned in bowls of oil secured on carved sticks stabbed into the sand. Tables low to the ground – previously arranged for dinner seating – had since been moved to the side after the banquet was served and the meal complete. Incense smoke spiraled up from bowls set on the tables, mingling with the heady perfumes of the hundreds of heated bodies that packed the court. The nobles of the city of Thinis circulated in a wide half-circle around the performance square in front of the raised platform that held the queen's throne and her special guests. Near her on the dais were also seated Bey, Merneith's cousin Penebui and aunt Bekeh, Ebrium's mother and sister, and a few other ladies of the queen's entourage. Batr and Makae still sat next to Bey. An empty seat marked the spot where Ebrium sat earlier that evening.

As was customary near the end of the harvest season, the queen was holding a banquet in honour of the goddess Renenutet, Lady of the Fertile Fields and Granaries. A shrine was set up in one corner of the courtyard for the goddess. Those nobles in attendance brought bouquets of flowers, loaves of bread, jars of wine, sacks of grain, and plates of fruit – all numbering in the hundreds. These gifts now ringed the goddess's shrine. Merneith – in lieu of a living pharaoh – gave a speech earlier thanking the goddess for this year's harvest.

Merneith had chosen to continue with all the festivals customary for the end of the year celebrations in the hopes that lavish feasts and generous gifts would help the people move forward from their speculations on the temple murders. So far, it was working. At least to all outward appearances.

Since they'd arrested Menkhaf, Ebrium had heard little from their network of spies regarding unrest. Rumours of the gods' displeasure quieted somewhat thanks to the swift apprehension of the murderous little priest. Following the arrest, they'd also seized Menkhaf's vast storeroom, where he'd been holding all the grain and goods he'd taken from the temple over the last two months. It didn't constitute anywhere near all of the stolen goods, but the queen's redistribution of the goods to the temple workers as a reward went a long way towards restoring their good faith.

Bey also arranged for some strategically placed people to praise the queen's abilities to manage Kemet in a time of crisis, and to root out corruption in even the highest ranks. The fact that the latest harvest numbers seemed to indicate some positive reversal of Kemet's fortunes didn't hurt either.

The main thorn in Ebrium's side, however, was the disappearance of the hawk-faced man who had stirred up dissent in the marketplace the morning of the murders. Menkhaf swore he didn't know who the man was, or who his associates were, and the men who'd been part of the hawk-faced man's group that attacked Ebrium and Satsobek were holding their silence. No amount of questioning or coercion could bring the men they'd arrested to provide more information. But Ebrium was convinced there was simply too much coincidence in the fact that Menkhaf and the men were all from the same region and, as he'd learned, the same town even.

He also wanted to know what had happened to the rest of the goods Menkhaf had stolen. The man claimed he sold them to traveling merchants from further south, and used the wealth to furnish his home and his wife and concubines with jewellery. Ebrium was still waiting for an estimate on the value of the man's home and wealth, but he was quite sure it wouldn't add up anywhere close to what the man had taken from the temple. By the priest's own reckoning, he'd taken enough to furnish a dozen manors, and heavily adorn twice as many concubines with the finest gold jewellery.

Having secured the favour of many of the temple workers and farmers, tonight's festival was a time to reinforce the nobles' loyalty. Earlier in the evening the queen had been quite liberal with her gifts and acknowledgements. She'd stood up on the raised platform situated in the centre of the southern edge of the large courtyard and called out the names of all the noble families in attendance, thanking them for their devotion and hard work. All together the attendees numbered around five hundred, and Ebrium had little doubt the pregnant queen was exhausted at the end of her speech. But like the admirable woman she was, she didn't let her fatigue show.

Queen Merneith was particularly striking this evening, having dressed with care. She wore only a plain white shenti wrapped around her waist and hanging straight down to her ankles. Her burgeoning pregnant belly and swollen breasts were as naked as the mounds of sand in the distant desert. Plain gold chains draped her neck, while matching earrings and wrist cuffs completed her jewellery. The flashing of the gold was a stunning contrast against her smooth, olivine skin.

Without doubt, her appearance was deliberate. Her pregnant, unadorned belly served as a reminder to everyone that she carried the next pharaoh in her. There could be no doubt of her power, her divinity, her ability to control Kemet. Or at least none that was openly spoken of tonight.

Ebrium had been particularly moved when the queen chose to publicly honour himself, along with Batr and Makae, for their services in catching the murderous priest. It was why they'd been given seats of honour near her on the dais. She presented Ebrium with several pieces of gold jewellery, a quantity of beautifully carved furniture to furnish his new home, and a stunning, decorative gold knife. He'd been embarrassed, amused, and humbled. From atop the dais his eyes had swept the audience, looking for Satsobek's face, expecting to at least see her looking in his direction. He thought he'd caught her eye for a moment, but she'd bowed her head, twisting her hands in her lap.

Satsobek. Merneith told him she'd asked not to be publicly named for her involvement in Menkhaf's arrest. Because of her Ebrium had spent the last eight nights in his new home, laying half-awake in his too-large bed, expecting to hear the mad little woman rapping on his door in the middle of the night.

If she had, Seret would have been there to open the door for her. Ebrium found he liked the boy too much to turn him out on the street and so Seret became his manservant. Since Ebrium had little idea what that entailed, and Seret had limited experience in such a position, the two were learning to muddle along together. It suited them both. Ebrium had few expectations or needs and Seret, eager to please as he was, had time to learn his way. In some ways, their positions in society were not so different. They both teetered in a nebulous state of half-belonging. Seret was an orphan, but also a favoured servant – not a slave – to the high priestess of one of Thinis's largest temples. Ebrium was a gardener's son who'd managed to befriend nobility in two different, far-reaching lands. Ebrium secretly acknowledged that, while he was as yet unused to it, the boy's obvious admiration for him – bordering, in fact, on awe – was good for his ego.

Hearing that he'd spent a night or two in the house, Ebrium's mother and sister sent over a cook. He couldn't turn the woman away, and he couldn't deny that he was enjoying having regular meals waiting for him throughout the day. Bereneith was a stout, bustling woman, older than his own mother, with a bald head, flat nose, and sharp, twinkling eyes. Ebrium enjoyed flirting shamelessly with her in good fun. She'd taken to swatting at him with her reed broom when he came into the kitchen to steal honeybuns.

Whether he'd intended to or not, it seemed that Ebrium had moved into his new manor. And it was all because of Satsobek, a woman he hadn't seen since the morning after they'd coupled in his bedroom.

On the day they'd caught Menkhaf he'd sent Seret – who insisted he was well enough to walk the distance – to her home with a message to apprise her of the arrest. He knew she was upset he hadn't let her attend Menkhaf's arrest, but her response was even less than he'd expected. She'd merely thanked Seret for informing her, telling him she was pleased to hear that the temple killer was captured at last.

That was all. Nothing for him, and nothing to indicate when, or if, he might see her again. So he sent Seret again two days ago, inquiring after her well-being. Her response had been to thank him for his enquiry and to let him know she was doing well. Seret assured him he'd seen her himself, and there was no doubt those were her very words.

He hadn't expected such coldness from such a passionate woman. Rather, he'd anticipated her scolding Seret for being up and about. He'd imagined she would also send Seret back with an earful of insults to pass on to Ebrium. In truth, he'd smiled when he envisioned her furious and adorable face scrunched in anger. He even allowed himself to imagine that if she were in front of him, reproaching him with her funny insults, he would take her face in his hands and silence her angry words with his mouth, turning her gestures of indignation into urgent caresses as he pressed her down into his big, soft bed.

He'd had plans for things he'd like to do with her – and to her – most of which involved her naked and laid out on some piece of furniture or other in his manor. Sometimes, she was standing, as she had been the first night in his hut in the village, and he thought of how light she was, how easy it would be to wrap her legs around his back and thrust up into her. He'd yet to taste the liquid heat of the space between her thighs.

Wanting these things did not surprise him. Since the time he was old enough to know the power of his dimpled smile over a woman, Ebrium hadn't felt the need for chastity. What surprised him was the frequency in which Satsobek haunted his thoughts, and that those thoughts sometimes involved more than just sex. They involved lying in bed and talking, as they had before Imhotep interrupted them, or attending the New Year festival celebrations, watching the sunset from his roof, and all other manner of things that came to mind throughout the day.

But Ebrium wasn't thinking about any of those things right now. His focus was on just finding a way to talk to her in the first place. Now, he wove through the crowd, following Satsobek from a distance. She was walking towards the palace, head bent towards her friend Betrest. Tonight he *would* talk to her and, whether she wanted to or not, she was going to tell him why she'd been avoiding him.

Satsobek's heart slammed into her chest, forcing the breath right out of her lungs as she stepped out of the room in the palace set aside for ladies to refresh themselves. Ebrium stood a short ways down the hallway, his large muscled shoulder resting against a column, one ankle crossed casually across the other. His arms were folded across his chest and his posture, along with the flickering torches that lined the walls and deepened the shadows, emphasized the ridges of his naked chest, biceps, and forearms. He was waiting for her, she knew it.

She'd seen him following them inside the palace, and warned Betrest. She'd already confided in the beautiful priestess, knowing Betrest had more than one indiscretion of her own. Betrest knew what Satsobek was about to do. What she *had* to do. Betrest would be waiting nearby in case Satsobek needed her support.

Ebrium's cerulean blue eyes fixed on her, and she felt like a hunted animal, pinned in the sights of an archer with arrow knocked and ready. The hard look on his face left no room for argument. She knew the time had finally come to talk to him. Although the hallway they were in was currently empty, it wouldn't be for long. She bit her lip and silently inclined her head to a room off to the side – a small greeting room, unlit and unused tonight. She didn't want to be alone in the dark with Ebrium, but there would be no other opportunity. And he deserved to hear the news from her before anyone else.

He followed her inside the dim room, closing the door so that only a small amount of light filtered in from the hallway's torches. She could see his body in profile, and as her eyes adjusted to the shadows she began to make out his face.

"Ebrium," she needed to say what she had to say as quickly as possible. His nearness, his scent, it was all too much. She didn't trust herself to remain long with him. "I cannot…"

With his hands on her hips, he turned her and pressed her against the wall behind the door. His lips slanted across hers, crushing them, taking her mouth in a bruising kiss. He stole her words away, along with the air from her lungs. She put her hands up to push him away but, like the first time he'd kissed her back in the House of Iput, her fingers skimmed the breadth of his broad shoulders of their own volition, greedy for the feel of him.

When her lips parted, his tongue delved into her, claiming her mouth more forcefully than he ever had before. Her back arched, tilting her breasts up towards him, aching for his touch. Eight days apart and she'd hoped the desire that burned between them would lessen. Instead, it had only been heightened. She'd fooled herself into thinking that their one night together had been a passing fancy for him. She'd never dared hope he would continue to want her. *Not that it matters if he does. Better if he does not at all.*

With that thought, she managed to break free of his kiss and wrench herself from his grasp, pulling to the side. Panting, she held up a hand to ward him off. "I can't, Ebrium. We *must* not. My father…"

"Damn him to Ammit." Ebrium growled. "I don't care. We'll find a way, Satsobek."

She shook her head. "No. It's not just that."

He stepped towards her again, catching her wrist and pulling her to him. His smooth, hard body pressed against her and she almost gave in. She made herself push at his shoulders. "Ebrium, I can't."

"Dammit, why not? What in the name of Dagon have you been doing these last few days? I sent Seret twice with messages. I was ready to come to your house myself, your father be-damned."

Her head shot up. "You were?" She sought his face in the darkness. She didn't realize he was that concerned, that he'd considered seeking her out. Collecting herself, she said, "I saw Seret when he came. Of course I'm pleased Menkhaf has been caught. But I…" She paused, licking her lips. Her chest hurt with the weight of what she had to say. It was harder than she'd expected, knowing that he might truly have feelings for her.

"Satsobek, what is it?"

She drew herself up. "I am to be married."

There was silence – silence that pressed harder against her than her secret had a moment ago. It thrummed, filling the room, crushing her head. The wings of silence battered at her ears.

"Ebrium? Did you…"

"I heard you." His voice was flat. "To whom? When?"

She forced the words out through clenched teeth. "Sekhemkare. The brother of the governor of the Aneb-

Hetch sephat. We marry in six days' time, after the Festival of the New Year."

His breath expelled in a whoosh, and he swore softly. "Since when?"

"The day you arrested Menkhaf."

He swore again with vehemence, and she flinched, not out of fear but in understanding. She knew what he was thinking. She'd gotten engaged just hours after they'd spent the night making love in his bed. Not that she'd had any choice in the matter. She was doing this for him, and for the queen, but they couldn't know that.

"Satsobek, is this your father's doing? You don't have to do this." He enfolded her wrists in a gentle hold. "Just tell me. I *will* put a stop to it."

Her voice was weak, her heart pounding too hard and her breath too shallow. She tried to control it, but that seemed to make it worse. Pain worked its way up her chest and lodged itself in her throat. "You cannot. You need not concern yourself with me any longer."

"Dammit, Satsobek," his grip moved to her upper arms. She was almost thankful for his support holding her up, as she was feeling weak, her head light. "We can go somewhere else, somewhere outside of Thinis, if that's the issue."

That was precisely what her father had warned her about, although she hadn't believed Ebrium would suggest it. When she'd found her father waiting for her that morning she'd snuck into the kitchen, she tried to explain her absence by telling him about Seret, and how he'd needed her help. *It's not what you think*, she'd lied. She'd told him they'd learned something new about the temple murders and were arresting Menkhaf as a result. Her father didn't care. It was enough that she'd been with Ebrium in the middle of the night. He had what he needed to force her to his will.

He'd laid it all out for her, and told her exactly what she must do. Sekhemkare had agreed to take her father on as a partner in trading the *hul gil*, the plant of joy, on the grounds that Satsobek marry him. Her father had actually laughed when he'd told Satsobek, saying that he'd never believed he'd be able to use his homely little daughter as a bargaining tool. He'd expected to have to offer a great sum of wealth to anyone who'd marry her. Instead, Sekhemkare was giving *him* a profitable gift *and* taking his daughter off his hands.

She argued that there must be some confusion. Sekhemkare couldn't want her. She'd hardly made herself agreeable to him. Her father disputed it, promising that the man had been very clear about his wishes. He wanted to marry Satsobek, and as soon as possible. The only delay was that her father wanted to ensure the contracts were written out clearly, so that he could be sure Sekhemkare couldn't opt out of the business at the last minute.

When she'd tried to refuse, her father promised to destroy Ebrium. He'd make it public that a low-born commoner had ruined Satsobek - forced her even - and that the queen enabled it all by giving a foreign thief a position of power and then pairing him up with a daughter of the nobility. Her father even knew that she'd corresponded with Ebrium after he'd saved her life from the tiger. Amenia, her own sister, had been the one to intercept the messengers eight months ago, and set Satsobek and Ebrium against one another. She'd been biding her time to tell their father and her timing helped ensure that the snare their father laid for Satsobek was complete.

By sneaking out to Ebrium's house and then getting caught, she'd made it possible for her father to compel her to do anything he wanted. He didn't even have to restrict her movements or prevent her from attending events, such as tonight's banquet. All he had to do was threaten two of the few people who'd ever shown her kindness, and she had no choice but to scorn Ebrium and marry Sekhemkare.

Satsobek roused herself, her voice firm with resolve despite the trembling of her legs. "No. Think of your mother and sister. We can't just run away together. It would ruin your family's reputation, and your sister's chances at a marriage. It would ruin the queen's trust in us. It could ruin *her.* You don't mean it." She couldn't even allow herself to contemplate the possibility of running away with him. He would regret it eventually, and hate her for it. She said,

"You're only saying this now because you're angry. But you would never do that to your family. I know you wouldn't."

"But you can't want this. We *will* find a way around it. Stop being such a damnably stubborn woman and let me help you."

He was more determined than she'd imagined he'd be and she could see that he wouldn't give up easily. She steeled herself to do what was necessary to get rid of him, however much it might hurt the both of them. Her father had scripted this for her, but she'd doubted then she'd ever have to say it. She told him, "But I *do* want this. Sekhemkare is powerful and wealthy and will make a strong trading partner for my father. I think he will make a fine husband. I see no reason to refuse the offer. Trust me, Ebrium, in time you will see that it is better this way."

His grip on her arms tightened. "I don't believe you."

She drew herself up and made her voice as cold as possible. "Believe me, it's true. I enjoyed my time with you, but we both knew it would come to an end."

For good measure, she added, "I have no doubt that in a few days' time you'll have forgotten about me, as I am sure I will forget you. After all, I forgot all about you after I sent that messenger putting you in your place eight months ago. You would do well to remember your place now."

His grip on her slackened and she took the opportunity to pull from his grasp. She slipped out the door and left him standing in the dark, hurrying back into the ladies' room so he would have no chance to follow her. There she found Betrest alone, biting the inside of her cheek, waiting for her. Betrest asked. "Did you do it?"

Satsobek's legs finally gave out on her and, back pressed to the wall, she slid down to the floor. She covered her face with her hands while painful sobs wracked her body, choking her, making it impossible to breathe. Betrest sighed and sat down next to her, putting her arms around Satsobek in order to let her cry on her shoulder.

Ebrium stood in the dark room, trying to even out his breathing. Not long ago he would have gotten angry at Satsobek, whether she was in the room or not. He would have left the room and let the impulsive side of him get the better of him, possibly picked a fight with an obnoxious drunk, and gotten drunk himself. He probably would have reveled in it, even. He used to take satisfaction in letting his resentment carry him away. As a little boy he'd learned that it was better to get angry at his enemies – better yet, to get even with them – than let them see that they had caused him pain, embarrassment, or shame. Anger felt better than hurt.

But anger was also both selfish and self-destructive. In the end it accomplished nothing. As Satsobek had reminded him during one of their arguments, anger was like an open wound, an insect bite that always itched and bled. In the end it was unproductive. Directing his ire at Satsobek or her father or Sekhemkare wouldn't help him to think clearly now, and it wouldn't help him to help Satsobek.

And he was pretty sure she needed his help.

Even in the dark she was an unconvincing liar. He'd felt her tremble under his touch. He'd heard the waver in her voice, the hesitation when she'd told him her betrothed's name. Most importantly, she'd kissed him back with all the passion of the first time he'd trapped her mouth with his that night at the House of Iput.

No. He didn't believe she wanted to marry Sekhemkare. And even if some part of her did, she would regret it. Ebrium remembered the man from their brief encounter in front of the queen's tent the morning of the temple murders. Sekhemkare was an arrogant bastard. He would never treat Satsobek as she deserved. Furthermore, Ebrium had a hunch the man was somehow involved in the temple murders. He came from the same region as Menkhaf and the missing men who had attacked him and Satsobek. It all felt *unfinished*.

He had to find some way to stop their marriage. If Satsobek didn't want him after that, well, he'd just have to deal with that later. As it was, he had six days to save her from making the worst mistake of her life.

Chapter 16 – Amenia

In the days to follow Satsobek did her best to prepare herself to marry a man she didn't care for, failing miserably all the while. She prompted herself to hope for something positive to change her situation, and to not fall into utter despair. It was hard to think clearly, though, when panic rose up in her chest, clawing at her throat, every time she thought about Sekhemkare laying his hands on her. *Women often marry men they don't know or that they dislike,* she kept reminding herself. The knowledge did not exactly help.

She *had* gotten to know Sekhemkare, to some extent at least. In the few times she'd seen him, he'd been pleasant to her, friendly and attentive. Watching him, she'd also learned that he was condescending to servants, cruel behind the backs of his supposed friends, and that he increasingly enjoyed the usage of hul gil, the plant of joy. He was also fast becoming one of her father's favorite companions. That alone was enough to make Satsobek scorn her husband-to-be.

Every moment spent with him was a moment spent comparing him to Ebrium, with Sekhemkare coming up short each time. It was pointless, she well knew, to think of Ebrium now but at every turn something reminded her of him. When a servant smiled, she remembered how he'd made Seret laugh. When a little boy ran by in the street, she thought of Ebrium sneaking in to the temple to pray for rain to help his father. When Sekhemkare's eyes rolled over her in his unusual stupors, she'd close her lids and draw up Ebrium's comforting scent, enveloping her as it had when she'd lain in his bed the last night she saw him. He was everywhere around her, intangible yet pervasive.

The one good thing that she could see was that her engagement had prompted her to try to make amends with her sister. Sekhemkare had told Satsobek that he intended for them to travel to his home city, Inbu-Hedj, the capital of the Aneb-Hetch sephat in central Kemet, after their marriage. She wanted to sort things out with those whom she had wronged, and who had wronged her, before she left Thinis.

Satsobek hadn't spoken to her sister since their argument the night before their father caught Satsobek sneaking back into the house. While she understood it was her own fault for sneaking out to see Ebrium with Seret, Satsobek blamed Amenia for being malicious enough to run straight to their father. The impending confrontation filled her with a mixture of determination, anxiety, and exhilaration.

She found Amenia alone one afternoon, sipping wine on the rooftop, reclining on some cushions in the shade of the tent. It was another blistering hot day, and Amenia fanned herself with a white ostrich feather fan, mounted on a handle of cream-coloured ivory. The handle was designed in an L-shape, so that Amenia hardly had to lift her hand as she swished the feathers in a lazy arc near her neck. The red beaded bangles on her wrist clicked with each indolent movement.

Amenia's eyes opened as the reed mats crackled under Satsobek's feet. "What do you want?" Amenia sneered.

"I want to know why."

"Why what?"

Amenia's apathetic attitude didn't help Satsobek's mood. Anger simmered below the surface of Satsobek's skin, but she tried to school her voice to be calm. "Why did you tell our father about Ebrium? Why would you do that to me?"

Amenia shifted her legs in a languid motion. As if she didn't care at all that she had destroyed any chance of happiness Satsobek might have had. She took a big gulp of her wine and poured herself another mugful.

A small smile lit in Amenia's eyes and her lip curled up. "Why would I *not* tell Father what you did?"

"Amenia," Satsobek's voice was a plea. She couldn't believe her sister could be so unfeeling towards her. How could anyone take pleasure in the suffering of a sibling like this? "I know you were upset about the things I said to you the other day, and I'm sorry if I hurt you. But did it really warrant this? Father is forcing me to marry Sekhemkare. He's threatened to ruin Ebrium. He doesn't deserve that."

Amenia's fan stopped and her eyes grew hard. She snapped, "So what if you have to marry a man you don't want? You will be no different from me then." Amenia took three quick sips of her wine.

"But you *wanted* to marry Rekhmire. Father gave you a choice. You could have said no."

"Really? And then what? Maybe the next offer would have been worse. You said it yourself, the men were not exactly lining up for me, were they? Father is not wealthy anymore, and I had little to offer beyond my youth. When Rekhmire offered for me I thought he was old enough that he might die soon, and I would be able to live as I pleased once he was gone. As you can see, it's been years and yet he lives on, rutting away like some disgusting animal. I can only thank the gods that he has not impregnated me; else I might be dead in childbirth like our mother, or forced to raise Rekhmire's filthy little brats." Amenia poured more wine, slopping some over the edge of the mug and licking it off her fingers before taking a sip.

Satsobek shuddered, thinking it was an awful thing to wish death on one's husband. Then she realized that she had done something similar with Sekhemkare when she first met him. She still hoped something would happen to prevent their marriage, and if it meant an accident befell him… she was ashamed to admit she would not be overly distraught.

Her voice softened somewhat when she asked, "But if you're so miserable how could you force that upon me?"

"How could I?" Amenia's cool demeanour was gone. She began to whirl out words like a maelstrom. "Who do you think you are that you can turn down an offer that I would have jumped at? Sekhemkare is a *governor's brother*, and he is handsome and fit. Why do you think you're better than any of the rest of us? Was it not enough for you to be everyone's favoured child?"

"What are you talking about? I was no one's favoured child. Father has always preferred you to me."

"Oh please," Amenia scoffed. "You know you were. When we lived in the palace our aunt preferred you. She always said what a *sweet* disposition you had." Amenia said it like it was an insult to be good-tempered. "And I was always the ill-behaved one."

Satsobek did recall Amenia being chastised often, but it was because she had a tendency to hit other children when they didn't obey her fast enough, or if she wanted something they were reluctant to give up immediately.

Amenia continued her tirade. "And then when we were sent to the hwt, everyone liked you better than me. Tiya chose you to learn to write instead of me, and the other priestesses spent more time teaching you the songs and dances." She paused to tilt her wine glass to her lips.

Even Amenia had to know her accusation was unjust. Priestesses typically didn't learn to read or write. They didn't go to the scribal schools that boys were sent to in order to learn, following in the footsteps of their fathers. Tiya herself was an unusual case, having learned from her father. She'd offered to teach Satsobek because Satsobek would always stand by her and watch over her shoulder as she wrote, asking question after question about the craft. Once given the opportunity to learn, Satsobek spent countless hours tracing her fingers over the hieroglyphics Tiya gave her as samplers. She would sometimes even scratch the symbols in the sand when she ran out of papyri to write on. Tiya didn't simply choose Satsobek over Amenia – Satsobek practically gave her no choice.

Since it wouldn't help to remind Amenia of that, she said instead, "But you never *liked* working in the hwt. You said it was a chore. You never expressed any interest in learning to write. You never even tried to understand it."

Amenia dismissed her argument. "There was no point in practicing. You and the other girls were all jealous of me. I was beautiful and you were *plain* and so they took pity on you. You and the other girls manipulated the priestesses so that they wouldn't like me."

Satsobek blinked at her sister. "I-I had no idea you felt that way. You always said you didn't care what the other girls thought of you." If anything, Amenia spoke badly about them behind their backs, and whenever a girl confronted her about the things she'd said, Amenia dismissed her with a verbal assault.

"Of course I cared, you selfish fool. Who wouldn't? It was *your* fault they didn't like me. You have always thought you were better than me." Amenia's throat worked as she swallowed several gulps of wine before pouring yet another glass. Satsobek frowned, worried her sister would make herself ill.

"Amenia, I am sorry. I had no idea you believed that. I never thought I was better than you, I just wanted us to get along."

But Amenia didn't want to hear what Satsobek had to say. The invectives tumbled from her mouth in a jumbled, contradictory rant. "Why should you get to be with the queen's guardsman when I had to marry a filthy old man like Rekhmire? Yes, I was there the day the messenger came from Ebrium. I didn't tell father then. I did you a favour by sending the messenger away and putting a stop to your correspondence. He would never have married you.

"And I saw you sneaking across the grounds the other night with that cripple from the hwt, running off to your *precious* Sumerian, ruining yourself without even thinking about it. *I saved you* by telling Father and now you get to marry a handsome, powerful man." Amenia waved her mug of wine at Satsobek. "And how do you thank me? By coming up here and accusing me of being cruel to you."

Amenia hissed out the next words with such vehemence they hit Satsobek like a slap across the face. "You are an *ungrateful bitch*, is what you are."

Satsobek gasped. An awful realization dawned on her. *Amenia is a truly horrid person.* Amenia had become so twisted over the years with jealousy, bitterness, and wine that there was nothing rational or kind left in her. She wanted Satsobek to be as unhappy as she was. Satsobek had warned Ebrium about the dangers of harbouring animosity. It wasn't until now that she realized just how dangerous it could be. Festering resentments could warp a person beyond recognition, beyond redemption even.

As much as Satsobek hated to think it, she didn't see that there was any point in trying to rationalize with Amenia now. Nor ever again, if she could help it. There was too much venom and hatred there to ever be spent. Satsobek might, one day, forgive her sister for what she had done, but she'd never be able trust her.

The afternoon of the Festival of the New Year Satsobek sat cross-legged on a reed mat in one of the sitting rooms in her home. Sweat beaded between her breasts, it was so hot, but she paid it no mind. She was preparing to write. She'd always found comfort in the ritual of preparing her reed quills and paper, along with the meditative process of writing itself. Since she was certainly in need of comforting these days she'd taken it up again. Although it brought back painful memories of Tiya and Yuny's deaths it helped to know that, because of her ability to read, she had aided in finding their killer. Perhaps one day her skill might come in useful again. Perhaps she'd find a place in one of the temples in her new hometown, once she and her soon-to-be-husband settled in the north.

Rather than go through the process of making her pigments and sheets of papyri, which would take several days, Satsobek had sent a servant out to obtain some from a scribe and artisan who lived near the Temple of Mehyt. The man was well known for his mastery of the craft. He collected the necessary papyri reeds from the banks of the Iteru himself, then stripped the skins and sliced the stalks into long strips. These he soaked in water for two to three days to soften them and release the sticky substance that helped bind the stalks together. Then he layered the stems, pressing them between sheets of linen to dry, changing the linen every day or two to speed the process. Finally, in order to smooth the surface to a glossy sheen, the sheets of papyri were burnished with a smooth stone.

As part of her training, like every scribe, Satsobek learned to make papyrus scrolls. She'd proven her skill by layering the wet reed strips to create scrolls up to one hundred feet long. She'd also learned to make writing implements from dried papyrus stalks, as well as paints made from various minerals and clays. These implements were now all arranged on the floor next to her, along with a granite slab to rest on her folded legs to serve as a table.

Before she could begin writing, she needed to pray to Seshat, Mistress of the House of Books and the goddess who created writing. She asked Seshat to direct her hand and make her writings true and strong. Satsobek also decided to pray to Thoth, Seshat's consort. Thoth was the counterpart to *ma'at* – chaos and disorder – and the mediator between good and evil, ensuring that neither ever overbalanced the other. Satsobek hoped that by praying to Thoth, Ebrium might be guided in the work that he did for the queen, and be kept safe. She assumed that, with Menkhaf's arrest, the case of the temple murders was closed. But whatever else Ebrium was tasked to do, she knew he was worthy of the gods' protection, if not a place in the Afterlife.

Once her prayers were complete she took up her granite slab, laid a scroll across it, and began to write. She'd chosen to work on the story of Mehyt and her consort – one of the first stories she'd learned to write. Satsobek remained that way for more than two hours, until her writing was interrupted by a knock on her door. Upon her command, the door opened and Sadeh popped her head in. "Nebet-i, it's time to ready you."

Satsobek blinked, her eyebrows creased in a frown. "Ready me?"

"For Sekhemkare, nebet-i! He's coming to pick you up shortly so that you may attend the Festival of the New Year with him."

Satsobek stared at Sadeh for a moment. Then she remembered. "Dammit!" She swore. Her father had given Sekhemkare permission to take Satsobek to the festival. She'd not wanted to go with him, but her father insisted she at least pretend to want to see her betrothed. At least until he'd secured the trading contracts and the marriage contract was signed. It would be the first time Satsobek was alone with her husband-to-be.

Sadeh flapped her hands. "Oh goddess Hathor, did you forget?! Come, come, now." Sadeh waited for Satsobek to move the tablet and scroll from her lap before grabbing her hands and pulling her up. "Oh not again!" Sadeh griped as she saw Satsobek's fingers. "You know how hard it is to get that ink out of your fingers. They will be tipped in black and green for days."

Satsobek submitted to Sadeh's ministrations, allowing the woman to scrub her down and rub scented oils into her skin. She braided a few strands of Satsobek's hair with red carnelian beads, but left most of it swinging free. Given the excruciating heat of the day, Sadeh wrapped a long shenti around Satsobek's waist, leaving her torso bare, adorned with several long strings of carnelian. She draped gold earrings from her ears and latched a thick gold bracelet on one wrist. Lastly, she thickened the lines of kohl that rimmed her eyes and dabbed red ochre to her lips. Sadeh stepped back and admired her handiwork. She nodded. "You look fit for the governor himself, nebet-i, never mind his brother."

Satsobek muttered defiantly, "I would rather I look like I had been dredged in from the desert. Maybe then Sekhemkare would change his mind about marrying me." She still had no idea what the man saw in her.

A flurry of sound drifted in from the hallway, along with her father's jovial tones. Sekhemkare had arrived. A queasy feeling took up residence in her belly.

In the entranceway her father attended the governor's brother, who appeared to have taken extra care with his grooming tonight. He wore a gold necklace, and a gold chain draped over his head. His side-lock of hair was braided and looped to hang low, brushing his jawline as he turned his head. His bare chest and the shenti neatly pleated around his waist displayed his lean, muscular torso to full advantage.

In one hand Sekhemkare held an intricately carved *wass* sceptre, like a tall walking stick. The top was engraved in the image of Seth, the god of violence and chaos who mutilated and killed his own brother for personal gain and power. The jackal-headed Seth had a long curved snout and tall ears.

Satsobek recalled how on her first meeting with Sekhemkare she had seen the constellation of the Foreleg of Seth.

Something about the sceptre held her attention, sparking a glimmer of a memory. But Sekhemkare cut into her thoughts as he drawled, "Ahhh, Satsobek, my darling bride. You look positively lovely tonight." He held out his hand, but she pretended not to see it, having ducked her head in a false display of shyness.

Her father puffed his chest up over his rotund belly. "Sekhemkare, I trust you to take care of my little *sat* tonight."

"Of course." Sekhemkare swept a bow. "She is, after all, my wife-to-be. Her well-being is my greatest concern." Satsobek wondered if that was a faint note of sarcasm she detected in his voice. She wanted to turn and leave, but knew her father would never let her get away with it. She pushed herself to step forward. This man was going to be her husband, and sooner or later she'd have to get used to him.

Not long afterwards, Satsobek found herself walking next to him through the crowded festival grounds on the outskirts of Thinis. The setting sun in the distance cast a cheerful glow over the white tents set up around the grounds. Every year the pharaoh – or in this year's case, the queen – arranged for the entertainment, food, drink, and games at the Festival of the New Year.

Hundreds, possibly thousands, of people of all classes milled around. Children ran past them, screaming and laughing, while mothers and fathers hoisted infants onto their shoulders and young lovers held hands. Satsobek saw Betrest further ahead, arm in arm with some man she'd never seen before, and smiled to herself. Betrest was making another conquest.

Sekhemkare, who loomed over her by several inches, reached down and took her hand, tucking it into the crook of his muscular arm. "So that I do not lose you in the crowd," he grinned down at her. His skin felt strange under her touch, and it took her a moment to realize why. *It is not*

Ebrium's. She wanted to snatch her hand back, but he wrapped his other hand around hers, trapping her in place.

Sekhemkare stopped in front of a stall selling jewellery. "Tell me, my love, which do you like?" He gestured to a display of rings, carved from gold and bone.

"Truly, I need nothing." She murmured. She didn't want anything from him, anything that would mark her as belonging to him.

"No? You are not like all the other ladies who wish a man to prove his love with the weight of his purse? Is my wife so modest then?" His eyebrow was raised, and she couldn't tell if he was goading, or genuine.

"I do not know what *other ladies* you are familiar with, tayi neb, but no, I neither need nor want you to spend your wealth on me."

"Truly? Well this is a first. Obviously I have chosen my wife well. A quiet, modest little woman who will not demand much of me. Will you be so obedient always?" He cocked his head, studying her. His tone was light, but Satsobek shivered despite the heat, and rubbed her arms.

"You are mistaken if you think I am ever obedient at all, tayi neb." She looked up at him, defiant. "Perhaps you have been listening to my father's assessment of my character too much."

His lips quirked up in a smirk and his voice was languid as he said, "I do listen to your father, but in truth I often hear little of value, and trust even less." She was so shocked by his openly callous appraisal of her father that she didn't know what to say. If he disliked her father so much, why had he spent so much time with him?

He turned to the jeweller then and pointed to a ring, one carved with the jackal head of Seth. "That one. For my future wife." She wondered if she should protest again. Surely choosing a ring made in the image of the god of chaos as a token of love was a bad omen for their marriage? But then, Sekhemkare did nothing but inspire disorder in her life. Furthermore, he and the god of chaos were entwined in her mind. The night she'd met Sekhemkare she'd been twice reminded of the Seth god, and his own sceptre of power was carved with Seth's image.

The eager jeweller, a thin, bald man with sunken cheeks and skin the colour of a walnut shell, seized his chance to make a sale. His chattering cut off any protest she might make. "Congratulations, tayi neb. And you are?"

"Sekhemkare. I am brother and chief advisor to Narmen, governor of Inbu-Hedj, the capital of the Aneb-Hetch sephat. I want something for my wife so that she may remember me always, on this plain and in the hereafter. You see, my dear man, in two days' time I shall marry this darling little woman, daughter of Sobek, the merchant nobleman."

Satsobek disliked the way he threw his shoulders back when he announced who he was. She didn't know why he was making such a big deal now about their marriage, calling attention to the both of them in such a self-important way. She clutched his forearm. "Please, tayi neb, you really need not get me anything."

"Nonsense! I will not hear you argue again. If you do not like this design, chose another." She began to wonder if he was putting on his own display for the jeweller, making a show of his affection for her. But to what end?

He put his arm around her waist and steered her closer to the display. Seeing that he wouldn't take no for an answer, Satsobek looked over the jewellery, hoping that they could move on from this awkward situation of his creation. Finally, she settled on a ring carved with the wings of Isis, the goddess who pieced Osiris' body back together when the Seth god had cut it into little pieces and sent it around the world. It was a fitting counter to Sekhemkare's apparent Seth worship.

"Wonderful!" Sekhemkare exclaimed, clapping his hands once. "You must get used to this, my love, as I wish nothing more than to shower you with jewels and fine linen." He made a show of sliding the ring on her finger and admiring it. As he did so, though, his grip on her hand tightened, and he drew her fingers up to his face for closer inspection. He glared at the ink stains on her fingertips, as if they offended him in some way, before dropping her hand.

He turned to the jeweller and made a show of drawing a lump of gold from a pouch slung around his waist. The jeweller protested, "But tayi neb, this is worth far more than the value of the ring."

"Then you may keep the remains, my good man. This gift for my wife is worth far more than a lump of gold to me." Sekhemkare's met the man's confused and hopeful eyes with a level gaze.

"Oh thank you, tayi neb." The man's slender fingers folded around the gold, secreting it away in the wink of an eye. "You are truly a kind man. I wish you all the blessings of the gods in your marriage and will pray for you to have many children."

"Thank you. Blessings for the new year."

"And you, sir!" The jeweller called out as Sekhemkare gripped Satsobek's elbow and steered her away.

Satsobek didn't believe for a minute that Sekhemkare had paid the man extra out of good-will. She'd heard him complain about peasants who always seemed to want more wages, and greedy merchants who wanted to charge him more for their goods. He'd once told her father he would rather throw a lump of gold in the Iteru than give it to an undeserving peasant begging in the street. But she couldn't imagine any other reason for his generosity. Could it be possible he truly was trying to impress her?

They meandered in silence around the stalls for some time, stopping here and there. At several of the locations, Sekhemkare made a show of introducing her, and himself, as he had at the first jeweller's. As the light failed she began to notice a change in his appearance. His face took on a waxy sheen, his eyes more hollow. From time to time he would swipe his forearm across his forehead, wiping away perspiration. Although the night was still warm, it had cooled since the sun had set. She wondered why he would be sweating now, and not earlier in the heat of the day.

They'd meandered for some time, and seen most of the stalls, when Sekhemkare said, "I see that you have stains on your fingers." He reached down for her hand and pulled it up, turning her fingertips for her to look at. Oil wicks and torches had been set up on sticks and in the tents around the grounds with the setting of the sun. In the darkness now she could barely see the ink stains. "What have you been doing?" He asked.

Satsobek shrugged. "Writing."

"Surely you are not working at the temple again?" His eyes sharpened and she was reminded of a crocodile's eyes, floating deadly calm just above the surface of the Iteru.

"No. I… sometimes I just like to write. It relaxes me."

He was clearly not interested in what she *liked* to do, as he next asked, "Tell me, do you ever see the queen's Sumerian, the one you worked with on the murder investigation?" He waved his hand nonchalantly, as if Tiya and Yuny's deaths were a mere trifle, yet he watched her closely as they resumed walking.

"Ebrium? He is Eblaiti, not Sumerian. And no. I have not seen him since…" she faltered. Since when? What could she say? That she saw him early the morning of Menkhaf's arrest? Her father would kill her if she told him that. "I did see him in passing at the queen's banquet last week. You were there, you probably saw him also. He is rather hard to miss."

"Yes." Sekhemkare drawled. "The man stands out like a jackal in a flock of ducks." Satsobek was not fond of the comparison, but decided it best to keep her mouth closed.

He tapped the fingers of one hand against his thigh in a restless gesture and asked, "So you have heard no more about the investigation then?"

She looked up at him, confused. "No. As far as I am aware they arrested one of the temple priests and that was the end of it." She paused, considering. "Do you know something more?"

His eyebrows rose and he tented his fingers on his chest. "I? Of course not. What do I know of these things?" Sekhemkare made a quick switch of topics. "My dear, you must be tired with all this. Come. Let us take rest in the home of a friend of mine just off the festival grounds. We can find some refreshment and relax for a time before returning to the festivities, or your home if you prefer."

She realized they were already on the outskirts of the grounds. He had somehow managed to lead them there as they walked. "Oh, I'm fine, thank you. I have no need to rest." She was unwilling to go anywhere outside the festival grounds with him. He seemed increasingly agitated and his movements had taken on a jerky quality. His strange behaviour was making her uncomfortable and she had no desire to be alone with him.

"Please, I insist." Sekhemkare's voice hardened. "I promised your father I would take care of you, and that includes ensuring that you are not overly fatigued. It is not far and we need not stay long." He tugged her along as he continued walking.

"Wait!" Her voice was loud enough to draw a few looks. She tried to shake loose from him but his fingers dug into her arm. "Please, tayi neb, I am not interested in meeting your friend tonight." Panic was beating at her throat. Something felt wrong. "I…I am not feeling well. Perhaps you could just take me back to my father's house? Or if you must see your friend, I can make my way home alone."

"Oh no, my dear. We shall only be a few minutes, I promise."

They were still walking and Satsobek looked around for an excuse to move them back towards the heart of the festival. She saw a familiar face not far off and, without thinking, called out to the woman.

"Iput!" She waved. "How nice to see you again." Sekhemkare had no choice now but to stop alongside her.

The older woman did a good job of covering her shock at being hailed in public by a member of the nobility. As she approached them Satsobek discerned her wig was quite fine, braided with turquoise beads and piled high atop her head. Turquoise earrings hung from her lobes, and she was draped in a thin white linen dress, adorned with only a plain braided belt of flax. She looked like a lady of class, not a woman who ran a tavern where men could procure women for a night.

Beside her, two younger women Satsobek recognized from Iput's tavern were also dressed modestly in plain white dresses that covered their chests and legs. Ironically, with her shenti knotted below her breasts, Satsobek was the most exposed of them all.

Iput raised her eyebrows in curiosity, but gave Satsobek a warm greeting, "My dear little one, how kind of you to take notice of me." Satsobek breathed a sigh of relief that the woman had decided to play along with her. Iput gave Sekhemkare a slow look of assessment, a sultry smile on her lips. But Satsobek noticed how her eyes lingered on Sekhemkare's hand, gripping Satsobek's upper arm hard enough to cause indentations from his fingers. Her brows drew together when she took in the sweat rolling down his cheeks.

"Iput, allow me to introduce Sekhemkare, the brother of one of our northern governors. Sekhemkare, this is Iput. She is a..." Satsobek hesitated for only a second, "successful local businesswoman."

Iput held out her hand, palm down, and propriety required Sekhemkare to take it. As he still held his sceptre in one hand, he was compelled to drop Satsobek's arm, and give a slight bow of acknowledgement as he took Iput's hand. Iput purred, "My, but it is a pleasure to meet you, tayi neb."

Sekhemkare straightened and took up Satsobek's arm again in his strong fingers. He said in his smooth voice, "It is indeed a pleasure to meet *friends* of my wife-to-be. Particularly one such as yourself."

Something about the way he said it made Satsobek stiffen. *Oh gods, he may know who Iput is.* After all, hers was one of the best known establishments in Thinis, although a man like Sekhemkare would be unlikely to have the need to frequent such a place. Men like him usually had women brought to them, or they had concubines or slaves. He could not be happy that the woman he was to marry knew a tavern owner, and was openly acknowledging her in public, forcing him to do the same. Her heart thumped against her chest. Perhaps she had made things worse.

Iput flicked a glance to Satsobek. Satsobek wondered if Sekhemkare saw the brief question in the woman's eyes.

Then Iput returned her attention to Sekhemkare and her mouth curved into a smile. "Well this is good news indeed. Please accept my congratulations."

"Thank you." Sekhemkare gave her a brief bow, then said in a firm voice. "Please, you must excuse us. I was just taking Satsobek to meet some friends of mine. I promised to introduce them to my wife-to-be tonight and they are eager to meet her."

His grip on her arm tightened and he began to steer her away. Satsobek pulled back a little, hoping to delay him. "Wait, *where* exactly did you say we were going? My feet *are* a little tired and if it is far perhaps we could rest on a bench here." Some small part of her hoped that if Iput overheard where they were going... well... at least someone knew where she was. Just in case...

Sekhemkare made a sound of irritation. "My friend has a hut north of the grounds, near the Iteru. It is just before the port where the merchants come in to dock. It is not far and we will not be there long. I promise you, my dear."

Satsobek twisted to look over her shoulder at Iput, wishing that somehow, in the darkness, she could convey her concerns to the woman. Satsobek had no idea if Iput would understand, or even care, or know what to do even *if* she cared, but it was *something*, and it was all she had. Iput was still facing them, although back-lit by the oil wicks of the festival grounds, so that Satsobek could only see her silhouette, blacker than the night sky on a moonless night.

"Goodnight, Iput." She called out. "I do hope to see you again soon." Ridiculous of her to say, but what else could she do? If she broke away from Sekhemkare and fled, her father would be furious, and do everything he'd threatened to do, possibly more. She had no real reason to fear Sekhemkare, but her instincts were screaming at her to run. If she could raise Iput's suspicion then perhaps...what? She didn't know.

An image of Ebrium flashed through her mind, but that hope flickered only for a second. Ebrium must hate her for what she'd done to him. And what could he do anyway? Sekhemkare hadn't done anything wrong.

Yet. The little voice of fear whispered.

That little voice was validated a moment later as Sekhemkare's fingers pressed painfully into the sensitive underside of her arm. He steered her faster into the darkness outside the festival. His voice was a hiss as he leaned down by her ear. "I hope you have had your fun, introducing me to that *whore* of a woman, because it is over now. We will go where I say we will go, or else your friends Ebrium and Iput will never see the light of day again."

Satsobek jerked to a stop in shock, but Sekhemkare dragged her along beside him. "Oh yes," his voice seethed with satisfaction. "I know all about your little escapade to the village, and that slut's tavern."

"How did you…?"

"Later. Don't worry, *my love*," sarcasm was thick in his voice as he waved his sceptre at her, an awful leer spreading over his face. "I shall reveal all to you in good time."

An awful realization dawned on her, more important than trying to convince him of her innocence. She'd suddenly remembered why Sekhemkare's sceptre was significant.

Frantic with fear, Satsobek sought some form of escape. Short of dropping to the ground, there was no way to break from his claw-like grip. And she had no doubt that if she managed to break free of him, he would only grab her and throw her over his shoulder. They were far enough from the festival grounds now, and walking deeper into the thick reeds alongside the Iteru, that she doubted anyone was near enough to hear them. She had no choice but to go along with him and bide her time.

Satsobek's eyes adjusted to the night sky and the sliver of moonlight that illuminated her surroundings, shimmering a silver trail along the dark waters of the Iteru that ran next to them. It wasn't long before a hut loomed ahead of them. Sekhemkare pulled her forward and, using the carved Seth head of his sceptre, banged on the door. The door swung open and Satsobek gasped, recognizing the face that materialized in the gloom.

And that's when Satsobek decided to turn and run.

She made it about ten feet before a weight fell on her back, knocking her face first into the scratchy reeds and dry earth, causing her to bite her tongue hard. She cried out, but a hand clapped over her mouth. The hawk-faced man's distinctive accent sneered in her ear, "How nice to see you again, nebet-i. Scream again and I'll snap your neck."

Chapter 18 – The Hut in the Reeds

The last rays of the setting sun slanted through the narrow windows in Ebrium's greeting hall, casting a warm glow on the white-washed walls that was in direct contrast to Ebrium's black mood. It was the evening of the Festival of the New Year and Ebrium had been pacing the greeting hall of his manor for over an hour. His mind was churning over utterly useless facts and memories.

Satsobek was due to marry in two days and he still had nothing of consequence to put a stop to the marriage. Every day since Menkhaf's arrest Ebrium had visited the house of the boy said to have witnessed the mysterious late-night visitor to the temple. The man who supposedly carried a *wass*. And every day the servants told him the boy had not yet returned from visiting family in the north. Three days ago Ebrium stationed a man in front of the house to watch it and report back the moment the boy appeared.

Each day he visited the *hnrt* to question the men who attacked him and Satsobek the night they left the House of Iput. Unfortunately, one of the men took it upon himself to hasten his punishment and slit his throat with a shard of a mug he'd broken. That left only one other man and Menkhaf, the priest. Both stayed true to their stories, no matter what Ebrium did to press them.

A knocking at the front door broke off his pacing. He'd been expecting Batr and Makae. The men had insisted that he was too obsessed with a case that, to all outside appearances, he'd solved. They'd forced him to agree to join them for the Festival of the New Year tonight, at least for an hour or so.

Ebrium opened the door of his manor and Batr gave a low whistle as the brothers stepped inside. Then he clapped Ebrium on the shoulder. "This is something, brother. You've done well for yourself here."

Ebrium shook his head. "I did nothing."

Batr scoffed. "Of course you did. You caught some bad men and were rewarded by the queen for your efforts. Accept it as a well-deserved commendation. But why are you answering your own door? You should have a servant do it." Batr waved his hand in an imperial fashion. "You are almost nobility now. How does it look to entertain esteemed guests such as us and answer your own door like a peasant?"

Ebrium snorted, his mood slightly lifted by his friends' presence. There was amusement in Makae's voice as he said, "My brother seems to think that once you move up in the world you should also behave like you have the *asastru* of a donkey."

Batr turned to his brother, mock seriousness written on his face. "If I had donkey *asastru*," *donkey testicles*, "I would spend my days amongst a harem of women and let whoever is at the front door be damned to the underworld for all I care." Ebrium's mouth twitched in a smile, shaking his heads at Batr's typical train of thought.

Batr moved through the entranceway and Ebrium and Makae followed. Batr peeked into doorways as he went, causing Ebrium and Makae to exchange wry looks at the man's curious and brazen nature. "Now, I hear you even have yourself a few servants. I know you have yet to entertain guests here, but let me tell you how it's done. Call for a boy – or a handsome woman if you have one – to bring us some wine and a plate of those sweet honey buns I so love. We'll dine on the rooftop and watch the sun set over our fair city before joining the festivities."

Well familiar his friend's audacity, Ebrium called out to Seret to bring wine and some food as he led the two brothers through his courtyard and up the steps to the rooftop. Just as they were mounting the stairs, another knock at the door stopped them. Ebrium turned and made it to the door at the same time Seret limped in to answer it. He let Seret do his job and pull open the heavy wooden door.

There, standing on the doorstep, was the lanky village boy Ebrium had hired to watch the temple boy's house.

"Sir," the boy's voice was eager, "the one you were waiting for is back. He came back not long ago. But you gotta hurry. I heard him say something to his father about going to the festival tonight."

Twenty minutes later Ebrium, Batr, and Makae were still catching their breath as they were led into a small hut near the Temple of Mehyt. They introduced themselves to the boy's father, who produced his son – a short, lean, tanned boy of about fourteen years. Ebrium set about asking him questions about what he'd seen. The boy, Pentu, was reluctant to speak at first.

"I... I don't recall exactly, sir. I may not have seen anything out of the ordinary at all."

His father, a well-muscled, stocky fellow who'd introduced himself as a stone-cutter, elbowed his son and growled in warning, "Whatever you saw, Pentu, tell 'em. They're the queen's men."

The boy looked uncertainly at his father, still hesitating. His father sighed. "Boy, I'll not punish you this time if you've done something wrong. Just tell 'em what you know. It's important."

Pentu tightened his lips and nodded. "Yes. I snuck back to the temple kitchen late one night, about three weeks ago, when I knew no one would be there." His eyes flicked to his father and he hunched, as if waiting for a blow. The father rolled his eyes, shook his head and said, "Go on, boy."

"I just wanted to get a honey roll. We... we can't afford the honey, and I wanted to try it. It was dark and I was just inside the kitchen when I saw one of the priests, Menkhaf. He was out back of the temple near the door, the one near the kitchen."

Ebrium nodded, he remembered the back door of the temple opened onto a short pathway that led to the kitchen, a separate building behind the temple. The boy continued. "There was another man with them. He was carrying a *wass*. The head was in the shape of a Seth head, the jackal."

Ebrium's eyes narrowed. "Did you see the man? What did he look like?"

Pentu bobbed his head. "He was tall, not quite your height, sir. Broad shoulders and good muscles. A long side-lock braided on the side of his head. I heard one of the other men call him tayi neb, and I think his name was something like Sekhmare, or Sekhemk," the boy frowned, shaking his head. "I'm not sure, sir. I don't recall exactly. Only I remember the man because of the *wass*, and because it seemed odd that they were there late at night."

Ebrium's heart was pounding in his chest. *This is it.* It wasn't concrete, it might not be enough to arrest Sekhemkare, but it was damned close to enough.

"Wait," Ebrium frowned, "what did the *wass* look like again?"

"Like a Seth head. You know, the jackal's head." The boy cupped his hand at a sharp angle, his fingers straight out and pressed together, like the head of a swan. With his other hand he added a finger sticking straight out from the knuckles of the curved hand. "With the ears, like this." He wiggled the finger.

And there it was. The detail Ebrium needed to make the connection. Yuny had been beaten with something that had the exact shape the boy was making with his hands. Something hard enough to bruise, to knock a man down. Something exactly like the sceptre that a very wealthy, powerful man would carry.

"Pentu, did you see the man at any other time?" Ebrium asked.

The boy glanced up at his father again. "Boy," the stone-cutter rumbled, "tell 'em everything you know, or you had better start running now and not look back."

Pentu hung his head. His voice was so low Ebrium almost didn't catch his words. "I was there the night of the murders. I was in the kitchen." He drew his shoulder up to protect the side of his head as his father's lips tightened and he frowned at the boy. "I – I was waiting for one of the kitchen girls. But nothing happened between us, I swear to Mehyt! She never showed up."

"What did you see, Pentu?" Ebrium was losing patience. At the moment he couldn't care less if the boy impregnated the girl and fled Kemet. He needed to find Satsobek and make sure she was alright.

"I… I saw the man again. There were others with him this time. I only saw them because I heard a shout from inside the temple. I peeked inside the doorway and saw a body lying on the ground…" Pentu licked his lips; a pained expression crossed his face, as if the memory hurt. "I suppose it must have been the high priest. I heard shuffling inside the goddess's chamber, then I saw the man with the *wass* come out of the chamber. That's when I ran. I think… well it's possible they heard me in the corridor."

The father looked startled. "And that's why you asked me if we could travel to visit your sick uncle."

Pentu nodded, shame written on his face. "I was afraid the man with the *wass* might come looking for me. I didn't know who they'd killed, only that they had to be powerful. I… I didn't want to get you involved, dad. And then I heard about the murders, and that the priest was arrested. I thought it'd be safe to come back after some time had passed." He addressed Ebrium and the brothers. "I… I'm so sorry. I should have come forward right away, but I was afraid of getting in trouble for being there in the first place. I didn't know who I could trust. If someone powerful had killed the priest and priestess, well…I was afraid there might be some conspiracy."

"I understand," Ebrium said. And he did. The boy had every right to be suspicious after seeing something like that.

The men took their leave of the boy and his father. Outside the hut, Ebrium rapped out to the two brothers, "We need to find Sekhemkare and Satsobek. *Now.* If Sekhemkare's *wass* matches Yuny's bruises then we have him." A feeling of urgency pressed against his sternum, one he couldn't explain but wouldn't ignore. He trusted his instincts and if they told him he had to hurry, he would do so.

A look passed between Batr and Makae, and Ebrium growled. "What now?"

Makae held a hand out, palm up. With obvious reluctance he said, "It is only… are you sure…"

Batr cut him off. "How do you know the girl isn't in on it with him? She did drop you as soon as you'd caught Menkhaf. Is it possible she had something to do with this?"

Irritation flickered across Makae's face and he elbowed his brother. Hooking his thumbs into the belt of his shenti, he leaned back on his heels. "What we're trying to say is, is it possible she might've gotten close to you in order to find out what you knew?"

Ebrium blinked. The brothers didn't know everything that had transpired between him and Satsobek, but they knew enough. It never crossed his mind to consider her involvement. Doubt niggled at him. She *had* been reluctant to blame anyone for the crime, but then she was the one who implicated Menkhaf with the faulty accounts. It had taken her a couple of days to tell him why she left the temple – had she made that story up to get his sympathy? Had she planned a marriage with Sekhemkare all along, or did he somehow convince her to help him cover up his involvement? Could she have been telling the truth when he last saw her? Did she truly *want* to marry Sekhemkare?

Several images flashed through his mind: Satsobek's sudden appearance in the House of Iput, her fingers tracing his tattoo while she ran her tongue over her lips, her showing up at his manor with Seret, then slipping to her knees between his legs and taking his hard length into her mouth.

But then he remembered other things as well. Her getting sick after seeing Tiya's necklace, her fighting for her life when they were attacked by the hawk-faced man and his group, the look in her eyes when he entered her, and the way she cried out his name.

"No." His voice was firm. "It's not possible."

Batr snorted. "Listen, friend, I know you have a soft spot for the girl, but don't let your cock lead the way here."

Ebrium's hands clenched and he took a step towards Batr. "And if you're not careful, I'll let my fists lead the way straight to your face. Now enough of this."

Batr put his hands up in surrender and smiled. "Alright, then! Let's go find this bastard."

The hawk-faced man hauled Satsobek to her feet, trapping her arms at her sides, and carried her past several men into the gloom of the brick hut. The inside consisted of one large room, and a smaller one off to the side. Reed mats covered the floor, a couple of small crude tables rested against a wall with jugs on them, and three low stools crowded the centre of the room. Sitting on one of the stools was a man she recognized. The man she had kicked between the legs the night of the attack outside the House of Iput. The feral look he gave her froze her breath in her chest.

The hawk-faced man dropped her and she stumbled, falling to her knees. Sekhemkare followed them into the hut and Satsobek realized he was starting to look very ill. He was perspiring heavily and his eyes flicked around the room. "You must excuse Mernon here, Satsobek." He gestured to the glaring man. "He is not very pleased to see you. Or perhaps I should say he is a little *too* pleased to see you."

Sekhemkare stepped past her, dipping a shaking finger into one of the jugs, testing the temperature. Nodding, he poured the water into a mug and tapped some hul gil in.

He swirled the mug around to dissipate the sticky residue before taking a long drink and continuing. "You see you really damaged one of his *asastru* – his testicles – when you kicked him. Mernon hasn't been able to walk properly since, have you Mernon?" Sekhemkare clapped a hand on the man's shoulder, a smirk on his face. "But then, I suppose it is lucky for you that his asastru are not working well, or else he might try to use them to take revenge on you."

Satsobek quelled, but drew herself up to her feet, giving Mernon a wide berth. "Why did you kill them?" She didn't know what Sekhemkare's plan was for her, but whatever it was she wanted to know why he'd killed her mentor and the high priest. Sekhemkare must have been there, or at least been involved.

Sekhemkare jerked his head at the two men. "Get out." The hawk-faced man hesitated, and Sekhemkare snapped at him, "I said GET OUT, you fool. You've caused enough problems already. Send the messenger and then stay hidden outside with the others and wait for the queen's man. This is your last chance to fix your mistakes and if you do not do it right I will hand you to the queen myself and watch them cut your ears off."

When they were alone a minute later Sekhemkare turned his back to her, poured a mug of warmed wine from one of the jugs on the table, and offered it to her. She accepted it, needing something to steady her hands and her thoughts.

"Sit, sit." He gestured to one of the stools. He sat across from her and sipped again from his mug. His eyes rolled back and he closed them as the hul gil began to take its effect. That feeling of watching something perverse and intimate washed over Satsobek again, stronger this time because she was alone in a dark hut with the man.

Tired of waiting for him to answer after a few moments, she asked, "Why did you ask to marry me? What does it have to do with Tiya and Yuny?"

Finally, he opened his eyes and a lazy smile spread across his face. He seemed more relaxed now that he had a cup of hul gil in his hand. He said, "I'm sorry, but it was never about you." The remorse in his voice was almost convincing. "Having you is like having a safeguard, so to speak. But let me start at the beginning, to answer your first question. We have some time before your lover is due to arrive."

"My what?" Satsobek's heart clenched. *Ebrium*. Hope swelled, then turned to cold fear as she realized that Sekhemkare must have something awful planned. She had a vision of her and Ebrium lying dead on the floor of this little hut, and a wave of nausea overtook her. She took a gulp of wine. It was warm, and soothing. Her muscles relaxed, and she took another deep sip.

"Yes," Sekhemkare watched her beneath his half-closed lids. "As you can see, the fools that attacked you work for me. They didn't know who you were that night at Iput's, they just thought you were a whore, spending time with a foreign bastard who had gotten in their way of having a good time. They followed you back to that dog's hovel in the village. I know exactly what kind of woman you are, so you need not pretend otherwise."

Satsobek didn't bother to argue. She took another sip of wine, feeling her heart beat return to normal pace.

The repugnant man across from her continued. "It was all an accident, really." His shoulders lifted in a nonchalant shrug. As if discussing the murder of two people was an everyday occurrence of little concern. "The priest and the woman were never supposed to die."

His older brother was aging, he said, but refused to die and give up governorship of their sephat, something Sekhemkare had coveted almost since childhood. Several years ago, Sekhemkare began building resources to help overthrow his brother. He couldn't recruit fighters from within his own sephat, where his brother was well-liked. Infiltrating the temples seemed the best way to gather assets to pay mercenaries and bribe other powerful nobles and officials. Menkhaf was only one of many he'd managed to either blackmail or put into positions of power across Kemet.

Satsobek sipped more wine. She understood now why she'd been so focused on the Seth god lately. The gods rarely bothered with human affairs, but she felt sure that the pervasive images of the fratricidal jackal-headed Seth had been a warning from the gods. Her mind began to meander, wondering which of the gods it could have been. Mehyt? Horus, perhaps? Or maybe even Ra. Her body was relaxing with the wine, and her fear of Sekhemkare diminishing. As if from outside herself, she wondered why the sense of urgency she'd had was evaporating, and why she'd even been afraid in the first place.

Sekhemkare watched her over the rim of his mug, his lips quirked upwards, then continued. "But you see, I'm cursed with inept associates. First the high priest discovered what Menkhaf was doing – helping himself to the inventory. The fool got sloppy and kept his records out in the open in his workspace. Yuny didn't realize, of course, that almost all of the wealth was being shipped to me.

"Menkhaf was able to keep the high priest under control for a time, a few months or so, by threatening to reveal his… *relationship* with the carpenter." Sekhemkare bared his teeth in a parody of a smile at the reference to Imhotep. "But after a time Menkhaf said he feared the priest was getting jumpy, that he might just take his chances and reveal everything. That's when I came to visit Thinis with my men here. Menkhaf thought if Yuny realized the magnitude of what he was up against he would be more… *pliable.*"

Satsobek shook her head, realizing the wine must be clouding her thinking. She was having a difficult time focusing and couldn't recall when she'd eaten last. Her voice sounded thick in her ears as she asked, "But what about Tiya? Why Tiya?"

"Ahhh. The priestess." Sekhemkare steepled his fingers. "Let us not get ahead of the story here." Sekhemkare told her that he'd seen Menkhaf a few nights before the murder. He was nervous, afraid he'd soon be detected by someone else. They didn't know then that Tiya had, in fact, somehow already discovered inventory was missing from the records. She'd gone to Yuny and, after questioning him about the accounts, he'd told her about the blackmail. They devised a scheme to catch Menkhaf. She would sneak into the temple each time Menkhaf and Yuny met in order to witness and keep track of their interactions.

"If we hadn't caught them when we did, their scheme might have succeeded. But if she'd stayed out of it they'd still be alive, you'd be free to whore yourself to your Sumerian, and I wouldn't be in this position. Do you understand now? It was never about you." He said it as if he expected that knowledge to comfort Satsobek.

"But how do you know all this?" Satsobek frowned, trying to keep track of everything. She understood now why Tiya had a list of dates and numbers. The dates were the days Yuny and Menkhaf met to do the inventory and fix the accounts. The numbers represented the items stolen.

"Ahhh, yes this is where that idiot out there got out of hand." He gestured to the door, and Satsobek assumed he meant the hawk-faced man. "It was a mixed blessing of sorts, you see. The last time I saw the high priest, the night he died, he was very agitated. He insisted that all activities cease, he was concerned we'd be caught. I refused, of course. The hwt of Mehyt is one of my more lucrative sources of wealth.

"Yuny was angry, and he moved too quickly for Arned's liking," he jerked his head again towards the door, and Satsobek took it to mean that Arned and the hawk-faced man were one and the same. "There was a *light* scuffle," Sekhemkare made a twisting motion with his hand, as if to downplay the significance of the scuffle.

"My *wass* was resting against the wall. Arned grabbed it and hit the priest. From there, well…" the evil man shrugged. "Arned can be a violent man sometimes. He has his uses, and he is quite loyal, but his temper is a little… difficult. Once he hit the priest there was nothing for it but to finish the job. I heard a noise in a room nearby, and found your priestess hiding in the goddess's cabinet. She was, of course, reluctant at first to tell me how she came to be there, but a little persuasion can go a long way. And that, my dear, is how I know what they were plotting."

Satsobek felt bile rising up in her throat. The sense of urgency and fear that had slipped away suddenly slammed back into her chest, and she pushed herself out of her chair. She needed to run for the door, to throw up, to get air, to *get away.*

But her feet weren't working. Too heavy, too clumsy, they tripped over each other and she tumbled to the ground, not even able to make her hands reach out to break her fall.

She banged her hip on the floor and her shoulder smacked the stool she'd been sitting on. The pain hardly registered, though, and even in her haze of fear she wondered why not. She blinked at Sekhemkare's sandal-shod feet, now very near to her face. His toenails, she noticed, were in desperate need of a shortening.

He smiled down at her from where he sat on his stool. "You see now why hul gil is such a wonderful thing. A small amount is useful for pain relief and a little extra now and then makes you nice and relaxed. A large amount, such as what I slipped into your wine, can be very useful for incapacitating someone. I had a feeling it might be problematic getting you to sit still for a few hours while we waited for that foreigner to show up to save you. I thought you might enjoy the chance to test out what your father and I have been haggling over lately."

His face loomed large as he leaned down close to her. "I am also not without mercy. When I kill you and the Sumerian, or whatever you call him," he lifted his shoulders to show how little he cared what anyone called Ebrium, "the hul gil should help dull the pain."

Satsobek's heart sped. Or at least she thought it *should*. She couldn't tell for sure what her body was doing. She tried to pull herself off the floor, but her legs and arms were slow to respond, as if she'd fallen into a barrel of date syrup. It took great effort to open her eyelids. "No." She croaked. "You cannot."

Sekhemkare shook his head, an obscene look of innocent reassurance on his face. "I have no choice. You see, it is really all that big bastard's fault. Blame the queen's man. I only asked your father to let me marry you because I wanted to keep an eye on you and the investigation. Best to keep your enemies close, and all that. By that point I knew you'd been whoring around in the village, and you can trust me when I say I had no intentions of following through with a marriage. When Menkhaf was arrested and your father told me he had insisted you stop your involvement, I thought you might not be of use anymore.

"But then, you see, that bastard of yours wouldn't give up. I hear he has been visiting Menkhaf and my other men in prison. *Every. Single. Day.*" Sekhemkare was clearly angered by Ebrium's efficiency. His fists clenched on his thighs. Then he took a deep breath and smoothed his palms over his shenti. "You see, I had to find some way to make him stop. He cannot pursue me when he is dead."

Sekhemkare shrugged. "So I have sent someone to find that lame boy that works for him, and tell Ebrium you must speak with him alone. That you will be here waiting for him. Once he's found, I have no doubt he will come running to you. Then it's easy. I kill you, then him. I tell everyone that I lost sight of you at the festival and the bastard kidnapped you in a jealous rage. He brought you here and killed you. I searched for you, found you lying here dead, and I killed the rabid dog who stole my dearly beloved wife-to-be. I even had a boy from the village procure this hut from the fishmonger who lives here under Ebrium's name, so nobody will know I arranged all this."

He rubbed his palms together and his lips hitched up in a smug smile. "I think it is my best plan yet. I will be the poor man who lost the woman he longed for and the queen will be discredited for her ill decision-making in pairing you together in the first place."

Satsobek realized now why he'd made such a big deal at the festival of buying her the ring. He wanted witnesses to his supposed affection for her so that he'd appear innocent of any wrong-doing. Even in her drug-induced haze, it sounded like a desperate attempt to cover his crimes. Covering up two murders with two more was absurd. Perhaps he had been taking too much hul gil. If he got anywhere near as intoxicated as she was when he took it, it was a wonder he could think of anything at all. But bad plan or not, she'd likely still end up dead. And Ebrium along with her.

She floundered on the floor, like a fish out of water, managing to propel herself towards the nearby wall and prop up against it. "No," she murmured. "Your plan is wrong. Ebrium will not come for me." After what she'd said to him at the queen's banquet she didn't think he'd ever want to see her again.

"Oh, I'm quite sure he'll come. But we also have quite a bit of time before that happens, and I think I know just how we can pass it." She looked up to find Sekhemkare towering over her. "We may not be marrying in two days' time, my dear, but I think it is only fitting you should get to sample just what you'll be missing." He crouched down next to her and reached for her ankle.

It was dark enough to see the stars in the sky by the time Ebrium, Batr, and Makae hurried up the steps of a large manor roughly halfway between Satsobek's home and Ebrium's own manor. Ebrium had learned several days back that Sekhemkare had spent the last three weeks living in the home of a cousin of his. He was glad now that he knew where to look for the man, and that it wasn't far from the temple grounds and Pentu's home.

A servant answered the door and informed them that Sekhemkare had left hours before. When pressed, he suggested they check Sobek's house, as that was where he spent a great deal of time lately. They rushed to Satsobek's father's house, where Ebrium ran up the steps ahead of the brothers and banged on the door.

A lean, elderly servant with short, curly grey hair opened the door. "Yes?" He ran a disdainful eye over Ebrium.

"Your master. *Now.*" Ebrium growled. The man hesitated, but just then a young girl appeared next to him. She was about Satsobek's height, but broader and heavier, and she laid a hand on the older man's arm. "Paser," she addressed the older man. "This is Ebrium. The queen's man who saved Satsobek from the tiger."

Paser's eyes widened and he pulled open the door. Ebrium nodded to the girl, who ran to get Sobek. Batr and Makae joined Ebrium in the entranceway and a moment later an older bald man came striding into the room. The man was tall and, despite the rotund belly that preceded him, he carried his weight well. His meaty shoulders were thrown back, his chest out.

"What's this all about?" He pointed a thick finger in Ebrium's direction. "*You* are not welcome here. I told the girl that days ago. Now get out of here before you force me to do something you'll regret."

The girl? Was that how he referred to his daughter? Things began to fall into place in his mind. Ebrium's sense of urgency turned to calm wrath. "And just what exactly, will you do, tayi neb?" Ebrium drawled, his voice laced with deadly sarcasm as he called the man *my lord.*

Sobek's eyes narrowed. "Exactly what I told that obstinate little bitch I'd do. I'll tell everyone how you defiled my daughter, and the queen enabled it to happen. I will *ruin* you, and your precious queen, too."

Ebrium was slightly taken aback that the man knew about him and Satsobek. But then he chuckled. "You fool. If you do that you'd ruin yourself, also, wouldn't you? Would Sekhemkare still have her if he knew? I can see by the look on your face you don't believe he would. You'd lose your new business partner. Yes, I know you're entering into a shipping contract with him, and that the scrolls will be signed the same day as their marriage."

Ebrium still didn't know all the details — such as *what* they were shipping — but a couple of days back he'd found the scribe involved in drawing up Satsobek's marriage contract, and he'd learned the details of her father and Sekhemkare's business arrangement.

Sobek sneered, wiping the back of his hand across wet lips. "I'd rather lose the contract and *any* marriage prospects than give her to a bastard like you. I'll sell her to work in the fields before I let you have her."

As if sensing his urge to do violence to the man, Makae placed a hand on Ebrium's arm, but Ebrium shook him off and instead said, "Tell me, did you know Sekhemkare was a murderer before or after you forced Satsobek to agree to the marriage?"

Sobek blinked. "No. You're lying." But he didn't sound very confident.

Ebrium smirked, savouring the moment of triumph. "I assure you I'm not. He'll likely be disemboweled within a few weeks for the crimes he's committed." The severity of Sekhemkare's penalty would depend on how much Ebrium could prove, but Sobek didn't need to know that.

Unrelenting, he'd stepped closer to Sobek with each point he made until he was looming over him and Sobek was forced to take a few steps backwards. The rotund man might have been imposing in his youth but Ebrium towered over him, and was fitter than the other man had ever been.

"If you persist in trying to compel Satsobek to marry, I'll ensure that you're brought up on charges for conspiring with Sekhemkare. Whether for murder or treason doesn't matter, either will do. Anything you say to besmirch the queen's name will only work against you. So you see, it's not *you* that will ruin me, but *I* that will ruin you. If you still intend to incriminate yourself, I urge you to do so while I have two more of the queen's men here to witness it." He gestured to Batr and Makae who stood just behind him.

Batr grinned, raised a hand and waggled his fingers. "Hello. You have a lovely daughter, by the way."

"In the future, you'll let Satsobek marry whomever she chooses, whenever she chooses. Or I'll make sure you're the one who ends up working in the fields. The hnrt can always use extra slave labour and traitors are quite welcome there. Now tell me," Ebrium made a point of clenching his thick fists. "Where is your daughter?"

Satsobek tried to jerk her leg and shake off Sekhemkare's hand, but at best managed to make her knee twitch. He grasped her ankle before sliding his fingers up her calf, pushing her dress up as he went. He watched her face, seeming to enjoy her panic.

"You see," he purred in his low, smooth voice, "you are not really my type, my dear. I like my ladies with a little bit more to grab on to." His gaze brushed her bared breasts, and she shivered. Or at least she did inside, even if her body was slow to react. "But I find that circumstances have heightened my interest. You do look rather better than usual tonight. Red becomes you." He reached out and slipped a finger under the strings of carnelian beads that rested on her chest between her breasts. He skimmed his finger along the beads, coming perilously close to her nipples.

With a massive effort she was able to lean away from him, pulling the beads, and her breasts, away from his touch. "Go to Ammit," she swore, wishing him to the underworld.

She spat at him but, lacking force, she couldn't spit far enough to hit him.

He chuckled. "I *do* like that you have a little wild streak in you. It makes it that much more fun knowing that right now, I can do *anything* I want to you. Does your foreign bastard play rough with you? Because I think that's what a woman like you needs, is it not?" He grabbed both of her ankles and yanked them out at right angles in front of her.

"NO!" She shouted, or she tried to. It came out more of a hoarse whisper. Her head lolled as she searched for something, *anything*, to help her. Nearby was the stool she'd been sitting on. She'd knocked it over when she'd fallen to the ground. One leg was just out of arm's reach. If she could just grab it... if she could muster the strength to hit him with it...

"Fight if you like, my dear," Sekhemkare crooned, "if it makes you feel better. I don't mind. In fact, sometimes I like it better that way. But it will be less painful for you if you just give in." With a quick motion, he flipped her over on to her stomach, scraping her bare skin on the rough dirt floor, and began to pull at the ties of her shenti around her waist.

The movement put her within access to the stool and, with a burst of energy, Satsobek grabbed the wooden leg and twisted, hitting him across the head with it. The blow wasn't as hard as she'd hoped – the angle too awkward and her strength too weak – but it surprised him and he reared back from the blow, enabling her to roll onto her back again.

"Bitch!" He swore, and backhanded her across the cheek. Her head snapped to the side and this time, when she cried out, her voice worked. A little voice inside her actually gave thanks to the hul gil – at least she didn't feel the pain much. He positioned himself between her legs and shoved her shenti up. His hands touched her thighs and she squeezed her eyes shut, praying to every god she could name that the hul gil would just knock her unconscious.

Ebrium and the brothers waded through the crowds at the festival, searching silhouettes for any resemblance to Satsobek or Sekhemkare. Their height gave them an advantage over the smaller people of Kemet, but their eyesight was no better than anyone else in the dark. It was the stuff of nightmares, searching for one short woman in a sea of people with only the stars and a few torches to see by. After what felt like hours Ebrium swore and turned in a circle, dragging his hands through his hair in frustration.

Batr shrugged and said, "Maybe there's nothing to worry about. We have no indication that he wants to hurt her."

Ebrium snorted. "Why would he ask for her when he must've known she was investigating the murders? No, he's planning something. I'm sure of it. The longer she's with him the greater her danger." The sick feeling in the pit of his stomach told him he had to find her, and soon.

Makae murmured, "Perhaps they've left the festival already and gone elsewhere? They may even be on their way back to her house."

The men were standing near the road that led out of the festival. Ebrium looked over the tops of the heads into the gloom beyond the festival grounds. Two shadowy figures emerged from the darkness, hurrying towards the grounds. One was unusually large, while the other had a distinctive, loping gait. Ebrium began shoving people out of his way as he rushed towards them.

Within moments Bey and Seret stood before him. The boy was panting. "A messenger, sir." He clutched at the robe over his chest, gasping out the words. "They came by the manor for you. Satsobek sent him. She needs to see you."

Bey frowned. "I thought to catch you at dinner for a visit before the festival, but instead found Seret ready to leave to look for you. Is everything alright? You look…" Bey made a gesture that suggested Ebrium looked as frantic as he felt.

"No. Thank the gods you're here, brother." Ebrium grasped Bey's forearm. "Something's amiss." Just then a woman's voice called out Ebrium's name, causing the men to turn back towards the festival entrance. Iput was making her way over to them, two other women at her side.

From then it was only a matter of minutes before Ebrium and the other men were running towards the docks north of the grounds, with Seret doing his best to keep stride.

"There," Bey whispered, pointing into the murky darkness. Ebrium squinted, and the figure of a man formed, separate from the tree trunk that rose up beside it. The men had spotted the hut based on the directions the messenger gave Seret, but given what Iput told them about her encounter with Satsobek and Sekhemkare, they'd decided it best to approach with caution.

Thank the gods they had. The great Iteru was close by, and the waning moon shone like liquid silver on the water's surface. The hut was surrounded by tall reeds, spotted here and there with leafy date palm trees that helped hide Sekhemkare's men. How many men were lurking in the brush? It was difficult to tell. Their silhouettes were black on black, against a midnight blue backdrop. When Ebrium's eyes flicked past the hut, light from the oil wicks flickering inside temporarily blinded him, so that he could see their tiny flames in his line of vision even when he looked away.

Around them the sounds of the burbling river at night were deafening, masking their careful steps, but also those of their enemies. Cloaked in the papyri thickets, crickets chirped while toads buzzed and croaked. An owl hooted. Something slithered through the reeds nearby and Ebrium shuffled his feet, suppressing a shiver as an image rose in his mind of one of the enormous, deadly cobras that made their homes in hidden places.

He blinked, surveying the area around the hut and clenching his curved blade in his hand, as did the others with him. Batr had even handed Seret a small blade that he kept strapped to his calf. At least they were not unarmed. The men spread out and moved forward, hunched to make use of the reeds as cover. Ebrium took a more direct route towards the front door. Out of the corner of his eye, he saw Batr sneak up behind a man and silently snap his neck. Off to his left a man leaped up from the reeds and ran at Makae, calling out as he did, alerting his companions to their presence.

That's when a familiar face rushed towards him, cutting a path through the reeds with his thick thighs. It was one of the men who'd attacked them outside the House of Iput, the one Satsobek had kicked between the legs. He brandished a long, thick stick and raised it to rap at Ebrium's head. Ebrium stepped to the side, swinging his blade and slicing the man's bicep.

At the same time, blinding pain exploded in his flank underneath his blade arm, sending him staggering to the left. Looking over his shoulder in shock, he caught a glimpse of another familiar face before his ribs received a second punishing blow, forcing the air from Ebrium's lungs in a loud whoosh.

The hawk-faced man. With a smirk on his cruel face, the man wielded both a short stick and a blade. He quickly struck out with the stick again, this time aiming for Ebrium's head, but Ebrium was prepared and caught the brunt of the blow with his left forearm, lashing out with his blade. The hawk-faced man parried and spun out of reach.

He sneered at Ebrium as he bounced his weight from foot to foot. "I am so glad we could meet again."

Arrogant bastard, Ebrium thought, not bothering to answer as he circled the other man, assessing his handling of his blade instead. He was smaller, thinner, and lighter on his feet than Ebrium. Probably faster, too. Ebrium was certainly stronger, and in a bare-knuckled fight he'd have the advantage. He was always better with his fists anyway. But the man Satsobek had kicked was now coming back up on his other side and he was out-numbered and under-armed.

The hawk-faced man lashed out with his blade, and Ebrium blocked it. But then the hawk-faced man lunged forward and, too late, Ebrium dodged to the side, the long knife opening up a cut across his left pectoral. At the same time, he used the hand that held his own blade to cuff the hawk-faced man on the skull, sending him reeling.

The first man stepped forward, stick raised to attack but, with an upward assault of his knife, Ebrium struck the stick out of the man's hand and into the air, where it landed somewhere in the reeds behind him. He drove his elbow into the man's chin, snapping his head to the side and stunning him.

Again the hawk-faced man came up alongside him and bashed his ribs with several short, rapid hits with the stick before Ebrium could drop his arm and trap the stick against his side, wrenching it from the man's grasp. The cut on Ebrium's chest was now bleeding freely and he'd felt something crack on the last blow to his torso, probably a rib. His blade arm was growing weak.

He was still trying to draw in breath when the hawk-faced man tricked him by stepping back, as if in retreat, before lunging forward to thrust at Ebrium's flank. At the last second Ebrium deflected, the hilt of his blade catching the other man's knife, pushing it to the side, but it scraped his abdomen, opening another wound. Ebrium used the man's forward momentum to drive his fist into the hawk-faced man's cheekbone, snarling as he did so.

His big hand hammered once more, causing a satisfying crunch, before the man could leap back. The hawk-faced man twisted around, slicing open Ebrium's bicep with the edge of his knife. Blood began to flow down his arm and the man smiled in triumph, but his lopsided smile and bloodied face betrayed the now-crushed cheekbone.

A thick arm wrapped around Ebrium's neck from behind, cutting off his air supply. Ebrium had momentarily forgotten about the first man, the one he'd stunned. A mistake, of course. The man tightened his hold on Ebrium's throat and the hawk-faced man brought the butt of his blade down on Ebrium's wrist, causing him to drop his knife. Then he thrust at Ebrium's abdomen. Ebrium managed to writhe and bend to avoid the worst of the slash, but still a deep wound opened on his side. The top of the blade, however, also caught the abdomen of the man behind him, who cried out in shock at the gash in his side.

Taking advantage of the confusion, Ebrium dropped his weight and, with a burst of his failing strength, flipped the man over his shoulders to land at the hawk-faced man's feet. Breathing heavily, his abdomen and arms on fire from more hits and nicks than he could recall, Ebrium stumbled a few steps back. In doing so, his heel hit something and he tripped, falling backwards and landing heavily with a jarring thud. With his weight on his elbows Ebrium panted, each breath an agony, his arms and chest slick with blood, watching the hawk-faced man bouncing his weight again on the other side of the first man's body. As if he was trying to decide how to finish Ebrium off. Ebrium wasn't sure he had any force left to do anything about it.

In the course of their fighting they'd moved nearer to the hut, and suddenly, over the sound of scuffling feet and swishing reeds Ebrium heard something crash inside. He heard a man swear and a woman shout. *Satsobek.*

In the same moment, the hawk-faced man rushed at Ebrium, raising his blade for a downward slash. Ebrium turned to the side and kicked out, the outside edge of his foot connecting with the man's kneecap, smashing it and dropping the man to his knees. In a reflexive movement, his hand released his blade. He looked down at Ebrium, shock registering on his face even as Ebrium rolled over, grabbed the other man's blade, and hauled himself up to his feet. He didn't waste time in pulling the man's forehead back, and drawing his blade across his throat. *A fitting and unceremonious end for a fool of a man.*

Ebrium staggered to the door of the hut, crashing clumsily through it. He was met by the sight of Sekhemkare laid out between Satsobek's splayed legs, fumbling with the folds of her skirt. Sekhemkare looked up in disbelief, then scrambled backwards over Satsobek's lifeless body as Ebrium made two quick strides across the room and grabbed the man by the lock of braided hair on the side of his head, dragging him to his feet.

"What did you do to her?!" He roared. Sekhemkare hardly had time to answer before Ebrium dropped the knife in his hand and proceeded to work over the man's body with his fist. Sekhemkare got out a few hits of his own, landing a strong right to Ebrium's face, splitting open the skin over his left eye. It didn't matter, Ebrium could hardly see past the rage that consumed him. The sticky blood coating his skin, the cracked and bruised ribs, were nothing compared to the knowledge that he'd been too late to stop the man. He hung on to Sekhemkare's braid in an iron grip, punishing him with his knuckles.

Then there were hands grabbing his arms, elbows locking around his, and Bey yelling in his ear. "For the love of Dagon, man, stop it! You'll kill him." Sekhemkare slumped to the floor as Batr pried Ebrium's fingers from his hair.

Ebrium struggled against Bey and Makae. "Let me do it!"

Bey hissed, "There will be consequences if you do. Let him face the judges. He *will* suffer. I promise you." Ebrium jerked again, trying to tear away from the two men that held him.

"Let me do it." Ebrium his voice was ragged. "Dammit, let me go!"

"Ebrium!" Seret's voice cut through the men's argument. He was crouched on the ground next to Satsobek, cradling her head in his hands. "She's alive. Her breathing is strong. I-I think she might be okay." Ebrium forgot all about killing Sekhemkare, struggling now to get free so he could scoop the woman up in his arms.

Chapter 20 – Resolutions

Satsobek dreamt she was sailing. In her dream she'd left Thinis, and Kemet, drifting away on a large vessel. The crew disappeared, and she was alone, laid out on her back on the warm, smooth planks of the deck with the smell of wood and the salty sea air filling her nostrils. The waves lapped rhythmically against the hull, the rocking of the creaking boat causing ropes to twist and groan noisily. Even in her sleep, she marveled at her ability to absorb so much detail when she'd rarely experienced sailing, and only then on the great Iteru, never at sea.

Aside from a sense of utter aloneness, it was quite peaceful. She wondered where the craft was headed. She turned her head and saw a great pelican perched on the guardrail to her right. A beautiful thing, its feathers the purest white she'd ever seen, with a long bill as pink as a kitten's nose, and a gullet the colour of a buttercup's petals. His majestic head was turned towards the side, looking out over the sea.

"Hello." She called to the pelican, and made a clicking with her tongue, as if to call it over, or to get its attention. The way one might do to a puppy.

It cocked its head, glaring at her with one black, inquisitive eye. The pelican spread its wings, an impressive span of over eight feet, then flapped them a couple of times before lifting up and soaring away. She turned her head the other way and saw a small shelter at the back of the ship and, as she watched, a figure stepped through the doorway out onto the deck. It was Anhur, the lion-headed consort of the goddess Mehyt. He shook his long, thick black mane and stalked towards her, an imposing figure. He wore a white shenti, and a leopard skin draped over his shoulders.

She wasn't frightened, as she realized that if he was Anhur, she must be Mehyt. He'd come to spirit her somewhere they could be together, just as she'd always hoped he would when she was younger. He knelt beside her and brushed a piece of hair from her face before taking her up in his arms. She suddenly wondered why she was so sore; her whole body ached as he cradled her head against his powerful shoulder.

She stretched an arm out around his neck and murmured into his neck. "*Anhur.*"

"Who?" His voice was rough in her ear. She gasped as he held her out at arms' length, her back and neck protesting against the pain. "Who in the name of Dagon is Anhur?" He growled.

Dagon? She thought. *No. There is no god named Dagon in Kemet. But there is one in Ebla.* Satsobek realized that, despite his lion's head, Anhur looked very much like Ebrium, and the smell of wood and sea air was also much like Ebrium's scent. She blinked, and suddenly *it was* Ebrium holding her in his grip, frowning down at her. She was lying on a large, soft bed and he was standing next to it, hunched over her.

"Ebrium?" She ran her knuckles over his freshly shaved cheek and noticed a cut over his left eye. Strips of white linen wrapped around his bulging bicep and abdomen, spotted with blood. Purple-green bruises marred the bronze skin of his torso, and she reached out to brush them, but her fingers couldn't quite make the distance. "What happened to you?"

His jaw clenched and his eyes stayed sharp and wary. He ignored her question. "You were making noises, so I came in to check on you."

"I – I think I was dreaming." She must *still* be dreaming, if Ebrium was there. Then again, this wasn't the first time she'd dreamt of an Ebrium-Anhur god spiriting her away. Her head ached and she slumped back against the cushions. She took in her surroundings - the white-washed walls with their cheerful images of children playing along the Iteru, the big white bed with its linen curtains, a wide cupboard in the corner, and late afternoon sunlight streaming through narrow windows in the wall. For a moment it was all unfamiliar. Then she realized why. She had only seen it at night, in the darkness.

"Oh gods," she sat up, "what am I doing here? Ebrium, I must leave. My father…" She couldn't tell him what her father might do. Sobek would do everything he threatened to, and more. She moved to roll off the bed but her body screamed against it, and she lost her balance. Ebrium caught her up in his arms as she struggled weakly against him.

"Shh shhh shhh." Ebrium gently pressed her back down to the bed. "Your father won't be a problem any longer."

"No! You don't understand. He'll kill me if he finds me here. He'll kill me, and then he'll kill you. And ruin Merneith. Please, let me go. I must go. I have to stop him." She was babbling, terrified that she had somehow done something in her hul gil – induced state to devastate them all.

He shook his head. "No, *you* don't understand. Your father won't ever compel you to marry again. I promise you. But right now you need to rest, and eat. I've brought someone to help you. When you're ready later, I'll explain everything. For now, though, you're safe here as long as you need it."

Accepting no arguments, he scooped her up, though she saw him wince in pain, and carried her to the bathing room. Even in her confused state, she was pleased to see a large tub full of steaming water, scattered with scented jasmine flowers. She was also stunned to see a familiar figure waiting for her by the tub. "Sadeh!" Satsobek exclaimed at the sight of her maid. "What in the name of Ra are you doing here?"

Ebrium put her down and Sadeh bustled over, tucking Satsobek's arm over her shoulder and helping her towards the tub. "His lordship insisted I come tend to you while you're here." Sadeh turned to Ebrium and flapped her free hand at him. "Now off with you, sir. This is ladies' business here." Ebrium raised an amused eyebrow at the stocky young woman but bowed his head and left them alone.

Sadeh helped strip Satsobek and get her into the tub. Satsobek moaned as the water scalded her skin, but it felt delicious, helping to burn off the terrible images of last night, and the memory of Sekhemkare's touch. Sadeh began to scrub her down, taking care to be gentle with her bruises and aching muscles.

Satsobek questioned Sadeh for details and the girl was more than happy to comply. "You should have *seen* his lordship storm into your father's house and demand I be brought to you to help you. He is quite ferocious." She gave a shiver of delight. Ebrium must be the *his lordship* the girl was referring to, and another jolt of shock went through her. In a way, she supposed, Ebrium was a lord of sorts now as the queen had acknowledged him with favours beyond most of the rest of the nobility.

Sadeh chattered on. "And he's so incredibly handsome, nebet-i. My goodness, he's got your father in such a rage, threatening him the way he did last night. He's like a vengeful god striking down from above, he is. Like Horus, avenging Osiris against Seth."

"What in the world are you talking about, Sadeh? How did he threaten my father?"

"Oh, nebet-i, it was truly something to behold!" Sadeh proceeded to tell her everything Ebrium had said to her father last night. "Of course, we were *all* listening at the door. I hope you don't mind, but it was too spectacular not to! Your father can be so frightening, but the queen's man there, his lordship, had no fear at all. Not a shred. He just told him, neat as you please, that if he tried to compel you to do *anything* against your will ever again he would have him charged with treason, and for conspiring with Sekhemkare. He promised to send him into exile, or worse! I'm sorry to say your father said some terrible things to him, about how he'd never let you marry a low-born foreigner. But his lordship just said that you could do as you please from now on, and that was that. He made sure to tell your father that you could marry whomever you wanted, whenever you wanted, and there was nothing your father could do to stop you."

Satsobek sat forward to let Sadeh rinse her hair. Her heart was beating fast and there were questions she needed answered. "Yes? And is that *all* Ebrium said about marriage?"

Sadeh helped her out of the tub, rubbing her dry. She proceeded to pull some jars of scented oils from a sack she'd brought with her, and massaged the oils into Satsobek's skin. "Well, naturally I don't think that would have been the best time for him to ask your father's permission. Although I suppose he doesn't need it anymore, now does he? Your father can't force you to marry anyone now. But don't you think the fact that he was there at all means *something*? Why would he insist you be allowed to marry who you want if he didn't intend to ask you himself?"

Satsobek wasn't so sure, though. Not after what she'd said to Ebrium the last time she'd seen him. Sadeh told her all she knew about the events of last night and how Ebrium and his men saved her from Sekhemkare. But how they'd known to look for her in the first place was still a mystery to her.

Sadeh finished applying the kohl and ochre to Satsobek's eyes and cheeks, stepping back to smile at her accomplishment. "There you are, nebet-i, nice and simple. I didn't braid your hair so it won't be an impediment to anyone's hands, or put any ochre on your lips. *Just in case.* You might not want to smudge them, you know."

"Sadeh! Now really, that is quite enough." But Satsobek smiled a little. A little flicker of hope sparked in her chest that Sadeh might be right.

Ebrium paced the main greeting room of his house again. It was late and he had long since sent the servants to bed. The twinkling constellations against the blue-black sky were visible through the slim windows. He hadn't bothered to light oil wicks, preferring the soft light of the stars reflecting off the hard sand and the white-washed walls. His ribs ached, but the pain was bearable now that they were tightly wrapped with fresh bandages. He was no stranger to cuts and bruises, and had endured far worse over the years.

He'd urged Satsobek to go back to sleep after she'd bathed and eaten a small bowl of mashed lentils and barley – all her stomach could handle. He'd like to beat Sekhemkare all over again for giving her so much hul gil it almost killed her. Ebrium had seen the stuff before. In port cities in the far north, and amongst some sailors. Usually, they used it temporarily in very small doses for pain relief. It wasn't a common drug – too difficult to obtain and too expensive to make a habit. Sekhemkare had obviously found a new use for it, though.

Soft footsteps sounded behind him, and he turned to see Satsobek padding on bare feet into the room. Her shenti flowed out behind her, a sharp contrast to her copper skin, black hair, and large, dark eyes. He was reminded again of a water nymph, a mysterious little being that flitted in and out through the night. The stuff of dreams. Or at least the stuff of *his* dreams. He pushed that thought aside. The fantasies he'd had of lifting her up against the wall and sliding her down over his throbbing erection were not in the least bit useful right now.

She hesitated in the doorway, watching him. He kept his distance. He had little doubt that her maid had told her everything by now, and he wasn't sure how she would take it. While he didn't think she'd really wanted Sekhemkare, he had no idea how she felt about *him*. Their last parting, when she'd told him to *learn his place*, had hardly been enlightening. Pair that with the way she'd murmured the name *Anhur* in his ear when she'd been sleeping earlier and he was left more confused than ever.

"Ebrium." Her voice was hushed as she stepped into the room and out of the gloom of the hallway. She moved to him and he crossed his arms over his chest. He recognized it as a defensive move, and wondered that he felt the need to protect himself from this one, tiny woman.

"Ebrium, I cannot thank you enough for everything you've done. My father... he was..." her throat worked as she swallowed, searching for words.

"It's fine. I understand. He threatened you." He looked away, wanting to pace, to move, but remained rooted in place instead.

"No, you don't understand. Maybe not all of it. I – I said some horrible things to you. I didn't know what else to do."

He nodded, jaw clenched. There didn't seem anything to say.

"I'm so sorry if I hurt you. I never wanted that."

He pulled his lips in, biting on them. He didn't want to look at her. Didn't want to see sympathy on her face, as if he were a heart-broken teenage boy. The last time he'd seen her, at the queen's banquet, he'd offered to risk everything for her. And now all she could do was apologize for hurting him.

Aggravated, he scowled. "Who's Anhur?"

"What?"

"Anhur. When you were sleeping earlier you were making noises. I came in to check on you and you said his name."

"Did I?" She laughed. A light, relieved sound. "Anhur is Mehyt's consort, remember? The god of soldiers. I dreamt he'd stolen me away, that he was taking me away from my father. But it was you."

She moved around him into his line of vision, forcing him to look down at her. She scraped her hands through her smooth hair, tucking it behind her ears and turning her dark, round face up to his. "In my dreams – and there has been more than one – *you* are Anhur, and he is you. You saved me, just like I always imagined Anhur did for Mehyt. Ebrium, I never thought you would say the things you did the last time I saw you at court. I didn't think you would care what happened to me."

He blinked. "Why wouldn't I care?"

"Why *would* you?" She shot back. "I drove you crazy when we worked together. You were always mad at me. I make everything more difficult, and you constantly have to save me from doing dangerous things, like sneaking out at night and going to Iput's. Like what happened last night."

Being almost killed by Sekhemkare was not her fault. Yet here she was taking the blame for the horrible things other people did. He realized they were both struggling under the weight of their own insecurities. He with his unwillingness to get hurt and be rejected because of his background, and she with her long history of being told she wasn't worthy of love.

"Satsobek," he unfolded his arms and wrapped his hands around her narrow waist, almost completely encircling it, drawing her to him. She came hesitantly, her eyes wide. He thought he detected fear, and maybe hope, in them. "I think I know how to solve that problem, to make it easier to stop you from doing crazy things."

"How?"

"Simple. If you moved in here with me it would make it a lot easier to keep an eye on you." He bent his head, brushing his lips along her neck. He smiled when he felt her shiver.

"Wait. Do you mean…"

"Since it's me you keep creeping out to see, after all, wouldn't it make sense to just spend your nights in my bed?"

She pulled back and glared at him, but he was sure her lips were quirking up. "I was *not* sneaking out to see *you*."

He tugged her back to him and buried his nose in her cardamom scented hair, running his lips along the fine hairs of her ears, flicking his tongue out to tickle her lobe. "Admit it." He skimmed his mouth down her neck to kiss her collarbone. She leaned towards him, her soft hands fanning gently out over his chest, avoiding the bandages. "I was right when I said you wanted to get into my bed."

"Well," she whispered, pushing herself up onto her tip toes to nuzzle his neck. She slid one hand down his abdomen, down, down towards the top of his shenti. She slipped one finger underneath the fabric, running it inside along the edge and making his skin thrum and his shaft painfully hard. "That part may be true. I *did* want to get into your bed. And do you know what? I still do. That is, if you think you can handle it, wrapped up as you are in all these bandages."

With a growl, he turned her around and ushered her to his bedroom.

Satsobek reveled in the feel of Ebrium's skin against hers. She almost wondered if she were dreaming again, it was *too* good. She felt like she didn't deserve this, like she didn't deserve *him*. This man who, time again, had protected her and fought for her. She would do anything for him. Her body was sore, but desire dulled her discomfort, filling her with a pleasurable ache instead.

Once in his room she untied her shenti with shaking fingers. Her skin was too tight and too hot. She needed him to touch her, to be inside her. Her shenti fluttered to the floor to pool at her feet. A moment later his landed beside it. She reached for him, but Ebrium put his hands on her shoulders, pressing her down to sit on the edge of the bed. Her heart pounded in trepidation, wondering why he was delaying.

He smiled, and her pulse beat faster. It was a wicked smile, one that deepened the dimple in his cheek and sparked a mischievous gleam in his eyes. He knelt beside the bed in front of her, reaching down to encase her delicate ankles in his large hands. He lifted them up onto the edge of the bed, near her hips, forcing her to lean back on her elbows.

"What are you...?" She gasped, watching that sly grin spread across his beautiful, boyish face. She tried to bring her knees together to cover the mound of her centre. She felt exposed and shy, as if it were her first time with him.

"Uh uh uh." He wagged a finger. He slipped his hands between her knees. "You still haven't answered my question." Pushing her legs apart, he slid his calloused hands slowly from her knees down her inner thighs, moving towards the molten core of her sex. She knew she was slick, impatient for him to be in her, moving against her, striving for that great moment of exaltation that only he could bring.

His thumbs made little circles on her thighs, near to but not quite touching her most tender of places.

"What question?" She panted, fascinated by the sight of his big hands on her legs. She gripped the sheets beneath her.

He dipped his head and kissed along the path that his hands had left. The light stubble on his cheek rasped against her sensitive skin and she gasped. She wondered if it was possible for her heart to burst in anticipation. She ground out again, "What question, dammit?"

He chuckled against her leg, his breath teasing. With one rough finger, he slid along the slippery lips of her inner thighs, stopping to rub the sensitive peak and making her cry out. She swore and she didn't even have to look to know that he was smiling. He leaned in and flicked his tongue along where his finger had just been. Her fists twisted in the bedsheets.

His hair brushed her thighs as he slid one finger inside her. At the same time he placed his lips against the nub of her sex, sucking even as he swirled his tongue around it. His finger curled up into her and everything that had been holding itself tight inside her tensed and knotted even harder. He pushed another finger into her, working in and out while he sucked and twirled his tongue. At some point she realized she wasn't breathing and heaved in deep, ragged breaths. The tension inside her rose up like a wild musical crescendo, rising and rising until it came crashing down over her in a discordant jangle of whimpers and flailing, shaking limbs.

She fell back on the bed, shivers wracking her limp body. He moved up over her, his elbows depressing the mattress on either side of her head. He brushed her forehead and cheeks with his lips. His scent wafted over her and in her dazed state she associated it with being *safe*. And free. Free from her father's harassment and her sister's taunting. Free from the need to marry a man not of her choosing. She reached up to twine her fingers in the soft black curls at the back of his head. She buried her face in his neck and breathed him in. *So this is what love smells like.*

Ebrium reached down to draw her knee up to her chest, hooking her calf over his shoulder. He nestled the tip of his shaft against her sex. "Tell me." He challenged.

"Tell you what?" She wiggled her hips, trying to push herself towards the edge of the bed. He was driving her crazy, teasing her by applying just the lightest bit of pressure at her entrance.

"Tell me you want to do this again."

"I - what? Of course I do. Isn't that obvious?" Heat pulsed from her core as her whole being focused on that one small patch of space. She was watching the muscles of his honey-coloured abdomen flex and heave as he drew breath.

His voice was gritty as he said, "Tell me you want to stay."

She looked up at his face, poised above hers. His jaw was tight, his nostrils flared in that way she remembered from their first time. He was holding himself back, needing something from her. His blue eyes were guarded.

Satsobek reached up and placed the palm of her small hand against his jaw, rubbing the pad of her thumb over his cheek. The other she cupped over his massive shoulder, pulling him down to her. Her lips sought his and their kiss was long, deep, and tender. His tongue probed her mouth with a gentleness so unlike the desperate kisses they'd shared in the past. This was sweet, filled with longing and unanswered questions.

He pulled back, watchful and almost pained-looking. "Yes." She murmured. "Yes, I want to stay with you. For tonight and more. For as long as you will have me. I want this."

Ebrium hadn't realized he'd been holding so much tension in his body until it all drained away, leaving him weak with relief. "And if I asked you to marry me tomorrow? Or whenever you wanted?"

"Yes." She brushed her slim fingers over his collarbone, resting them over his heart. He was sure she could feel it pounding beneath the bandages and the hot flesh of his chest. Her full lips lifted in a smile so sweet he wanted to see it every day for the rest of his life. "Tomorrow."

Ebrium couldn't hold back any longer, he was shaking he wanted her so bad. He pushed the thick head of his shaft inside her and she cried out. "Yes! Definitely yes!" He smiled as he drove deeper into her clenching depths. She was so wet, so tight, so soft. He knew he wouldn't be able to last long this time. He'd waited too long for her and it only increased his desire knowing that he was going to have the rest of their lives to make it up to her.

He pressed Satsobek's knee closer to her beautiful breasts and thrust himself to the hilt. He let her adjust to his girth for a moment before he began to move in earnest. He dipped his head to swallow her moans in his mouth, nipping at her neck and jawline. He paused when he heard her whisper in his ear, "I love you." He reared back and searched her eyes, as though he trusted his eyes more than his ears. She repeated herself, more forcefully. "I love you, Ebrium." She propelled her hips upwards to force his length even deeper.

"By the gods, woman." His voice was strained. "You'll be the death of me, but I love you too." Ebrium picked up his speed, pumping into her molten core. He needed to finish, needed to bring them both to that perfect peak of exquisite ecstasy. With one hand, he cupped her breast and flicked her hard, copper-coloured nipple. She called out his name and then he could feel the snug walls of her sex contract around him. His own completion wasn't far behind. He thrust harder until he lost control of himself, spilling into her along with a few choice swear words. His shaft spasmed and his gut clenched until he finally went limp.

He maneuvered his large body over Satsobek's and, wrapping an arm around her waist, pulled her up alongside him on the bed. He tucked her soft little body against his. He was on the verge of falling asleep when she wriggled around under his arm to face him. Their knees bumped and he opened his eyes a crack.

"Ebrium?"

"Mmm?"

"You never told me why you waited so long to move into your new house." She paused and he got the sense she was hesitating to ask him something. He prompted her, "And what else?"

She bit her lower lip and placed a hand lightly on his chest. Her eyes were huge, dark nervous pools. She asked, "Was it so that you could be closer to Iput's? I – I understand if that's why. I got the impression that maybe the two of you… I want to be your wife, Ebrium. But if there's another woman, a concubine, I believe I would prefer to know."

His body was aching, and he turned awkwardly to face her, resting his head on one hand. With the other, he tucked a lock of her hair behind her ear, his fingers lingering along her jaw. "Iput and I had… an arrangement. It was never meant to be long-term. Neither of us wanted it that way. I'm not some randy youth, Satsobek, that I need more than one woman. I'll have more than enough to keep my hands full with you, I think."

Despite the gloom he knew she was blushing at his teasing, and he smiled. "There is a reason I didn't move into the manor sooner though."

"Oh?' She ran one suggestive finger over his collarbone, dipping her hand down the length of his chest.

He tightened the arm that was draped over her waist, pulling her closer until the mound of her sex was pressed against his growing fullness. "I was waiting for something to add to the house. The last piece I needed to complete it, to make it a home."

"Mmmm?" She slowly ground herself against him. "What was that?"

He slid his hand up the smooth skin of her waist, over her shoulders, tipping her face up to his. Skimming his mouth across hers, she responded by pressing harder against him. "You." He murmured. "It needed *you* here to make it a home." He pulled her over on top of him, positioning her over his rigid member. He proceeded to show her just *how much* he needed her.

ꔍ **Epilogue** ꕤ

Three months later

Satsobek leaned back into the cushions on their rooftop. The early evening was blissfully cool, and she pulled her scarf a little tighter around her shoulders. Next to her, Ebrium turned from his conversation with Bey, Batr, and Makae. He smiled and rubbed a large hand along her forearm to soothe away the goosebumps that rose on her flesh.

Around her an assortment of friends and family chattered to one another. Ebrium's mother and sister sat to her left, along with Betrest and one of Satsobek's distant cousins, Penebui. Penebui was a beautiful young blonde woman, the granddaughter of a slave concubine and the queen's grandfather, pharaoh Hor-Aha. She was also a close friend of Ebrium's sister Akshaka. Amongst the women was Queen Merneith and in her arms she held a swaddled infant – Den, the next pharaoh.

Den's birth had been a difficult one. Childbirth was dangerous for women at the best of times, and if a woman didn't die in childbirth she could just as easily die within a few days of it due to various complications. And Den was a big boy, larger than most. The word was put out to the masses – in part thanks to Bey, Ebrium, and their network of strategically placed people – that Den's size was a good omen, a blessing from the gods and a sign that the queen wasn't to be held accountable for the temple murders. The implication being that waiting for the next pharaoh to come of age – thereby enabling Merneith to continue her regency of peace and stability – would be worthwhile, as Den was destined to be strong and powerful.

Since Den's birth, rumours of dissent in the north had died down. This was probably also due in part to the arrest and subsequent execution of Sekhemkare. The governor himself hadn't protested his brother's demise. Once he'd learned that Sekhemkare stole from the temples in order to raise an army to overthrow him, the governor was happy to see his brother make the journey to the underworld. He even came to Thinis to watch it happen. He'd promised the queen to use his position to garner support for her regency. Ebrium, who'd been present at the meeting, said that he believed it possible the governor was actually telling the truth. At least for the moment.

Earlier that evening Merneith had pulled Satsobek aside, asking for a few moments alone.

"Satsobek," the queen leaned in close and lowered her voice. "I know you've had your issues with the hwt of Mehyt in the past, but I am very happy to hear that you've returned to serve the women there as a scribe. They tell me your presence is very comforting, and that you've taken up many of Tiya's duties."

Satsobek nodded, a glow of warmth warming her chest. "Yes, the priestesses asked me to come back. It was the least I could do after all Tiya did for me. She would want me to help them." While it was bittersweet sometimes when she remembered the awful things that had happened in the temple, Satsobek was once again able to find solace in the rituals of worship. After all, she couldn't help but think that Mehyt had somehow led her and Ebrium to one another, while at the same time warning her of Sekhemkare and his worship of Seth, the god of chaos and destruction.

Merneith smiled and took Satsobek's hand. "I realize this might come as a shock, but I would sincerely like you to consider taking up Tiya's position as high priestess."

Satsobek *had* been shocked, and tried to protest. She was still young for the position and had kept away from the temple a full year until Tiya and Yuny's deaths.

But the queen persisted. "I need someone capable that I can trust. With all that's happened there, the temple is in disarray. And we still don't know how many temples

Sekhemkare infiltrated, and who might be aligned against us. You know that the duties are not so onerous there. You may fulfill the rituals and worship and still have time to raise a family, if you and Ebrium wish for one. You yourself just said Tiya would want you to help, and this *is* what she trained you to do, and I believe you can do it. I do not need you to answer immediately, but please do think on it."

Satsobek had promised she would provide an answer soon, after she spoke with Ebrium. While he still had no great love for the gods, he'd been happy to see her return to the temple and to her work, knowing how much it meant to her. He'd never stand in her way if she chose to take up the position of high priestess. And the more she thought on it, the more it seemed fitting. What better way to honour Tiya's memory than to do the job the woman had trained her for? And what better way to help smooth her husband's transition into the nobility than to be in a powerful, high ranking position herself? Whether they liked it or not, it would be difficult for anyone to be openly rude to the husband of the high priestess of the Temple of Mehyt.

A discussion from the men on her right pulled her from her thoughts. They were debating fighting maneuvers and training schedules. Batr flexed a bicep and said, "Push-ups. Nothing better for arms and back. A hundred or so at a time."

Makae nodded. "Running, also. A man needs stamina."

Batr chortled. His voice was low but Satsobek overheard him say, "I can think of other ways to build stamina, but I sure wouldn't do them with a group of other soldiers around."

Ebrium's arm shot out, back-handing Batr on the shoulder. "And you won't mention them in front of my wife again, either." The other men chuckled.

Just then, Seret appeared with a large tray laden with deserts, setting it down to arrange plates of honey buns, and bowls of nuts and fruit. Satsobek marvelled at how well the welts on his back were healing. Soon they would be nothing more than a few white lines, and perhaps one day they wouldn't be visible at all. *He's not such a boy anymore*, Satsobek realized with a start. In fact, he was of an age when many young men married.

Makae looked at Seret thoughtfully and said, "Ebrium mentioned that you've begun training with him. Does it cause your leg any pain?"

Seret stood up tall and drew his shoulders back. "No, but thank you for asking, sir. Ebrium's also teaching me to fight. I believe it has been good for my leg, making it stronger. It pains me less already." Satsobek was pleased to see him doing so well. Seret admired Ebrium greatly and worked hard to impress him. As a result, Ebrium took the boy's training seriously.

"Well then, we might make a decent soldier out of you yet." Batr joked and Seret smiled, ducking his head to hide his gratified blush.

Makae nodded. "A few more months of training under Ebrium here and we might be able to find you a position somewhere."

Satsobek smiled at her husband, pleased that he'd recognized Seret was too smart, too ambitious, to serve solely as a house servant. The military was one of the few options for advancement for a young man like Seret. One who had been left on the doorstep of a temple with no family to his name – or even a name at all. Most of the military was conscripted labour, farmers and slaves who were called upon in times of need to fight. But to be employed solely as a soldier provided an opportunity to rise through the ranks, higher than Seret could ever aspire to as an illiterate house servant or farmer.

"Thank you, sir." Seret's words were clear. "I would like that above all else." But Satsobek saw his eyes stray to the side, where Ebrium's sister Akshaka sat. The look of longing that flashed through Seret's dark eyes, the clench of his jaw, the slight flare of his nostrils, told her that perhaps there might be something he'd like more than just a position in the military ranks.

Akshaka must have sensed his gaze because she looked up. Satsobek saw their eyes meet and hold for just a moment before the pretty girl looked away.

Ebrium's eyes narrowed and he growled, "But don't forget, boy. If I catch you looking at my sister like that again I'll be sending you out to train in the desert where you won't see another woman for the next ten years. Until long after she's married."

Seret blinked, looking stricken, while the other men hooted with laughter. Batr said, "Watch out, boy, he means it. Besides, I've had my eye on that girl longer than you. I'm just waiting for Ebrium here to say she's old enough to marry."

Ebrium snorted. "She could be older than my mother and she still wouldn't be old enough to marry you."

Satsobek had to cover her mouth to hide her smile. "Don't worry, Batr. I am sure we can find you another girl. But darling," she turned to Ebrium, "what's wrong with marrying a soldier?"

He pursed his lips. "Pfft. They're a disreputable bunch. I know exactly what kinds of trouble they can get into."

She laughed. "Ah yes. Soldiers. Pirates and brigands are a much more noble lot."

Ebrium nodded sagely, his eyes wide and feigning innocence. "By the gods, you're right. I knew you were smart."

Their banter was interrupted by Satsobek's old manservant and confidante, Paser, clearing his throat. As part of the marriage contract Ebrium had negotiated with Satsobek's father, Satsobek was allowed to bring along any servant or slave from her father's household she liked. Sadeh and Paser were amongst the handful of servants to join them in their new home, thereby saving Ebrium the problem of staffing his new manor.

Paser inclined his head when Satsobek gestured to him, and he announced a late arrival. "Imhotep, the temple hmww."

The tall, handsome man bowed and Satsobek beckoned for him to join them. "Imhotep, we are so pleased you could make it. Everyone, allow me to interrupt you for a moment please." She waved to get the attention of her guests, thrilled they could all be there to share in this pronouncement.

Ebrium took her hand and bestowed a bright, dimpled grin on her and, like a giddy girl, she grinned back. She turned to the assortment of friends and family around her.

"Ebrium and I would like to introduce you to our friend, Imhotep. Imhotep has been the carpenter in the hwt of Mehyt for over twenty years now. We've hired him to help decorate a room in our home. One for the baby we anticipate joining us in about six months' time."

A loud murmur rose up amongst their guests and one voice was loudest. "I told you!" Batr elbowed his brother. "She isn't just getting fat."

Ebrium glared at his friend but Satsobek smiled. Three months ago she'd never imagined she could be as happy as the night Ebrium asked her to marry him. Now she had something that was at least comparable. She had the love of a group of friends and family. And soon enough, there would be one more of them to love.

The End

Looking for more?

Check out my website for Q & A about some of the facts in this story, as well as some of my pictures of Egypt.

www.DanielleSLeBlanc.com

And please consider leaving a review on Amazon, Goodreads, Barnes & Noble, Kobo, or elsewhere. Your reviews mean a lot to me, and help others to decide if this series is right for them.

Read on for a blurb on the next book in the series!